ARSEN'S RULES SERIES

A BILLIONAIRE ROMANCE NOVEL

MICHELLE LOVE

CONTENTS

Made in "The United States" by:

Michelle Love

© Copyright 2021

ISBN: 978-1-64808-753-0

❀ Created with Vellum

ABOUT THE AUTHOR

Mrs. Love writes about smart, sexy women and the hot alpha billionaires who love them. She has found her own happily ever after with her dream husband and adorable 6 and 2 year old kids. Currently, Michelle is hard at work on the next book in the series, and trying to stay off the Internet.

"Thank you for supporting an indie author. Anything you can do, whether it be writing a review, or even simply telling a fellow reader that you enjoyed this. Thanks

BLURB

Arsen Sloan is a thirty-five-year old monster of a lawyer. Highly successful as a criminal lawyer, specializing in murder cases, he has only lost one case in his career. Allen White was the second defendant that he represented some ten years earlier. He was convicted of murdering one of his high school teachers after kidnapping her for a period of two months and eventually killing her.

Arsen is aware that the man who lost ten years of his life in prison has been released after serving only part of his sentence, gaining his freedom on parole as he turned his life over to God, or so he has made everyone believe he has turned into a prison evangelist.

Things begin to go very wrong for Arsen and very quickly his freedom is at stake as not one, but three of his kink-inclined lovers have been found murdered. Arsen is into some dark and shady things in the city of San Francisco where he works defending some of California's worst criminals. With his life hanging in a balance that he never thought possible, Arsen avoids his usual BDSM clubs, and goes out to a nice, normal club that many law students frequent in San Francisco.

1

PART ONE: FOR HER

Cool air hit his face as he left the building he'd been stuck in the last eight hours. His tie couldn't get off fast enough as his large hands pulled it away from his neck, letting it hang loose.

He'd felt his throat closing in on him as he was accused of things that were beyond him to execute, beyond him to perform and beyond him to even think of doing.

Arsen Sloan was a thirty-five-year-old criminal lawyer. Tall, at six feet and nine inches, he dwarfed most of his colleagues. To make sure they all had even further insecurities in his presence, he kept himself in peak physical condition. Pecs and abs that most men would die to have and biceps the mere sight of made women wet with desire for him.

Arsen prided himself on his appearance which he used to his advantage whenever possible. He was a machine of a man, using everything he could to get the results that he was seeking, whatever they were.

In law, he used his well-educated brain to find every last law or case to make sure he won his client's cases. Arsen Sloan had never lost a case since he began his career as a criminal lawyer, ten years prior. Well, there was that one, but it had only been his second ever case.

Arsen tended to forget about the first few cases, the first two anyway. He never mentioned the first two, as a matter of fact.

WHEN IT CAME TO SEX, Arsen used everything in his personal arsenal to make sure that he stayed on top of that game. Love had played no role in his sex life.

Love was a word he hadn't used since he was a naïve kid in his late teens before the girl he thought loved him watched him become broken and near dead.

Arsen kept his shoulder length waves in perfect order, accenting his dark brown, brooding eyes. Thick, dark lashes surrounded them, giving the slightest hint of a soft side to the hard as nails man.

After the day of horrible accusations, Arsen just needed a drink. A stiff drink and to be able to unwind, and get rid of at least a little of the tension which filled his muscled body.

As he got into the backseat of his Escalade the privacy window went down. His driver and long-time friend, Paul, looked at him through the rear view mirror.

The tension Arsen felt radiated off him and Paul knew better than to ask any questions.

"To the club, boss?"

Arsen nodded and closed the door, then ran his hand over his face and rubbed his temples. He pulled a bottle of beer from the little fridge and took it down in one gulp. The evening sky was growing dark and a thin fog was already moving in as they made their way up the coastline of the San Francisco Bay.

Arsen's eyes followed the lights that were coming on along the edge of the road. He was wondering when it had gotten so bad. When had his world started to rule him rather than he rule it?

After the first five years as one of the top criminal lawyers in the entire state of California, Arsen Sloan had not only managed to gain a reputation as a winning lawyer who would do anything to win his cases, but also had become a billionaire. His ability to make great investments proved to be yet another thing Arsen did with near perfection.

PERFECTION WAS a thing he made great strides to achieve in every part of his life. Up until that day, he'd done pretty well at keeping his life near perfect at all times.

The alley was already dark as they pulled up to one of the main clubs that he frequented. Though, if not a member of the exclusive club, no one could tell what type of social gathering was going on there.

People tended to get dropped off at the clubs he went to. Clubs that catered to his tastes some considered to be immoral and worse. The rusted metal door was closed and only a small sign at the very top of the old door let on that it was a bit more than an old storage facility.

'FIERCE,' was the word etched into a small metal sign and suddenly Arsen's stomach was in knots. He knew he shouldn't go in there. He knew that was why he was in the precarious situation he was in.

"You know, Paul, I better find another place to go from now on," Arsen's deep voice called out to his driver and friend.

Paul was a friend who knew all about Arsen's past, and present, but he was being left out of why Arsen had been so moody when Arsen told him he had a meeting at the main police station in San Francisco.

"Sure thing, boss," Paul said and pulled out of the alley and headed back to the part of the city where the regular people went to get drinks and socialize with one another.

"I'll take you to the club my younger sister likes to go to, but if you see her in there, she's off limits, bro," Paul told his old friend. "Lots of young law majors in that place. You should find someone to your liking, boss."

.   .   .

ARSEN'S THROAT was growing tight again, so he unbuttoned the two top buttons of his stiffly starched white shirt he wore under a black suit jacket. The tie came all the way off and he stretched his long, lean-muscled legs out. Another beer he grabbed and popped the top, this one he took a long drink of, but stopped short of downing the whole thing.

"Paul, let the boss shit go for tonight. I need a friend, not another employee. Shit's coming down on me and without any family to support me, I'm going to need you to keep me from jumping off a bridge." Arsen looked out the tinted window and felt his eye twitch.

The first of many physical signs his body was sure to start exhibiting, just like it used to do when he was young and things were out of his control. Things he worked hard to get under control, and here he was with things beyond his control again.

His stomach hurt, another sign and another thing he'd left behind him, or thought he had anyway. Paul pulled along the curb and jumped out to open Arsen's door. He gave him a clap on the back and said, "Arsen, things will work out, man. You're beyond smart and whatever has you this worried I know you can figure out how to take care of it. You're good at this shit."

Arsen wished he had the faith in himself his old friend had, but the truth was his marks were all over the accusations made against him. He'd represented tons of people that he knew were guilty and managed to get them off the charges.

He just needed to figure out how to get himself off charges where the evidence pointed right at him and he had to tell the men who questioned him things he never thought he'd have to explain to anyone.

"I NEED a drink and a piece of hot ass would do wonders for me," Arsen said with a deep chuckle. "I'd ask you to come, Paul, and help me drown my sorrows, but one of us has to drive and I think I pay you to do that, so I'll go in alone and hopefully come out with a wicked little thing on my arm to take home."

"There's no doubt you will, Arsen," Paul said and gave Arsen a smile. "Get in there and get rid of that frown."

Arsen turned and walked into the door of the nightclub. The dance music was cranked up and a herd of young women were on the dance floor already, though the night was only beginning.

He took a table near the dance floor so he could watch the people dance. Arsen was not into dancing, but he appreciated the way women could bend and move their bodies to the beat.

He preferred a hard rock sound to the bubblegum pop that the DJ was playing in the social norm of a club. A pretty, young waitress came and placed her hand on his shoulder.

"What can I get you, sir?"

His dark eyes looked at the small, pale hand with perfectly manicured pink fingernails that was touching his left shoulder. In the clubs he went to, no female would ever approach him that way, and he had to fight the urge to grab her and toss her over his lap and teach her how to act accordingly.

After swallowing hard, he answered, "How about a whisky sour?"

The young woman with red-stained lips and blue eyeliner, her black hair pulled back into a tight and high ponytail smiled at him and said, "You should try our Eastern Sour. It has bourbon, OJ, lime juice, and Orgeat in it. It's really popular. I think you'd like it."

He blinked at the dimwitted thing and thought about what would happen to a female who dared to suggest the thing a man wanted was anything but that. Through gritted teeth he said, "Bring me what I asked for."

SHE REMOVED her hand from his shoulder as her smile quickly turned to a frown. "Touchy! Okay then. A whisky sour it is. Top shelf bourbon or does it matter?"

His dark and now very moody eyes rolled with her endless questions. "Top."

She hurried off, and he hoped his attitude didn't earn him a good bit of her spit in his drink as well. Arsen had a hard time dealing with normal women. He liked women who knew their place. Not that he was chauvinistic.

Arsen knew strong women. Women who were smart and capable of doing anything a man could do. Those women he could respect and appreciate. But the little dimwitted things like the waitress would be so much better off if they let a man take control of them, even if just in the confines of the bedroom, or dungeon.

The song ended just as the waitress brought him his drink. She placed it on the table.

"You wanna pay now, or run a tab?"

"I think I'll run a tab," he said and took a credit card out of his wallet and handed it to her. "Keep 'em coming and your tip will reflect my approval."

She laughed and made a low bow in front of him. "Thank you, Master." She sauntered away, shaking her head as she went.

"Okay, that's ten bucks knocked off right there," he mumbled to himself.

He'd sat back one table away from the dance floor and was glad to see a group of about six young women had taken the table in front of him. Now he had a front-row seat behind a bevy of young beauties to pick from.

He sipped his drink and let his eyes roam over each young woman at the table. One was tall and pretty in a Barbie doll kind of way. Her voice was high and a little squeaky.

He thought about the kinds of sounds she'd make as he took her the way he wanted to. Maybe tied to his bed or the railing of the balcony outside his bedroom.

He shook his head as she laughed and a snort came out of her mouth.

On to the next girl.

. . .

SHE WAS DARK HAIRED, plump, and wore little make-up. He noted how she could've used more and then when she spoke, her voice was deep.

No, he couldn't take a voice nearly as deep as his. That would make anything hard go soft in an instant. The next girl was intriguing as she had long, red curls that floated down her back.

She showed promise, but he knew from experience that red heads could be feisty and it took a lot to get them to understand what he would and would not tolerate. He watched as a man approached her and asked her to dance.

Her eyes ran over him like he was a piece of crap rather than a decent-looking man who was just being nice to her. "What do you want?" she asked with her nose squished up like he smelled bad or something.

The guy kept his cool and even smiled at her.

"Would you like to dance?"

"With you?" she said and rolled her eyes to look at the other girls who watched her, most likely sure she was about to annihilate the poor guy.

His laugh was getting a little nervous as was his demeanor as he switched his weight from one foot to the other.

"Yes."

The red head's hand ran over her too small for Arsen's taste, breast, then down her small waist and landed on her too skinny ass, according to Arsen.

"Does this look like something you'd like to get into your bed?" she asked the guy.

THE GUY TOOK a step back with her loaded question and should've turned and ran away from the obvious bitch. Arsen had to fight not to get up and take the young man out of harm's way.

"Sorry," the poor guy mumbled and turned to leave.

"Wait!" the red head called out.

He turned back with hope in his eyes and Arsen found himself rooting for the poor kid. "Yes?"

"What the hell made you think you could come over here and ask a woman who is clearly out of your league to dance?" The girl who now Arsen thought looked really ugly asked the poor guy.

The guy spun around and took off as the table full of young women hooted and hollered at him vulgarities and put downs. It was more than Arsen could take anymore. The whole lot of them needed their asses spanked until they couldn't walk, in his opinion.

The waitress arrived with another drink and placed it on the table then picked up his empty one. Just as she began to make another bow, Arsen took her shoulder in his strong hand and stopped her. "Your antics are not lost on me, girl.."

Her face went white, and she hauled ass away from Arsen who smiled as she fled. It was the first smile he'd made since he got the news the night before that he was a man of interest in some terrible crimes. The smile faded with his thought and he took a sip of his drink.

THE NOISE of the club faded as he thought about why it was he ever became involved in the seedy underworld that he'd become a part of. There was his first and only love at the beginning of it all.

Beth was a sweet young thing. At sixteen, she was fresh and everything he wanted. Arsen had been a young seventeen and not as ready as he thought he was to delve into the romantic world.

After a year of dating, Beth finally gave into him and the two lost their virginity to one another one fateful night in her bedroom. Her parents caught them and her father beat the hell out of him.

As he laid on Beth's bedroom floor, he saw it in her eyes as she looked at him. Her father had beat him into a bloody pulp. His jaw was broken and one arm was too. It laid out next to him at an awkward angle.

Beth's eyes held no compassion for the young man that she had just been claiming she loved, had just given her innocence to. No, the only thing there was disgust.

Her words he could still hear, "Get up, Arsen! Defend yourself or something!"

She held the blanket over her naked breasts as she sat up in the little twin bed they'd just made love on. Her blonde hair fell across her tanned shoulders and her blue eyes drooped at the outer edges as she looked at him with so much disappointment that he couldn't believe it.

"Help," he'd managed to get to come out of his broken mouth.

The same mouth that had lavished her with sweet kisses moments before her father came in and caught him on top of her. Arsen had been pulled away and slung across the room before he knew what was happening.

He lay naked and twisted on the floor and all he could do was look at Beth and feel like a complete loser who let this happen to himself. She needed him to be so much more than he was.

It was her mother who finally came to his aid. She'd found something and knocked her husband out as he wasn't going to stop his assault on Arsen until Arsen no longer was drawing breath.

Arsen was confused as Beth jumped off the bed, wrapping the sheet around her naked body and yelled at her mother, "What did you do to Daddy?"

Her mother shoved her back onto the bed and shouted, "He was about to kill Arsen!"

Beth looked at him with disgust again. "Get out! We're done!"

His body was in agony as her mother picked him up the best she could and took him to her car. She took him to the hospital and left him at the emergency room, alone.

ARSEN CAME BACK to reality and took the last of his drink which seemed to be disappearing way too fast. Another drink came, but a waiter brought it and left it for him.

Shame filled him as he realized he'd scared the waitress. He was always doing shit like that. He seemed to have no real filter as to who he could talk to in his dominant way and who he couldn't. It was a fine line, and he seemed to always be on the wrong side of it.

A popular song came on and the table full of girls in front of him shrieked, making him cover his ears. They all grabbed each other and ran to the dance floor like a heard of elephants.

Arsen looked around and saw table after table of young women doing the exact same thing and he shook his head and mumbled, "This is not going to work for me."

His drink was new, so he knew it'd take him until at least the end of the upbeat song before he was done with it. The night was still young, and he had no desire to go home all alone. The women in that club were not going to be anything he needed on that night.

"Oh, hell," he heard a young woman's voice say as she walked past him.

He turned his head and watched her take a seat at the table the women had vacated. She watched them for a moment then took her cell phone out of her back pocket and started looking at it.

Arsen looked her up one side and down the other. She was tall and curvy. Her breasts were exactly the right size, a little bigger than most women's. Her ass was round, and he liked the way that her tight jeans fit it perfectly. She had on leather cowboy boots that she had her jeans tucked into.

Her hair was long and dark, falling in waves to the top of her plump ass. His mouth was watering already. Looking all over her, he noticed the absence of a drink and looked back to find the waiter near him. He motioned him over and told him to take the same thing he was drinking to the young woman who stood alone at the table in front of him.

He sat back and watched as the waiter took the drink to her and when she asked who had sent it, he pointed to Arsen. She smiled and waved and mouthed a 'thank you' to him.

He liked her manners already. She knew how to accept things and that was a thing he had to have in a woman. He believed in lavishing gifts on them. It had been years since he had a submissive that he had felt enough for to do that.

The women in the last three years had all been people he felt nothing for. Just women who liked things the way he did, nothing more. The fact that three of his previous subs were gone was a thing which made him sad, only he wasn't given the time to mourn them.

HIS ATTENTION WENT BACK to the young woman he'd sent the drink to. She had gone back to looking at her phone and occasionally tapping the screen. She was too far away for him to see the color of her eyes, but the shape of them were like almonds and she had thick, dark lashes that fluttered occasionally as she smiled at her phone's screen.

The herd of bitches came back off the dance floor and the tall blonde Barbie hugged the new girl and started wagging her finger at her, obviously admonishing her for not being on time like the rest of the mindless young women at the little party.

The red head lifted her arm high in the air and the waitress came to them with a lit up cake. It was the blonde's birthday it looked like and the other women sang happy birthday to her then she blew the candles out. The dark haired beauty looked completely out of place with the mob of air heads.

Another song came on and the girls made another screaming shriek and ran to the dance floor. Barbie grasped at the gorgeous dark-haired girl, but she shook her head and stayed at the table, alone.

ARSEN SAW his chance and took his half empty glass and glided the distance between the tables, coming up behind her. He hesitated and took in her essence. The vague aroma of lavender wafted past his nose and he leaned closer to smell her hair that was shiny and full.

His hand fisted at his side as he had to stop himself from taking a handful into his fist and pull it to make her come to him.

"Hi," he said, and she spun around, nearly knocking his drink out of his hand.

"Oh! Sorry," she said. "You scared me."

His first thought was that she was right to be afraid. "You should run."

She smiled and blushed. "Oh yeah?"

He nodded as he leveled his dark eyes on her deep blue ones.

"I think your eyes are gorgeous. I had to come and say hello. I had to see the color and I have to say I'm not one bit disappointed."

Her smile sent waves of some unknown sensation through him. She could be dangerous to him he thought. She could push him out of his comfort zone and he knew it without any doubt.

"Your eyes are pretty nice too," she told him then took a sip of the drink he'd sent her. "Thanks for the drink. I'm not really knowledgeable about alcohol yet. I only turned twenty-one a few weeks ago."

"I see," Arsen took a drink as he looked at her. "What is it that you do?"

"I'm in school. I wanna be a lawyer when I grow up," she said with a giggle.

Her voice was soft and easy on the ears. Her giggle was too. Not silly, or sexy, just kind of a sweet sound he thought he could listen to a lot.

"I'm a lawyer."

Her eyes brightened. "Anyone I may have heard of?"

His impending legal problems sprung to the forefront of his mind and suddenly his name was not a thing he wanted her to know. Just in case it ended up on the news in the near future.

"Name's A.C. I'm nothing big, just a small time lawyer." He took a drink and watched her reaction.

"We all have to start somewhere," she said with a smile. "One day you'll make it big, I bet. You have the look of a powerful attorney."

He smiled and thought she had a look about her too that showed she was capable of great things.

"You don't really fit in with the bitch pack, do you?"

HER EYES TRAVELED to the dance floor where the other girls had gone. She shook her head, making the dark waves of her hair move across her shoulders and one strand fell across her breast making Arsen's cock twitch.

"The tall blonde is my roommate. She turned twenty-one today and made me come. I'm not real big on hanging with, what did you call them, the bitch pack? That's funny, I'm stealing it." Her smile revealed straight, white, perfect teeth. Pink, plump lips pulled over them and everything about her was genuine.

"Steal it," he said and stopped himself from telling her the corny words that ran through his mind.

Arsen had thought to himself that she was already stealing his heart, but those were not only thoughts he never had at least since back in the days of his naïve innocence and Beth. The words would never pass his lips.

His time was limited before the bitch pack would come back so he asked, "Would you allow me to take you home. I have a car outside. I'd love it if you'd let me give you a ride."

"Sorry, I'm not that kind of girl," she said and sipped her drink. "You're a complete stranger after all."

THE FACT she was no easy piece made him thrilled, but he wanted her much too badly to take no for an answer. "Smart girl," he said.

"Thanks," she looked him over and frowned. "You're most likely married anyway. Have a house full of kids you're here to get away from."

"What makes you say that?" he asked as he'd never been told he looked domesticated before.

She bit her bottom lip as she looked him over. "Can't say really. You just look like you're used to getting your way. Not many single guys get their way very often."

He held his left hand up for her to inspect. "You will not find a tan line around this finger. I've never been married."

"Can I ask you a question?" She looked up at him and he found himself loving her basic character. She would be able to be what he wanted in a sub, he saw it in her.

"Sure." He moved a little closer to her, feeling the warmth which came from her.

"How old are you?"

"Thirty-five." He moved a step closer and touched her waist. "Old enough to teach you things that you've never thought about knowing before."

Heat came off her body as her faced turned pink. "I bet you could."

"You should let me take you home." He leaned into her, his hand moving from her waist to the small of her back, gently moving her body to his, their hips touching.

HE KNEW she'd fit him perfectly and his dick stretched the giving fabric of his slacks. Her body trembled with the contact and he knew she'd be fantastic in bed... and the living room, the hallway, the backseat of his Escalade.

"I'm really not that kind of girl. There are plenty of easy ho's around here though." She peered up at him as she tried to take a step back, but his hand on the small of her back stopped her retreat.

"I don't do easy," he said and found his mouth moving to take hers.

She licked her lips and for a second he thought that he was home free. "Don't." Her voice was but a whisper, but her word stopped him.

He moved back a little. She would be begging him soon enough. "Smart girl."

"I am and you, sir, I dare say seem a little bit dangerous," she took in a deep breath and backed another step away from him.

Arsen shook his head. "A little dangerous, no." He was very dangerous, and he knew it. A young innocent thing like she was didn't stand a chance under his expert hands. He'd bend her to him as easily as a young sapling to a post.

She surprised him as she leaned back in close to him and whispered, "I have to tell you that you are the first man who actually made me think about doing what you asked though."

He smiled without realizing he was doing it. She was a bit dangerous herself. He felt a pull like he never had before. It was a thing he couldn't even afford to have at that time in his life.

There were no guarantees he'd even be walking the streets the next day. He could be scooped up by the authorities and placed in custody at any moment. The detective had made that abundantly clear to him just that afternoon.

The other young women were coming back to the table, and he wasn't about exchange pleasantries with any of them. He kissed his fingertips and placed them on her lips. "See you around then." He turned and left before she could say another word.

After paying the tab and taking care of the bill for the party that the young woman was a part of, he took his credit card back from the bartender and went out to get in his car.

Paul jumped out and opened the back door for him. "No girl, boss?"

"Not yet," Arsen said as he sat in the back. "Give her time. She's coming, she just hasn't realized it yet and I don't want to hang out with her idiotic friends."

HE TOOK a beer and sipped on it as he contemplated his day and all he was up against. His mind wandered off to how it was he got involved in the life he led.

All the way back to how he was living out of his car in Los Angeles after he got out of the hospital. His mother had left him there, leaving him alone after Beth's father's beating had put him in the hospital.

It was her chance to have a valid excuse to finally abandon him the way he knew she'd wanted to for years. She said the hospital would make her pay if she stuck around. It was in his best interest if no one could find her, then the state would have to pay his hospital and doctor bills and he'd only have to live six months in a foster home after that.

She told him she was doing it all for him. He'd be eighteen in six months, a month after that he'd be out of high school and being in the system would ensure him that he could go to college, like he always said he wanted to do.

Yes, she was sacrificing all for him.

HE FROWNED WITH THE THOUGHT. After a long drink from the tall bottle he nodded and thought, at least he was able to go to college and make something of himself.

And physically, with the help of Beth's mother, he made sure his body toughened up as well as his heart. It was she who set him up in a small apartment near Stanford University where he got his law degree and learned about the life of a sub under her tutelage.

Under her firm hand, he learned to turn pain into something else. Power and pleasure. While the professors in law school worked his brain out and made it work in a way that would take him into a productive future, Mistress Sinclair taught him how to take his power in his own hands.

The apartment was where she had taught him all there was to know about BDSM. She was a closet case who had to hide her obsession from her family. Her husband would have been a terrible Dom, she'd told him. He was too mean spirited and lacked self-discipline.

She taught him to be strict and to dole out the proper punishment when it was called for to get the sub to do what made the Dom happy. She taught him, what she would later tell him, was a little too well as he quickly outgrew his desire to be a submissive to her.

He was made to be a Dom and when he sought out the underworld where people went to find others who wanted the lifestyle, he had begun to enjoy Mistress Sinclair who tried hard to punish him back into submissiveness to her. All the lashings in the world would not see him spend a lifetime in that role.

ARSEN'S back still carried the scars from the whips she used to try to subdue him, but the lashes healed eventually and she came to realize he was not going to bend to her will any longer. He'd grown into a huge man, muscles on muscles and a determined spirit that refused to follow anyone.

He held the reins. He held the chains, He held the whip, and she had no want to be at the stinging end of it. That's when he moved out to his very first place and found his very first sub at one of the clubs he'd found. Kyla was his first and now she was gone.

They'd spent a year together. He never loved her, but she was good at doing what he wanted. In the end, it was her entire devotion to him and what he wanted that soured their deal. One couldn't call what they had a relationship.

He took her on no dates, sent her no flowers, and called her no sweet names. He did take care of her. Gave her a car, kept her in a nice place, though not the same place that he lived in. He gave her money so she didn't have to work. She was to be available to him whenever he wanted and she did have to come to his office many times to give him what he needed there as well.

People asked about her and him and what they were to each other, but Arsen only told them they were acquaintances who occasionally fucked. He thought about the one legal aid he had. She was an older woman who'd helped her lawyer husband before he died.

She often told Arsen he was wandering down a path that would never make him happy. He found it odd the woman in her sixties had even an inkling into what he was really doing.

She never came out and told him she knew, only hinted that she did and let him know it would grow old one day and he'd want someone to love and cherish. Not bend to conform to his will and dominate with his authority.

So far, Arsen had found no one who made him want to open his hard and dark heart to allow to come in and possibly hurt him or take control of him. But the young woman who was inside the club with her friends had nothing in common with what had made something twitch not only in his pants but also in his heart.

Now was not the right time for any type of relationship. Definitely not one of traditional means. No normal woman would understand the things that were most likely about to become public knowledge about him.

The young law student certainly looked like a girl who'd run if she knew his dark and troubled secrets. His eye twitched as he thought about her pretty, little face that was so full of life and hope falling as she heard the things he'd done.

She'd hate him for sure. He should just leave and stop waiting for one more chance to get her to let him take her home. She wasn't the type he usually went for. She wasn't one of the girls from the club who was looking for that sort of thing.

She was a nice girl in a normal club. She wore cowboy boots and jeans, not stilettos and ripped stockings. Her blouse covered her ample breasts, not torn and leaving nothing to the imagination.

She stood tall and held herself with confidence even though she was young and had yet to start her law career. He envisioned her in a tiny leather corset, a collar around her long and slender neck, with a chain he held as she made her way through a dark room on her hands and knees.

The men in the clubs he went to would be so fucking envious of him if he took her to any of them. She was a true woman of great beauty and confidence. To have her doing for him as he wanted would be some big feat.

Arsen shook his head to clear it. What in the hell was he thinking? Women should be the last thing on his mind. They were the reason his freedom might be taken away.

Everything he worked so hard for might be gone in a flash because of women and how he chose to have sex with them. He needed to go home and be alone. Contemplate his case and his whole damn life.

BUT JUST AS he was about to tell Paul to take him home. The door to the club opened and out she walked. "I'll be right back," he told Paul as he got out of the car.

He followed her as she walked down the busy sidewalk of downtown San Francisco. She was all alone, and he found himself thinking that she was too pretty to be walking alone. Something bad could happen to her.

Arsen slowed his pace as he thought what it was he wanted to do to her and that it wasn't entirely good for her either. He wanted to hold her down and make her beg him to fuck her after all.

Some young guy took notice of her as he walked towards her.

"Hey, baby, where you off to?" he asked as he approached her.

Arsen's body filled with tension as the guy spoke to her. She turned her head, ignoring the guy, but the idiot had the balls to reach out and grab her arm, making her stop. Arsen stopped only feet behind them, his hands balled into fists.

"Too good for me, or what? Not even a, fuck you, can you be bothered with saying to me," the guy said as he glared at her.

"Let me go." Arsen watched as her hand slipped into the purse she had hanging from her shoulder.

The bottle she was pulling out had Arsen stopping and falling back to be sure he got none of the pepper spray near him. A little doorway offered him protection from the stuff which was about to fill the air, but he could still keep an eye on her.

"Who do you think you are, bitch?" the man slurred at her and yanked her arm hard.

Arsen had to cover his mouth to keep the laugh quiet as he watched her pull the pepper spray out of her purse in one swift motion and spray the fucker right in his baby blues.

He screamed and let her go. She turned around and went right back into the club she'd just left. Arsen smiled all the way back to his car and climbed in, telling Paul all about the tenacious young woman and how much more her actions had him intrigued.

PAUL TURNED AROUND and leveled his eyes on his long-time friend.

"Okay, Arsen, give me the news."

Arsen stopped smiling and looked at his friend turned employee.

"My ways have caught up to me, Paul. That's all it is."

"Your ways, while questionable, are not illegal. So how is it they've caught up with you?" Paul asked with a frown.

"I'm not sure how much I really want you to know. You see as a person who is aware of almost all of my comings and goings, you're sure to be brought in if they decide to make a case against me. It's best you only know what it is you truly know, not what I can add." Arsen leaned his head back on the leather seat and looked at the ceiling.

"So, I can expect to get called in myself. Fantastic!" Paul groaned. "Crap! The shit I've seen you do are not things I ever wanted to talk to anyone about, Arsen."

"Sorry," Arsen said as he continued to look up. "As far as a friend to you goes, I haven't been the best, have I?"

"Don't think like that, Arsen. I love you, man. I'm not judging you by any means. So you should tell me what I say and not say. If they ask me if I've seen you hit a woman, how would I answer that?"

"Fuck if I know," Arsen said with a moan. "Maybe something like, everything he did was mutually accepted by all parties he engaged in those types of activities with."

"That's a fucking mouthful, isn't it?" Paul asked and had to laugh. "What about that time you had me hold that chick for you while you took your tie off. I tried to get the hell out of the room before you got started but I saw you tie her up and hang her up on that door and smack the shit out of her with your belt. I remember her begging you to stop."

· · ·

ARSEN RAN his large hand over his face which had gone ashen with the memory his friend brought up.

"It's part of the act. Our safe word was rose, and she knew that. She wanted to beg, that's all. Man, that's one of the girls this shit is about. This is bad, Paul. This is really bad."

"Not that chick!" Paul ran his hand over his face as well. "Man, Arsen, she was into that crazy violent shit. There was the time she begged you to choke her. Then another time when she came out to the car completely naked, and you two went to one of the clubs and when you two got back in the car, her body was covered in bruises."

Arsen's stomach was hurting again, and he felt like he might throw up. He grabbed another beer and downed it.

"I'm in so fucking deep, Paul."

"And why are we waiting out here for yet another female, Arsen? I can't tell you what a bad idea this is. Does the word, 'stalking,' ring in those ears of yours?"

"I fucking know! Fuck!" Arsen balled up his fist and hit the back of the seat next to him. "If this girl was one of them I'd tell you to take me home and lock my ass up until I came to my senses. But she's not into that at all. Well, I don't think she is, but she seems like she might like some aspects of it."

"Stop! Do you hear yourself?" Paul asked.

ARSEN TOOK in a deep breath and let his mind work like the lawyer he was. Was he that self-destructive that he was on the verge of the end and still he was consumed with sex?

"Drive away, Paul," Arsen said finally. "This is ridiculous. Drive away."

Paul turned around and pulled his seatbelt on and turned his blinker on to pull away from the curb.

"Good decision, Arsen."

The sound of metal smacking against metal made the men look

out the left side of the car and Arsen moaned as he saw there was no way they'd be leaving and getting him away from what would surely be part of his downfall.

A truck had run into a car right next to them. The wreck had them sandwiched between the mangled cars and the sidewalk full of people making their way to the various clubs and restaurants along it.

"Fuck me," Arsen swore.

"Just stay in the car," Paul said. "Don't even look over there to see if she comes out of the club again."

Arsen laid his head back and tried not to think, but the other woman who was no longer around, his second sub, filled his mind. Her dark skin had always been a thing he thought beautiful about her. Meagan was tough at first. A real spit fire.

He'd broken her down until she was a shell of her former self. Arsen had thought it was up to him to teach her that her place was where he said it was. He wanted her home all the time. He had her order the groceries instead of going out to get them.

When she went out, her beauty had other men gawking at her and it made him insane. She was his. They'd drawn up a paper which said so. He wanted no other eyes falling on her.

One night as she laid in her bed in her apartment he had her in, she asked him to stay the night with her. She was alone too much and was beginning to hate it. She asked him to please stay with her and he hadn't wanted to start that kind of thing.

He'd been taught that was not what people who lived that lifestyle did. It made them weak, and that was a thing he didn't want to be. And look where that had left him. Alone and accused of things he could've easily done.

No alibi for any of the things he was accused of and the fact he'd recently met with each one of his old subs. One last go round he wanted with each one as the lifestyle was beginning to grow boring, just like the older lady who used to work with him said it would.

Arsen wanted to see if any one of the women made him feel like they had a spark. Like the life he'd been living was something maybe one of them could spark an interest in again.

WORK and more work had been filling his days and nights. Random hook-ups weren't filling the emptiness that had begun to grow in him. He gave each woman one last shot to see if it was one of them who could fill him, or begin to at least.

The last sub he had was named Lacy and their contract was short-lived. Her quiet nature, he soon found out was due to her being a complete air head. Arsen knew she didn't really have the brains to decide if she really wanted what he dished out or not.

And when she even forgot their safe word, and he went on with his spanking of her until she was sobbing uncontrollably, he knew that she wasn't cut out for that kind of sex life.

But for reasons that made no sense he took one last shot with her anyway and now she was another who was gone and he might stand accused of that too.

POLICEMEN BEGAN to show up to the scene of the accident and as the two drivers' of the wrecked cars argued over who was at fault, one cop knocked on the driver's side window and asked Paul and any other witnesses in the car to please step out so they could talk to them.

Paul and Arsen stepped out of the car and Arsen quickly told them he hadn't seen a thing and had no idea of who was at fault. Something brushed up against his arm and a voice filled his ears, "What happened?"

He turned to find the deep blue eyes of the girl he should be avoiding for not only her own good but his too.

"They wrecked. Um, hit each other, I mean, they smacked into one another. Fuck, you know what I mean, right?"

His stammering made her giggle, and he had to ball his hands into fists to stop himself from grabbing her hair in his hands and pulling her mouth to his. Her lips, plump and pink formed a smile.

"Nervous?"

"Me?" he asked and found his voice going high.

That was not like him. She did make him nervous, and that was odd.

"Do I make you nervous?"

"Hell no!" He slipped his arm around her waist.

PAUL CAME to his side after telling the cops he had no idea who was at fault either.

"Hi," he said to the girl who would be running away from Arsen if she knew what he really wanted with her. "I'm Paul."

Arsen gave him a look that told him to go get in the car. The wreckers were pulling the wrecked cars away, and they'd be able to leave in minutes. Paul walked away and got in the driver's seat.

"As you can see that's my driver, Paul. So you won't be completely alone with a stranger if you allow me to drive you to your home." Arsen told her as he moved her along with him, his arm tight around her waist.

"I don't think so. It's very nice of you, don't get me wrong."

"It's really not safe for you to walk. Please, just get in. I swear we'll take you straight home. If anything happened to you and I saw you were hurt or God forbid something worse, it would haunt me forever," Arsen told her as he opened the door and gently pushed against her.

"I'd hate it if I haunted you. I think that would mean bad karma for me," she said and looked into his dark eyes. "Promise me something."

"Anything," he said. "I think I could promise you anything?" His finger trailed over her collar bone and he looked deep into her eyes.

They were full of trust, even though they shouldn't be. If she only knew what he wanted to do to her beautiful porcelain skin, watch it turn a nice shade of pink after he had paddled it well.

"Promise that you won't hurt me." Her words hit him hard.

"Why would you say that?" he asked as he pulled his hand back and searched her eyes.

"It's just that I don't go places with strangers. I don't do stupid or dangerous things," she said as she looked at him with such innocence. Too much innocence.

Arsen took a step back. "You should run, little girl."

"SHOULD I, REALLY?" she asked as her eyes danced. "A little while ago I tried to walk home, and a guy grabbed me. I had to empty my pepper spray on his ass. So I'm quite defenseless and a nice, strong lawyer seems a safe bet. A hell of a lot better than taking the chance the prick I sprayed may be waiting to get even with me."

"You know I saw you do that. You seem quite capable of taking care of yourself in situations you feel threatened in."

"I know a little self-defense." She watched his reaction carefully. "If you did something I didn't want you to for instance, you could be sure I'd take your balls in a vice-like grip and make you beg me not to rip them from your body."

His laugh came from deep in his chest. "You're pretty sure of yourself. And what if I did something to you, you wanted me to? What then?"

"I'm a big girl, I can take care of things. So, are you going to give me a ride or should I catch a cab?" Her arms crossed over her chest and he knew he should put her sweet little ass in a cab and move on without looking back.

"I should definitely put you in a cab. To be honest, I'm a bit afraid of you," he said with a smile.

"I'm a bit afraid of you too," she smiled back. "But what's the fun in always playing it safe?"

"By all means, climb into my lair, little girl."

· · ·

HE HELD her hand as she lifted one leg to place her round ass on the leather seat. Arsen sucked in his breath as he pictured that ass beneath his palm.

He balled his hand into a fist again to stop himself from making a swift smack to it as she lifted it some to scoot over so he could take the place next to her. She stopped just short of moving all the way to the edge, staying in the middle.

His arm draped over the back of the seat and she leaned back and took a deep breath. "I love the smell of leather," she said as she let the breath out.

"Good," he said, thinking that she'd really like the good amount of leather he kept in a closet in his penthouse.

"Good?" she asked as she turned her face to look at him. "That's an odd thing to say."

Paul turned and looked at Arsen.

"Where to, boss?"

Arsen looked at the young woman.

"Your place or mine?"

"Take me to my house, scoundrel. 555 Bayview Drive." She looked at Paul. "Please, Paul."

"Yes, my lady," he said with a laugh and the privacy window between the front seat and the rest of the large SUV went up.

Arsen's arm moved down off the back of the seat to touch her shoulders. He felt her shiver and pulled her closer.

"Cold?"

"No, just out of my comfort zone," she answered and ran her hands over her bare arms as she wore a sleeveless shirt.

"You know, it's okay to get out of that boring old comfort zone every now and again." His mouth touched her neck for just a moment then he pulled it back.

SHE TURNED to face him and he found her breathing had increased and came a bit heavier than normal. She was getting ready for him, he knew it, but was she ready for all of him?

Slowly, he ran his fingertips over her lips as he gazed at them. His cock went hard in an instant as she parted her plump lips and pulled his finger into her hot mouth.

She sucked it gently and ran her tongue around it. He watched her and took one of her hands, placing it on his growing cock. Her eyes went wide, and she pulled her mouth off his finger and looked at the lump he held her hand to.

Her eyes darted up to his as she put her fingers on the button of his slacks. She seemed to be silently asking if she could let the beast free and he gave her a nod.

His stomach tensed as he knew he'd be taking her anyway he pleased in just a little while. He watched her open his pants up and his large erection sprang out at her.

She gasped and sprang back, her eyes went wide and he was pleased with her reaction. His big male member was a thing of beauty and she seemed to realize that.

Her eyes went to his again, and she licked her lips. He gave her a nod of approval and she lowered her head to his lap. The touch of her lips sent shivers through him.

His hands moved through her dark waves and he groaned as she moved her mouth over his throbbing cock. Her mouth moved over him so fluidly he knew her innocent demeanor had to have been a farce.

SHE STOPPED and looked at him.

"Why'd you stop, baby?" he moaned as he pulled at her hair.

"I wanted to know if I was doing it right. It's my first time and if I'm doing it wrong and you're up here laughing at me, it would make me very upset. So, am I doing it right? Is there anything I should be doing better? Do you think I should just stop even trying?"

"Seriously?" he asked in disbelief.

She nodded, and he pulled her hair, making her face come to his. He took one deep, hard kiss then released her mouth.

"So, should I continue?" her face was full of innocence and he knew she really was telling him the truth.

"You're doing a fantastic job. Please, get back to it." He let her go, and she resumed her position, placing her hands on his massive member and her mouth on the tip of his dick.

Arsen had been given so many blow jobs he couldn't even keep count of them, yet never had one sent the sensations through him this young woman's sweet mouth was doing.

He laid his head back on the leather seat and tried not to think about a thing as she ran her tongue up the underside of his cock and sucked gently as she pulled her hot mouth back up his long length.

All he could think was this was not going to help his situation at all. Red and blue lights lit up the back window and had Paul slowing the car down and pulling to the side of the road.

ARSEN'S HEART stopped as he knew his time was up and they must be about to officially charge him for the murders.

2

PART TWO: FOR HIM

Steele Gannon

A thin vein of light fog rolled in under the barn door. Steele Gannon had just finished brushing her horse's mane after taking an evening ride to clear her mind from the long school day.

Steele Gannon was a college student in her first year of law school at Stanford University. She'd found a passion for criminal law at the tender age of fifteen when a murder happened in the town she lived in.

At that time her family was living in Baltimore and Steele, and in a rare instance, was watching the nightly local news. The story of a young sixteen-year-old girl who was missing from her sister's apartment was headlining that night.

Steele found herself worried about the girl and she kept up with the news story as the weeks, then months played out with no sign of the girl. After being missing for four long months, Phylicia Barnes' body was found floating in the Susquehanna River and later her sister's onetime boyfriend was accused of the murder.

It seemed he'd made sexual advances towards the young girl and when she thwarted him, he'd strangled her. A death that Steele found eerily brutal and scary. She'd not wish that death on anyone.

She'd read up on how long it takes to die that way and how aware the victim is of what's happening to them. The brain takes a long time to stop working with a lack of oxygen. So the victim is helplessly aware they are going to die.

As the trial went on, it was obvious to most that the young man had murdered young Phylicia and Steele was glad the family would get justice. Only the young man had a couple of female lawyers who somehow managed to get the clearly guilty man acquitted from the murder charges.

Steele, though terribly disappointed with the loss for the family, was intrigued by how the lawyers managed to win such an open and shut case. She became fascinated with the law and started reading any law book she could get her hands on to find out more about the complexity of criminal law.

HER CELL PHONE buzzed in the back pocket of her blue jeans. She looked at it and found a text from her roommate, Gwen. It was Gwen's twenty-first birthday, and she was bugging Steele to hurry to the bar so then they could do the cake.

Steele was not a fan of the bar scene. She preferred wine and a good book, and that was exactly the way she'd spent her twenty-first birthday six months before. She wasn't one to hang with a pack of girls either. The little birthday party for her roomie wasn't a thing she was looking forward to.

But it was her roommate, and she'd never let her live it down if she didn't at least show up for the cake. So Steel gave her horse, Tripper, one last hug and closed his stall for the night.

"Good night, big boy. I'll see you in the morning to let you out into the pasture."

Gwen would be pissed at what she was wearing, tight blue jeans, a white cotton sleeveless shirt, and her cowboy boots, jeans tucked into them, a thing Gwen hated. But if she wanted her there anytime soon, she'd have to put up with her appearance.

She climbed into her truck. One look into the rear view mirror had her ditching her cowboy hat and pulling the braid out of her hair, leaving it in waves that cascaded over her shoulders. The dark waves fell clear to the top of her ass.

Her hair was about the only thing Steele found attractive about herself and she took excellent care of the long, thick, dark, silky mass. She'd somehow managed to get a mix of her parents' hair colors. Deep, rich browns and golden glows along with a smattering of copper strands made up her hair color. Her sky-blue eyes contrasted with her dark hair and she'd been told she looked exotic by more than a few people.

Her skin was a light tan and her butt and breasts were larger than most young women her age. At twenty-one, she was no innocent, but she wasn't promiscuous either. Only a couple of boyfriends she'd had that ended after short bursts of affection.

Steele wasn't the mushy gushy type, but the two she'd dated were and she found herself bored with them after mere months of their attention. She liked a man's man, but had yet to find one.

She was a strong young woman with goals and aspirations, she wasn't interested in the guys that she'd met so far in life. Gamers, most of them were, and that bored her to tears. She liked the outdoors and doing things that made her mind work.

The way the two guys she'd been intimate with had touched her and treated her left her empty. She'd never climaxed with either and found them annoying when they'd want a little action, but couldn't manage to pique her interest.

In the end both had told her she was frigid and would have to get over herself if she was ever to find happiness with a guy. At that point in her young life she could've given less than a shit about hooking up with men. Her mind was on law school and learning all she could so someday she could be a criminal lawyer who won cases no one would ever guess she could.

Steele pulled up into the parking garage of her apartment building. She knew Gwen would make her drink something, and she wasn't a drinker and had no idea of how she'd handle the liquor. She wasn't about to try to drive home after consuming even one alcoholic beverage.

THE EVENING AIR WAS NICE, not too crisp, and she had a bottle of pepper spray in her purse if anyone should try to bother her as she walked the mile to the downtown San Francisco area where Gwen and her friends were having the little party. Though not excited about the bar, she was excited about getting out for a little while. It wasn't a thing she did, and she prided herself on pushing her comfort zone's barriers from time to time.

The music leaked out of the bar's door and she found the bubblegum pop annoying already. She liked hard rock, much unlike every other girl on the planet she'd been told about her taste in music.

After her eyes adjusted to the dimly lit bar, she found her room-mate and gaggle of girlfriends shaking their asses on the dance floor. A thing she wasn't about to get caught up in. Too sober and too embarrassed to be shaking it yet.

She saw Gwen's purse sitting on a table right next to the dance floor and knew she'd be trying to get her to dance with them, a thing that had her wanting to leave already.

"Oh, hell," she muttered to herself as she made her way to the table.

Steele took a seat on one of the tall chairs that surrounded the little table and reached back and took her cell phone out of the back pocket of her jeans. While she waited she might as well see what her Face book peeps were up to on that Thursday night.

To her surprise a waiter showed up with a drink in his hand.

"From the gentleman at the next table, miss." He placed the drink on the table in front of her.

"What is it?" she asked. "I mean, I'm new to this drinking thing. Is it going to knock me on my ass?"

The waiter smiled.

"No, you'll be fine. Sip, don't chug. It's a whisky sour, just like the man who sent it to you is drinking." He turned and gestured to a man with dark waves which hung to his broad shoulders.

Steele smiled and gave the man a little wave and mouthed, 'thank you' to him. She turned back around and had to take in a couple of deep breaths. The man who'd sent her the drink was the best looking man that she'd ever laid her eyes on.

The fact he'd even noticed her was making her wet, and she wasn't one to go all wet and wiggly so quickly and easily. But the way he looked at her with his dark eyes that seemed to narrow as he took her all in, made her knees weak.

Steele prayed he wouldn't come talk to her. She was sure she'd get all tongue tied and make a complete ass out of herself if he did. She wanted desperately to take another look at the magnificent specimen of manhood.

He had a beard which was not a thing she'd ever thought attractive before, but it was meticulously groomed close to his face which was so symmetrical it looked perfect. She guessed he was some type of lawyer or business man because he had on an expensive suit, but his tie was gone and the top buttons on his shirt were undone. He must've had a rough day, she thought.

He's got to be married!

HE LOOKED to be in his thirties and had to be a successful something or other, she just knew it. The gang of girls made their way back to the table and Steele was caught up in Gwen's long arms before she knew it.

The tall blonde was a sweet girl, but her taste in friends left a lot to be desired. The red-head, Tracy was a complete bitch and her other friend, Laura she thought might be a lesbian, but she didn't claim to be. Then there were a couple of stragglers she didn't know but recognized from their college.

Gwen started wagging her finger in Steele's face.

"Why are you so late? And what the hell are you wearing? Did you come straight from that smelly old barn you keep your horse at? Oh, will you ever decide to clean up for anything?"

"Nice to see you too, Gwen," Steele said with a laugh. "I hope your birthday is going well."

"It is," Gwen said and changed her mood quickly as she saw the birthday cake coming her way and the girls began singing her the birthday song. "Yes, cake!"

Steele took a step back and got out of the way so Gwen could blow out her candles. She could swear the gorgeous man who'd sent her the drink was looking at her. She wasn't about to do more than glance from the corner of her eye, but she was pretty sure he was looking at her.

Why would he be? She thought. I'm nowhere near his league. I'm sure he has a beautiful wife at home waiting for him to get there and tuck their three kids in for the night.

Another song came on and the girls around Steele burst into a simultaneous scream and ran to the dance floor. Gwen tugged at Steele's arm to get her to join them, but she wasn't budging and adamantly shook her head. Finally, Gwen could take it no more and gyrated her body out to join the other girls.

Steele picked up her drink and took a sip, happy she got out of her roommate's clutches. Something stirred her hair, and she turned around quickly, finding the gorgeous man right behind her. Her arm hit the drink he held and nearly knocked it out of his hand.

"OH! SORRY. YOU SCARED ME."

"You should run."

Steele smiled nervously and found herself blushing. "Oh yeah?"

His voice was deep and velvety. He stayed close to her. So close that she could smell his cologne which she knew had to be expensive because she'd never smelled any like it before. His elbow touched her upper arm and a constant stream of electricity was flowing across her bare skin.

The way he told her she should run had her thinking all kinds of crazy thoughts, a thing she never did. He was beyond intriguing and he gave off a dangerous vibe.

He nodded as he leveled his dark eyes on her. "I think your eyes are gorgeous. I had to come and say hello. I had to see the color and I have to say I'm not one bit disappointed."

OMG! He thinks my eyes are gorgeous!

"YOUR EYES ARE PRETTY NICE TOO," she told him then took a sip of the drink he'd sent her. "Thanks for the drink. I'm not really knowledgeable about alcohol yet. I only turned twenty-one a few months ago."

"I see." He took a drink, and she found herself mesmerized by the way his lips conformed to the glass. She licked her lips as she noticed a drop of the liquid on his bottom lip. With a quick flick of his tongue he got it and she felt her panties get a little bit wetter. "What is it that you do?"

His words had her looking back at his eyes and feeling like an idiot for starring at his lips.

"I'm in school. I wanna be a lawyer when I grow up," she said with a giggle.

"I'm a lawyer."

Steele was even more intrigued...

"Anyone I may have heard of?"

"Name's A.C. I'm nothing big, just a small time lawyer." He took a drink, and she doubted he was a small time anything.

"We all have to start somewhere. One day you'll make it big I bet. You have the look of a powerful attorney." She shifted her weight as she let her eyes run up and down his fit body.

The man was muscled like a machine. She just knew there was a tight little six pack hidden under his starched white shirt and she bet his ass was solid as a rock.

He smiled and said, "You don't really fit in with the bitch pack, do you?"

·   ·   ·

HER EYES TRAVELED to the dance floor where the other girls had gone. She shook her head. "The tall blonde is my roommate. She turned twenty-one today and made me come. I'm not real big on hanging with, what did you call them, the bitch pack? That's funny, I'm stealing it," she said with a smile, finding him funny and great looking.

What a fantastic combination! Now, if he's great in bed that would be a trifecta!

"STEAL IT," he said as his dark eyes twinkled with amusement.

She took a sip of her drink and peered at him over the ridge of the glass. He was much too good to be true. He held himself like a man, not some boy who was trying to get into her pants. This man had the look of a man who got his way.

"Would you allow me to take you home? I have a car outside. I'd love it if you'd let me give you a ride."

"Sorry, I'm not that kind of girl," she said then took another sip of her drink as he was getting under her skin and making her itch for him in a way she'd never done before. "You're a complete stranger after all."

"Smart girl," he said with a smile.

Am I? Or am I just being a big chicken?

"THANKS," she looked him over and just knew he had to be married. He was too good looking and well put together to be single. "You're most likely married anyway. Have a house full of kids that you're here to get away from."

"What makes you say that?" he asked, looking a little confused.

She bit her bottom lip as she looked him over.

"Can't say really. You just look like you're used to getting your way. Not many single guys get their way very often."

He held his left hand up.

"You will not find a tan line around this finger. I've never been married."

She looked up at him. Her mind was spinning a bit with the knowledge he wasn't married and that made him fair game. "Can I ask you a question?"

"Sure." He moved a little closer to her. Her body warmed with the closeness and she wondered what it would feel like to be wrapped in his strong arms.

"How old are you?"

"Thirty-five." He moved a step closer and touched her waist, making her legs shake. "Old enough to teach you things you never thought about knowing before."

HER INSIDES MELTED. He was actually coming on to her. There was an actual chance she could feel this powerful man's arms wrapped around her. His naked body touching hers.

Steele blushed with the naughty thoughts that were running through her head.

"I bet you could."

"You should let me take you home." He leaned into her, his hand moving from her waist to the small of her back, gently moving her body to his, their hips touching.

Steele had to fight the urge to give into the man. His face was so handsome and his body so rock hard. There had to be some downfall with the perfect man.

"I'm really not that kind of girl. There are plenty of easy ho's around here though." She peered up at him as she tried to take a step back, but his hand on the small of her back stopped her retreat. She found she loved the way he made her do as he wanted.

"I don't do easy," he said, and she found his mouth moving closer to hers. He wanted to kiss her. Right there in front of the whole bar, he wanted to take her mouth, and she wanted to let him so damn bad that she could already taste his lips.

He was so close to her she could feel the softness of his whisker covered face. Steele licked her lips.

"Don't," she whispered.

She was still the same young woman inside no matter how crazy her brain was thinking. Steele did not make out with strangers and she sure as hell didn't do it in a bar with people watching.

He moved back a little. "Smart girl."

"I am and you, sir, I dare say seem a little bit dangerous," she took in a deep breath and backed another step away from him. Her body was yearning for his, a thing she knew wasn't smart to give into.

He shook his head.

"A little dangerous, no."

She surprised herself as she leaned back in close to him and whispered, "I have to tell you that you are the first man who actually made me think about doing what you asked though."

He smiled, making her happy to see he really did want her. It was still running around her mind that he had to be fucking with her. He was gorgeous and out of her league in every possible way after all.

The other young women were coming back to the table she could tell by the way his eyes darted to the dance floor and a frown covered his handsome face. He kissed his fingertips and placed them on her lips.

"See you around then." He turned and left, leaving a chill covering her body as he did.

Almost instantly she regretted not going with him. Gwen had her by the shoulders and steered her out to the dance floor not taking no for an answer any longer. Steele watched as the gorgeous man paid at the bar then left.

Her chance had gone, and she felt like an idiot for not taking him up on his offer. As she danced to the crappy music, she felt disappointment in herself. She'd wanted a man's man, and he sure seemed like one.

His body and attitude commanded respect and attention. She was sure he could make her do just about anything he wanted her to. What did she want with a man like that anyway?

She wasn't sure what she wanted with a man like that, but she did want him. And she'd missed out on that chance.

I'm an idiot!

THE NIGHT WENT on and after an hour, she managed to sneak away from the bitch pack. She smiled and thought to herself that the man from earlier was clever and it was hard to find clever.

Out the door she went, the cool air making the skin on her bare arms goose-pimple. She ran her hands up and down them and silently cursed herself for wearing a sleeveless shirt after dark.

Down the sidewalk she went, making her way back the mile-long walk to her apartment. Her eyes darted up as some damn guy focused his drunken gaze on her as he came towards her.

"Hey, baby, where you off too?" the drunk guy asked as he approached her.

Steele turned her head, ignoring the guy, but the drunk had the audacity to reach out and grab her arm, making her stop.

Oh no he didn't!

SHE LOOKED up to find his glassy ice-blue eyes glaring at her.

"Too good for me, or what? Not even a 'fuck you', can you be bothered with saying to me?"

Placing her hand in her purse to retrieve the pepper spray, she warned the fool, "Let me go." She pulled the bottle out.

His words were slurred as he said, "Who do you think you are, bitch?" He yanked her arm hard, and that was all she could stand out of the asshole.

Steele pulled the pepper spray out of her purse in one swift motion and sprayed the drunk right in his drooping eyes.

He screamed and let her go. With the man out there, she had no choice but to go back to the bar and wait for him to leave the area so she could go home. She turned around and went right back even though it was the last place she wanted to be at that time.

Steele really wanted to go home and get into bed and think about the gorgeous man she let get away. What a fool she'd been, and it was highly doubtful she'd get a chance like that again.

She went back to the table and Gwen frowned at her.

"Where did you go, Steele?"

"I tried to go home, but a drunken asshole messed with me. I pepper sprayed him and now I have to wait for him to get lost before I can go home." She sat back down, but Gwen took her hand and pulled her back out on the dance floor and made her dance some more.

The night was turning into exactly what she expected it would; a nightmare.

THREE DANCES later Steele could take no more. Crazy drunk guy or not, she was leaving. The party had gone on too long for her and she headed out after letting Gwen know she was going and wishing her a happy birthday.

Just as she opened the door, she saw a wreck had happened right in front of the place and to her complete joy she saw the gorgeous man, sans his black suit jacket, standing at the back of a shiny black Escalade.

His back was to her, and she'd had just enough liquid courage to have her acting on her whim. She walked quietly up behind him, brushing her hand against his arm. "What happened?" she asked.

His eyes went wide as he turned back and saw her. "They wrecked. Um, hit each other, I mean, they smacked into one another. Fuck, you know what I mean, right?"

His stammering made her giggle. She was glad to see her presence had unnerved him. She smiled. "Nervous?"

"Me?" he asked in a high voice.

Her mind raced with the fact she made him nervous.

"Do I make you nervous?"

"Hell no!" he said and slipped his arm around her waist.

Steele felt complete with his arm securing her as if she belonged to him. His arm was strong. She could feel his bicep beneath the long sleeve shirt pressing against her back. She longed to actually see the muscled arm.

ANOTHER TALL MAN in a black suit came up to them. "Hi, I'm Paul."

Steele gave the man a nod and a smile. She took notice of the way the man who had his arm wrapped tightly around her looked at the other man. Paul walked away and got in the driver's seat.

"As you can see, that's my driver, Paul. So you won't be completely alone with a stranger if you allow me to drive you to your home," he told her as he moved her along with him.

Not entirely sure it was smart to actually go through with accepting the man's ride, she said, "I don't think so. It's very nice of you, don't get me wrong."

"It's really not safe for you to walk. Please, just get in. I swear we'll take you straight home. If anything happened to you and I saw you were hurt or God forbid something worse, it would haunt me forever," he told her as he opened the door and gently pushed against her.

The way he gently was forcing her to do what he wanted secretly thrilled her. Though she knew it was most likely the most stupid and dangerous decision she'd ever made, she said, "I'd hate it if I haunted you. I think that would mean bad karma for me." Looking deep into his eyes, she searched for the truth. "Promise me something."

"Anything," he said. "I think I could promise you anything?" His finger trailed over her collar bone and he looked just as deep into her eyes. Her body tingled with his touch and she was hot and ready for the man in an instant.

Feeling very vulnerable in the stranger's hold she found something in his dark eyes that told her she could trust him. "Promise you won't hurt me."

"Why would you say that?" he asked as he pulled his hand back and searched her eyes.

She felt compelled to tell him how she really was. "It's just that I don't go places with strangers. I don't do stupid or dangerous things."

He took a step back. "You should run, little girl."

His choice of words had her knowing she was about to show him she was no little girl.

"Should I, really? A little while ago I tried to walk home, and a guy grabbed me. I had to empty my pepper spray on his ass. So I'm quite defenseless and a nice, strong lawyer seems a safe bet. A hell of a lot better than taking the chance the prick I sprayed may be waiting to get even with me."

"You know I saw you do that. You seem quite capable of taking care of yourself in situations you feel threatened in."

"I KNOW A LITTLE SELF-DEFENSE. If you did something I didn't want you to for instance, you could be sure I'd take your balls in a vice-like grip and make you beg me not to rip them from your body."

His laugh came from deep in his chest and she loved it.

"You're pretty sure of yourself. And what if I did something to you, you wanted me to? What then?"

"I'm a big girl, I can take care of things. So, are you going to give me a ride or should I catch a cab?" She crossed her arms over her chest and waited to see if the man was all talk and no action.

"I should definitely put you in a cab. To be honest, I'm a bit afraid of you," he said with a smile.

"I'm a bit afraid of you too," she smiled back. "But what's the fun in always playing it safe?" She didn't even recognize the woman who was saying the words that were coming out of her mouth. This was not her, but her body was overruling her brain.

"By all means, climb into my lair, little girl."

He held her hand as she got into the Escalade. Her heart pounded in her chest as she couldn't believe herself. She stopped just short of moving all the way to the edge, staying in the middle.

His arm draped over the back of the seat and she leaned back and took in a deep breath. "I love the smell of leather," she said as she let the breath out.

"Good."

"Good?" she asked as she turned to look at him. "That's an odd thing to say."

Paul turned and looked back at the man. "Where to, boss?"

He looked at her with a smile. "Your place or mine?"

"Take me to my house, scoundrel. 555 Bayview Drive." She looked at Paul. "Please, Paul."

"Yes, my lady," he said with a laugh and the privacy window between the front seat and the rest of the large SUV went up, making Steele shiver as they were completely alone in the very back of the long SUV.

The man's arm moved down off the back of the seat to touch her shoulders. He pulled her closer. "Cold?"

"No, just out of my comfort zone," she answered and ran her hands over her bare arms.

"You know, it's okay to get out of that boring old comfort zone every now and again." His mouth touched her neck for just a moment then he pulled it back. The way her stomach tightened had her thinking the man was probably going to be able to make her orgasm.

She turned to face him and found her breathing had increased and came a bit heavier than normal. He was exciting the shit out of her without even really trying.

Slowly, he ran his fingertips over her lips as he gazed at them. She decided to let it all go and be the bad girl that she never was until that night. Steele parted her lips and pulled his finger into her mouth. Sucking it gently and running her tongue around it.

He watched her and took one of her hands, placing it on his

growing cock. Her eyes went wide, and she pulled her mouth off his finger and looked at the lump he held her hand to.

Her eyes darted up to his as she put her fingers on the button of his slacks. Steele had never given a blow job, but for some reason she could think of little else other than getting the man's cock into her mouth.

He gave her a nod, and she found herself giddy with excitement. She unbuttoned his slacks and pushed the black underwear down and a giant cock sprang out at her, making her gasp in awe of it.

Steele found that it was one of the most beautiful things she'd ever laid her eyes on. It surprised her how large it was, with a perfect tan color to it and not too veiny. She looked at him and silently asked if she could take the monster into her mouth.

He gave her another nod of approval and she took the thick cock in her hands, finding it felt like silk wrapped around a steel rod. Slowly, she placed her lips on top and licked the head. His hands ran through her hair and he moaned.

She ran her tongue along the underside of his dick as she moved her mouth up and down the long length of it a few times. Her hands holding it to cover where her mouth left. With no idea if she was even doing it right as it was her first time after all she found herself wanting to ask him if she was okay at it.

She stopped and looked at him.

"Why'd you stop, baby?" he moaned as he pulled at her hair.

"I wanted to know if I was doing it right. It's my first time and if I'm doing it wrong and you're up here laughing at me, it would make me very upset. So, am I doing it right? Is there anything I should be doing better? Do you think I should just stop even trying?"

"Seriously?" he asked as confusion riddled his handsome face.

She nodded, and he pulled her hair, making her face come to his. He took one deep, hard kiss then released her mouth. Just that one kiss was better than any she'd ever had. Her body tensed with need, but she was still worried she wasn't good at giving him the oral sex she was attempting to please him with.

"So, should I continue?" she asked.

"You're doing a fantastic job. Please, get back to it." He let her go, and she resumed her position, placing her hands on his massive member and her mouth on the tip of his dick.

Steele took him in again with renewed passion as he'd told her it was fantastic and that was more than she'd thought she'd get for her first blow job. Faster she moved her mouth up and down him. His hands fisted in her hair, pulling it and making her ache for more.

She's never had her hair pulled and found it very stimulating. He was aggressive as he pushed her head down with each stroke, making her take him all the way down her throat. She was hot with the knowledge she could even do that without choking on the massive organ.

THE CAR BEGAN to slow down, and she felt them pulling over. Her heart pounded as she heard the man say, "Fuck! It's over!"

She pulled her mouth off him as the car stopped and saw the police lights out the back window. "What happened? Did your driver run a red light or something?"

The guy was looking at her with such sadness in his dark eyes that she couldn't understand it. His hand ran over her cheek and he pulled her up and kissed her.

The kiss was so deep and she felt like he was kissing her like he might not ever get to do it again. She pulled his pants back up and buttoned him all back up so if the cops did look in the back then they wouldn't see his giant dick out.

He finally ended the kiss and looked into her eyes. "You give great head, baby. I wish I could've felt the ending, but I can't control everything."

SHE WAS REALLY CONFUSED by his behavior. Steele got back on the seat and waited to see what was going to happen. After a minute they saw the cop walk up to the driver's window and then he walked back to his car and the light went off as the driver pulled back onto the road and drove away.

The window rolled down and Paul said, "Seems I accidentally left my driver's license with that police officer back at that accident scene." He laughed and rolled the window back up.

Steele kind of giggled as the man next to her grabbed her by the shoulders and growled.

"Thank God. Now no more fucking around."

The buttons on her shirt flew everywhere as he ripped it open. Her expression had to have been full of surprise as he did it and she found him ripping her bra off next.

Sitting in front of him with her large breasts exposed had her not daring to breathe. He'd turned in an instant. She was afraid but excited as well. He pulled her off the seat and down to the floor with him. Flipping her over, he unbuttoned and unzipped her jeans and yanked them back to her knees.

She gasped as he easily ripped her panties off and said, "Put your hands on the seat."

Steele did as he said with no hesitation. She heard his zipper go down then felt him force his cock into her. She was as wet as she'd ever been with the rush of excitement, but he was huge and he spread places that had never been spread.

It burned, and she screamed with the sensation. He yanked her hair hard. "No noise!"

Somehow, she cut the scream off and he pulled nearly all the way out then thrust back into her. It burned like fire and she wanted to scream so bad, but she didn't know what he'd do if she did. She moaned a little with the intense burn and he smacked her ass hard.

Now she knew what he'd do if she didn't do as he said.

No noise!

.   .   .

HE POUNDED her with his massive cock and eventually the burn turned into more pleasure than she'd ever known. She rocked back against him, loving how savage he was. The little grunts he made and the sound of his body slapping against hers filled her ears.

One of his hands ran around and pinched her nipple then pulled it hard. She wanted to moan and tried hard not to but one slipped out and he moved the other hand and smacked her ass hard twice.

Her body started shaking on the inside and she knew she was about to have the first orgasm that she'd ever had with a man. He stopped his assault and leaned over her.

His hard chest was against her back and it felt like pure Heaven to her. His words hit her ear hot as he said, "I can feel you about to come. You don't come until I tell you to or you'll feel the sting of my hand until tears run out of your pretty blue eyes."

Steele had never been talked to that way and even though she knew she should tell him to fuck off, she found herself wanting him even worse. His hand twisted in her hair, pulling her head back.

"Tell me you understand me."

"I understand you," she said then he kissed her hard.

BEFORE HE PULLED his mouth off hers, he bit her bottom lip hard, but not hard enough to break the skin. Her body was on fire as he pulled his body back and resumed plunging deep into her from behind. His hands on her hips, dragging her back to him with each hard stroke.

"Fuck, you're tight as hell. When's the last time you got fucked?" he asked her through gritted teeth.

Every thrust was knocking her breath out and she gasped out, "About a year."

He laughed "Fuck me, that's seems impossible."

AN INTENSE FEELING was filling her, but she knew without a doubt that if she let the orgasm go he'd spank the shit out of her. She didn't know if she was up to that so she held on.

"Good girl," he said as he continued to pound her from behind. "You hold it like I told you to. It's going to be better than you ever imagined it could be."

To further make things harder, he reached one hand around her and pinched her clit between his fingers. The tiny pearl had swollen with desire and his touch nearly sent her over the edge. Only the fear of his punishment stopped her.

Steele closed her eyes and thought of nothing as she held back the thing her body wanted to do the most. His fingers left her clit and she let out the breath she didn't even realize she'd been holding in.

He moved his body down on hers, pressing his chest to her back and his strokes went slow and somehow even deeper. "You on birth control or do I pull out when I come?"

"I'm on birth control," she said with a hard pant.

"You want me to come inside you?" he asked.

"Yes," she said with a little moan.

She wanted to feel his heat fill her body more than she'd ever wanted anything in her life.

His mouth fell hot on her neck and his teeth grazed her flesh as he sunk his cock into her with slow movements that she felt deep inside her. He pumped short hard strokes then bit her neck hard.

Finally, he released her neck and whispered, "Come."

Steele was nearly shocked as her body did what he said the instant he said it. She felt him tense behind her and his dick throbbed as heat shot into her as the most intense orgasm crashed through her body.

She shook with the sensation and her mind went to another place. There was no way that she could hold the moan back, and it slipped out of her mouth. She heard his follow as he pulsed inside her.

She knew without a doubt that no one would ever be able to make her feel the way that this man did. He pulled out of her, leaving her feeling empty. She hated it and loved it all at the same time.

He pulled her jeans back up and picked her shirt up and helped her get it on as she tried to catch her breath. He handed her the bra which was torn up and the ripped panties and looked a little guilty about tearing them up.

He looked at her as she held the shirt closed. "I'll have some new ones sent to you. What's your apartment number?"

She shook her head. "No, that's okay. Truth be told I'm most likely going to keep these to remember this by." She laughed a little, but knew it was true.

He tapped the glass of the dark partition. "We can take her home now."

Steele looked out the window and saw they were very near her apartment. The driver must've been circling the block. His boss must do this type of thing often.

Suddenly she felt pretty dirty and more than a little dumb. The car stopped, and she grabbed her purse off the floor and reached for the door handle.

His hand on her shoulder stopped her.

"I had a good time," he said.

"Me, too," she mumbled, not daring to look at him.

"When I talk to you, I want you to look at me," he said with a commanding tone.

Her eyes moved up to meet his. "Okay."

"Good girl," his voice was soft. "I wish things were different, but they're not so this is goodbye."

The door opened as Paul held it for her.

"Bye," she said and got out of the car not looking back.

She held her bra and panties in one hand and held her shirt closed with the other and felt bad because she should be feeling shame and disgrace at what she'd done.

Instead she felt elated and nearly overjoyed as her body felt like it had been cleansed. The car waited until she was inside then it drove away. She stopped and turned to watch it pull away once she was inside the lobby doors.

It was over. The brief moment of complete pleasure was over and she wouldn't see that man again. She turned and walked to the elevator. She wondered what was happening in the man's life that he would say he wished things were different.

The elevator doors opened, and she stepped out and went to her apartment. She mumbled out loud, "Why did it have to be goodbye? What could possibly be the reason we can't see each other anymore?"

She unlocked the door and went inside, finding Gwen passed out on the sofa, a bottle of wine clutched in her fist. Steele took the half empty wine bottle out of her hand and took it to the kitchen.

The trash can was half full, and she contemplated tossing the bra and panties into it. Maybe it would be best to forget about what had happened if it could never happen again.

The memory would only serve to torture her and make it where no other man could ever please her again. She shook her head and kept the panties and bra and went to her bedroom. Tossing them in the dirty clothes hamper, she decided she would keep them.

God only knew when she'd ever get laid again, she may as well have a memento of the one time she let a man treat her like his property. The one time she allowed a man to take her the way he wanted to. The one time she had allowed a man to boss her so much he made her control a function she didn't even know she had the ability to.

She pulled her clothes off and got in the shower to wash away his smell which was all over her. His cologne, sweat, and semen. It was the best smell she'd ever smelled, and she thought she must be more of a freak than she ever let on.

Steele ran her hand between her thighs and over her wet inner thigh. Wet with the mixture of him and her. Starting the shower, she climbed in and poured body wash on a rag and ran it over her legs then her arms and over her breasts.

The nipple he'd pinched was sore, and she smiled as it hurt when she ran the rag over it. Her whole body was a little sore, her vagina would hurt like a mother fucker in the morning, she was positive she'd have a hard time walking.

The memory of his huge cock in her mouth made her lean back against the wall and her eyes closed.

Why does it only get to be once?

SHE LEANED up and let the water run over her face. She knew it was stupid, but she felt like crying that there would be no more. He was a onetime thing, and that made her stomach ache with the knowledge.

He was a thing she'd never tell a soul about. A secret she would keep forever from everyone. How could she tell anyone that she liked the way he threated to spank her until she cried if she climaxed without him telling her she could?

Gwen would tell her she was crazy and probably make her go talk a counselor or something. Maybe she was a little crazy. She never thought in a million years that she'd do something like that, much less find it so damn fantastic.

Rinsing off, she got out of the shower and went to lie in her bed with no clothes on. She never did that, but she felt like she was going to take this being bad thing all the way at least for that one night.

She climbed under the pink blanket and ran her hands over her body, another thing she didn't do. She closed her eyes and pictured him. The man she only knew as A.C. Not even his real name did she know and she'd never even told him hers. Perhaps because he never asked for it.

He knew she was a onetime thing all along. Offering her no more than a nasty little tryst in the back of his Escalade. He'd called it his lair and her lips quirked up into a half smile as she thought that was an apt name for his car.

How many women had he taken in that car? How many rounded asses had felt his hand's sting? How much more could he do to a woman?

Maybe he could be found in one of those clubs she'd heard about.

She racked her brain to try to recall what she'd heard they were called.

Would she venture out and find a club like that and see if he was there? He had to be into that type of thing. Whips and chains were not a thing she ever looked at with any excitement. But if that man was holding a whip, she didn't think she'd mind it.

She thought she might like it a lot more than she was supposed to. Steele stopped touching herself and closed her eyes tight. That wasn't her. That was not the person she was or even wanted to be.

A powerful lawyer was not a person who wanted to be strapped to a bed and taken the way some man wanted. A powerful lawyer was not a person who was told what to do by some man. No, that was not what her future was about.

The gorgeous man had no place in her future anyway, so why did she have an empty place inside her that hadn't been there until he took her the way he did? She felt like she was his, even though she knew she wasn't.

Why couldn't things just be easy?

3

FOR DESIRE PART THREE

Steele

Slow strides Steele made as she walked to her first class. The previous night's activities with the sexy stranger had her body aching in a way that she'd never dreamed would make her so happy. A smile was plastered across her face and no matter how much she thought she should be ashamed of what she'd done and allowed herself to be treated, she just couldn't feel a thread of guilt about it.

Her mind continued to replay certain scenes from the back seat of that Escalade and every single time the gorgeous man's face entered her memories her smile went a little bit wider. She'd never felt more alive and hoped the afterglow of the night would never go away.

Steele entered the small classroom where her professor, an extremely successful criminal lawyer, seemed to be waiting for her arrival. She was one of his favorite students as she had such passion for the law and his criminal law class was her favorite.

.   .   .

TANNER GOLDSTEIN WAS a tall man with classic good looks for a forty something man. Salt and pepper hair made him look smart and seasoned. He was smiling at her as she walked into his classroom.

"Good morning, Steele," he said as he moved from behind his desk to run an arm around her narrow shoulders. "I have something I want to offer you. Stay after class so we can talk. You and Rowan are getting a rare opportunity to learn more than any class could ever teach you."

He let her go as she went to her seat on the front row. Rowan sat at the desk next to hers and offered her a small smile. He most likely wasn't super happy about having to share the opportunity with her.

Rowan was extremely competitive. Steele smiled back as the smile had yet to leave her face anyway. She leaned over a bit and whispered, "Did he tell you what this is about?"

He shook his head. "He said he'll tell us both after class. I do have an idea though. A criminal lawyer named Arsen Sloan is being looked at for a triple homicide. Serial killer style. Three young woman all bound and strangled to death. And all three of them were his past girlfriends. If you can even really call them that."

Steele's smile faded as she thought about the idea all the women had been strangled. A death she'd thought brutal and had turned into a real phobia for her. "That's awful. I don't know if I want to be on the man's side."

Rowan rolled his dark green eyes at her and ran a hand through his blonde curls which were closely cropped to his head. "Then you clearly don't have what it takes. You should just let me do this on my own, Gannon."

SHE SAT BACK and thought about what the young man had said. Maybe she didn't have what it would take to defend people she knew were guilty. But it was a thing she'd dreamt of.

She took notes as Professor Goldstein talked about a case where all the evidence pointed to one of his defendants, but when it came down to it there was a reasonable doubt and that alone had the jury giving the man an acquittal.

Steele decided by the end of the class she would accept the offer her professor gave her, no matter what it was. This was her passion after all and she'd have to toughen up if she was to become the success she wanted.

Rowan and Steele remained seated as the class was dismissed and Tanner came to talk to them about his offer. He crossed his arms in front of his chest as he said, "Arsen Sloan is a man in a tough spot and he's retained my services in case he's charged with the murder of three women who he knew well. I'd like to offer you both an internship on this particular case. It could lead to a permanent internship with my office."

Rowan spoke up quickly, "I'm in, Tanner."

Steele's eyes shot to Rowan. She wondered when it got to be okay to call the man by his first name. She looked back at her professor.

"Count me in as well, Professor Goldstein."

He smiled and said, "Call me Tanner, Steele. I want you to feel just like a real part of the legal team I'll be putting together if Arsen is charged. We all are pretty informal with each other and I don't want you two made to feel you're anything but part of the whole team."

She nodded.

"Thank you, Tanner. It'll be quite a privilege to get this opportunity to work with you. So, Rowan told me a bit about what he's accused of. Do you think he did it?"

"I don't ever think like that. I just need to know the facts, every last sordid detail and there will be sordid details. The relationships Arsen had with the deceased women were violent in many people's eyes. Have you heard of the term BDSM?"

STEELE NEARLY PASSED OUT. That's a term she'd been thinking of last night. Though she never could come up with the term exactly. She nodded, and a chill ran through her. "Whips and chains, right?"

"Among other things. Anyway, I want you two to accompany me

to my first meeting with Arsen this afternoon. We'll take my car over to his office, so meet me here at four-thirty and we'll be on our way to meet the man." He gave Steele a wink. "And Steele, try really hard not to be repulsed by his demeanor. He's what you would call an alpha male. He may come off chauvinistic. You'll come up against that a lot in this line of work and it is best you learn how to deal with that sooner rather than later."

Steele nodded and gathered her things to go to her next class.

"I'll be okay. See you this afternoon."

Rowan walked alongside her as they left the room.

"Think you can handle the BDSM thing, Gannon?"

Inwardly she cringed as she'd thought of little else last night.

"I'll be able to handle it. I'm no baby, Rowan."

"No, but you aren't exactly well experienced in sex." He grinned at her as they walked down the long hallway.

"How the hell would you know?" she said as she blushed.

He shrugged his shoulders. "I just know. So, don't you think the sordid details might make you sick? You really should consider dropping this case. Maybe the next one won't be so bad. More your speed, you know."

She found her fist balling at her side as she wanted to knock the crap out of the annoying man.

"I'm not dropping this opportunity, Rowan." She sped up and walked away from him.

"See you at four-thirty, partner," he called out after her.

The only reason she saw not to take the opportunity was the fact she'd have to spend so much time with Rowan and his way of trying to get her to quit just so he could gain the permanent internship with Tanner's office. But she wasn't about to hand the position over to him.

.   .   .

STEELE SAT between the men as they rode into downtown in Tanner's town car. His driver let them know they were there and parked in front of the large building Arsen's law office was in.

Steele's heart was jerking in her chest and her stomach was tight as she went inside with Tanner and Rowan. The building was magnificent, and she looked around, hoping that one day she'd have her own suite of offices in a building like that one.

The elevators were in several banks in the huge lobby and Tanner took them towards one set of gold elevator doors. Etched in them at the top were the words, 'The Law Offices of Arsen Sloan; Criminal Lawyer.'

"He's loaded, huh?" she asked as they got on the elevator that went straight to the top of the building to the entire upper floor.

"A billionaire to be exact," Tanner told her.

"How old is he?" she asked with raised eyebrows.

"Thirty-five," Tanner answered. "Now, I don't want you to think I agree with any of the things he does, but please don't speak, either of you, unless he directly asks you a question. Just sit back and take notes."

ROWAN AND STEELE gave him a nod and the elevator doors opened. Steele's jaw dropped as she saw a monster chandelier hanging in the reception area. A giant salt-water fish tank was the other centerpiece of the large and richly furnished room.

A tall blonde woman sat at a Cherry wood desk and smiled at them as they came in. Rowan's shoulder brushed hers as he said, "Close your mouth, Gannon."

Steele slammed her lips together and knew she had to be turning all kinds of shades of red. She was overwhelmed with the office and she'd yet to even see but the very front. She made a mental note to make sure her lips stayed closed, so she didn't look like an idiot in front of the powerful man they were about to meet.

The receptionist who she noticed was a complete knockout led them to a large office with four overstuffed leather chairs that sat in front of a massive oak desk. It was meticulously cleaned and only one small stack of papers sat on it.

The man who they'd come to see was nowhere around. She took a seat on one side of Tanner and Rowan took the other as she tried hard not to drop her jaw again at the different crazily expensive items he had on a bookcase behind his desk.

Her mouth had gone dry, and she pulled out her notepad and a pen, getting ready to take down every word that was said at the meeting. She was determined to get the internship and one day an office just like this one.

"OKAY GUYS, remember the rules. This man is professional to the hilt. Maintain that, or he'll tell me I have to let you off the case. He puts up with nothing, and I do mean nothing."

Steele's mind went to the fact the man was into BDSM and said, "I suppose that would be how a man who likes the kinky stuff that he does would act."

Tanner leveled his eyes on her.

"That's right, so watch what you say. I can't be sure he won't threaten to spank the shit out of you if you talk without being spoken to and for God's sakes, do not look him in the eye. So many rules with this man, but follow what I tell you or he does or you'll get dropped and I'd hate for you to miss out on this."

Steele nodded and the door to the office opened. Not sure if she was supposed to look, she just looked at her lap as Tanner got up and shook hands with the man who'd walked in.

"Hello, Arsen. I hope your day has been going well."

"Not as well as I'd like it to," Arsen said and Steele's ears prickled with heat.

His voice was deep and sounded like the man from last night. She continued to look at the notepad in her lap and shook her head slightly, knowing that she just wanted to hear the guy's velvety voice again that was all it was.

That had to be it!

· · ·

TANNER CAME and sat back down. "These are a couple of students I may use as interns if we end up having to go to court." He tapped Steele's knee that was exposed as her black skirt had ridden up as she sat down on the large chair that barely allowed her feet touch the floor. "This young lady is Steele Gannon."

Steele let her eyes flicker up, but not long enough for the man to think she was eyeballing him or whatever the dominating people called it.

"Hello, Sir," she said quietly.

"Look at me when you're speaking to me," he told her.

Her heart was pounding as she'd heard the man from last night say nearly the same thing and with the same tone to his deep voice. Her eyes snapped to his, and she stopped breathing.

It was him. His hair had been cut, the silky waves shorn, leaving only the slightest curl at the end of his dark hair. His face was still covered by the meticulously groomed dark beard and his dark eyes danced as they stared into hers.

"I am Arsen Sloan, Steele Gannon. What a strong name. I don't believe I've ever heard a woman called something that strong before." His tongue ran over his lips with a quick motion that made her heart speed up.

"My father named me. Thank you for the compliment, sir." She had no idea if she was supposed to drop her eyes or not, but she couldn't stop looking at him. All she wanted to do was jump over the desk and pull his mouth to hers in a hot kiss.

"No thanks necessary." He looked at Rowan. "And who is this, Tanner?"

"Rowan Stevens, my other top student," Tanner said as he gestured to Rowan.

"Nice to meet you, Mr. Sloan," Rowan said.

"You too. Now tell me are the two of you supposed to work closely together if this becomes a case?" Arsen asked Rowan.

Rowan gave him a nod.

"Not to worry sir, we can work well together, I assure you."

STEELE WAS BACK to looking at her lap as all types of thoughts were storming her brain. The man from last night might be a murderer. Never had she done something so reckless and she'd gotten into a probable murderer's car and allowed him to fuck her like a damn prostitute. Her stomach was twisting on itself and bile was rising in her throat.

"Can you?" The way his voice sounded he must be looking at her and she lifted her eyes and found he was.

"Of course, Sir," she answered.

"Arsen, call me Arsen, Steele," he said with a commanding tone.

"Of course, Arsen." Her hands twisted in her lap and he looked at them.

"No need to be nervous, Steele," he said, his voice much softer, reminding her of how soft he could be.

BUT HE COULD BE hard as hell too and she was still mentally berating herself for being so foolish and doing what she did with him. She wasn't fool enough not to realize that telling Tanner she knew Arsen was not a thing she was supposed to do. But she felt like saying it then running from the room.

Tanner patted her knee and her eyes flew to Arsen. He was frowning as Tanner said, "She'll be fine, Arsen. It's just this is her first case."

Steele could tell that Arsen didn't like Tanner touching her, so she shifted in the chair, crossing her legs away from Tanner so he didn't tap her knee anymore. Her actions had Arsen's eyes darting to her and his lips pulled back into a smile.

She smiled too, happy for some damn reason that she saw what he wanted her to do and did it without thinking much about it. Steele knew she should stay far away from the man who might be a killer, but she was drawn to him like she never knew possible. To make him mad at her for any reason was a thing she didn't want to do.

The meeting went on as Tanner talked just a little about the way the women were murdered, but Arsen put a quick stop to it. "There's really no reason to remind me, Tanner. It's really not a thing I like to talk about and won't unless they charge me and I have to."

Tanner looked at Steele then down at the notes she'd been taking.

"I understand that, Arsen. I would like to get ahead of the police on this thing just in case they do throw the charges at you with rapid fire. Your phone records I'll need and access to all your email accounts."

Incredibly, Arsen's already dark eyes darkened even more as he said, "I know you need those things, Tanner. I'll send it all to you in an email later today. For now, I really need to get out here. So, we'll keep in touch." He stood and so they then left Arsen alone in his office.

STEELE FOUGHT the urge to stay and when Arsen called out after them she thought he might be about to ask her to stay. Instead he said, "Leave all of your cell numbers with the receptionist. In case I want to talk to the interns."

Her heart sped up, and she thought he might be looking for a way to talk to her again. Steele knew that wasn't safe or the right thing to do, but her body was overriding her mind by leaps and bounds.

After leaving their numbers they went back to Tanner's car and were barely inside it when Steele's cell rang. She pulled it from her purse and saw a number she didn't recognize.

She nearly refused the call when Tanner looked over her shoulder at the phone.

"Answer it, it may by Arsen."

She did as he said. "Hello, Steele Gannon here."

"Save this number, Steele Gannon," she heard Arsen's voice tell her.

"Yes, Sir," she said, trying hard not to smile.

"I want to meet with you alone," he said.

She looked at Tanner with wide eyes. "He'd like to meet with me."

Tanner nodded, and she said, "Of course. Where?"

"Get out of that car and into mine. Don't you see Paul holding the door open for you a couple of cars over?" Arsen said.

She looked out the window and saw Paul dressed in a black suit holding open the back door of the Escalade Arsen had taken her in last night. She was sweating bullets as she looked at Tanner.

"He wants me to go get in his car." She pointed to his waiting driver.

"Do it," Tanner said.

"Okay, I'll be in the car," she told Arsen, and he ended the call without another word.

Before she got out she asked Tanner, "Are you sure about this? I mean he might be a murderer."

"He'd be a damn fool if anything happened to you with the two of us knowing he asked you to meet with him and had his car take you. You can't be a chicken, Steele. You have to get to know your clients and they all will be accused of terrible things. The closer you can get, the more you can find out and the better you can help them to get off the charges." Tanner patted her leg. "Keep your wits about you."

She nodded and got out of the car and walked up to Paul who smiled. "You," he said under his breath. "Imagine that."

"Hi, Paul. Yeah, it's me." She climbed into the car she had gotten into less than twenty-four hours earlier and found the smell of leather and Arsen's expensive cologne making her head lighter than it already was.

Paul pointed to a small refrigerator.

"Get yourself something to drink. You should really calm way down before you see him again."

"Is it showing how much I'm freaking out?" she asked with a nervous laugh.

He nodded. "By the way, Arsen told me your name. It's nice to officially meet you, Steele Gannon."

"You too, Paul."

The door closed, leaving her in the dark backseat of the car. The buttons from her shirt he'd ripped open the night before were still all over the floor. She smiled and took a beer from the fridge.

What was his plan for her?

4

ARSEN

Pacing in his office, Arsen had never been more nervous. It was infuriating him that the young woman had such an effect on him. Never did a woman make him nervous, yet she did somehow.

When he'd walked into his office to meet with the legal staff he'd just hired to represent him if he was officially charged with the murders, he nearly dropped to his knees when he saw her.

The woman from last night. The woman who he thought he'd never see again. He didn't know her name because he hadn't asked it. He kicked himself all the way home for not getting her number, name and apartment number.

He knew he'd want to see her again, but the things hanging over his head were not things he wanted to tell her about. But now she knew about them, so that was an issue no longer. And she was being taken to his penthouse and would be waiting at home for him.

Arsen knew that he should leave the young thing alone. He had so much going on after all. He may not be around to keep her anyway.

She had to be freaking out about what she had done. Steele didn't seem the type who did that sort of thing. Her tight as hell pussy sure didn't seem to be used much, but she sure seemed to like it.

She did so well following his commands. Not many could hold back an orgasm just because he said to. She showed great restraint, and he loved that. Steel showed promise she'd make an excellent sub. But would she even want that?

The girl was trying to become a lawyer. A criminal lawyer. Would the lifestyle he led be a thing she could accept? Could she let him control her? Is that even a thing he wanted?

Why break a free spirit? If that's what she was.

He took out a bottle of Jack Daniels and tossed a shot of it down his throat. Arsen should be calling Paul and telling him to get the girl out of his penthouse. That was the smart thing to do.

But his body was overruling his brain, and he was walking out the door to take his Jaguar to his penthouse. Thinking could come later after he saw if she'd let him have a piece of her again.

If she was smart, she wouldn't!

He got into his car and crossed his fingers that she'd not be smart, at least for the rest of that day, anyway.

5

STEELE

A large window overlooked the San Francisco Bay and Steele held her third beer as she gazed out at it. The alcohol had taken the edge off and she was feeling quite lucid.

The sound of his shoes clicking and clacking as he walked out of the elevator which led to the penthouse she heard coming up behind her. She spun around and placed the beer bottle on a small table beside her and readied herself to tell the man she'd slept with the night before that she was never going to do that again.

HIS DARK EYES leveled on hers as he pulled his dark blue tie loose and ripped his shirt open at the top, the top couple of buttons flying away. Her heart pounded as he strode towards her. His face was set, jaw tense, and muscles bulging.

Her mouth opened to speak, but he was on her before a word could pass her lips. His mouth crashed on hers hard and his tongue thrust into her mouth. His tongue raked over hers and his hands were everywhere, holding her body to his.

One hand grabbed one of her legs hoisting her up to wrap her legs around him. Steele's mind was gone, and she did as he wanted.

Because she now knew that she wanted it too and no matter how strong her mind was, the attraction they had was stronger.

His erection throbbed against her soft core and she moaned in desire for him and quickly stopped. But he did nothing to stop it as he began walking, carrying her to another room.

His mouth held hers as he kissed her like a man who thought he might never get to again. The sound of a door opening then slamming shut she barely heard as her heart was beating so hard and loudly she could barely hear a thing except that.

His mouth left hers and she looked at him as he tossed her onto a bed. She looked around the room and found it done in dark colors, red, and dark chocolate browns. It looked like something a man with his wants would have.

"STRIP," he said as he stood back and started unbuttoning the rest of the buttons on his white shirt.

She noticed the black jacket he'd taken off, and he was stepping out of his dress shoes. Steele thought about saying they should talk, but once he dropped his pants and his huge erection sprang out, she forgot what she wanted to say anyway.

Steele shimmied out of the tight, black pencil skirt and pulled the blue blouse off over her head. She managed to get the bra unclasped before he pounced on her as he had finished undressing.

He pulled it off this time without ripping it, but her black lace panties were history as he ripped them off. Arsen pinned her body beneath his and kissed her again. Hard and wanting, he kissed her as his huge cock pushed into her.

The pain reignited, and she writhed under him. He pounded into her as she wiggled as the burning sensation was nearly unbearable. His hand wrapped up in her hair and he pulled it hard.

His mouth left hers and he ran his tongue up her neck then his teeth bit her earlobe. "Be still," he said.

Steele stopped wiggling. "It burns."

"After how I fucked the shit out of you last night, it better burn," he said as he continued to thrust hard strokes into her.

His words had her going to another place and for some reason she thought how hot it was that he was so brutally honest with her. She raised her knees to better accommodate him and he pushed even harder into her.

The pain turned to pleasure quickly, and she arched up to meet his thrusts. The wind left her lungs with every hard thrust he made. Her hands ran over his short hair and she moaned at how silky soft it was.

He let her moan, and she whispered, "I wish I could've run my hands through it when it was longer."

"Shh," he said in her ear. "No talking, only fucking." His hot mouth moved down her neck then over her chest. He landed on her breast and bit her nipple hard.

"Oww!" she yelped and he let it go and stopped moving.

His eyes searched hers, darting rapidly back and forth. "Did that really hurt you?"

His eyes were narrowed at her and she found herself wondering if it did really hurt. "Not really, just surprised me I guess."

"If I really hurt you, our safe word is rose. Okay? Do you understand me?" He ended his sentence with a tender kiss to her nipple which kind of ached for him to bite it again.

Steele nodded. "Rose, I got it. Okay, and just so you know, you can bite it again. It's kind of nice."

His smile went all the way over his gorgeous face and she couldn't help herself as she took it between her palms and pulled him into a kiss. Her lips touched his softly, and he returned a gentle kiss. His tongue stroking her lips.

Arsen pulled his head back and looked at her. "You're beautiful, Steele. I'm so glad I saw you again."

"Me too. I could hardly get you out of my mind," she confessed.

"Me too," he said then kissed her again softly as he made long, slow strokes.

His hands roamed over her soft body, and he moaned as he caressed her silky skin. Her hands ran over his muscled back and she loved he way the muscles felt.

His body was perfect, and she wanted to taste every inch of it. He was being gentle with her and she liked it, but she loved it when he was rough. She raked her nails over his back and his kiss hardened.

Arsen ran his hands back and took hers into them, pulling them over her head and holding them down with one hand. He pulled his mouth off hers and smiled.

"Scratching, huh? I can fix that."

He got up and left her lying on the bed. She watched him grab his tie off the floor and come back. He looped it around her wrists, then the other end over the bedpost. She smiled at him as he resumed his position above her.

"Now I'm going to let you have it. Remember, no coming until I say or I will have to."

She smiled and interrupted him, "I know, spank me until I cry. I remember, don't worry."

His eyes went dark, and he growled. "Why did you have to come into my life at this horrible time? You're fucking perfect for me."

With that he took her breast and bit it hard, her body arched up but she stifled her scream as he slammed back into her. Her body shook with relief as he pounded her again.

The way he took her like a savage was a thing she found more than exciting. Every nerve was on fire. Every fiber of her being was relishing in the assault his body was making on hers. One of his hands fisted in her hair and he pulled it hard.

Her arms strained against the bond he had her in and she ached to run her hands over his body. She could see the muscles as they rippled over his back with his harsh thrusts. He was using every one of them to pound his hard cock into her tender pussy.

She shuddered as an orgasm began to build and she knew she

couldn't let it go. She wrapped her legs around him to try to hold herself back. She found herself aching to let it all go.

She knew damn well he knew she was fighting to hold on and he reached between them and squeezed her clit between his fingers. He sucked on her breast hard, making her stomach tighten in some deep place with every hard suck he made.

He was going to make her come and then what would he do to her? She held on, clenching her teeth and then she decided to try to make him come so he'd let her.

She did a few Kegel exercises and after about ten of them he groaned and took one last pull on her breast then looked up at her.

"Come."

Steele found the sound she made a thing she didn't know she was capable of as her body let go and she felt as if an enormous wave was crashing over her.

Arsen's body tensed as he shot into her. He groaned like an animal then lay on top of her, letting their bodies pulse around the others.

6

ARSEN

Arsen had never let anyone control him sexually since Mistress Sinclair. He wasn't about to let the young thing get the best of him. He finally pulled his head up after both had caught their breaths. He kissed her lips softly then pulled back to look at her.

Her skin was flushed, and she smiled weakly at him.

"My arms hurt."

He rolled off and untied her, then rubbed her wrists and arms.

"Better?"

She watched him as he carefully rubbed her shoulders.

"That was something, thanks."

He tweaked her nose and put his hands on either side of her.

"I know what you did to get me to come, Steele."

She blushed. "You did?"

He nodded. "Sneaky, don't you think?"

She shook her head. "It got the job done is what I think. You were torturing me."

One eyebrow raised. "Was I?"

"Well, you know, not actual torture, but my body wanted to release so bad and you were adding more and more stimulation until

I was about to come without you telling me to and I knew where that would leave me," she said and ran a hand across his cheek.

Arsen ran his fingertips over her collarbone and spoke softly, "Steele, I can't allow that sort of thing. I realize you didn't know that, so this time there'll be no punishment for it, but if there is a next time then there will be."

"Well, what will the punishment be because I may be able to put up with that to get what I want," she giggled, and he kissed her to quiet her.

"That isn't how this works, Steele. The punishments are meant to get you to stop the behavior I don't approve of. If it doesn't detour you from doing what it is I don't want you to do, then I'll have to go to the next level and you don't want that, do you?" He stroked her arms.

"Arsen, I'm not one of those women. I don't want to be controlled."

His laugh came from deep in his chest.

"You sure about that? Because your body begs to be controlled by me."

Steele looked away and sighed. He pulled her face back to look at him and kissed her softly again. When he released her lips, she said, "You're right."

He smiled. "Another thing I think is perfect about you is that you're truthful. Many women are stubborn and hate to admit things. I wish I didn't have this thing hanging over my head. I wish you weren't on my legal team and not really a woman I should be even thinking about making into my submissive."

"Wait? What?" she asked her face riddled with confusion.

THE WAY her eyes went wide had him thinking he'd jumped the gun and said too much.

"I can see that's something which hasn't occurred to you."

Steele pulled her body to sit up, and she leaned against one of the mountainous pillows on his bed.

"Okay, time to talk, Arsen. Those women who you might be accused of killing. Tell me about your relationship with them."

HIS FACE WENT VOID, and he got up, strolling in all his glory to the bathroom adjoined to his bedroom. He left her waiting for him to return and when he did he brought in a bottle of water. He took a long drink then handed it to her.

"Drink."

She took the bottle and a drink then handed it back to him.

"Okay, now tell me."

She'd wrapped the blanket around her tightly, covering her breasts.

"Steele, I didn't ask you to come here to tell you anything. I don't want to talk about them."

"But I kind of need you too. You see, you're accused of some bad shit, Arsen. Should I be afraid of you?" Her blue eyes hammered him as she looked at him more than he'd ever allowed anyone to.

"Yes and no," he said. "You see, I'm sure to make you do things you never thought yourself capable of doing. But as far as killing you, no, you have nothing to fear. I'm innocent of those crimes."

She let out a sigh, and he knew she was thinking that he might have been guilty.

"I didn't think you really could kill anyone, but I don't know you at all."

"No one really does, so don't feel bad," he said as he climbed up next to her and ran his arm around her shoulders. "My story is long and full of terrible things I don't like to recall. The things I've done with women I think are my business and mine alone. Don't you feel like your sexual business is yours to keep to yourself?"

STEELE WAS EERILY QUIET, and he found that disturbing. Finally, she said, "I don't want to tell anyone about how much I enjoy what it is you do to me, if that's what you mean."

"Why is that, do you suppose?" he asked then left a kiss on top of her head.

"The obvious reasons. It would make me seem weak and you seem controlling and mean," she answered.

"As long as you don't see me like that is all that matters to me," he said. He tilted her face so he could see her expression. "You don't think that, do you?"

She shook her head and smiled. "I just never knew I'd want to be done that way. But I don't want to tell a soul about it, to be honest with you. And to stay in the strain of being honest, I don't want to be your submissive. I wouldn't mind dating and seeing where this leads though."

"Dating," Arsen said as if he'd just tasted something awful. "I'm not a dating kind of man."

"I bet you're not. And the fact is that we can't really be seen going to the movies and holding hands as we walk through parks," she said then laughed a little.

"Not that I'd do that sort of thing anyway," he said with a chuckle.

"Nah, you'd never stoop to such a low-brow thing." She ran her hand across his chiseled chest.

"You get me, Steele. Somehow I can see that you get who I am without really knowing a damn thing about me," he said as he ran his fingers along her neck. He pushed the blanket away from her breasts and ran his fingers over one of them. "Your body is beautiful."

"Said the man with the perfect body." Steele sighed. "This is such bad timing. But maybe it's really the perfect time as you don't seem the type to conform and I, well, I have a goal to get to and being anyone's submissive isn't on my agenda."

With her words Arsen felt himself shifting inside. Could he bend the rules for her? Could he live life a bit differently? Or could he manage to get her to come to see why he needed things the way he did?

"I have no idea if I even have the time to do this with you, Steele. I could be picked up by the police at any given moment after all. But I might not either. The thought of not being with you like this anymore is a thing that makes my stomach hurt. And I've already exhibited way too many of my past weaknesses with what's happening to me. You make me feel strong and hopeful. With you a part of not only my life, but my legal team as well, I think I can manage to live through this crisis in my life."

She looked at him and took his face in her hands. "Arsen, please never talk about not being able to live through anything. You can make it through whatever is thrown at you. I'm sure of that. The thought of dropping your case and walking away from you is a thing that would break me down. I think above anything else, you can teach me strength. In more than one way."

Arsen was confused by his feelings for this young woman who laid in his arms. She was a child in so many ways, but she had something about her that told Arsen she was so much more and she was meant to be in his life. Maybe his life needed changing. Maybe hers did too.

"The things I could teach you are things you've never even thought about, I bet. For instance, did you know you hold so much power to influence people using your body, and I don't mean giving it to them?" He stroked her hair and had to lean in and smell it.

"Body language, you mean?" she asked as she lay her head on his chest and ran her fingers in circles over his abs.

"Yes, but it's so much more in depth than just how you do little things. The moment I saw you, I had a strange reaction to you that I've never had before. I also have never talked this much to anyone, especially a woman. You do something to me, Steele." He leaned over her and kissed her cheek. "This is crazy and I know it, but please try this thing with me. We can hide it until all this legal shit is over."

Steele's body froze in his arms as she tensed up.

"Arsen, are you asking me to see you in secret?"

"I am, but much more than that. I want you to start to learn about how it is I want this relationship to be. Fuck, I can't believe I used the word, relationship. I haven't had one since, well, in forever. And that one ended horribly, but I always say that you should do what scares you or your life is no life at all. It's time I follow my own advice." He pulled her up so they could be face to face.

Her large breasts were a bit distracting, and she was breathing a lot with what he figured was excitement. "Arsen, I can't be everything you want in a woman. If you expect me to not look at you unless you tell me to, I can tell you right now, that shit will get old quick. Some crazy sex I can handle, but all the rest, I think that's going to be impossible."

"All the rest can come in baby steps, and it doesn't have to be any more than what you want." He cupped her chin and gave her lips a feathery kiss.

"I could be really good for you and you for me, once I show you how great life is when you follow my rules."

"YOUR RULES," Steele said. "I do have to say that you must be right about holding onto an orgasm until the other person is ready to climax too. That was right. You do have to speed up your climax though." She laughed.

Arsen frowned.

"If I asked that of you would that be appropriate?"

Steele looked as if she was contemplating what he said, yet another thing he absolutely adored about her was the fact she would think about things before answering. Steele said, "No, it wouldn't."

"SO A SMALL SET of rules for you to get used to wouldn't be too much to ask for a woman who is not my sub as of yet?" he asked.

"Or maybe never," she said. "How would you feel if I never felt like being put in that category?"

. . .

ARSEN HAD to stop and think. He had to be honest with himself as well. He was a man who had a single purpose for women in his life. Not a night had passed with him staying in a sub's bed or her staying in his. Would Steele understand that?

"How about we both bend some of our own personal rules for ourselves? For instance, I've never allowed a sub to stay in my bed all night, nor did I stay in theirs. But, I'd like you to stay the night with me. This is a huge rule that I'm letting go for you, so you can let something go for me. I'm all about your safety at all times."

Steele's face pinched as she asked, "Your girlfriends never got to spend the night with you?"

Arsen frowned. "None of the women who have been my subs or other sexual partners were my girlfriends. For that matter, nor will you be. I don't do girlfriends, Steele. I do business transactions."

"You're the one who said the word relationship, not me," Steele reminded him.

Arsen found himself at a loss for words. He was being a man that he wasn't. He was being the same stupid boy he was with Beth, offering her all he had to give only to be tossed away like trash when he couldn't stand up to her father.

"I might be wrong about this whole thing," he said. "Forget about it. I'll have Paul take you home. Go get a shower and dress."

STEELE COULD TELL something had gone through his mind that shut him down. "I'll do it, Arsen. I'll take your secret relationship offer and we can see how this works out with no one being any the wiser if it doesn't. You can set some rules for me and I can see if I can live my life while following them. You have proven to me that at least one of your rules makes me quite happy after all."

Arsen shook his head, had she said what he thought he'd heard?

"Are you sure, Steele? I mean, I can't make you any promises. I can't tell you there won't be punishments for breaking my rules. You have to understand that."

She snuggled into his wide chest and smiled up at him. "As you told me, that's how I learn to stop doing the thing that makes you crazy, right?"

"Right," he said.

"So, what are your rules, Arsen?" she asked.

He had so many he had to think. He couldn't dole out any hard ones or she might not stay and he wanted her to stay more than he'd ever wanted anything in his life.

7

STEELE

After a hot shower while Arsen left her alone to go write his rules down for her, Steele toweled off and wrapped the fluffy white towel around her body. Her arms ached a little from being tied up, but she loved it and ran her hands up and down them, remembering how awesome the whole thing had been with Arsen earlier.

The bedroom door opened and Arsen came in wearing only black pajama bottoms. Steele's breath halted as she thought him the most beautiful man she'd ever seen.

"Hey," she said.

His reaction was instant.

"Don't speak to me until I speak to you, Steele."

She looked down as his tone was harsh and it was a reaction she didn't seem to be able to control. She pressed her lips together in a hard line. Standing still, she had no idea of where he wanted her.

He took her arm and pulled her to sit on the edge of the bed. Arsen handed her the paper that was full of his rules. She looked up at him as he paced in front of her.

"You want me to read these now?"

He stopped.

"Yes. Out loud please and ask me about anything you don't understand."

Steele cleared her throat as Arsen resumed his pacing.

"Steele must do as Master says at all times."

She stopped and shook her head. He looked at her.

"What? Of course you know that's the first rule, Steele."

"Um, I'm not your sub and you're not my Master, so that word will have to be stricken from this document if you expect me to take it seriously." She looked directly into his dark eyes and found them boring into hers.

"It's just a term, we use. How would you have me write it?" he asked.

"Just put your name in place of every single use of the word, 'Master.' I can't express to you enough how degrading that feels to me. I will not be degraded at any time, Arsen." She looked back at the paper.

"Fine, I'll change that since this is not a dom/sub contract. So, go on and read the rest," he said as his eye twitched and his hand flew to cover it.

Steele noticed though and frowned. "I'm making you upset, aren't I?"

He shook his head. "No, I'm just not used to this kind of behavior out of any woman of mine and it's taking some getting used to. Please continue."

With a shrug of her shoulders she read, "I'll just read this as if you've already changed the word then. Steele must do as Arsen says at all times. Steele will stay every night with Arsen." She looked up at him. "You want me to live with you?"

"I don't want to call it that, no." He stopped his pacing and looked at her. "You share an apartment with another person and that's not appropriate. Your things can stay there, for now anyway. You sleep in my bed, so I know you're safe."

"But Gwen depends on my financial help. And I don't really want her all alone every night. That makes her not safe," Steele argued.

"She's not mine to worry over. You are, or will be, if you accept this. This rule is non-negotiable I'm afraid. Perhaps you could help her find another roommate. You can still help her pay the bills if you want to as I'll be giving you a credit card to take care of all of your expenses. And you should, as you need to keep that room, you know in case things don't work out." He resumed pacing. "Keep reading."

"We'll discuss the credit card thing later as I will not be taking money from you. That's a thing a prostitute does and I'm anything but that. Okay, next rule is, Steele will make herself readily available to Arsen at all times. She will be given a cell phone that is to be used only to communicate with Arsen and she will answer his calls and texts, if not immediately, then within thirty minutes. It should be noted that there will need to be a valid excuse for not answering right away and any excuse deemed unworthy will have repercussions," she said then shook her head. "I have school, Arsen."

"And I'm aware of that and would never ask you to come to me or answer my calls when you're in classes, Steele. You need to trust me. I have no intention of ruining your education. I'd only like to enhance it and will if you allow me to exert my expertise with you. You can be assured I'll never do something that would harm your career or your mind, body, or soul. I'll care for you more than you ever thought possible."

"Okay then, moving on," she said as she continued. "Steele will not pleasure herself unless Arsen asks her to. What the hell, Arsen? Gee that's really gross." She kept reading. "Steele is not allowed to orgasm until Arsen tells her to. Yeah, I got that one. Moving on. Arsen has a say on who Steele is friends with."

"That red head is out, Steele. She's a real bitch and I don't want her to have any influence on you." He took her chin in his hand. "That won't be a problem, will it?"

She shook her head. "I hate her anyway. I will have to stay firm on Gwen though. She's my friend and will always be."

"Then I will schedule a time for us all to be together so I can see how you two interact with one another and I will deem if the relationship is one that enhances your life.." He let her chin go and walked over to grab a bottle of water from the night stand. "Please continue."

"Steele's body is only to be given to Arsen to do with as he wishes." She looked at him and frowned. "So you want to be exclusive I see, but I'm not your girlfriend. Okay. And what about you? Are you going to be only with me?"

"You have to trust me. I don't plan on being with anyone else and if I am, I will be honest with you about it. But you have to realize I am the master of myself and as such, I can do as I please. As long as you are pleasing me then I see no reason why I'd even want to have sex with another, but that is my decision to make. Also, if you ever do decide to move all the way with this thing and become my sub then I can allow another to have sex with you if I want as your body will be mine."

"Fuck that, Arsen!"

"I SHOULD'VE PUT that in there as well, but I'll be sure to add it soon. That language is not to be uttered out of those precious lips of yours. For now, just know that it does not please me for you to utter curse words. And when I'm not pleased, it will reflect on how I treat you. Do you understand me, Steele?"

"I sure do. But please be advised that I will not be given to anyone else at this time. Not unless we do make a dom/sub contract. Which is getting more and more unlikely. And just so you know, if you think I'm going to be the only faithful one in this relationship then you're far from correct."

Arsen frowned and said, "Like I said, as long as you're pleasing me I don't see that happening."

Steele smiled. "It's just that I think I'd be really jealous is all, Arsen."

"Noted," he said as he ran his hand over her cheek.

. . .

"Okay then, Let's see. The last thing here is pretty long. Steele must follow a diet and exercise program that Arsen develops for her. If she is caught straying from the diet and exercise program in any way, she will be punished. All foods and drinks must be consumed within a twenty-four-hour period. The program will include required times to go to bed and wake up." Her eyes moved to him. "So, you want me to lose weight?"

Arsen got on his knees in front of her. He took her hand in his and kissed the top of it then looked up at her. "Not at all. I love your body and as such I want to keep it healthy. I want you around for a long time after all. These rules are all only to help you be the best you can be. The addition of punishment for falling off the program serves to help you stay on the plan, that's all. You're beautiful and I want you to know that. Everything I will do is only to your benefit."

"I see, okay then." She laid the paper on the bed. "So these are the rules for now anyway. I suppose as time goes on you'll be adding to this."

He nodded and got up and sat beside her, still holding her hand. "In time when you see just how much I'm doing for you, making things better for you, I think you'll understand why the dom/sub thing is important. You should want to please me in every way that I want. You should want to show me how thankful you are for me. You should want me to dominate you and make you mine in every way possible."

"You make it sound kind of romantic," she said and ran her hand over his leg.

"Romantic? I wouldn't say that," Arsen said then stood up. "So, if I change the word Master to my name then you'll sign it and we can start this?"

"Let me really look it over one more time before I say yes to that.

It's a lot to take in you know," she picked up the paper and gave it one more read through.

ARSEN WATCHED her carefully as she read. He seemed to be noting every little frown she made and Steele was wondering if he was second guessing some of his rules. In the end, she found they were all something that she could live with, or try to anyway.

"Change those words and I'll sign, Arsen."

Arsen looked as if he had to stop himself from jumping up and down and Steele was shocked to find him grabbing her up into his strong arms. So un-dominate-like, she thought.

Her next thought was what had she gotten herself into?

8

PART FOUR: FOR ACCEPTANCE

Steele

S tep for step, Steele matched Arsen's strides as they ran side by side in the park near Arsen's penthouse. Both were wearing the running shoes Arsen had researched and bought them, New Balance 1500v2s.

After only one week, Steele knew more about Arsen than she thought possible. The man himself that was. Not the man he had been or anything about his dealings with the women who had been found dead.

No, not the past Arsen. Only the present Arsen and that man she was falling for more and more with each passing day. He was strict and demanding in many ways, but he was also caring and at times she saw something in his dark eyes that told her he was beginning to soften.

HE MADE his list of rules and she'd followed it better than he thought she would be able to. Arsen showed her respect for how well she managed to understand what it is he wanted from her and why. Her only real weakness with the rules thus far was her love of soda.

The diet he placed her on did not allow any soda ever. Nor caffeine in any form. Her mornings had been hard and the one glass of orange juice that she was allowed each morning was just not cutting it. That's when he came up with the morning's activities to get her juices flowing each day.

Steele could say this about the man. He may have strict ways, but when she told him how her body was reacting to the sudden loss of the things that she'd used to get her going, he came up with alternative ideas to get it going again. Though he seemed tough as nails and a real chauvinistic bastard at times, he really was thoughtful and concerned with her overall health and safety.

They ran in the dawn's light. Earlier than most so they wouldn't be spotted together. Their relationship was being hidden because of his legal problems. But he had managed to fit in some lunches and a dinner as he introduced her as part of his legal staff when people who knew him came around.

PAUL WAITED at the end of the trail for them. Each morning he took Steele back to her apartment to get ready for school and Arsen back to his to get ready for his day at the office. Then he'd take Arsen with him. They'd pick up Steele and drop her at college, then go downtown to take Arsen to his office.

Steele thought that it was absurd, but Arsen refused to let her take her truck to school. He was more than over-protective and that was about the only thing which grated on her about the man.

THEY SLOWED their pace to a walk as they finished up their run. Without looking at her, he said, "I have to commend you on how well you're keeping up with what I'm asking of you. I think next week I'll add a little more to our run, maybe another mile."

"Sounds good," she said and grazed his hand with the back of hers as if on accident but it was on purpose.

"Thank you for the compliment, Arsen."

He gave her a sideways glance and took her hand in his.

"It's deserved, Steele."

Paul was waiting and opened the door for them to get into the Escalade. "Morning."

STEELE SMILED AT HIM. "Good morning, Paul. Thank you again for the ride."

Arsen helped her in first then climbed in behind her. He did as he had done every morning and tapped his leg for her to put her foot up on. He unlaced her shoe and rubbed her foot for three minutes then did the same thing to the other one.

He'd explained to her about the tendons that needed massaged as she had never been a runner and it would take some time before her feet were in the shape that his were. She found it endearing. People thought he was a man who thought himself better than all women, but that just wasn't the case with Arsen.

Steele was feeling especially thankful for him and asked, "May I run my hands through your hair, Arsen."

He nodded without looking at her. She ran her hand up and felt the damp hair under her palm and wished they could go back to his penthouse and shower then dress and go off to their day, like normal couples.

She let out a sigh, and he looked at her. "What?"

"I wish we could just do this thing out in the open is all." She ran her fingers lightly over his bearded cheek.

"Soon, I hope." He looked back at her foot that he'd been massaging and after a couple of more seconds he stopped and placed it gently on the floor.

"Is your roommate asking you any questions about why you're never there?"

Steele shook her head.

"No. She usually doesn't come in until late anyway and I've been telling her I started this new diet and exercise plan so I get up really early. She thinks I'm insane and told me I didn't need to change a thing about myself."

"And you said what to that?" He looked at her and her eyes migrated to his.

"Nothing, because it's none of her business anyway." Steele's eyes lit up as she said the words. She knew that was what he wanted to hear. And they were true after all.

HIS SMILE TOLD her he was happy. The warmth of his hand on the back of her neck sent chills through her body. "So perfect," he muttered as he pulled her face to his and took her lips with his.

Steele melted into him and her hands ran over his shoulders and down his muscled arms. She nearly moaned with how well developed his biceps were, but thought better of it.

She'd done so well with his rules that she hadn't earned even one punishment. Only fantastic sex was her reward for making each day with no infractions of his rules. Steele found it easy so far, but she had to be honest with herself, the soda thing was beginning to haunt her.

He ended his sweet kiss and pressed his forehead to hers. "Since it is Friday I can take you to visit your horse this evening before it gets dark. I assume that you miss him since I hired that service to see to him."

"It would be nice to see Tripper. Thank you, Arsen." Her fingers trailed over his shoulder.

THE CAR STOPPED in front of her apartment and after one more kiss she got out and went inside. It was only when she physically got away from Arsen that her brain would begin to work again. His mere presence seemed to take the air from her lungs and replace it with some need for him.

Even as she walked into the house and made her way to the bathroom to shower she ran her tongue over her teeth relishing the taste of him still fresh on them. She sighed as she put toothpaste on her toothbrush and cleaned the remnants of him away.

The shower finished the job and she no longer could smell him on her. But soon enough she'd be sitting in his car with him as he took her to school. Then she'd get a fresh kiss and as he ran his arms around her with a hug before she left him for the day, his cologne would linger through the day, making memories of the night before crop up in her head. Usually at the most inappropriate times.

After dressing and grabbing her laptop Steele found her cell buzzing at her, telling her Arsen was back. Gwen surprised her as she came out of her room, rubbing her sleepy eyes.

"You didn't come home last night. Where were you, Steele?"

"Um, oh, just out with a friend. I'm going out again tonight, I think," Steele said with an edge of nerves that suddenly cropped up.

"Well, let me know at least. I was worried about you." Gwen gave her a wag of her finger.

Steele laughed and opened the door. She didn't realize that Arsen was already walking up to the door, a frown covering his handsome face. "Okay, Mom," she said to Gwen.

Gwen's face looked odd and when she turned to see what she was looking past her at, she saw Arsen. "What's taking you so long?" he barked.

GWEN WAS QUICK TO ASK, "And this is your friend, Steele? The one you've been staying with all these nights?"

"Yeah, I have to go, Gwen." Steele hurried out and Arsen took her by the arm, hurrying her along to the car.

"You know my time is important. Standing around and chatting it up isn't a thing you should do while I'm waiting for you." He threw the door open, and she slid in.

"Sorry, she caught me off guard." She positioned the laptop on the seat next to her as Arsen got in. "And I was coming, you shouldn't have gotten out of the car. What if someone saw you?"

"I don't give a fuck!" He straightened his tie and looked at her. "You're a person who works for me after all. It's not beyond the realms that I might give you a ride here and there."

"Okay. Man, you're kind of grumpy. Did something happen I should know about?" She ran a hand over his thigh as a tiny piece of lint had somehow found its way to his slacks. "You look incredibly handsome today in this dark blue suit. Is it an Armani?"

He nodded. "Very good, Steele. You are learning about fashion like I told you to."

"I'm trying. It'll take some time. I've never been into clothes and shoes and things." She moved her hand to run it over the tan skirt she was wearing and noted it looked nowhere near as nice as his suit.

"Once this is over, you're throwing away every last piece of clothing you have and I'm buying you a new wardrobe. One that's fitting for the woman in my life. I provided those things and cars as well to all my subs." He took her chin in his large hand and made her look at him as her eyes had not left her lap. "You're coming along so well. I think you should really start contemplating what it will mean to be my sub, Steele."

"I'll think on it then. So far it's been a breeze, but something tells me I won't cotton to every aspect of that lifestyle." To make her point she ran her hand up his arm, stopping to feel his bulging bicep. "That arm there tells me you can probably wield a belt like nobody's business."

"I can do that to you now if you break any of my rules. You do realize that, don't you?" He reached out and ran his hand over her breast. The white shirt she had on wasn't buttoned up entirely, and he ran his hand from her breast the mere inch to her bare skin and shook his head. He buttoned the buttons all the way up. "I don't want to see that again, understand me?"

She sighed, making her chest heave and said, "Yes, Master."

His eyes cut to hers but she was looking away. "Look at me, Steele," he said, sharply. She did as he said as it seemed nearly impossible to not do what he said to when he used that tone of voice. "That sighing shit is proving something that pisses me off, so no more of that. Understand me!"

Steele nodded. "So two more things to add to your list of rules for me then?"

"Seems so," he said and picked up his phone and clicked away on it.

"May I ask what you're doing?" she asked and leaned over a little to try to see.

"Adding those things to the list." He tapped away, and she found herself getting angry. "And the one about no cursing as well, so it's officially on the list now so watch yourself or you will feel the sting of my belt."

"Arsen, are you being for real? I mean, are you keeping that list on your phone?" She managed to see he had a page up on his notes and there was the list of rules. "That's not smart. What if the police take your phone and see that?"

"Your name isn't on it." He turned it so she could take a good look. It was headed with the words, 'Terms of Agreement.' "A contract is made up of the things we've mutually agreed on up until that point and it's essential that I keep up with the rules so I can make a contract up when you agree to."

"Which I may never do. By the way, I didn't really agree to the last few, you just told me you were adding them." She saw the school ahead and took the laptop onto her lap.

His eyes narrowed as he gave her a sideways glance. "Eager to leave my company, Steele?"

"Never, but thanks to Gwen, I'm running about one minute late and will need to rush to my first class now." She leaned forward. "A goodbye kiss?"

He sighed, and she looked at him as she pulled back. "Oh you can sigh but I can't?"

"THERE ARE a great many things I can do that you can't." He took her chin and pulled her back and pressed his lips to hers. She started to run her hands around his neck and press her body to his, but he stopped his kiss which remained only on her lips, no tongue and no hug. "You were a bit disagreeable this morning, so no mind-blowing kiss for you. Think about that for future reference."

"But, I kind of need one to get through my day. I was kind of counting on it," she said as she stayed leaning in as close as he'd let her.

"I suppose you'll think better of making me wait and leaving your top buttons open and making over the top sighs then, won't you, if you need my kisses so badly?" The car stopped and Paul was opening her door before she could even think of what to say to that bull crap.

She scooted out and turned back. "Have a nice day, Arsen. I'll miss you."

"You too," he said not looking at her but at his phone instead.

His cold nature was making her stomach hurt for some reason and she turned back after she got out. "Arsen, I'm sorry."

He glanced at her. "Thank you for the apology. We'll be here at four-thirty sharp." He looked back down at the phone in his hand. "Let's go, Paul."

Steele felt as if she'd been slapped and when Paul's hand touched her shoulder, she looked back at him. "Oh, sorry, Paul."

ROWAN STOPPED short as he walked from behind the car. "Steele, what the hell?"

Steele took off, trying to hurry away from Rowan, but he easily caught up to her and grabbed her by the shoulder, making her spin back around. "Rowan, don't," she said under her breath.

"What are you doing with him?" he demanded.

Her eyes went wide as Arsen came up behind Rowan. Arsen's voice was low and stern.

"Hands off her, boy."

Rowan lifted his hand from her shoulder and turned to face Arsen.

"This isn't right. You could be a murderer."

And just like that Arsen knocked him out.

"Oh, God!" Steele fell to her knees as Rowan lay on the ground. She looked up at Arsen. "Not necessary, Arsen!"

She patted Rowan's reddened cheeks. He moaned and his eyes fluttered open.

"Bastard, you sucker punched me."

ARSEN LEANED OVER AND SNEERED. "That was no sucker punch and you will keep your hands off her and mind your fucking business." He looked at Steele. "What are you doing? You need to get to class, Steele."

She stood up and took off towards her class. She glanced back once to see Arsen pulling Rowan up and dusting him off roughly. Steele was shaking as she went into the classroom of Professor Goldstein.

"Mornin' Steele," he said happily.

"Good morning," she said back and Rowan came in after her, a bit of grass on the back of his head and a swollen jaw.

Rowan went straight to Tanner and said, "I need to talk to you after class."

Although Tanner was whispering, Steele heard him.

"What the hell happened to you?"

"Arsen Sloan happened to me and it seems he's been happening to Steele as well." Rowan looked directly at her as he said it and she dropped her head.

This will be very bad!

9

ARSEN

A rsen had pulled a bag of ice from the office freezer and he held it over his red knuckles. He cursed Rowan. His cell phone rang, and he cursed again. When he saw it was the San Francisco Police Department, he cursed one more time.

"Arsen Sloan," he answered.

"Hi, this is Detective Riddle, Mr. Sloan. I need to talk to you this morning. Now I can come to you or you can come to me, but I need this taken care of before noon."

"I'll come to you. I'll leave now," he said and hung up.

After making a stop in his office to purposely leave his phone in a locked drawer, he left his office. Before he left it, he called Paul from the office phone and told him to be outside.

Something told him this day would not be a good one, and it was all falling into place. A numb sensation was filing his body, and he thought about not being able to hold Steele anymore if he went to prison.

THE YOUNG WOMAN was creeping under his skin. Her subtle defiance was a thing he couldn't stand in most women, but she had him thinking of her as strong instead of head-strong. He never thought he'd find himself experiencing such feelings again, not after what Beth did to him all those years back.

Arsen cursed again as he realized he needed Tanner to be there. He pressed a button and the privacy screen went down.

"I need to borrow your cell, Paul."

Paul handed it back and Arsen made the call to his attorney. Tanner told him he'd meet him there and not to say a damn word until he got there. Arsen gave the phone back and tried to settle back into the seat. His eyes caught something on the floor and he picked it up.

He saw one of her buttons from the first night they'd been together. Letting her go is what he should do. He was nothing but trouble and the poor thing would be devastated if he went to prison. But his selfishness knew no bounds as he wasn't about to give her up.

HE PUT the button in his pocket for reasons he didn't even know. It was a piece of her that he could keep close to him and it brought him a tiny thread of security. In this insecure world there was Steele, and he was beginning to hate himself for needing her so damn much.

Arsen had never found it so hard to maintain his disciplined demeanor. When she was looking at him, when he refused to give her the goodbye kiss he had given her each morning before dropping her at school, he had to mindlessly look at his phone in order not to give in to her.

He shook his head and sighed deeply. His world seemed to be falling apart. It seemed almost nothing was in his control any longer and he hated it all. The car pulled to a stop and when he looked up, he saw the police station.

What can they possibly have found?

10

STEELE

Heart pounding, Steele followed Tanner up the stairs of the police station. He'd taken her and Rowan out of their second class to go with him to be there. Some detective was going to talk to Arsen.

Fear was coursing through her veins and she wanted to break down and cry so badly it physically hurt to hold it all back. Rowan had told Tanner what he saw and suspected. Tanner told Rowan there was not a thing illegal about it so he should mind his business with a man like Arsen. Steele was relieved Tanner didn't ask her anything about it.

She bound up the stairs in front of Tanner and Rowan, making Rowan remark, "Worried about your boyfriend, Gannon?"

She ignored him and made her way inside. Finding him sitting on a chair, waiting. His eyes met hers as she came through the glass doors and he stood up. "He brought you?" he asked her.

She nodded and stopped short as she nearly had thrown her arms around him and this was not the place to be doing that.

"Are you okay?"

He nodded.

"I'm glad you're here," he whispered.

Her heart pounded with his admission and she brushed his hand with the back of hers.

"Me too."

Tanner and Rowan made it in and Arsen's eyes darted to the young man he'd punched earlier. His jaw still swollen.

"He brought him too, huh?"

"Yes, Tanner is his mentor as well." She looked back to find Tanner telling the officer at the main desk something then he gestured for them to follow him as a man in a white shirt and tan slacks opened a side door. "Here we go then."

She and Arsen walked side by side behind Tanner and Rowan as the officer greeted them with a smile and a nod. "This way please."

THEY FOLLOWED the detective down a long hallway and eventually into his small office. Only two other chairs, besides his, were sitting in front of his small desk that was strewn with papers. She and Rowan had to stand behind Tanner and Arsen.

Steele took out her notebook and pen and prepared to write down every word. She stood right behind Arsen and looked at the detective as if he was the devil himself.

The detective sat down.

"Mr. Sloan, I have a few questions about your relationship with Meagan Stanley, the first homicide victim."

Arsen nodded but kept his mouth shut. Steele's stomach knotted as the detective turned over a picture on his desk and revealed a caramel-colored woman who was naked and had marks around her neck that clearly showed where someone's fingers had gripped her throat. Her wrists and ankles were bound with rope.

The detective pushed the picture towards Arsen. "Would you like to tell me when you made these marks on Meagan Stanley's neck?"

Without any hesitation Arsen answered, "At two in the morning on the date of September third of this year."

Steele wrote the words with a trembling hand. He had choked the young woman and had just admitted to it.

"Care to clarify why?" the detective asked.

"She asked me to do it." Arsen ran his hand through his hair and Steele knew he was nervous.

"I SEE. So this is a thing you practice often? Choking women?" The detective leaned back in his chair and his eyes roamed up to Steele. "You're a woman near Miss Stanley's age. Do you like to be choked, Miss?"

"Miss Gannon," she answered. "And no I don't."

The detective looked back at Arsen.

"Was Miss Stanley your current sub at that date, Mr. Sloan?"

"No. I had no sub at that time." Arsen's foot began to tap a little.

"But she had been your sub at one time. I do have the contract you gave me on your relationship which had ended about when was that?" The detective moved some papers around and picked up a stapled stack of three pages.

Steele knew it was the contract he'd made with the dead woman and her heart was pounding so hard she was afraid they all could hear it. She had to swallow hard to get the bile which had gathered at the top of her throat to go back down.

Detective Riddle looked at the papers and turned to the very back. He turned it for Arsen to see. "See here at the bottom where she and you both signed, terminating the contract some two years before you choked her?"

"I do, and I understand there was no written agreement about that at that time, but it was consensual. She was into that kind of thing. I don't know what to tell you. But we both know that was not what killed her. Those marks were days old."

"A couple of days old, Mr. Sloan. Forensics also found your semen still in her." The detective laced his fingers and placed them behind his head.

"I don't see how. I used a condom," Arsen argued.

"I didn't say it was in her vagina, did I?" Riddle smiled. "I'm sure I don't have to spell it out for you."

Arsen shook his head. "So are you telling me that she was murdered after I left her house?"

"You tell me. It seems you two were having sex pretty often."

ARSEN FIDGETED IN HIS CHAIR.

"Three nights in a row. The first night is when the marks on her neck were made. The second night was different, and no marks were left and the third night there was no actual penetration but there was oral. But she'd made me remember why it is we didn't work out in the first place and after she gave me oral sex, I left with no intention of seeing her again."

Steele was reeling and had to lean against the wall. Her face had paled and the detective saw that. He stood up and excused himself then left the room, coming back with a chair. He placed it next to his then went to Steele and took her by the arm, placing her in the chair.

SHE HATED IT. She was able to see Arsen's face then, and she found she could barely look at the man. He wasn't happy with it either. His eyes bore into hers and she looked down at the notebook.

Arsen let out a sigh and said, "Look, there had to be someone who went to her house after I left it. That's where you need to be focusing on. I'm not a killer, Detective Riddle."

"But it does seem that your hands are the ones on the other two women as well. Do you mean to tell me they all liked to be choked?" The detective leaned over and looked at the notebook Steele was writing in. His shoulder touched hers and she turned her head, finding him much too close. "Do you know any women who like to be chocked, Miss Gannon?"

· · ·

SHE LOOKED up and shook her head. Then her eyes traveled to Arsen's finding him frowning at her. She crossed her legs in the opposite direction and leaned more to the other side so the detective was no longer touching her.

Arsen spoke between clenched teeth, "I do believe Miss Gannon does not frequent the clubs those women did. If you had ever been in one, Riddle, you would find the majority of the women there beg for it. They want the marks left on them. Personally, I didn't enjoy it nearly as much as they did."

"HMM," Riddle said then tapped his fingers on the desk. "I've been reading up on this whole dom/sub thing that you seem to be all about. You must have a lot of controlling issues that you should most likely be seeking therapy for, Mr. Sloan."

Arsen stood up and Steele's eyes flew to him.

"Now you listen to me, you sawed off piece of shit. I did not kill those women and you are wasting precious time finding out who did while you fuck with me. My sex life is not what's illegal here and you damn well know it. Now if you have nothing better to do then I have business to tend to and really need to get the fuck out of here."

Riddle smiled as if he'd gotten just what he wanted from Arsen.

"Temper issues too. Hmmm."

Arsen slammed his fist on the desk and Steele stood up abruptly.

"Arsen! Stop!"

EVERY MAN in the room looked at her as if she was insane. But Arsen sat back down.

"I'm sorry, Riddle. Perhaps I should see someone about my quick temper."

Steele sat back down and looked back at her notes. Riddle cleared his throat and said, "Okay then. I do need you to go ahead and give us your prints and we'll be taking some whole hand prints for our forensic specialists to verify the marks on the women's necks. You see, they all were strangled and if the prints match then you are our only suspect."

Arsen's tanned skin paled a bit and Steele knew it was because it was his hands that had made the marks and he would be taken in and most likely proven guilty. Her heart ached for him, but her mind was asking her how the hell she could trust he was telling the truth.

11

ARSEN

He wiped the black ink away from his hands with a towelette they had provided him after taking his prints. The things which would damn him. He took the stairs out of the police station as Steele walked by his side.

Arsen could hardly look at her after all he'd said. He wondered if she thought he was a murderer.

"Will you ride with me?"

"I think that's a bad idea," she mumbled as Tanner came up on the other side of Arsen.

TANNER SAID, "Look, I know it's just a matter of time until they pick you up. The prints will come back as yours and we both know that. But the plan is that I'll get you out as soon as they set bail and then we can begin an investigation into the murders on our own. I'll need you to really think about all you did with the women so we can see if any of the places you went had surveillance cameras that might have caught someone of interest following you when you were with the women."

Tanner's car was parked in front of Arsen's and they all stopped at it. His driver opened the door and Tanner gestured for Steele to get in first. Arsen grabbed her hand and pulled her back and whispered, "Steele, I really need you."

SHE PULLED BACK and looked at him. Then she looked at Tanner.

"I'm going with him."

Rowan rolled his eyes and said, "Are you an idiot?"

Tanner gave Rowan a swift pat on the back.

"Get in the car, Rowan."

He did as Tanner said but looked at Arsen.

"Nothing better happen to her."

Fire flashed through Arsen.

"Little boy, you should watch what the fuck you say to me and her for that matter."

Tanner tried to ease the tension.

"Watch your temper, Arsen."

Steele took Arsen's hand in hers and gently pulled him.

"He'll be fine, Tanner. Come on Arsen."

He allowed her to pull him away and as they walked he squeezed her hand. "Are you mad at me?"

She shook her head. "How can I be?"

"Are you disgusted with me?" He stopped and turned her to look at him.

The way her eyes darted back and forth answered him and he dropped his eyes and led her to the car where Paul waited for them with the door open.

Steel slid in and Arsen moved in next to her. After Paul had closed the door she turned to face him and took his face between her palms.

"ARSEN, you can tell me anything. Even if you did do it, you can tell me."

Fury filled him and he pushed her hands off his face.

"So you don't trust me! Steele I have to have your trust or we have nothing!"

"Arsen! How the hell can I just blindly trust you?" she shouted back.

"Cursing, that will cost you," he said in a low growl. "Or are we done?"

She looked away, and he could tell she wasn't sure.

"I'm sorry. It's just that I'm very confused and I know it all happened before me, but I'm jealous too."

"Jealous? We both have pasts, Steele. Nothing can be done to change that." Arsen grabbed a bottle of liquor from the little fridge and took a long drink. He sat back and held the bottle.

After another long drink, Steele placed her hands over his around the bottle. "Arsen, that's not a wise decision."

"I know that, Steele. Believe me, I know that I make poor, mother fucking decisions all the fucking time. You are a poor decision. I should leave you the fuck alone and I know that. I'm about to rot away in prison anyway. If I can't get you to trust me and believe I didn't kill those women, then I'm fucked for sure." He took another long drink then let her have the bottle.

She put it away and got on her knees in front of him, placing her hands on his thighs.

"Arsen, don't think like that. I'm sorry. I wish it was as easy as you telling me you didn't do it and all the doubt could disappear, but I would be lying to you if I told you that."

He took her chin and ran a finger over her lips.

"I need you to believe me, Steele. Or this is over."

He could see her thinking and pulled her up to sit on his lap. He had to convince her. She looked at him and he saw she desperately wanted to believe him, but her brain was battling her heart.

. . .

ARSEN PRESSED his lips to hers and felt her body turn into liquid. He pushed his tongue through her lips and ran his hand up her skirt, finding her warming already. One finger he pressed against her clit and she moaned and ran her arms around his neck.

He stroked her clit until she was squirming with the need to release. He stopped moving his finger and took his hand away then pulled his mouth from hers. She was panting and looked at him with confusion.

"Steele, do you trust me?" Arsen looked hard into her eyes and he found the answer behind them.

"I do," she whispered.

"You cursed and you have to be punished. Do you understand that?" He searched her eyes again.

They actually brightened.

"I do."

He lifted her off his lap.

"Drop your panties and get on your hands and knees and lift the skirt up over your hips."

She looked at him for a moment then did as he'd told her. She turned away from him as she went to her hands and knees then lifted her skirt.

He pulled his leather belt from his slacks. Arsen ran his hand over her smooth, white ass then placed a kiss on one ass cheek. He knew this would make them or break them, and he gritted his teeth as he swung the belt.

12

STEELE

The sting as the leather bit into her flesh had her making a small scream before she choked it back. Steele had no idea how many times he would hit her and she was trying hard not to let any tears get away from her.

Another hard whack and she flinched with the pain. Arsen's voice was tight as he said, "Do you think you'll curse again?"

She shook her head but didn't answer out loud. Another smack across her ass, this one harder had the tears springing forth.

"Out loud, Steele."

"No, sir. No, Arsen," he words were laced with her tears and she felt his hands running over her ass.

Sobs began to come out of her and she knew it was from so much more than the pain. It was for everything. She was about to lose the man she was pretty positive she was beginning to love deeper than she imagined possible.

His arms were suddenly around her and he turned her to him. He pulled her into his wide chest and shushed her with soothing sounds and soft caresses.

"It's okay, Steele. It's all going to be okay."

She took his lapels in her hands and pulled at them as she leaned back and looked up at him. Tears ran in rivers down her reddened cheeks.

"No it isn't. None of this is going to be okay. They're going to take you away from me. I just found you and they're going to take you away."

His hand ran over her hair and she found him smiling at her. He kissed her slow and soft.

"I just gave you your first punishment and you're thinking about what might happen to me instead of being angry with me?"

She sniffled and said, "How can I be angry? You just did what you said you were going to. And it did hurt and it will definitely make me think about what comes out of my mouth." Steele eased her cries. "The truth is I don't think I would've even cried if I hadn't been holding it back since Tanner came and told me they'd called you in."

Arsen moaned as he pulled her hair back, exposing her throat.

"You're so fucking perfect, Steele." He pressed his lips to her neck then ran his tongue up until he reached her mouth.

He kissed her hard and laid her back on the floor. Her skirt was still hiked up, and he ran one of his hands to hers and moved it to his swelling cock.

"Take it out," he told her then continued his kiss.

His mouth was hard on hers as she fumbled to unbutton his slacks and release him. She knew she should be mad at him for spanking her, but a part of her wanted to know what it was like.

The fact was it allowed her to release the tension she'd been holding and with that came a lot of freedom. Unbelievably, she found it had stimulated her as well and she was wetter than hell and aching for Arsen to be inside her.

She finally freed his erection and guided it to her. He pressed into her as soon as she lined him up and she moaned with how fantastic it felt as he filled her.

Hard, deep thrusts he made, as she wrapped her legs around him. She arched her body up to meet each thrust and ran her hands through his hair. He ran his hands back and took hers in them, holding them over her head.

She wondered if he hated being touched during sex. He seemed never to want her hands on him. He pulled his mouth from hers and looked at her as he pounded into her.

"Say it," he said, and she found herself confused.

"Say what?" she asked.

He shook his head and took both her wrists and held them with one hand as he took the other and smacked her thigh.

"Say it."

She searched his eyes as he continued to thrust into her. Something in them was making them shine, and she suddenly knew what he wanted to hear.

"I love you, Arsen."

He smiled and kissed her hard, thrusting his tongue to the back of her mouth, claiming every last part of it as his. She found her heart pounding with what she'd said. But was aware he'd not said it back to her.

Somehow it didn't really matter as she could tell he did have love for her. She arched up as her body was aching to release. And for the first time he pulled his mouth from hers and said, "You come when you want to. As many times as you want to."

A knot formed in her throat and tears began to fall as he watched her. She let the orgasm overtake her and he watched her as it did. A smile moved over his face as he continued to thrust in and out of her.

"My God, you're beautiful when you come, baby." He kissed her long and deep and she felt more for him than she had before.

His body tensed and he spilled into her. She was shocked to find herself coming again with his release. They lay on the floor, flooding the car with their gasps. Arsen released her mouth as their bodies began to stop throbbing against the others.

. . .

THE PRIVACY WINDOW opened just a little and Paul said, "Boss, you might want to get yourself cleaned up. The police are waiting in front of the building."

"Fuck!" Arsen said as he rolled off her.

Steele sat up and looked for her panties.

"Arsen, I'm so sorry. What should I do?" She found the panties and pulled them on quickly.

He buttoned his slacks and zipped them after tucking his shirt back in. He put the belt back on and grabbed his jacket. As he sat back on the seat, she ran her hands through his hair, taming it since she'd ran her hands through it, messing it up before.

Arsen took her wrists in his hands and said, "You are to stay at my penthouse. Promise me you won't go anywhere. I'll be out as soon as I can."

She nodded and said, "I will. Don't worry about me."

"I can't not worry about you, Steele. Just as long as I know you'll do as I've said, it'll help me not to go crazy until I can get back to you." He kissed her again. "Tell me again, before they take me away."

"I LOVE YOU, Arsen. I'll be there waiting for you. I promise." She gave his hair one last smoothing and managed a smile.

He pulled a set of keys from a hidden compartment.

"Take these so you can get into the penthouse."

The car pulled to a stop and Paul came around and opened the door. "She should probably stay in here," he said.

Arsen nodded.

"Take her to my place, please." He looked at Steele. "One more rule, Steele."

"What is it?"

"That little dick, Rowan. I don't want you around him without me present. Tell Tanner about my arrest and do not go with him to do anything. I don't want the little shit head to mess with your mind about me."

"Okay, Arsen." She found she couldn't stop touching him as she ran her hand over his cheek.

His hands ran up her arms, and he kissed her one last time. Then got out of the car. The door closed behind him, shielding her from the officers' view.

Steele watched as the police officers came straight up to Arsen and both took out their guns and pointed them at him. His hands went up, and he stopped moving.

Her breathing stopped and more tears found their way out. She pressed her hand to the dark glass as sobs racked her chest. One officer cuffed him and put him in back of the police car. They drove away with him and Paul started driving her away.

She watched out the back window as they went in opposite directions and cried hard as she lost sight of the police car. She'd never felt that much pain before and it hurt more than she knew she could actually live through.

It was as if she was in an alternate reality as Paul pulled up to the building where Arsen's penthouse was. He opened the door and when he saw her state he opened his arms.

Steele same into them and cried on his shoulder.

"I'm so scared, Paul."

"I know. So am I," he said. "Somehow he'll make it out of this. He didn't do it you know."

She nodded.

"I know. There has to be something we can do to help find the real killer, then this will be over and we can move on."

"You're a smart girl. Think on it," he said and let her out of his tight hug. "Now go on up and have a nice, stiff drink and relax."

She gave him a weak smile.

"Okay, thanks."

Steele wiped her eyes and walked inside. The place felt odd without him there. She wandered to the bathroom and picked up his bottle of cologne. After dabbing a little on her wrist and taking a sniff of it, she made her way to the kitchen and made herself a small glass of cognac.

THE KEYS she laid on the counter top and noticed one of them looked different. Like an old key, maybe to a box or something. Curiosity overtook her, and she took the keys and went to Arsen's office. He'd never taken her in there, but she'd seen him come out of it.

The aroma of leather filled her senses as she opened the door. The chair behind his large oak desk was leather and there was a leather sofa against the opposite wall. A large set of cabinets lined another wall, and she went to them, opening one at a time. Careful not to disturb any of the contents, she looked around in them.

At the back of the third cabinet, she saw a dark box. When she pulled it out, she saw it would take an old key to open it. She placed it on his desk and put the key in the slot and the box opened. Inside was one thing, an old tattered notebook with the words, 'life sucks' scrawled across it in black marker.

Steele pulled it our carefully and opened it to the first page. At the top of the first page was written, 'Day 1 - The Day I Met Beth.'

She read the page and saw it was about Arsen's first love. And by the end of the fifteenth page, she found out why he didn't think love was something for him.

It seemed that Arsen had been beaten nearly to death by the girl's father and the girl was actually mad at Arsen over it. Seemed he hadn't stood up to the man who was older and larger than he was.

The rest of the little notebook told her about how his mother abandoned him while he was in the hospital and how he had to go live in a foster home. Then the girl's mother, who was a secret BDSM lover, took Arsen as her sub.

By the time she was done reading, Steele was livid with the two women and one girl who had damaged Arsen so badly. She replaced the notebook and put it right back where she'd found it.

Her stomach hurt as she thought about Arsen as a skinny teenager who got beat up so badly he had to spend a week in the hospital. And he had described some of the things the woman he called Mistress Sinclair had done to him, to make him be submissive to her.

Steele was seething with anger at the women. In an effort to better understand the man she'd fallen in love with she went through his desk and a note in the top drawer caught her attention.

In feminine handwriting the note read; I know what you did, and you won't get away with it. The initials, K.P. were at the end.

STEELE PUT the paper back in the exact same spot she'd found it. One of the victims, the last one killed was Kyla Peterson. And by the file Tanner had on Arsen, she was his first sub.

MEAGAN HAD BEEN KILLED FIRST. A week later, Lacy Andrews, Arsen's last sub, was killed. Kyla was killed last and somehow she must've seen something that led her to leave him the note.

Steele pulled every drawer on his desk open and in the back of one of the drawers was a small length of rope. She didn't touch it, but she knew it was the same type of rope the three women were bound with.

She closed the drawer as her body went numb and her brain quit working.

He did it!

13

PART FIVE: FOR APPROVAL

Description

Even though Steele knew the rule about being anywhere alone with Rowan, she found herself all alone in a room waiting to see Arsen as he was supposed to be brought in to see his lawyer. Tanner had yet to arrive, leaving the two alone, and both were surprised as a free Arsen walked in and found them talking about things that Rowan had found out about Arsen.

Arsen flew into a rage and Rowan found himself punched before he knew what happened. Steele managed to get Arsen away from the young man and out to his waiting car before he did anything else to Rowan, getting himself into even more trouble.

Arsen went strangely quiet as they left the area of the police station as he saw someone he knew. He refused to let Steele in on what was wrong with him, making her furious and she argued with him about his need for her complete trust yet he wouldn't give her his.

He told her she'd proven herself untrustworthy so far and until she proved different, he would continue to question her and leave her out of things.

Once they got back to his apartment, he let her know she had to be punished for staying in the room alone with Rowan. Steele found that she wanted to show Arsen the lengths she'd go to for him. To get closer to him, she was willing to accept a little pain if it would bring them closer and help him to let her in.

After administering the punishment, Arsen found himself feeling guilt for spanking her. Something in him was changing, and he felt things needed to change between them.

At the same time that he was feeling bad about how he was treating her, Steele was feeling bad about how she was making him soften. She knew the weak young man he'd been and didn't want him to lose all the confidence he'd managed to gain after all that had happened to him.

When Arsen told her he wanted things to be different in their relationship, he was surprised she didn't agree with him. Instead she wanted him to make a dom/sub contract, a thing he told her they both needed to think about some more.

A bit later as the two showered, Steele saw the man that they had seen outside of the police station looking up at Arsen's penthouse. She decided the man needed to be looked in to. Especially after Arsen let her in on who the man was.

Arsen was opening up to her, and she was ecstatic. Steele pushed for him to make her his sub as she felt intrigued by the lifestyle and wanted to know about every aspect of the man.

After a bit of being treated like his sub, she found it not entirely what she'd thought, but wanted something solid binding them. Arsen decided to make up a contract and book for her. He was confident she was too strong willed to truly be happy with that lifestyle.

But is Steele wanting to commit to be his submissive before she really understands all which goes with that?

14

STEELE

Cool air blew over her face as the vent in the ceiling of the small room in the police station poured the cooled air out. Her chair was directly beneath it as she waited for Arsen to be brought in.

Tanner had called her early that morning and asked her to meet him there so he could talk to Arsen and she could take notes.

After what she had found in Arsen's office the day before, she had a pretty restless night. But when it came down to it, she thought there had to be someone setting him up. The man she was beginning to know just couldn't do those terrible things.

The door opened, and she stood, ready to see Arsen, but instead saw Rowan. "What are you doing here?" she asked as she sat back down.

"I work on this case too, Gannon." He took the chair next to hers and she knew Arsen was going to have a fit if he got there before Tanner did and found them alone.

"Want to know what I found out about your boyfriend?"

"It's most likely rumors but go for it, Rowen." She crossed her arms over her chest and listened.

"After snooping around, I found the woman who made the man."

"Let me guess. Her last name wouldn't be Sinclair by any chance?" She smiled.

"Yes, and it seems he and her daughter had been high school sweethearts and your boyfriend got his ass beat pretty badly by the girl's father," he said.

"Look, I already know this. I know she was his Dom and that doesn't make him a killer."

"It certainly gives the man the psychological past which could make him into a man who hates women. A man who might kill women, Gannon. Don't you see that?" He smirked as if she was stupid.

Steele scooted her chair away from his a bit as she was beginning to get uneasy Arsen would catch them alone.

"You have no idea about him. He doesn't hate women. I have reason to believe he's being set up."

"I gained access to a club called, Fierce. Arsen has his own room there and what it's filled with is more than kinky. It's downright sinister, Gannon. More than mere whips and chains." His eyes narrowed at her.

"How did you get into his room?" she asked in disbelief.

"A FRIEND of a friend works there and let me in early this morning. Tanner knew about it," he told her and she found herself furious he had gone through Arsen's private things. "Choke collars, some things on the wall to hold women up off the floor in chains. You wouldn't believe the assortment of paddles and even long poles. And two of these long poles looked like there were blood stains on them."

"Blood?" she asked. Her body tingled with a chill.

Would he actually hurt someone?

"WHAT DO you think happens to flesh when something like that strikes it, Gannon? There was even this wooden thing where it looked like he could trap a woman in it and take her or beat her and there'd be no way she could get away. It was a room of nightmares for any woman." He leaned forward and placed his hand on her leg and looked into her eyes. "It's not a place for you and you really need to think about what the hell you're doing with him."

"I don't know what to say. I don't entirely believe you."

"Not only is the man most likely a serial killer, he's an awful monster who gets his rocks off hurting women, Gannon."

And then the door opened and Arsen stood there. He was alone and free and his face was red with anger.

"What the fuck are you doing alone with him, Steele?" His eyes went to the hand Rowan still had on her leg and she jumped up.

"Arsen! You're free!" she said and took a step towards him.

He reached out and grabbed her arm, moving her behind him as he glared at Rowan.

"I heard you, you little piece of shit! How dare you talk about things you have no idea about? I'm no killer and what I do in private is just that, private!"

Rowan was up and in Arsen's face. A very stupid thing to do.

"Look, Sloan, you don't intimidate me and she needs to know the truth about you and your sick ways!"

And in an instant, Rowan was falling backward as Arsen had punched him. In the eye this time and it was already red and swelling.

"Arsen, no!" she screamed.

Steele grabbed his arm and found him shaking with rage. She pulled at him and he finally allowed her to get him out of the room.

"I told you he would tell you things to interfere with us."

What Rowan had told her was making her think she might be in over her head with Arsen. But the man had some kind of hold over her and her body continuously overruled her brain.

Maybe I am stupid!

15

ARSEN

The entrance to the police station was rather busy that morning and as Arsen and Steel made their way to his car, he stopped dead in his tracks. A man was standing at the back of his car, looking directly at Arsen and tipped his head in a hello. He walked away slowly, without looking back.

Steele noticed Arsen's reaction to the man.

"Do you know that guy?" she asked.

Arsen began to move forward again.

"No."

Steele watched the man walk away. His brown hair was cut short, and he wore tan slacks and a white collared shirt. He looked a bit like an accountant or a computer nerd.

Paul was quick to get out and open the door for them.

"Nice to see you, boss."

"You too, Paul," Arsen said as he let Steel get in first.

Once inside the car and alone Steele pressed him about the man.

"You know that man, Arsen. Who is he?"

"Never mind, Steele. It's not important anyway. What is important is why you decided to be alone with that prick when I told you not to." He took a bottle of liquor from the little fridge and took a long drink.

Steele didn't say a word. After he took one more long drink she took the bottle from his hand and put it back in the fridge. "For God's sake, it's nine in the morning, Arsen."

As she sat back down he looked at her and ran his hand over her cheek. "You have no idea how much I missed you last night as I lay on the tiny, hard bed in the cell they put me in."

She took his hand in hers and held it to her face. "I missed you too. I hardly slept."

"Me too," he said.

"TELL me who the man is, Arsen."

His eyes went dark, and he pulled his hand from hers. "Drop it, Steele."

Her arms crossed in front of her and she frowned.

"Damn it, Arsen! You're always telling me I need to trust you, but you don't trust me enough to let me in on anything."

"Maybe that's because you've proven yourself untrustworthy." He reached over and buckled her seatbelt. "Try to remember to buckle your safety belt, Steele."

"How in the world have I proven myself untrustworthy?"

"I told you not to be alone with that prick and you did it anyway. I'm not an idiot. I know you thought Tanner would get there before they brought me in to talk to him. You sat there and listened to what the moron had to say. Your curiosity overrode your want to follow the rules I have for you." His hand tapped her thigh, and the other took her chin and made her look up at him. "We'll deal with that little indiscretion when we get home."

HE COULD TELL that she was fighting the urge to roll her eyes at him. And he had to give her credit for not doing it. His hand left her chin and cradled the back of her neck, pulling her to him.

As mad as he was that she'd gone against him, he had missed her like he never imagined possible and needed to feel her. His body tingled as their lips met and he allowed himself to need her at that moment.

She was so far under his skin that he had no choice it seemed. He loved her and he knew it. With his impending arrest and trials, he felt an urgency to have her in a contract with him. His intention was to draw one up and hopefully she'd decide to enter the contract with him. He needed some security with the woman in order to stay sane with all the craziness in his life.

When he finally stopped his kiss and released her he pressed his forehead to hers.

"I love you, Steele."

He saw her lips quirk into a smile.

"I love you too, Arsen."

16

STEELE

After showing Arsen the note and the rope which he seemed to have never seen either before, Steele was sure that he was innocent and being set up. They took both things and burned them in a small metal trash can. Then for good measure, threw the ashes into the garbage disposal and cleaned everything with bleach afterward.

She was waiting for him in his bedroom as he had told her to go in there and wait for him. He had to punish her for breaking his rule about Rowan and she understood. She'd known the moment Rowan had walked into the room she should've went out and waited in the hallway.

And for some damn reason, she wanted him to do it. Wanted him to discipline her for not doing what he told her to. Steele was a strong woman and had never felt she needed anyone telling her what to do.

It wasn't so much she thought she needed the discipline as she thought Arsen did. She felt if he felt she trusted him and would be submissive to him, he'd really let her in. Let her into his mind, his soul, and the past that made him the intricate, dark man he was.

She sat on the bed and looked down as he came into the room.

She was willing to take the pain his punishment would bring if it would somehow help her take the pain which filled him away.

ARSEN WAS NEARLY a part of her. She loved him more than she thought possible. When he told her he loved her, she knew she'd do anything for the man. Anything to help him get past the terrible things which were done to him.

She was ready for whatever he was about to do to her. She'd read a little about what the punishments in the dom/sub relationship were about. She knew she was supposed to cry to shed tears. It would show him she understood what she'd done to displease him and that she was sorry.

Then she was to thank him for what he'd done for her. She was prepared to do those things for him. To show him she was his and in the process if things went how she hoped they would, he'd become hers as well.

It wasn't her plan to remain in a dom/sub relationship. She knew to get to the place she wanted though she had to go that route.

The sound of the leather belt sliding from his pants made her heart race. "Stand up!" She did as he said and continued to look down. "Turn around."

She turned and felt his hand at the small of her back. The zipper of her skirt he pulled down and pushed it off her hips. It puddled around her ankles and then her panties were ripped off.

His hands grasped her shoulders, and he turned her around slowly. He ripped her shirt open, buttons flying in all directions. His arms went around her to unclasp her bra and he gently pulled it off her.

He took a step back and sighed as she could tell he was looking at her naked body, but she didn't dare look up at him. She stepped out of her heels as he took her by the arm and moved her towards the closet.

He opened the door and said, "Raise your arms."

She did and felt something cold go around each wrist then the sound of metal clicking and she knew she was in handcuffs. He pulled her up until she was on her tippy toes. He looped the cuffs over some kind of hook at the top of the door. Her arms ached already.

He stepped back and when he came back something went around her eyes, covering them with a soft material. Arsen leaned close to her. His breath hot against her ear and neck.

"Do you trust me, Steele?"

"I do, Arsen." Her body was tense, and she was surprised to find she was aroused.

His fingers trailed over her back, sending chills through her.

"What was it you did that brought this punishment on?"

"I broke your rule about being alone with Rowan."

The crack of the belt across her butt made her wince. It stung, but it wasn't unbearable. Not yet anyway.

"Why did you break my rule?"

She had to swallow to make sure her voice was steady.

"My stubborn curiosity."

Another loud crack and the belt bit into her flesh. She had to bite her lip not to scream.

"Why do I make rules for you Steele?"

"Because you care for me and want me to be safe and healthy."

THE LEATHER STUNG as it slammed across her ass. She couldn't hold the tears back any longer and a sob came out of her involuntarily. His hand reached between her legs and one finger ran into her.

"You reacted appropriately Steele and now you'll be rewarded. Tell me our safe word."

She choked back her sobs. "Thank you, Arsen. Our safe word is Rose."

He pulled her long, dark hair back and kissed her neck. "That's right, baby."

Arsen pulled her cuffed hands off the hook and led her to the bed. He bent her over the bed and she heard his zipper then felt his large cock press into her in one hard thrust.

Each hard thrust sent waves of pleasure through her. His hand fisted in her hair and he pulled it hard. She panted with excitement and her body began to quiver.

His voice was hard and demanding. "If you come without me telling you to, I'll give you five more licks of the belt, Steele."

She didn't want any more, so she held back. Her body was cresting, and it was growing more difficult to keep from letting go. Finally, she said, "Please, Arsen..." Her body was shaking from the need to release.

He stopped and pulled out of her. Then she was picked up and laid out on the bed flat on her back. Her cuffed hands looped over something and then she felt something go around one ankle.

It was cold and her leg was pulled and then it was obvious to her he had cuffed her leg to something that held it in place. The same was done to the other, and she was helpless to move at all.

"Do you trust me?" he asked her.

"Yes, Arsen. I trust you."

The swoosh of fabric she heard and then she felt his bare skin on hers as he pushed into her again. The wave which had built up had dissipated, and she was no longer in danger of climaxing without his permission.

With her sense of sight gone, she was able to concentrate on everything her body was feeling. The way his large cock was moving inside her felt amazing and his muscles rippled on his stomach, moving against hers.

His breathing was a thing she found amazing. Hard, deep breaths which came from deep in his lungs moved hot air over her cheek and some of her shoulder.

The way he smelled seeped into her senses. His expensive cologne, his sweat, and the unique smell of them together filled her nostrils and made her head feel slightly light. Intoxicating her with the aroma, distinctly them.

His mouth took hers and his tongue moved to the back of her

throat. Stroking against hers. It was all getting to be too much for her to handle and she began to feel the orgasm starting. In the position she was in she couldn't stop it. It was impossible.

His mouth on hers had it where she couldn't even ask him. Her body climaxed and shook under his. He kept going though. He didn't stop, didn't quit kissing her.

Instead she felt his hand move up her arm and take her hands from the thing he'd hooked them to. He pulled them to go around his neck. Stroking hard into her.

He pulled his mouth away and kissed her neck then nipped at her earlobe.

"I LOVE YOU, baby. I'm sorry, baby. I only want to bring you pleasure and happiness."

Steele began to cry. She was beginning to get to him. For some reason, making him soften felt wrong. Like she was making him weak.

She wanted in so bad, but to break him down wasn't what she wanted. "Arsen, I love you."

His body stiffened, and he groaned as he came. It made her body climax again, and they both were breathing hard as she felt him trembling. She was breaking him and she couldn't stand herself.

This isn't what I wanted!

17

ARSEN

As he un-cuffed her ankles one at a time, he couldn't stop the ache in his heart. He'd hurt her and he was finding that act unforgiveable. He had no idea what was happening to him.

She lay perfectly still, her eyes still covered. As he released her ankle he saw it was red from where she'd pulled at it. He ran his hand over it and flinched at the sharp pain which stabbed at his heart.

This wasn't a lifestyle she'd chosen. This wasn't some fantasy of hers. She wasn't the woman he was making her be. She cared for him – that was the only reason she even allowed him to do the things he did to her.

He was a monster. The fucking kid had been right about him. He was so set in his ways though. Was it in him to change? To be what the gorgeous woman strapped to his bed deserved?

He released the other ankle and then her wrists. When he pulled the blindfold away, he saw her red rimmed eyes and nearly lost it.

"Steele, baby, please forgive me." He took her in his arms and held her tight to him.

Her head was on his shoulder and he felt the hot tears rolling over his skin. It was breaking his heart, and he had to swallow the knot down which had formed in his throat.

He picked her up and took her to the shower. The warm water fell over them and he found she was still crying, not hard, but her tears were still flowing. "I've lost you, haven't I?"

She shook her head.

"Far from it, Arsen."

He was confused and kissed her cheek.

"So why the nonstop tears?"

"Because you told me you're sorry. I feel like I'm breaking something in you. The thing which makes you who you are." She looked up at him and he wiped her tears.

"You are changing me. Somehow, you're so under my skin it feels like you're a part of me. I brought you into a world you didn't seek out. I feel now like I was wrong to force you to accept my lifestyle."

"You don't want me anymore?" He saw fear in her blue eyes and it further hurt him.

He kissed the tip of her nose.

"Of course I do. Just maybe a little different though."

She shook her head.

"I want you the same way you had the other women. Arsen, you'll tire of me quickly if you can't live the way you have since…" She stopped herself from saying anymore and he saw it.

"Since what, Steele." He looked at her and lifted her chin.

"I snooped, I told you that. I didn't tell you that I read your little journal thingy you have locked away in one of the cabinets in your office." She bit her lip.

Arsen was mad, furious even, but he'd already felt far too much guilt over spanking her. He wasn't going to let his temper rule him.

"I SEE, so you know about it all then?" His grip on her loosened some. His mind wandered to the past. A place he hated to go to. "You know I was a weakling and then a submissive myself."

"Yes, and Arsen, I don't want you to feel weak again. I don't want you to feel that way because of me." She wrapped her arms around him and laid her head on his chest.

The fact was she'd already made him feel weak. His love for her made him weak. He wasn't in control of himself that was for sure.

"Are you saying you want to live my way so I can stay strong and in control?"

She nodded, and it made him sick. This strong woman was willing to let herself be treated in a way which was beneath her for him and he was ashamed of himself. For the first time in a long time, he was not satisfied with the man he was.

Her eyes met his.

"I want you to make the dom/sub contract, Arsen. I'm ready and willing to live that way with you. I trust you."

"You aren't ready and frankly, I doubt you'll ever be." Arsen let her go and poured shampoo in his hand and started washing his hair. His heart was pounding in his chest.

The truth was he longed to take her to the BDSM club, Fierce. He knew all the men would be envious of his gorgeous find. He envisioned her on her hands and knees, his collar around her long and slender throat. His leash holding her, telling all the others in the club she was his, and he was her master.

"ARSEN, what's wrong? Why do you think I'm not ready?" She moved to be in front of him. "You don't want me like that?"

"You have no idea of what you're in for, Steele. Tell me, has it ever been a fantasy of yours to crawl around on your hands and knees at the end of a leash I'll hold?" His eyebrows quirked up, and he grinned.

"I could do it for you," she said and ran her finger in the lines of his chiseled abs. "I could do anything for you, Arsen."

He rinsed his hair then took her hand from him.

"This wouldn't be allowed. You'd touch me only when I allowed. You'd be expected to do so much more as a sub. My subs catered to me. They washed my hair and trimmed my nails. They allowed me to take them whenever and where ever I wanted. That included in front of people."

He saw Steele take in a sharp breath. "Really? Where? Those clubs?"

"Clubs, elevators, semi-secluded booths in restaurants. Where ever whenever. Think you could do that?" He smiled at her again and ran his hand over her shoulder.

Steele wasn't answering right away, and he laughed.

"Like I said, it's not a thing you're ready for and may never be. It's something I'm coming to terms with."

"You certainly have done a lot you in your life, haven't you?" Steele asked as she shuddered.

Arsen ran his hands up and down her arms.

"I have. More than most and you'd be smart to run away from me, Steele. Not that I'll let you, but it would be the smart thing for you to do."

"You choked those girls. Why'd they want you to do that? I actually have a fear of being choked to death," she said as he turned her around and started shampooing her long, dark hair.

"WHY'S THAT?" he asked as he massaged in the honeysuckle scented shampoo he'd picked up just for her.

"A case I saw played out on television when I was fifteen. A girl came up missing and when they found her months later, they found out she'd been strangled. I looked it up and found it takes a good while for the lack of oxygen to make your brain stop working. The victim is aware they're dying. It's awful, so why would people want to be choked?" She looked up at him as he pushed her head back to rinse the shampoo out.

"It's because of exactly what you read about. They want to be brought just to the point of passing out, then once their throat is released the oxygen hits their brains rapidly and they have a euphoric experience. Add in an orgasm along with that and some people find it to be a phenomenal sensation." He filled his palm with a honeysuckle scented conditioner and ran it through her hair.

"Have you been on the receiving end of that, Arsen?" Her blue eyes were wide.

Arsen thought it over before he spoke. He didn't like to think about his time under Mistress Sinclair. It held too many bad memories. But Steele needed to know more about him. He couldn't expect her to be what he needed in his life without letting her in on some of his past.

He nodded.

"Twice and I hated it both times. It wasn't a pleasant experience for me. I was a young man, trying to impress my Dom. I should've used the safe word, but I refused to show my weakness and ended up passing out both times. I woke with a headache and an aching throat. On top of that, I was further disciplined for not using the safe word."

Steele ran her arms around Arsen and hugged him.

"I don't know what I'll do if I ever meet that horrible bitch, Arsen."

"Not a damn thing, Steele. I won't have you getting into any kind of altercation with her. She can take a fuck load of pain and you can't. Believe me she knows so many ways to hurt you it's not even funny." He wrapped his arms around her and thought how good it felt to be talking to her about things.

Arsen never realized he'd want to talk about such things and with a female at that. It was crazy what she had him doing. He kissed the top of her head and felt a shift in his future was happening.

18

STEELE

As Arsen held her in his arms, Steele was able to see out the one window in the bathroom. On the sidewalk below, was the same man from the police station. He was looking up at the penthouse. Just staring.

That man needed to be looked at as a person of interest in the murders. She pulled back and pointed out the window.

"Look whose outside, Arsen."

He turned and muttered, "Fuck."

After turning off the water in the shower, he got out and wrapped a towel around his waist then wrapped one around Steele.

"Who is he, Arsen?"

"An old client of mine. The one case I lost." He took her hand and led her out of the bathroom and into his bedroom. "This is probably not a good thing he's out there."

"What kind of case was it you lost?" she asked as he pulled one of his soft T-shirts out of a drawer and pulled it over her head.

"A murder case. Allen White was convicted of murdering his high school math teacher. He kidnapped her and kept her hidden away for a couple of months then killed her. Her body was tortured in many unbelievable ways." Arsen pulled on a pair of blue pajama bottoms and led Steele to the kitchen.

"How come he's out of prison then?" she asked as Arsen began to pull things out of the refrigerator to make sandwiches.

"Grab the bread, please," he said as he placed a jar of mustard on the island in the large kitchen. "I was called by a member of the parole board several months ago. It seems Mr. White managed to gain his freedom by becoming a jail house evangelist."

"So he found Jesus, and that alone got him out of prison?" Steele took a knife from a drawer and slathered fours slices of bread with mustard. "Is that all it takes to be set free after torturing and murdering a person?"

"Apparently." Arsen placed three pieces of turkey on two of the mustard covered slices of bread. "The thing is, he was let out approximately three weeks before the first murder. So he could very well be the murderer."

"Why target those women?" Steele asked as she placed slices of cheese on the two sandwiches.

Arsen piled lettuce on each sandwich.

"Well, I was feeling like I needed something in my life. The random women weren't doing it for me. I was feeling like I needed more in my life. I went to see each woman who had been my subs a few times to see if there was any type of spark. I suppose he wanted to take away anyone that I cared about."

Steele cut a tomato up and placed slices on the sandwiches then Arsen placed the other pieces of bread on top and placed each one on plates. He carried them to the table and Steele grabbed two bottles of water from the fridge and a jar of pickles.

She sat across from him. "Why haven't you told the police about your hunch?"

"Do you think it would do one bit of good to do that? I mean, it's my handprints on each of their throats. If it was him, he must've managed to kill them without leaving a trace of DNA anywhere." He took a bite of the sandwich.

Steele stabbed a couple of pickles out of the jar and placed one on her plate and one on his.

"We need to investigate him."

"I do," Arsen wagged his finger at her. "You are not to go anywhere near the man."

"I can help you." She wagged her finger right back at him and smiled.

"Minutes ago, you were wanting me to write up a contract and now you want to argue with me about something. Really, Steele," he said with a grin.

"So if I'm going to be your sub, my opinion no longer matters?" she asked then took a drink of the water.

"It's complicated. What I say goes. Arguing will get you punished. Let's face it, you can't really take punishment, Steele." He frowned and looked down. "And I really can't take dishing it out to you."

Steele reached across the table and ran her fingers over the back of his hand. "I really shouldn't have been alone with Rowan. He did exactly what you said he would. I'm not upset with you."

"I'm not happy with myself, Steele. Things have to change." Arsen put the half-eaten sandwich down.

"Take me to your club, Arsen. I want to see how it is. I want to know the you that you're trying to change. If you're trying to change for me, you need to know that I don't want you too," she said as her fingers traced a pattern on the back of his hand.

Arsen's tone went sharp and commanding. "Take your hand off me."

Steele pulled her hand back and looked down. "Sorry."

"So, that's what you really want?" he snapped at her.

Steele had to think. She wanted to know what his lifestyle was really like. Rowan had made her curious about Arsen's room in the BDSM club.

"Yes, Sir."

He let out a harsh laugh. "On your knees, now."

Steele's stomach went tight. A part of her wanted that, and another part was appalled she wanted it. She got off the chair and got on her knees.

Arsen got up and walked away, leaving her in the kitchen on her knees. When he came back, she didn't look up at him. He placed something around her neck. Then a clicking sound she heard near her left ear and a quick jerk she felt as Arsen apparently had attached a leash to the thing around her neck.

She swallowed hard as she realized he'd put a collar on her and had her at the end of a leash. Like an animal. And he was her master. "To my room."

Steele started to get up, and he jerked the leash hard. "On your hands and knees."

She began to crawl towards his bedroom and she was surprised to find herself getting turned on. Once she was in the room, he stopped and said, "If I take you to that club, you'll have to crawl in front of a room full of men and women while you wear clothes that show your tits and ass." He moved around in front of her. "Take my cock out."

Steele swallowed hard and reached up. Taking his cock out of his pajama bottoms. Then let it go. It was erect and near her face. His hand took the back of her neck, roughly. "Suck it."

He pressed her head to him and she opened her mouth and took it in. She tried to run her hands up to it and he slapped one away. "I didn't tell you to touch me, woman."

He moved her head back and forth, forcefully. Steele was aroused and moaned. But found her head pulled back quickly. Arsen pulled her hair, making her look up at him. "You make a sound without my instruction in that place and your ass will be hot before you know what you've done. Also, you will have to endure this as others watch. And if I want, I can make you suck any man's dick in the place. Sounding like something you still find intriguing?"

Steele answered with a smile, "You'd never allow any part of me to touch another man, Arsen. We both know that."

His smile grew sinister. "Baby, you have no idea what I'll allow. The fact is I made all my other subs do things with other men as I watched. They got ate out and I wouldn't allow them to come. If they did, not only did I punish them but so did the other man."

"ARSEN!" she said and found her stomach growing tight. "You didn't!"

He nodded. "I made them have sex with other men while I watched and dared them to enjoy it. I used their bodies any fucking way I wanted to and if that's what you want from me, then I can do that for you, Steele. Is that what you want? Me to take you in front of people and put you under other men and dare you to enjoy it? Dare you to tell me no about anything?"

Her heart was pounding. It sounded awful and amazing at the same time.

"I want that."

HE LAUGHED and took her by the back of her neck again, hoisting her up. Arsen looked into her eyes and she saw his had darkened even more. "It's not even about sex, it's about power. It's about taking your power and making it mine."

She had no idea why that intrigued her so damn much.

"I want it."

He picked her up and tossed her over his shoulder. All she had on was his T-shirt. He unleashed her then pulled it off over her head. Arsen placed her on the bed on her back. "Spread your arms and legs for inspection."

Steele did as he said and her eyes cut to the side to watch him as he reached into a drawer next to the bed. He took out a small box and pulled out two odd little clear things.

He gave one a couple of squeezes then placed it on her nipple and pumped it several times. It sucked hard, and the pain began right away. Arsen watched her as she closed her eyes and her lips pressed into a hard line. "Do not utter a sound."

He placed the other one on and she wiggled a little with the intense pain. A quick smack she felt on the side of her ass and she opened her eyes to see he held a thin piece of wood, like a paint stirring stick.

Arsen held a wooden clothes pin, and she began to wonder where he thought he was going to put it. His hand ran over her sex and down one leg. When he went back up he placed the clothes pin on her clit and she arched up in pain.

Things were not going as she expected and the pain was too intense. "Rose!" she shouted. "Rose! Get them off, Arsen! Please!"

He took the clothes pin off and then each suction cup. "Are we done here?"

She nodded. "I'm not ready."

His hand grazed over her cheek. "And most likely never will be. Your pain threshold is low. Most can take many more strikes than you can and can take the suction cups and clitoral pinning much longer than that. You need to face the fact that this isn't a thing you fantasize about or even want."

She began to cry. "Then I'll lose you. You'll never be okay with a... what do they call it, a vanilla."

He left the room, and she turned to cry into a pillow.

I can never be what he wants!

19

ARSEN

The woman was making him crazy. She was trying too hard to be something she wasn't. Something he didn't think he even wanted her to be anymore.

He grabbed a handful of ice cubes from the freezer and put them in a cloth. Grabbing a bottle of whisky, he went back into the bedroom and found Steele crying into a pillow.

He rolled her over gently and placed the cloth full of ice on one nipple. "Here this will stop the pain." He pulled her up a little and handed her the bottle of Jack Daniels. "Take a drink of this."

She wiped her eyes and did as he said, choking on the whisky.

"I'm sorry. I'm a wimp."

He shook his head.

"No, you're not. You're just not cut out for that. And it takes a while anyway. You want to go and rush things that take years to learn how to make your mind focus to take the pain it causes." He moved the cold cloth to the other breast.

"Arsen, it will get old and boring with me, won't it?" She sniffled and took another drink from the bottle.

He smiled and took the bottle from her and placed it on the nightstand.

"I doubt you'll ever bore me, Steele."

"The fact is I might be the one who bores you." He moved the cold cloth to her clit, and she tensed up. "And I'm sorry about doing that to you. You clearly weren't ready, and I went ahead and did it anyway. I'm not myself. I'm much more responsible than this."

"Perhaps the fact you have more murder charges hanging over your head." Steele ran her hand through his hair. "That could throw anyone off their game."

He laughed. "You think?"

She ran her hand to graze his bearded cheek. "You should let me run the clippers over that beard. You've always kept it meticulously groomed and here of late you've let it go a bit."

"AFTER WHAT I did to you, you still want to be nice to me?" he asked as he shook his head.

"I asked for it, didn't I?" she said with a smile. "Just didn't really realize what I was getting into. I do want to learn though. Maybe baby steps."

Arsen's eyes brightened. "If you really want to do this, I'll make up a contract. One we both agree on. Then maybe you'll feel like I'm letting you into my world."

Steele nodded. "I'll stop rushing this and let you take the reins."

"Good." He placed her hand on the cold cloth he held to her throbbing clit and went to his chest of drawers.

HE PULLED out paper and a pen then went and picked up the T-shirt he'd pulled off her. Arsen held out his hand for the cloth and she gave it to him. He pulled the T-shirt back over her head and sat next to her.

"Okay, let's discuss the things you can handle. Obviously, anything involving pain is going to be a hard limit for you." He wrote that down.

She leaned forward. "What the hell else is there?"

He smiled. "You'll see. So what about public orgasms? Where do you stand on those?"

"Never had one in public. Is it really embarrassing?" she asked as she bit her lip then added, "And how? Myself or one's you induce?"

"Both," he said as he looked at her. "For instance, we might be in a restaurant and I might make you keep a remote controlled dildo inside you while I have the remote. I may turn it on as the waiter approaches or something like that. And I may tell you to come. I can condition your body to come using one word. It doesn't have to be the word come, it can be anything I see fit. You'd be surprised how easily this is done."

"No shit?" Her hand ran to cover her mouth as he frowned at her. "Sorry! It slipped out."

"Hmm. Let's see, perhaps instead of spanking I could come up with some other way to punish you. I'm going to think on it. For now, I'm going to let that little slip up go." He tapped the end of the pen on the tip of her nose. "Please try harder. It's so unsuitable for you to curse."

"I know. Sorry. It's just I have a hard time believing what you're saying. My mind can be conditioned to orgasm with just a word?"

His finger ran over her bottom lip. His dark eyes danced.

"You'd be surprised what all our minds can do, Steele. Now is that a thing you think you can and want to do?"

"IT SOUNDS KIND OF exciting so yes." She smiled and giggled. "This is kind of exciting too."

He smiled.

"Glad you find it that way. Now how about sex in public places?"

Steele's eyes went wide, and she ran her hands over her arms as a chill went through her.

"That sounds kind of risky. I mean, I do want to be an attorney one day and a charge of public indecency wouldn't look good for me or you for that matter."

"That's where you have to trust me, Steele. To make sure we don't get caught. It's part of the excitement." His eyebrows raised, and he winked at her. "Trust is the main thing with this. You always need to trust that I won't hurt you or do anything that would cause you to get into trouble."

She smiled.

"Okay then, that's a yes for that one then. I do trust you, Arsen. I honestly do."

"Good. And always tell me if I'm really hurting you, Steele. Don't do what I did when I was a sub and try to push yourself past your limits. With time you'll build up to whatever your personal limits are. It's about testing them, but not going past that. Honesty and trust are essential in the dom/sub relationship." He pushed back a strand of her hair that had fallen over her face.

"You really are sweet, Arsen. Do you know that?" she asked as she searched his eyes.

"I never have been. Well, once a long time ago. You bring something out in me I thought was long gone, Steele. But you are right about me needing to keep the strength I've managed to build. I can't go back to the young man I was."

"IT'S NOT EVEN a thing I want. Your strength is very attractive. Your authority is also extremely attractive." Her hand moved up his arm and squeezed his large bicep. "To be honest, the way you spank me, the first couple of licks anyway, send me into a wet, quivering mess."

He looked down and smiled.

"So a couple of swats are good, but three is too many. Got it." He wrote it down.

Steele leaned into his shoulder.

"And the way you bite me is good. That sends me over the edge."

Arsen looked sheepish as he wrote that down.

"Biting is good. And now onto other points of business. Sharp objects. What do you think about those?"

"Like you'll poke me with them?" Her expression was horrified.

"No, just run them over your skin. But it's exciting, especially when you're blindfolded and have no idea of what the sharp object is and if I'm going to poke you with it or not. Especially if you move."

"Oh, the trust thing again. Then okay. It does sound kind of intriguing." She ran her hand over his thigh. "Arsen, can I touch you when I want to? I mean unless you specifically tell me not to."

He sighed.

"You really like touching me and running your hands through my hair, don't you?"

She nodded.

"I do. But I can take sometimes being held back from it. The frustration building is a thing I find I'm liking."

"I'LL ALLOW it more often then. And another thing I want to talk about is making love. I want us to do that as well." He looked at her and seemed to be nervous. "It's a thing I haven't allowed myself to do since that day. The day Beth's father caught us. I've built up a fear in my mind and I'd like to work through that. I trust you enough to try to do that with."

Steele's heart nearly burst.

"Of course, Arsen!" her arms went around him and she was almost shaking with the breakthrough.

IT WAS BEGINNING TO HAPPEN. Arsen was letting her in and she would be able to help him heal from what the women did to hurt him. Now if she could help him find some evidence against Allen White everything would be falling into place for them.

ARSEN

After painstakingly writing their contract in a book which would hold the things they'd agreed on and the things he expected out of her, Arsen took the book and a legal contract to Steele as she sat in the living room.

"Here it is, only thing left to do is sign the contract." He placed the three page stack of papers in front of her and handed her a pen. "You sign then I will."

"And then we'll really be bound by this?" she asked as she tapped the pen on the top of the coffee table.

"Yes. You will be bound to me and me alone." He found himself nervous and nearly pulled the paper from her. But she seemed to need it.

She looked up at him and smiled.

"And you will be free to do who and what you want, right?"

He nodded and something inside him was telling him to stop her from signing it. Signing away herself to him.

She tapped her chin with the end of the pen.

"I have to trust you." She signed the paper and moved it over to him and handed him the pen.

He signed it hastily. Arsen handed her the book.

"This is yours to keep. We'll add things to it as we move along. It's like a journal that will show our journey together. But it's more than that."

"Sounds romantic," she said as she ran her hand over the leather cover. Gold embossed letters spelled out one word on the front of it, 'Arsen's.'

"IT'S NOT. It's a guide of what I expect from you. I'll write certain sex acts. Perhaps draw positions I want you to become adept at. Add rules and even punishments as time goes along and I deem the additions necessary to get you to understand your position as my sub."

"You may not think it romantic but I do, Arsen." She held the book to her chest and hugged it to her.

She stood and reached out to touch him. He took a step back.

"Uh, uh. It starts now, Steele."

A frown covered her face. "So what we've been doing is over?"

HE NODDED and turned away from her. "I'll be in my office. I'm going to order you a new wardrobe. In that book, you'll find the recipes for the meals I expect you to not only learn to cook, but make them to my satisfaction. If not edible then we'll order out, but you won't get to touch me at all until tomorrow."

"My adjusted punishments are not being able to touch you rather than physical punishments?" she asked.

He nodded and walked away, leaving her to look through the book he'd left her with. So many pages were full, and she found it a bit overwhelming. She found the recipes and groaned as she was not a cook.

"I asked for this," she said out loud to remind herself.

The chicken piccata recipe he'd written in the book was one of his favorites so when he heard Steele pounding away in the kitchen then smelled the delightful aroma of the chicken breasts cooking, he had to smile as he opened the door to his office.

Arsen had ordered her a complete wardrobe which would be delivered in a couple of days. He made his way down the hallway to the kitchen to peek in on her. He stifled a chuckle as he saw her with flour all over one cheek and the front of an apron she'd managed to find.

She blew a puff of air from her mouth to move a stray lock of hair which had gotten away from her ponytail. Her cheeks were pink with the heat of the stove she stood over.

After wiping the smile from his face he put on a stern look and cleared his throat. Steele jumped and spun around.

"Arsen! You scared me!"

He tapped his watch.

"It's five minutes late."

She looked confused.

"What is? Dinner? No, it says it has to be ready at seven-thirty. I still have forty-five minutes."

"Look on page eighteen and I'll be in my office waiting. Every minute I have to wait is a minute you'll have to wait before I allow you to touch me." He turned and left, smiling all the way back to his office.

IT WAS JUST a matter of time until Steele found she was not entirely ready for the submissive lifestyle. He sat at his desk and began researching safe cars for her. He was going to put her in the safest thing he could find.

The clothes and the car were things he wasn't about to change in how he took care of her. His cell phone rang and when he picked it up his smile faded.

There it was, the San Francisco police department yet again.

"ARSEN SLOAN."

A woman's voice came through the phone.

"Hello, this is Detective Fontaine. I've been assigned to your case, Mr. Sloan. The other detective gave it up. I'll need you to come and talk to me and give me your statement. Seems he misplaced the one that you gave him."

The woman on the other end of the phone had him seeing red.

"Look, I'm an extremely busy man, Fontaine. The other detective's desk looked like a pigpen. I'm sure if you look hard enough or have him do it then you'll find what you need. I'm not coming back down there. I just left the fucking place this morning."

"I'm afraid I need the statement. How about I come to you since you're so busy?"

Arsen stilled as he thought about what might happen if they found out he had Steele with him. It might prove very bad.

"Be here around eight. I won't be home until then."

"See you then, Mr. Sloan. Thank you. Goodbye."

. . .

WITH THE HIGHBALL glass in hand, Steele knocked on the door before entering his office. He looked up and was about to bark at her for walking in before he told her she could, but couldn't muster the energy to do it.

"Here you are, Arsen. A Manhattan. I hope you like it." She placed it on the desk in front of him and saw a picture of a beautiful car on his computer screen. "Oh, that's gorgeous. Thinking of getting a new car?"

"Huh?" He looked like his mind was far away. "Oh, not for me, for you."

She got an odd look on her face.

"I have a truck and don't want you to be buying me a ton of things. The clothes I get because you want to me to dress a certain way and I can live with that. The car and credit card…"

"Oh, yes. The credit card." He pulled open the top drawer of his desk and pulled out an envelope. He pulled a platinum colored credit card from it.

"Here, take this. I ordered it last week for you."

"Arsen, I just said…" She went quiet as his finger touched her lips.

"You signed the contract. It's all in the book. You should really take some time to read the whole thing. As a matter of fact, I have to take you to your apartment for a little while after dinner. Another detective has been assigned to my case, and she's coming here at eight this evening." He took a sip of the drink and gave her a thumbs up. "Great job, Steele."

She smiled then turned to walk away.

"I have to get back to cooking. I don't want anything to burn." She spun back around. "Wait! Did you say she? Like the detective is a woman?"

He nodded. "And take the book with you so you can read it. You'll have a lot to do tomorrow and need to know what I demand from you, as a submissive. Oh, at dinner, please respond to me as Master instead of my name. That'll be all."

Her eyes went wide, and she spun around and left. Her cheeks had turned red in an instant and Arsen had to put his hand over his mouth to hide his smile.

It would just be a matter of time before she realized she was so much more than just a sub.

22

PART SIX: FOR HER SAKE

Steele

The second glass of wine finally took the edge off Steele's nerves. She sat in her living room with her roommate, Gwen, and drank wine while she waited impatiently for Arsen to return for her.

The fact he was having to talk to another detective was cause for concern and adding in the fact the new detective was a woman had her woman's intuition on alert.

Tanner was supposed to go to Arsen's for the meeting, but she wasn't sure if he was there or not. Arsen had instructed her not to call him. He didn't want the detective to get any idea they were seeing each other.

Gwen refilled their wine glasses and took her seat on the other end of the sofa and by her narrowed eyes, Steele felt she was about to get bombarded with questions.

. . .

"OKAY, so that's your third glass of wine and now it's time to talk, Steele." Gwen leaned back and tapped her finger on the rim of the glass. "Spill it! Tell me everything about you and this Arsen guy."

"Not much to tell, really. A normal relationship." Steele sat her glass down as she didn't want to become too loose lipped by the alcohol.

"Normal! No, it's not normal, Steele." Gwen sat up and placed her glass on the table. "He's been charged with murder, that's not normal."

"He's innocent," Steele said and picked her glass up as her stomach tensed with the reminder of his predicament.

"It was on the news, Steele. The woman had been his submissive partner. What do you know about that?" Gwen questioned.

"He's into that kind of thing. No big deal, really. Don't know why people make such a giant thing about that lifestyle. It's not what people think. That woman wanted it. That woman wanted him to choke her just to the point of passing out and he did what she asked." Steele took a long drink as her head was beginning to pound with the admission to her friend.

"While he fucked her. You know that's how that works, Steele."

Steele nodded.

"I'm completely aware of that. Thanks for reminding me though."

"HE'S NOT a real nice man, Steele. You're virtually innocent and he's capable of making you into something you're not. What has he made you do so far? Be honest." Gwen sat back and looked casual. A thing Steele was aware of and knew she was anything but that.

"He hasn't made me do a thing. The emphasis on, made." Steele sighed and looked Gwen in the eyes. "I've wanted to do it."

Gwen shook her head slowly.

"He's a Master, remember? He made you think you wanted it. So tell me the dirty details."

"He's really not like that. Everyone sees this man who is closed off and arrogant, demanding, and somewhat brutal at times. Ask Rowan, he'll tell you he's a monster, and he's hit Rowan a couple of times. But he's not that. He's more than that facade he shows the world. But I get to see more of him than that. I get to see some of who he was before he had to become that man to protect the hurt boy inside him."

Gwen smiled.

"Bullshit, Steele. He's only making you think he's letting you in. He's a master at getting what he wants and he wants little, innocent, sweet you to do what demanding, arrogant, BDSM master wants. End of story. Now you've yet to tell me what's happened in the bedroom between the two of you. So spill it."

Steele thought for a moment. Would it be a mistake to let Gwen in on at least a little of what she and Arsen had done?

She knew she needed not to hide so much. After another sip if wine she decided to let her good friend know about the life she was moving into.

"Okay, I'll tell you, but you have to promise not to jump to conclusions or judge either Arsen or me."

Gwen gave her a nod.

"I am in college to become a psychologist you know. I can be trusted, Steele."

"Yeah, I know. You're in your first year so try to remember that. You aren't thoroughly educated yet." Steele put the glass down, kicked off her flats and folded her legs, Indian style.

"The worst thing so far is that I've allowed him to punish me with spankings."

"Why?" Gwen's one simple word made Steele's mind go blank.

Why had she allowed that?

"I think I did it so he would see I was trusting him. I think you would have to have been in my head at that time."

"What made you think you needed to allow him to physically harm you for him to think you trusted him?" Gwen's face had paled a bit and her hand shook as she took another drink.

"I'm not really sure, Gwen. The truth is I'm not really sure why I've allowed the things I have. I fucking love the man and would walk through fire if he told me to. I don't know if its trust or what the hell it is. I'd do anything for him and let him do anything he wanted to me."

The admission had her feeling heavy with an odd guilt. She knew Gwen was trying so hard not to let her see how appalled she was but the look was spreading over her face and it made Steele think she'd made some poor decisions where Arsen was concerned.

"DOES he make you do things sexually that make you feel used or abused?" Gwen's finger tapping on her temple told Steele tons about how her friend was taking the news.

"No. I mean my body is his to do with what he wants. I am his after all."

Gwen jumped up and began to pace.

"I'm sorry, Steele. This is way too much! What the fuck, girl?"

Steele looked up at her.

"You promised! See, that's why people don't talk to others about this. Yes, I believe my body is his. But it's not like you think. I can walk away anytime I want. I just don't want to. His touch sends me to a place I've never been before. Everything he does to me feels like Heaven. Even when his belt falls across my ass, I fucking love it and get all wet with desire for him. The first two licks, anyway."

Gwen spun around and looked at Steele with wide eyes.

"How in the hell are you romanticizing this shit?"

"I'm not trying to. I'm just trying to explain why I decided to enter into an agreement with him. I'm his sub now. We signed a contract." Steele closed her eyes as she readied herself for the explosion.

Gwen's voice surprised her when it came out soft.

"You are his sub now. Wow! He wasted no time. It didn't take him long at all to break the strong woman you are."

"I asked him to do it. He didn't think I was ready. Told me I might never be ready. To me, that meant he might get tired of the boring vanilla I am. I don't want him to get bored with me, so I'm learning how to be what he wants, what he needs."

"You? You told him you wanted to be his sub? You, said that? Well, that's just crazy and I know you're not crazy. Tell him you want to tear that contract up. Tell him you want to be you, not the you who has changed for him, the you, you were." Gwen sat down next to her and reached out and touched her shoulders. "You can stop this. He needs to accept you for who you are, not what he can make you."

"I don't know if I can do that. You see, a big part of me would break if I made him go back to the soft way he was before his first girlfriend's father beat him nearly to death when he was seventeen. The man put him in the hospital and Arsen's mother abandoned him at the hospital. When he got out, he had to go straight into foster care. When he was eighteen, a woman, the mother of the girl he had loved, took him in and made him her submissive. She was cruel and nearly was the end of him."

"He told you this?" Gwen looked skeptical.

Steele shook her head.

"I found a journal he wrote all this in. But then I told him I read it and he confirmed the story. See, it took him building that wall to get to be the strong man he is today. He's a success story and his love for me is making him soft and I don't want to be the person who ruins such a magnificent alpha male."

"What do you mean by soft, Steele?"

"Don't get pissed, but he told me not to be alone with Rowan. He caught us alone and when we got home, he spanked me. I cried, and he told me he was sorry. He told me he would never do that to me again."

.   .   .

"Good. That's not going soft, that's getting his head straight. Be glad about that. Keep working for that. Not going the other direction, Steele. If he loves you, he'll accept you for who you are. That goes the same for you. If you love him, you have to allow him to be who he is with you. If that means changing some, allow that to happen. You said he's built a wall around his heart to keep himself safe. He must feel safe with you and is letting the wall down, a brick at a time. Let him do that."

"So, what you're saying is that I'm stopping him from being the man he is by having him make me his sub?"

"That's what it sounds like. You two have enough crap to deal with as it is. Don't go adding in your desire to keep him a certain way add to that."

Steele thought about what all her friend had said for a few moments.

"You know what. You might be right. But I want to stay with the contract for now anyway. You see, I want him to take me to the BDSM club. I want to see it and experience it. I know that sounds nuts but I want to know what he was like before me."

"Sounds like he was a real prick before you. A man better left in the past. It's not a thing I think you'll like," Gwen said.

"I kind of find it all romantic. Arsen says it's not, but I think the idea of taking such good care of a woman that she wants to give herself to a man in all aspects is romantic." Steele's eyes sparkled with her fantasy.

"You're quite delusional, Steele. If Arsen told you it's not romantic, you should take his word for it. He has been the master for a while now and who should know better than he?"

Steele sighed and said, "I know. But, I'm a curious person and want to see the damn club. So I'm going to push for it. If I hate it, we can always leave. I've found out a thing or two about myself since I've been with Arsen. I'm a little bit of a freak in the sheets."

Gwen laughed and got up.

"So, want to hear about my new guy?"

Steele sat up with excitement.

"You have a new guy? Yes, do tell."

Gwen smiled. "He's older, almost as old as your guy. He's cute, with dark hair and dark eyes. And he's like this awesome Christian man. He goes to different prisons and jails to talk to the inmates about God and stuff. He's great, Steele."

"Sounds awesome. So you two are serious?" Steele asked.

"He stays here a lot. You're never home anymore, so I didn't think you'd mind," she said with a laugh.

Steele laughed too.

"I don't mind. So, what's his name?" Her cell rang, and she saw Arsen's name and held her hand up to stop Gwen from answering.

"Hello, Arsen. Okay, be right out."

The way Steele hauled ass to get out to his car had Gwen shaking her head. "Bye, and don't forget what we talked about, Steele."

"I won't," Steele said as she walked out the door.

23

ARSEN

It was five minutes after eight p.m. when the doorman buzzed Arsen to tell him a young woman was there for a meeting she'd sat up with him. He told him to send her up and prepared himself to see the new detective who'd been put on his case.

He left Tanner out of the meeting on purpose. He was a criminal lawyer himself after all. He knew the rules.

ARSEN WAS NOT PREPARED for the gorgeous woman who walked off the elevator and stepped into the living area of his penthouse. Clad in an expensive tight fitting, short pencil skirt in black and a silk blue shirt, she'd left the top three buttons undone on, and sky high black heels. He had a hard time not letting his eyes roam all over her.

Her dark hair was falling over her shoulders in waves and her blue eyes were piercing.

He shook his head to clear it.

"You must be Detective Fontaine." He extended his hand as he walked toward her.

She took his hand and shook it with a slow movement and held it a bit too long.

"And you are the infamous, Arsen Sloan. What a pleasure it is to meet you. I have to tell you I'm not a fan of your work as you get way too many of the bad guys off the charges we work so hard to make stick."

With a shrug he pulled his hand away and said, "Someone has to defend the accused, Detective. Please come this way and we can talk in my office."

He WANTED her in there where he could be the one to sit behind the large desk and make her feel he was in charge and not the other way around.

"Can I offer you a drink? A Cognac or a glass of wine?"

She laughed a little as she followed him.

"Afraid I'm still on the clock, but thank you. Perhaps another time when I'm not working. You are a single man, aren't you, Arsen?"

He almost stopped and turned around as she asked him such a personal question.

"As far as anyone knows, I am," he managed to say with a laugh. "What woman in her right mind would give me the time of day with all the news out there that I'm a BDSM master with three dead subs after all?"

"I guess that would cramp your love life a bit." She took the chair in front of the desk he gestured to and he went around and took his large, leather chair.

He noticed her taking him all in and frowned.

"It has. Now, tell me what you need from me."

She bit her bottom lip, and he thought how easily he could bend the woman over his desk and take her anyway he pleased. And then it hit him. She had to be part of a set up against him.

"I need to know why your hand prints are on the three victim's necks. If you don't mind. I need explicit details."

He knew what she was doing and wouldn't play into her devious hands. He leaned forward and laced his fingers together and placed his chin on them.

"Those particular women were into something not a lot of people know about. They liked to be choked. You should really look it up on your own. It's not appropriate to discuss in mixed company."

She crossed her legs, leaving them open for a moment and Arsen saw the flash of red panties she'd meant him to. He almost laughed out loud at her antics. "Please, Mr. Sloan, let me into your world a bit so I can help you. Tell me about why the women wanted you to choke them to death."

HE LAUGHED and sat back in his chair.

"I didn't say to death, Fontaine. I didn't even choke them until they were unconscious. Merely until they could take no more and touched my forearm, telling me to let them go."

"Could you show me?" she asked as her eyes lit up.

He shook his head and laughed.

"No."

"But I'm asking you to and that's what you said the other women did. I want to feel that. Can't you understand? It could help me find out who really did this to them. I don't think it was you." She leaned forward and her breasts spilled over her bra and she moved in a way to make sure they jiggled.

"IF YOU WANT to feel that, I advise you to ask your boyfriend to help you out with that. I'm not going to. You see, there's a little more to it than just cutting off the oxygen supply to the brain for a little while. It's during intercourse, so you see how that's not going to happen?" Arsen opened his bottom drawer and pulled out a small glass and a bottle of Scotch.

"Am I making you nervous, Arsen?" she asked as she sat back and spread her legs apart, allowing the red panties to remain in his line of vision.

"You, no." He wasn't nervous, he was growing angrier and didn't want to lose his temper with the woman who thought she was so enticing. She was anything but that. And the fact is all he could think about was getting the meeting over with and getting Steele back by his side.

"I'd like to help you. But I need you to let me in. You see, I think you might have an idea of who the real killer could be."

He did, but he was unsure if he should share that information with the woman he felt more and more was some type of trap they thought he'd fall into. He shook his head.

"If I had any idea, don't you think I'd already have thrown a name out there?"

"It's occurred to me that you might be thinking you're smarter than we are." Her eyebrows arched, and she smiled as she looked intensely into his eyes.

"I don't think anything of the sort. Now, unless you have anything else to ask me, I have somewhere to be." He sipped his drink as she smiled.

"Oh, I see. Well, there is one more thing. It's about this club called Fierce and how you have a private room there and how we need to get in there and take some samples of any type of bodily fluids in the room. I was hoping you'd see fit to help us out on that, without us needing to get a warrant." She sat back and made damn sure her panties were showing as she hitched up her short skirt a little higher.

He smiled.

"Afraid I'm going to have to let you get a warrant for that. And you will find evidence of all three of them in there."

"I see. And how about in here?" she asked as she gestured around.

He shook his head. "I never let them come here."

"Never?" She looked surprised. "You never let your girlfriends come home with you."

"They weren't my girlfriends." He took a long drink, growing tired of her.

"But you have had a girlfriend before. Beth, right?" Her eyes sparkled as she knew she'd hit a nerve.

His eyes narrowed. "She had nothing to do with this."

"No, but her mother might. You see, I think your ex-mistress might have been the one who killed your ex-submissive partners. She actually came to us, asking us to protect her from you, Mr. Sloan. Tell me when you last contacted her." She leaned forward and smiled. "And try to remember to be truthful, as she's told us."

"I HAVE NOT CONTACTED her in years. Not since I got away from her. So whatever she said was a lie. She's prone to lying. She kept her lifestyle a secret from her family. I assume with her coming to you she must've finally divorced her husband or something." He sat back and refused to let the woman see how irate he was.

"He's dead, Mr. Sloan." Her face went emotionless.

His eyebrows rose.

"I hope you're not about to accuse me of that as well."

"No," she said with a smile. "He had a heart attack a few years ago."

He sat back with relief. "Fucking bastard," he muttered.

"SHE TOLD US, he'd beaten you nearly to death and that her daughter saw you as a weak coward. Mrs. Sinclair said she helped you to become the man you are today. A successful billionaire." She stood up and looked down at him for only a second as he quickly stood.

"She had nothing to do with my success. I became the man I am despite her. And I don't care enough for the miserable woman to bother to threaten her in any way. I have walked away from her, much to her disapproval and I have the scars on my back to prove she was a harsh mistress." He walked around the desk. "I'll see you out then, Detective Fontaine."

He walked down the hall to the elevator as she followed behind him. He pressed the button, and the door opened up. She stepped inside and smiled.

"Be seeing you soon, Mr. Sloan. As soon as we get that warrant." She gave him a wink just before the doors closed.

Arsen stood staring at the closed doors and cursed silently to himself. He had to get to the club and clean up some things before the police went in there. And he would need help. He knew the one person he could count on, but it really wasn't what he wanted for her.

HE HAD NO CHOICE THOUGH!

24

STEELE

Arsen's face was unreadable as she got into the car with him.

"How'd it go, Arsen?" she asked as she slid in beside him and buckled her seatbelt.

"Not well, and now it seems I need your help." He ran his hand over her shoulder and down her arm. "I need you to go with me to, Fierce. It's Friday, so we have the weekend to get things taken care of before the police manage to get a warrant to search my private room there."

Her eyes lit up.

"So, you're taking me there?"

"Yes, I wouldn't get excited about it if I were you." He looked past her as they waited at the exit of the parking lot of her apartment complex. A car went by them and he saw the man who'd been at the police station earlier that day and outside his penthouse as well.

"It's Allen White."

STEELE LOOKED out the dark window and saw him too.

"What's he doing here?"

Arsen called out to his driver,

"Wait a second, Paul. I need to see where the man in that car that just passed us is going."

They watched out the window as Allen pulled into the parking spot next to Gwen's car. He got out and used a key to go into the apartment Gwen shared with Steele.

Steele looked at Arsen.

"OH MY GOD. Gwen told me she was seeing a new man. It's him, Arsen!"

"This is not good, Steele. She's in real danger. We have to go in there. We have to let her know about him." Arsen looked worried and called out to Paul, "Go back and park, Paul. Steele and I have to stay here until that man leaves. We may have to stay the night."

Paul turned the Suburban around and took them back. As he opened the door for them, he said, "I'll stay here, in case anything happens, boss. I can sleep in the car. No problem."

"Thanks." Arsen took Steele by the hand and led her back to the apartment. "Your roommate didn't tell you the guy's name?"

"She was about to but then you called me."

"I SEE. Okay. Well, let's do this. Let's try very hard not to let things escalate. We don't need a scene to be made and the police to be called after all."

Steele opened the door and found a very surprised Gwen and a not so surprised Allen White. But Allen managed to quickly turn his expression into one of complete joy.

"Well, as I live and breathe, it's my dear friend and old attorney, Arsen Sloan." Allen stepped forward and Arsen was taken into the smaller man's arms in a hug.

Arsen let Steele's hand go to pat the man's back and gently push him back. "Allen. How are you doing?" Arsen asked with a smile.

Steele could tell he was playing along with the man. Allen

stepped back and ran his arm around Gwen. "I'm doing great, Arsen. Really, great."

"That's good to hear. So, when did you get out?" Arsen said. Steele guessed Gwen had no idea she was allowing a horrific murderer to put his hands on her.

Allen's eyes cut sideways to Gwen and his smile faded. "She doesn't know about that, Arsen."

Arsen's eyebrows raised. "Oh, sorry. It seems I might have let the cat out of the bag. Allow me to explain, Allen."

Allen nodded. "You're the one who is so great with words. Go ahead."

Gwen looked oddly at Arsen. "I'm Gwen, by the way. We've actually never been introduced."

"It's nice to meet you, Gwen." Arsen looked back at Steele. "Have anything to drink so we can all sit down and get to know one another, baby?"

Steele moved quickly to the kitchen. "Yes, oh, sorry, Arsen. How rude of me, sorry."

Gwen's eyes followed her, and she said, "No reason to get all apologetic, Steele." She looked back at Arsen. "Is there, Arsen?"

"No, no reason to apologize, Steele." Arsen took a seat on the sofa and Gwen and Allen sat across from him on the other smaller loveseat in the living room. He looked at Gwen. "I was Allen's attorney in a murder case. He was accused of kidnapping and torturing his high school math teacher when he was nineteen. After a couple of months of doing that, he killed her. I lost the case, and he went to prison. But it seems as if you managed to get out, Allen. Good for you. How'd that happen?"

"I found our Lord and Savior, Jesus Christ, Arsen," Allen said as he took Gwen's hand in his and looked at her. "But you know that, darling."

"But I didn't know you killed someone. And tortured and kidnapped." She pulled her hand from his and stared at him in shock. "That's a big thing to leave out, Allen."

Steele appeared with a tray of drinks. "Whiskey Sours, anyone?" She handed Arsen one first and made a little courtesy as she did, something which had Gwen's frown go even further across her face.

Arsen looked at Steele and made a little head shake. She found herself nervous. After placing the other drinks in front of Gwen and Allen, she took hers and sat next to Arsen. His arm ran around her and she leaned into him.

Allen looked at Gwen and smiled. "I've come to terms with what I did and firmly believe the Devil made me do that. With Jesus as my leader I have changed my ways and will no longer be following that terrible path of evil any longer. I've made it right with God and the Parole Board, Gwen. You have nothing to fear from me, baby."

Arsen took a drink and glanced sideways at Steele.

"Well, that's wonderful to hear, Allen," he said.

Gwen still looked to be in shock and took a drink.

"So, you're all better then?"

Allen nodded.

"Better, yes, I'm better. Completely not that guy anymore. I was a kid when I did that anyway. A crazy kid who listened to too much hard rock. The Devil got into me with his Devil music and turned me into his pawn. I'm looking into suing those rock bands I listened to back then." He looked at Arsen. "Say, you couldn't help me out with that could you?"

"Suing old rock bands?" Arsen asked in surprise.

"Yeah, you know those guys who let the Devil into my soul and robed me of years of my life. Those guys. Could you help me sue them all?" Allen smiled.

Arsen shook his head.

"Um, I'm not that kind of lawyer, sorry Allen."

"Perhaps you could refer one for me. I'd really appreciate it if you could help me. You have to recall that I told you the Devil was in my head back then." Allen took a little sip and looked at Arsen intently.

"I do, I recall you telling me that would be a great defense. I don't remember you saying anything about suing the people who made the music you listened to though," Arsen said.

"I came up with that later." Allen looked at Gwen. "Honey, our kids can't ever listen to that stuff, promise me."

STEELE HAD the glass to her lips as he said that and she spit the drink out and choked on the liquid.

"God! Sorry! What did you say? Kids? When you have kids? How the fuck close are you two? Shit, sorry!"

Her hand flew over her mouth and she looked at Arsen with wide eyes. He tapped the top of her thigh.

"I'll let that slide, Steele."

Steele nodded and looked down for a brief second then she looked at Gwen who was glaring at her. "We are very close, Steele. And why are you apologizing yet again?"

"I'm trying to stop cursing that's all," Steele said and took another drink.

GWEN'S GLARE moved to Arsen then back to Steele. "You see, Allen is a Christian man, and he doesn't want to sin so he has asked me to marry him because he doesn't believe in having sex without being married. He also doesn't believe in birth control. He believes we should have every child God gives us. We've talked extensively on the subject."

"YOU LEFT that out when we were talking a while ago, Gwen." Steele said. "So where's the engagement ring and when's the wedding?" She glared at her roommate.

"There's no ring," Allen said as he smiled at Gwen. "Those are for people who need to show the world they're married. We only need God to know that. And as soon as I find us a place to live, I'm going to marry us myself as I am an ordained minister."

Steele rolled her eyes and looked at Arsen. He tapped her leg and said, "Well, seems like you're really doing great, Allen. Um, it's been a long day and I have some things to talk to Steele about in private. We'll be staying the night here in her bedroom." He got up and Steele quickly followed.

Gwen watched them leave the room as they all exchanged good nights. Steele smiled at her as she walked by.

"Happy for you, Gwen."

"You too," Gwen said as she looked up at her friend. "You two have a good night now."

STEELE'S STOMACH was in knots as she led Arsen to her bedroom. She closed the door behind them and whispered.

"That guy's crazy. I can't see how Gwen doesn't see it."

Arsen nodded and pulled her to the bed. He sat down and pulled her to sit next to him. He kept his voice quiet as he said, "He isn't all there. I'm sure you can tell that. We have to get her away from him. I'm positive he's the killer. I mean why else would he be here with her? How'd they meet?"

"I don't know. She didn't tell me."

"Go and get a glass of water and ask them, but make it simple, you know not obvious that you're looking for information," he said.

She nodded and left the room. Gwen and Allen had moved to opposite sofas. Steele smiled.

"Just getting Arsen some water. Hey, how did you two meet anyway?"

Gwen smiled.

"He almost hit me with his car as I was walking to get into mine in the parking lot."

"Oh, glad he stopped in time." Steele said with a little laugh. "What parking lot?"

"Ours, right out there. He was visiting an old friend at one of the apartments down from ours." Gwen said.

Steele smiled.

"What a crazy coincidence, huh?"

Allen looked at her.

"God always finds a way."

Gwen nodded and Steele just kept on smiling.

"That's so true, Allen. So true. Well, good night again."

SHE STARTED to go back down the hallway when Gwen stopped her.

"You're forgetting Arsen's water, Steele. You don't want him to get angry with you and punish you for not bringing him his water do you?"

Steele spun around and gave Gwen a dirty look. Then Allen said, "Oh, I know all about Arsen and his dom/sub stuff. It's all over the news with the murders he's accused of. Don't worry, I'm not judging you guys. That's between you and God after all. Better hurry though, he's probably adding up the spankings your about to get. You did curse, and that has to be a big one for him."

Steele was embarrassed and somewhat pissed.

"He said he was letting that one slide," she said as her cheeks burned and she went to get the glass of water.

She overheard Allen say to Gwen in a quiet voice, "I don't know how your roommate can do that to herself, she sounds smart. She seems so confident and didn't you say she was in school to become a criminal lawyer?"

STEELE TOOK the water and went to her bedroom, feeling like a fool. She couldn't explain even to herself why she was so ready to be submissive to Arsen.

She went into the bedroom and right away when Arsen saw her expression he knew something was wrong. He got up and pulled her into his arms.

"What has you so sad, baby?"

There was no way she was telling him she was feeling ashamed of herself for being his sub and yet she knew it was part of their contract for her always to be honest with him about all things and that above all else.

Tears filled her eyes as she looked up at him.

"With it all over the news about you and your lifestyle, I told Gwen about us and our contract."

"You did?" He frowned. "How did that go?"

She shook her head.

"Not well. As you can imagine."

"Hmmm. I might like this Gwen. She seems to have your best interests at heart. It's what makes a good friend. So why the long face now? I mean you told her earlier, and you didn't wear this sad face." He pulled her to the bed and sat her on his lap.

"When I was pouring the water I suppose Allen didn't think I could hear him and he said I seemed too confident and smart to do this to myself." She looked down and sniffled.

"You are. The nut-job is right about that." He pushed a piece of her dark hair back and touched her chin, pulling it gently up so she had to look at him. "Tell me how you liked the way we spent today?"

"It was different, but that's okay. I mean, I'll get used to it and I don't really feel demeaned in any way. Not really." She searched his eyes to see if there was anything in them that told her he was really okay with her talking like this.

His dark eyes were soft, and he smiled at her.

"How'd you enjoy calling me Master during dinner?"

She'd hated it, and she knew he could read her like a book. "You tell me."

He smiled. "It wasn't a thing you wanted to do. You see, that lifestyle is for people who want that in their lives. Need it for one reason or another. It's not about making someone do what they don't want to. I'm just realizing that now, myself."

"But it's how you want things. How you want to live and I want to be with you." She nearly ran her arms around his neck then stopped herself. "Can I…"

Arsen put his finger against her lips. "Don't ask. For tonight let's do what I asked you to do with me. Let's leave the dom/sub stuff off the table for tonight. Do whatever you want. Tonight, I want us to make love. Show me how much you love me and I'll show you. No rules, just you and me showing how much we love each other."

"Really? Are you sure?" she asked as her eyes shined with the knowledge he was allowing her in so much further than she dreamt possible.

"I'm sure." His hand grazed her cheek. "I love you, Steele." His lips touched hers and the kiss was so gentle it felt as if silk was drifting over them.

His hands moved over her arms, lightly and left electricity in their wake. Steele found herself more nervous than she'd ever been with him. The fact this was only the second time the man had ever made love was weighing heavily on her. The first time had ended so badly, she was afraid he might have a flashback to that terrible day.

WHEN SHE LOOKED into his eyes though, any fear she had disappeared as she saw more love in them than she'd ever seen before.

25

ARSEN

Arsen laid Steele back and began to pull her clothes away. Piece by piece, he took them off and ran his hands over her smooth and satiny skin. He wanted to take every last bit of her in. Relish her beauty and see her for who she truly was.

Steele had been bending for him so hard he was afraid she was about to break.

"You are perfect, Steele." He kissed her neck and trailed kisses to her mouth.

Her arms ran around his neck and she held him to her. He so seldom allowed her to touch him when they had sex. The urge to take her hands and hold them over her head was one that he had to fight.

Arsen focused on the way he was kissing her. Slow strokes his tongue was making against hers. He ran his hands through her long hair and again found himself fighting the urge to pull it.

HE PULLED AWAY from her and stood up, looking at her as he undressed. She ran her hand over one breast and smiled at him. Slowly he undressed, trying to gain control over his dominating instincts.

Finally, naked he stood there and when she held her hand out to him, he took it and climbed onto the small bed with her. It had been so long since he allowed himself to have real feelings.

Slowly he trailed his fingers over her breast, he leaned down and took it in his mouth. Making lazy circles with his tongue, he sucked it gently. Her hands ran over his head and she moaned softly.

He almost smacked her on the side of her ass, but stopped himself and ran his hand over her hip instead. Softly, she ran her hands over his back and he tensed as it triggered a memory.

HE PULLED his mouth away from her breast and looked at her. It was Steele he was with, not Beth. No one was about to break the door down and start beating the hell out of him.

The way she looked at him made his heart pound. She ran her hand over his cheek and he took it and kissed it. He smiled, weakly.

"You have no idea how hard this is for me, Steele."

"Lie down, Arsen," she said as she sat up.

He sighed and did what she said. She kissed his lips then let her mouth graze his body as she moved it over him. All the way down she went until her mouth was moving over his cock.

Arsen closed his eyes and moaned. Slow strokes she made up and down his length. Her hand covering where her mouth left. The other hand massaged his balls and his body relaxed.

"That feels so good, Steele." He moaned again and found himself feeling different.

Her mouth was hot, her tongue ran along his cock and he was about to climax. He pulled her head up and smiled at her. She kissed her way up his body and straddled him, sliding down on his erection.

Her body shuddered as she took him all in and her eyes closed. He took her by the hips and lifted her up and down, keeping the rhythm slow and watching her body as it moved over him.

.   .   .

SHE WAS beautiful with her dark waves falling across her shoulders. Her breasts bounced a little with each stroke and all of a sudden it felt as if his heart was breaking. Arsen was falling in love with her so hard it hurt.

Arsen stopped lifting her up and down and turned her over to lie on her back, moving his body over hers. She looked up at him as he pushed back into her. Making harder strokes, he moved faster and looked into her eyes as he did.

Steele looked back into his and he saw the love she had for him and knew without a doubt she would do anything he asked her to. His power over her was absolute. He didn't deserve her, and he knew it.

SHE GRIPPED his arms and arched up to him.

"Arsen, can I ...."

"You don't have to ask, baby." He moved harder and quicker and she moaned as she came.

Her body took his along, and he groaned with his release. It was a bittersweet moment for him. He'd managed to put his need for total control away for her, but with the realization that she'd do anything for him it meant he had to be much more careful how he treated her.

Kissing her just behind her ear, he whispered, "I love you, baby."

"I love you," she echoed as she tried to catch her breath.

Arsen rolled over and pulled her to lie on his chest. Her heartbeat he could feel and her breath left the skin beneath it warm. She was becoming more to him than he could've ever imagined. Steele was like oxygen to him, he had to have her to live.

THAT KNOWLEDGE FILLED him with joy and dread at the same time as she held his heart in her hands and he was no longer in control.

If he was sent to prison, he'd have to let her go. It wouldn't be fair to keep her if he couldn't be there for her and keep her safe and protected. He had to figure out a way to prove Allen had killed those women.

Arsen was getting no closer, and that fact had him beyond frustrated. The man was right there in the same damn apartment with him and still he was no closer than if he hadn't found the man at all.

26

GWEN

"If you're really her friend, you have to do something about it, Gwen," Allen said as he held her hand and they sat on her bed. "I know the man, he's hard as a rock. I'm serious, he'll only destroy her."

"You do realize what you're talking about is kidnapping, Allen," Gwen stood up and began pacing and running her hands over her hair.

"It's not really that, Gwen. It's just getting her away from him for a while so she can see what he's done to her. She's blind to it right now. She thinks she actually wants what he's doing to her. No one wants that. No one wants to be so controlled." He got up and put his arm around Gwen to stop her pacing. "Don't you care about her?"

"Yes! Of course I do! Shit!" She looked at him and found herself near tears. "Allen, we can't do what you're suggesting. I'll talk to her more and get her to see things aren't right with Arsen. She'll leave him on her own. Taking her and hiding her out against her will is wrong."

"YOU'D RATHER he kill her like he did those other women?"

"He might not have done that. He hasn't been convicted yet." She pulled out of his grip and sat on the bed.

"It's just a matter of time. I can assure you he will be convicted and then he'll go to prison. Just like I had to. You have no idea of the hell the poor girl is going through with him. Constant criticism, the threat of beatings hanging over her head all the time, you saw how jumpy and skittish she is around him. You can't tell me that's how she's always been."

"No, she never was like that before him. But taking her isn't the answer here. I'll deal with this. You don't have to worry about her."

Allen sat next to her and ran his hand over her hair.

"God has told me what has to be done, Gwen. She has to be saved from him."

Gwen stood up and looked down at him.

"Allen, you're going to have to leave now. I'm afraid you're making me very uncomfortable with all this talk about kidnapping my room-mate. I think you should probably go talk to someone. God isn't talking to you. You really need to get help."

Allen stood up, his eyes drooping slightly at the corners.

"Gwen, I thought you could help me save your friend from that monster. I'm very sorry I have to do this." He reached into the front pocket of his tan slacks.

GWEN'S EYES WENT WIDE. Her mouth opened to scream, but no sound made it out as he ran his hand over her mouth and stabbed the syringe full of morphine into the vein in her neck. Her body fell to the floor with a loud thump.

"You made me do that, Gwen. Now let's get you out of here. Looks like I'll have to get another set of chains since I'll have to take you both now that you made me do this. You really messed up my plans for Arsen."

Gwen could still hear him talking as he picked her up and threw her over his shoulder, taking her out of her room and to God only knew where.

27

PART SEVEN: FOR OBEDIENCE

Steele

W arm breath on the back of her neck woke Steele up. Arsen's strong arms were wrapped around her. A smile crept over her face as she recalled the events of the last night and how Arsen had made love to her.

He had been tender and loving and she loved every moment he gave her. She knew he was getting a bit soft around the edges which had been so sharp, but she remembered what she and Gwen had talked about.

She would stop being so controlling herself. Arsen needed to become whoever he was meant to become. If that meant a little softer version of the man she'd met and fallen in love with, so be it.

His arms tightened around her and he groaned. His lips pressed against her neck and he said, "Good morning, Baby."

"Morning, Sweetheart," she said and turned in his arms to face him.

His hair was growing so fast, it was nearly as long as when she'd met him the first time and she ran her hands through it. His beard though, he had kept meticulous as always and his dark eyes blinked a few times as he looked at her.

"Thank you, Steele," he said with a lazy smile covering his caramel lips. "That was the most amazing thing I've ever felt."

"Glad to hear that. I was afraid it bored you," she said as she moved one hand out of his silky locks to run over his bicep.

"Bored with you, never." He kissed the tip of her nose, making her giggle a little. "We should get up and you should see if your room-mate is up yet so we can talk to her about Allen. Then we need to get going. I have to purchase you some things so we can go to Fierce and get some things out of my private room before the police get a warrant and get in there."

"So you're really taking me then?" Steele looked excited, and he frowned at her.

"You will most likely be disgusted by what you see there. But, yes I'm taking you there to retrieve a couple of things, then we'll leave. We'll have to get masks as I want no one to see you there. What you and I have going on is to be kept a secret from the police. You do understand that. Don't you?" His hand ran over her cheek.

"I do, Arsen. Don't worry. Let's shower and dress and I'll go find Gwen. You may have to get Allen to talk about something so I can get her alone." She rolled off the bed and onto her feet and padded away to the bathroom.

THE SHOWER WAS SMALL, much, much smaller than Arsen's. Steele had gotten into the shower and smiled as Arsen joined her. "Give me the shampoo and let me wash your hair."

She did as he said and he massaged the soap into her dark hair. "You really are very sweet, you know."

"Sweet, there's that word again no one has ever used to describe me." He leaned her head back to rinse her hair and placed a gentle kiss on her lips.

One hand moved in her hair to aid the removal of the vanilla scented shampoo and his other hand moved down to run between her legs as he kissed her a bit harder.

Steele moaned as his fingers found her center and moved right in. Pumping his finger inside her, he had her hot in seconds. He pulled his hand from her and ran his hands around her waist, lifting her.

She wrapped her legs around him and groaned as he entered her. The warm water flowed over them as he lifted her up and down, then backed her to the wall and thrust into her, hard over and over.

THERE WAS JUST no way which Arsen took her which didn't drive her over the edge. He was the master of her body and she knew that without a doubt.

The thought flashed through her mind if he was convicted of the murders she'd lose him to prison. A single tear escaped with the thought.

Her hands roamed over his muscled back and she moaned as her body began the dissent into climax. Arsen pulled his mouth from hers and watched her as she went into ecstasy.

"My God, you're gorgeous, Steele. When you come all over my cock like that, it makes me feel more than a mere man. It makes me feel powerful."

"You are powerful, Arsen." She ran her hands up his back and grasped his neck and pulled his mouth to hers again.

He kissed her hard, his tongue running over hers, stroking it with hard strokes just like he was pounding into her. His hands squeezed her ass as his body went rigid and he spilled himself inside her. A long groan he made as he let it all loose.

Pulling his mouth from hers, they both tried to catch their breath.

"You know how to get the day going, Arsen."

"I am quite good at it, aren't I?" He smiled as he let her feet touch the floor. "Now let's finish this shower up and get our day going. It's going to be a long one."

Steele's insides shook with excitement.

. . .

I'M FINALLY GOING to get to see the inside of a real BDSM club!

28

ARSEN

"**N**o one else is here, Steele. Try to call her," Arsen directed.

Steele called Gwen, and both heard her cell phone ringing in Gwen's bedroom. They followed the sound and found the phone on the floor near the bed.

Steele picked it up.

"Well, the blanket is gone from her bed. Perhaps she was sick on it or something and took it to get it cleaned and accidentally dropped her phone. Is her car still here?"

They went to look out the front door and Gwen's car was still there, but Allen's wasn't. Arsen shook his head.

"She must've went with Allen. I guess we'll have to talk to her tomorrow about him. I don't think he's crazy enough to do anything to her now that I know he's with her. That would be really stupid. Don't you think?"

Steele turned to go grab her purse so they could leave.

"It would be dumb and he didn't seem stupid, just crazy."

. . .

ARSEN TOOK her hand as she came back and they left the small apartment. Steele winced as Paul got out and opened the back door to the Suburban for them.

"Good morning, Paul. God, I feel awful about you having to stay the night in the car," she said.

"Aw, don't worry about me. I climbed in the back and slept like a baby. Sure I'm a little wrinkled this morning, but I can shower and change once we get back to the penthouse. You know I have an apartment in that building, don't you?"

"No, I didn't realize that." Steele slipped inside the car. "Paul, did you see when that car we followed back here left?"

He shook his head.

"No, I just woke up about fifteen minutes ago. It was gone already."

"Okay, thanks," she said as she buckled her seatbelt.

Arsen moved in next to her and frowned.

"It would've been nice if he had seen them leave."

"I'm sure they just went to eat breakfast and must've took her blanket to the cleaners. Gwen drinks often, but it still has her puking now and then." Steele ran her hand over Arsen's muscular thigh and left it there.

He looked down at her small hand on him and thought how he'd never allow anyone to touch him like that before. She was changing him and it was happening a lot faster that he even thought possible.

ARSEN RAN his hand over hers and lifted it to his lips, leaving a kiss on top. "You really are perfect for me, baby."

Her blue eyes sparkled.

"You are perfect for me too."

Running an arm around her he felt as close to normal as he'd ever been. But as they pulled away from the apartment a police car moved down the street in front of them, reminding him of his trouble and how he had to hurry to fix that problem.

Arsen knew his time was limited. He pulled out his phone and pulled up the website of a local shop that sold the clothes and masks they'd need to go to the club. He tapped on something he'd love to see Steele in and showed it to her.

"How about this for tonight?"

He smiled as pink stained her creamy colored cheeks.

"Really? That will show all of me! I mean every bit! You'd let me out in public like that?"

THE LEATHER GARMENT was a series of black belts which crisscrossed over the body, leaving the breasts exposed and the ass as well. The belt which ran between the legs was a little wider than the rest and managed to cover the goods, but that was the only thing which was covered.

Arsen stifled a chuckle and said, "Oh, it has a thing you wear over it, Steele." He tapped another place on the cell phone's screen and a sheer, black short dress came up. "See, this goes over it."

"It's nearly invisible, Arsen! You have got to be playing with me." She tapped her foot, nervously.

When his head shook her forehead wrinkled with a frown. Arsen's eyebrows went up.

"Steele, you said you wanted to see what it's like. Well, this is the type of thing the females who go there, wear. You'll look hot as hell. Don't worry. I'd never dress you in anything you wouldn't look good in."

He tapped at the screen again, pulling up a picture of thigh high, shiny leather boots with six-inch heels and grinned at her. Steele shook her head.

"Arsen, I can't wear that. It's crazy!"

AFTER SHOWING HER A CAT-WOMAN MASK, he said, "You'll wear this. You'll be anonymous. No one will even know who you are or ever recognize you on the street. Let yourself go with the character, Steele. You said you wanted to know and you will know after tonight."

"And what will you be wearing? May I ask?"

"An Armani suit and a batman mask." He put his arm around her again and pulled her tight to him. "Cat-woman and Batman. Sounds fun. Don't you think?"

"Only this cat-woman is naked," she said with a frown.

"Nearly naked," he corrected her as he placed the order for the things, having them delivered to his penthouse by eight that night.

Thinking about how hot she was going to look had him more excited than he'd been in a very long time. He had a bright red collar he would put around her long, elegant neck to show every male there, she was his and his alone.

Arsen toyed with the idea of making her crawl or not, but ended up deciding she could walk in as he led her with his leash. It would be his last time going into the place after all and he was going to make it count.

He nipped her neck, playfully and ran his hand over her sex.

"I cannot wait to show your hot ass off, baby."

The way she shivered let him know she was afraid, and for some reason that made him happy.

A LITTLE FEAR *is good for the soul.*

29

STEELE

"Arsen! This is just too much!" she whined as he buckled the last buckle on her little BDSM outfit, emphasis on little.

She turned her body in front of the mirror and frowned.

"My big ass is all out there!"

His large hand cupped one of her ass cheeks and he gave it a good squeeze. "It is and I'm loving it."

Steele watched his eyes light up in the mirror and knew he was in his element. It both excited her and made her nervous at the same time.

"Arsen, I'm sure to let you down. I know I will."

He pulled her into his arms, resting his forehead to hers.

"Baby, we're not going there to really do any more than retrieve a couple of things from my private room. None of the regular things that happen there are we going to be involved in. So you can't possibly let me down. Can't you see that? Plus, I kind of love the shit out of you, and that means whatever you do never lets me down."

"You love the shit out of me, huh?" she asked with a grin.

He popped her ass. "I can curse. You cannot."

She giggled. "Yes, Master."

HE SMILED and pulled away from her, picking up the sheer, black dress and pulled it over her head. Then went to a closet that when he opened it up Steele about fell over.

"Oh my God! That's why I smell leather in here all the time." She went to him and looked at all the leather inside.

He pulled out a long, red, leather coat and held it out for her. She put her arms through the sleeves then he wrapped it around her and tied it closed.

"Better?" he asked

She nodded and smiled.

"You fooled me, you rogue."

"Oh, once inside, the coat has to be checked. But you won't be walking around anywhere else like that." He led her back to the mirror where she looked at their reflections.

Arsen was in his black Armani suit, looking handsome as hell and she was in the long, red, leather coat with the tall boots. Her long, dark hair was pulled into a single braid which fell over her shoulder. Her make-up was impeccable, and she found herself feeling a lot sexier than she ever had before.

Then Arsen went to the leather filled closet again and took out a red leather collar and leash set. Her heart started to pound in her chest as it never crossed her mind she'd have to wear that and crawl on her hands in knees in front of a group of people.

AS HE REACHED up to run the collar around her neck her hand took his wrist. "Arsen, I'm beginning to think this isn't a thing I can do after all. Crawling around in front of people is too much."

His smile was a mixture of fun and evil.

"You will have to trust me, Steele. I am your master after all. You signed the contract."

The contract, yes she had asked for the contract between them and signed it. Ready to show him she could be what he needed. After gulping down the knot which had formed in her throat, she said, "I did. Go ahead, put your collar on me, Master."

Arsen placed the thing around her neck and attached the leash.

"How does that feel? It's not too tight, is it?"

She shook her head. The fact was it fit a little bit loosely. But she wasn't happy with the way it made her feel. Like an animal and not in a hot way either.

"I suppose I'll get used to this."

Arsen's silence left her wondering what the man was thinking.

WILL this become something we do often?

SHE'D SIGNED the contract and whatever he wanted to do with her he could. When she looked back up at him, she saw a slight droop at the edge of his dark eyes. He wasn't as happy as he had been.

His finger ran over her red painted lips.

"Think about things tonight when you see that lifestyle. Be true to yourself and to me. If you decide you want out of the contract, I'll let you."

Steele shook her head. No contract meant no Arsen, and she knew it.

"I'll get used to this. I can get used to anything if it means I get to stay in your life, Arsen."

"If I have my way, you will always be in my life, Steele." Arsen kissed her cheek and picked up the leash. "Remember to follow a step behind me when we get to the club, baby. I don't want one of the assholes there to smack your ass if you don't. It's not like any place you've ever been."

.　.　.

As THEY WENT DOWN the elevator to get into the car, Steele felt something inside her growing. It was fear and excitement and a little anger. She was feeling angry with herself for letting so much of herself go. But she couldn't seem to stop herself. The thrill was outweighing the shame.

30

GWEN

Water was dripping somewhere in the open room. Gwen opened her eyes and looked around. It was dark and musty smelling. She could hear the sound of water lapping against the shore outside a window.

Lights glowed in the darkness outside the window which had been covered with a plastic sheet she couldn't see through. She tried to move and found herself trapped.

Still groggy, she moved her head around and found herself chained to a small bed. It seemed like she was in an old warehouse, most likely down by the docks near the San Francisco bay area.

Though her mind was fuzzy she did remember telling Allen he had to leave as he was talking about kidnapping Steele for her own good. Now it seemed he must've kidnapped her.

Panic ripped through her as she recalled what Arsen had told her Allen had done to his high school math teacher that had him sent to prison. She wondered how anyone could be set free after what he did.

"ALLEN?" she called out.

Nothing came back, and she hoped he would leave her alone there rather than come back and do God knows what to her. Better to die of starvation and dehydration than to be tortured by the crazy man.

The sound of metal grinding against metal met her ears and then there were footsteps. She bit her lip and tried hard not to cry as Allen came near her. The light was dim, but she saw he was holding a whip in one hand and some type of odd contraption in the other.

"Allen, what are you doing, Sweetheart," she asked in a really kind voice, hoping to make him see her for who he knew she was. They were going to get married after all. Though crazy, he had to love her she thought.

"I asked you to help me and you told me to get out of your house. I guess you have no idea what your best friend is going through with that monster, Arsen Sloan, so I'm about to show you what he does to women, Gwen." He took a step towards her and placed something in her mouth.

The contraption he had in his hand had been some type of gagging device. After placing the ball in her mouth, he buckled the thing around her head.

She tried to talk and scream and it wouldn't allow either. She shook her head, and he looked at her with no emotion.

"You have to see. So you understand what he does to your friend, Gwen. You didn't understand me or maybe you didn't believe me, so you see, I have to show you or you never will understand."

He took a step back and let the whip fly, the thin leather fell across her stomach and she shrieked with the pain, only the thing in her mouth stopped it from ringing out in the air for anyone to hear.

Tears fell in streams down her cheeks. The whip flew through the air again.

So this is how I'm going to die.

31

ARSEN

The angels and demons residing in Arsen seemed to be at war with each other. On the one hand he found Steele beyond amazing in the outfit he bought her. On the other hand, that was not her.

She was tolerating too much, and he knew it. It was he who needed some change in who he was, not her. She was a sweet, innocent, young woman he met and radically influenced in a bad way.

Yet here he was taking her to a place he'd promised himself he wouldn't. The car stopped in the alley where the entrance to Fierce was. He watched as Steele looked around, confusion riddling her beautiful face.

"Where is it, Arsen?"

He pointed to the rusty metal door.

"Right here."

Paul opened the car door, letting them out.

"Call when you're ready to leave, boss."

Arsen nodded and placed the mask over Steele's eyes then put his own on. He took her leash and heard her sigh. His heart sped up, and he wanted nothing more than to tell her to get back in the car and wait for him to go get the things he needed to so the police wouldn't find them.

"Steele, would you rather wait in the car for me?"

"I want to see this place. I want to see what you found you had to have in your life these past years. I want to know all about you and what you need," she answered.

"The only thing I need since I found you, is you, Steele. None of this is me any longer. I need you to start understanding that, Baby."

She shook her head. "I'm no fool, Arsen. You will tire of me if I can't be what you need."

HE SHRUGGED his wide shoulders and took a step then turned back.

"Steele, if we get separated somehow, you need to immediately go into that little submissive sit I showed you. As long as you have my collar and leash on and take that position, no male will mess with you. If you're wondering around free they might mess with you even though you have the collar and leash on. If you're wondering around free and it's off, you're fair game to them. And all the screaming and yelling will be ignored or even stopped by a gag."

"You're just trying to scare me into staying in the car, aren't you?" She smiled and giggled. "So dramatic!"

Arsen shook his head and knew she was about to really freak out, but she was too tenacious to believe him. Once he opened the door, and she saw how dark it was she hugged up behind him. Her hand moved into his and he stopped and looked back at her.

"You can't do that here."

"Oh! Yeah, sorry. Okay, let me get into character. Wow, this place looks spooky. Don't you think it's creepy in here, Arsen?" She took a step back and seemed to be rambling.

"You have no idea, Baby. Now, keep your mouth shut and follow me. Remember all the rules, please. I don't want some mother fucker smacking you and pissing me off." He led her down the stairs and prayed she'd follow the rules he'd laid out for her.

When they rounded the corner to the coat check he heard Steele gasp at the freak show who was running the counter. The guy did look rather ghoulish with his spiked black hair and ruby red lipstick. The piercings all over his pale face were gruesome, and he was dressed in only tight leather shorts. His nipples were pierced, and a chain ran between them.

Arsen turned and took off Steele's coat and saw her eyes go wide behind her mask as he revealed her nearly naked body. Her chest rose as she held her breath.

"You need to breathe, Baby," he whispered in her ear as he pulled the coat completely away.

"Nice," the young guy said as he took the red coat. "Room 21, right?"

Arsen nodded as the guy placed the coat on a hanger and pressed a sticker to it with his private room number. Arsen looked back to find Steele biting at her lower lip and shook his head at her. She stopped and fell into place behind him.

With a few feet of privacy before they got into the main room he told her, "Walk with your head up high. You're proud to be with me after all and want all to know that. But don't make eye contact with anyone. Look forward and stay only one step behind me."

"Okay, man my stomach is full of butterflies. I guess I should've had a drink or something before I came in here," she said.

Arsen smiled knowingly.

"I wanted you completely sober to see this place. Now no more talking until we get to my private room."

Steele shut her mouth and Arsen walked into the room, holding her leash and loving the stares the men were immediately giving his woman. He walked through the crowd of scantily, leather clad people and had to hold back a smile.

She was stealing the show, just like he knew she would.

32

STEELE

Steele was amazed by the people she tried so hard not to look at as Arsen had instructed. Nearly naked women everywhere on leashes. Some on their hands and knees while others stood. But all seemed to be looking at her and Arsen as they strode through the middle like they owned the place.

The air was cold and had her nipples as erect as they could get. A good thing she supposed. A scene from the corner of her eye made her head turn just slightly to see a man who stood and looked on as another man fucked the woman he had on a leash, from behind as she looked up at her master.

The word, degrading, hit her mind like a brick and she looked at the back of Arsen's head instead. Her stomach was tense, and the butterflies had transformed into pterodactyls.

The six-inch heels were proving hard to walk in as the cement floor was a little slippery and she glanced down to see a fair amount of fluid was here and there on the floor.

Bile rose in her throat as she thought of being made to move through the room on hands and knees as some were having to do. It was disgusting. Arsen had been right about how she'd see it.

. . .

THE SCENE CHANGED as they walked into another room. A disco ball was suspended high on the ceiling and hard rock music played loudly. People danced, and it was an odd feeling as the lights flashed off and on.

Arsen turned to her and pulled her up in his arms and moved them to the hard beat of the music. He whispered, "Okay, so far?"

"I'm okay, Arsen. This is not what I expected though."

He pulled back and turned away from her, pulling her along after him again. Once they made their way out of that room they entered a dark hallway. Then turned and went down another.

DOORS WERE on each side of the dimly lit halls. Odd sounds leaked out of some of them as they passed by. Some good groans, some not so good groans, and some horrific groans had Steele second guessing coming into the club.

Arsen finally stopped at a door and used a key to open it. He led her inside and turned to close the door behind them.

"So, you like this place, Steele?"

"Um, uh, It's uh, different. I can't say I do or don't like it," she stammered.

He pulled the collar off her and smiled.

"Really? Maybe the full treatment will help you make a decision then." Arsen turned a knob on the wall near the door and the interior of the dark room lit up.

"Oh my God, Arsen," Steele said in a whisper as her eyes traveled over his extensive collection.

An odd wooden structure was in the middle of the room which she found to be rather large. She pointed at it and before she could ask, he said, "That's a bondage bed."

"It looks medieval. And anything but comfortable." She walked over to it and almost touched it.

"Stop!" he said with a sudden sternness to his voice. She stopped, and he walked up to her, then pulled some surgical gloves from a black box under the bed. He put them on her hands. "I don't want your finger prints on anything in here."

"Oh! Smart, Arsen." She looked around as he put the white gloves on her.

Two long poles leaned against one of the black walls. A rusty color was running down the tan poles and she knew immediately those were the things Rowan had told her about. She gulped and asked, "Is that blood on those things over there." She nodded her head towards the poles.

Without looking at her, he answered, "It is."

"You beat women until they bled?" Her mind was spinning.

"I did." He still didn't look at her.

A block of wood caught her eye next.

"Is that like a stockade? Like from the old days when people would get locked up in them for committing a crime?"

"It is." He finally looked into her eyes.

"So you would lock women up and then do whatever you wanted to with them?" Her lip was beginning to quiver as she was realizing the man she knew was so much more messed up then she imagined he was.

"I did, yes." His eyes were dark and hard as if daring her to tell him he had done anything wrong.

A LEATHER, full-face mask hung on the wall near a hook and silver handcuffs dangled from them. Along the wall was a line of various items used to flog people. Her heart began to race.

"There is not one thing in this room which doesn't bring pain, is there, Arsen?"

He shook his head slowly.

"So what do you think of this place now, Steele? Think it's a place you'd care to frequent? Think it's a place you belong in?"

If she wanted to stay in his life, she'd better figure out how to take all he was about.

"Show me how you take a woman on this hard wood bed, Arsen. Show me how it feels to be in here with you as my Master."

He chuckled and his eyes softened.

"You know stubborn isn't a strong enough word for you, Steele. I'm not going to be taking you in this room, ever. This is not for you. It's not a thing you want. Your mind was not made to handle the pain that this lifestyle is about."

"Show me how to do what you want, Arsen," she said and fell to her knees on the cold cement floor. "If this is you and what you want, then teach me. Teach me to take the pain you like to give out."

He turned away from her and put his head in his hands. "Get up!" he snapped.

SHE DID AS HE SAID. But her mind was racing with the newfound knowledge he had never really had sex that didn't involve pain. She had to be disappointing to him.

"If you won't take me in here then at least put me in some type of bondage thing you have so many of in here. I know you want to, so just do it. I want you to do it." She looked around and pointed to a table.

It looked benign enough.

"There, that table thing. Do to me what you did to other women on that table, Arsen."

He looked at where she was pointing then back at her with an expressionless face.

"I leaned women over that and flogged them with various things until they begged me to stop. Then I held them down and fucked them on it. Is that what you think you really want?"

"I want some of what you gave other women here, Arsen. I feel left out of a part of you." She stepped towards him and found him moving back from her.

"Be glad you're left out of this part of me. This part of me only wanted to cause pain the way pain had been done to me. You don't seem to understand. This is about overcoming pain, Steele. Learning to handle the harsh reality that some of us are dished out a hell of a lot more than others are. Learning how to overcome it." He spun around and pulled his jacket off, hanging it in a closet. He pulled his shirt off next and hung it up.

STEELE'S HEART began to pound, thinking he was finally going to give her what she'd asked for.

"Arsen, it kills me that you were ever hurt."

He picked up one of the long poles and carried it over to her. She looked at it and flinched.

Why would he want to use that?

ARSEN HELD it out to her.

"I want you to take this and match it to the faint marks on my back." He turned, and she held it to the three places on his back where faded scars were.

That woman who'd been his mistress had hit him with the thing and split his flesh wide open more than just one time. "Arsen, this is horrible."

He looked back at her.

"No, what's horrible is when I did that to others. When I first met you I told you that you should run and you should've. I am a monster, Steele. And now that you've seen this and what I have done, you know it's true."

"I don't think of you as a monster. You had tons of pain inside you. You still do. I can see now why the women asked you to do the things you did to them. I also want to take your pain away and would feel the bite of your strap or whatever you had to endure to take it away from you," she said then ran her hand over his cheek.

"That's not what I want for you, Steele. I don't want you to feel pain. Shit! You can't take it and you shouldn't have to. Your life wasn't bad. You have no reason to need to accept pain and learn how to deal with it and I won't be the one to make you." He took the pole from her, turned and walked away.

IN THAT INSTANT it all became crystal clear to Steele. Arsen was never going to be able to stay with her. She turned and ran from the room at full speed. All she could think was she had to get the hell out of that place and away from the man she loved more than she ever could've imagined, but he was never going to allow her to be what he needed.

33

ARSEN

The door slammed, and he turned to find Steel had gone. He cursed and ran after her, not sure which way she'd turned in the hallway. He took off the way they had come in, but he knew she might've gone the other direction and he hoped she hadn't done that.

After searching the two rooms they'd been in, he found nothing. He stopped by the coat check stand and saw her red coat still hanging and he knew she wouldn't go out without it.

He made his way back and hoped she was okay because if she found herself in the room at the other end of the hallway she was going to be in over her head.

Hearing the roars of laughter and shouts from a lot of men, Arsen went into the room where the auctions were held and sure as shit, Steele was on the auction block.

The daft woman had run right into the one place where she should never have gone. Arsen stayed in the back in the dark shadows as he saw her trying hard not to let her fear show as a man wearing nothing but ass-less chaps held a leash fastened to a black collar around her throat.

She must've been making a lot of fuss and a gag was in her

mouth, the straps ran around her head and her hands had been bound as well.

Oh, the fit she must've been throwing for them to do all that to her.

HE FLINCHED WHEN THE BLONDE-HAIRED, older man smacked her on the ass and said, "Whew wee! This one is wild and built to handle what you got to dish out. I tell you what!"

Steele glared at the man and Arsen winced as the man pinched one of her nipples, making her close her eyes and shake her head. Some man in front yelled, "Two hundred dollars."

The auctioneer's eyebrows raised.

"You have got to be kidding me. For this feisty piece of prime ass that's all you got. I'm starting the bidding at five hundred dollars. She's got it all men. The looks." He grabbed her by her braid and pulled her head up and ran one finger over her red cheek. "The body." His hand ran over her breast.

Arsen stiffened and clenched his fist at his side. Another man shouted. "I'll give you five hundred for her."

Another shouted out, "I'll give you six. She's about as wild as they come. I'd love the chance to break her fine ass." He held a whip in his hand and popped it in the air.

Steele's eyes went wide, and she shook her head, making the room full of men laugh. Arsen wasn't laughing though. He was getting increasingly pissed at how the auctioneer was touching what was his.

AN OLD MAN YELLED OUT, "I'll give you one thousand dollars for her. I could use me another sub and she'd make a fine one."

The auctioneer reminded him.

"This is only for the remainder of this one night, old man. Not forever."

The old man cackled then said, "Once she gets a taste of my dick, she'll beg to become my sub."

. . .

THE AUCTIONEER MOVED his body behind Steele's and acted as if he was fucking her from behind. He went so far as to push her shoulders forward and pull her hips back and slammed into the back of her. Only the thin leather strap of her outfit which ran between her legs and his chaps was stopping him from actually getting to her and Arsen had all he could take.

He strolled up to the very front and smiled at Steele who mumbled behind the gag and begged him with her eyes to save her. Arsen looked at the auctioneer. "How does five thousand sound?"

The man released Steele and said, "It sounds like you got a hankering for this little filly, sir. Your number please, so we can get our money."

"Twenty-one," Arsen said and took the leash the auctioneer handed him. "Thank you."

THE CROWD of men moaned and gave Arsen dirty looks as he led Steel off the auction block then threw her over his shoulder, smacking her ass one time. He took her all the way back to his private room before he took the gag and binds off her. She took in a deep breath and threw her arms around him.

"Arsen, that was horrible." She let him go and placed her hand on a small red bump on the outside of her thigh. "That man popped his whip, and it hit me as I realized once I got into that room I needed out of there fast."

He pulled her back into his arms and shushed her.

"You're okay now. I have you, Baby."

"I'm sorry I left the room. I was an idiot!"

"Look, that's over now. Let's get those poles and break them down and get them out of here. I think you've seen quite enough of Club Fierce." Arsen let her go and moved to unscrew the poles to make them manageable.

Steele pulled the black collar off and found the red one and put it on. She held her hands out to take the poles into her hands.

"Take my leash and do not let me go. I'll carry these."

Arsen handed her the six pieces of wood and chuckled.

"At least I don't ever have to hear you ask to come here again."

"No, you will never hear those words come from my mouth ever again. That's a promise. If you wish to leave this behind you, I'm all for that."

"Good." He took her leash and led her away from what had been his life.

HE LOOKED around the room just before he closed the door for what would be the last time if he had anything to do with it. Ghosts of the three women who had been his subs flittered through his mind and he found himself saying out loud, "I'm sorry girls. I'm really sorry and I hope you can forgive me."

HE CLOSED the door and had to swallow the lump which had formed in his throat. Arsen hadn't allowed himself to think about the dead women and with their memory came a flood of emotions. And Arsen was not one to allow many emotions.

34

STEELE

Sliding into the back of the Suburban, Steele opened the little fridge and grabbed the first bottle of liquor her hand landed on. One long drink she took then wiped her mouth with the back of her hand as Arsen watched her with a smile on his handsome face.

"That was rough on you."

She nodded and stayed on her knees on the floor of the car as he sat on the seat. Paul closed the door and Steele untied the belt of her leather coat. Pulling it off, she laid it out on the floor and got on her hands and knees and wiggled her finger at Arsen.

He looked at her for a second, obviously taking her all in. Arsen moved off the leather seat and came to her. Moving her to lie on her back. He ran his hand over her forehead, pushing some of her hair back off her face.

"Thank you, Steele." His lips brushed hers softly, and she moaned and ran her hand to the back of his neck.

She needed him. For reasons she didn't understand she needed to feel him inside her. Show her she was his in every way. What she'd seen was fresh in her head and worrisome. She needed to know he wanted her. Nearly plain old vanilla, her.

His tongue ran around hers and he pressed his body to hers. She arched up to him and said, "Arsen, please take me."

He reached between them and unbuckled the one strap that was keeping him from getting to her. His fingers found her wet and he unbuttoned and unzipped his slacks and pushed himself into her.

She moaned in his ear as he thrust into her.

"Fuck me, Arsen. Make me come all over you hot, huge cock."

Steele knew he didn't tell her she could talk and a small part of her wanted to test him. See if he was going to really be her master.

Arsen plunged deep into her and pulled one of her legs back. He held his body up and watched his dick slam into her over and over. Steele found him fascinating as she watched his reaction to their bodies coming together.

He looked at her.

"You like it? You like my cock buried inside you?"

She nodded and moaned then put one finger in her mouth and wet it. She reached down and touched her clit and moaned as she stroked it. She was pushing him and was waiting for him to tell her something.

"Fuck me harder, Baby," she groaned.

He pounded into her harder as she rubbed herself and moaned loudly. She knew he didn't allow much noise made, and made as much as she could. He pulled out of her just before she was about to come.

"Did I make you mad, Master," she said with a sly smile.

"Really, Steele." He leveled his dark eyes on hers. Then he grabbed her and turned her over and slammed into her from behind as he pushed her face and chest to the floor. "Is this what you want from me?"

HE POUNDED her like any other piece of ass he'd fucked, Steele thought. Her breath was coming out in spurts and she was thinking that was exactly what she wanted. She wanted to feel him do to her what he'd done to all the others. Fuck them and care nothing for them. Then he stopped again and pulled out of her.

She lifted herself off the floor and turned around to find him setting back on his haunches. His hands over his face and he was shaking.

"Arsen?"

Steele reached out and placed her hands on his and gently pulled them away to find tears streaming down his face. She pulled him to her and hugged him as he cried.

"I'll never lay my eyes on their beautiful faces again. I'll never run my hands over their exquisite bodies again. I will never get to tell them how sorry I am for hurting them both physically and mentally."

She had no idea he'd break like this. Selfish is what she felt like. She was so busy wanting him to do to her what he'd done to the others, she never thought about how it might affect him.

"ARSEN, IT'S OKAY." She hugged him tight. "They know now, Baby. They know everything now. And they no longer hurt."

He pulled back and looked at her, breaking her heart for him as the strong man sat on the floor of his expensive Suburban, wearing an Armani suit that cost more than the rent on her apartment, and cried like a baby.

"I never even bothered to talk to any of them about why they felt they needed to be submissive. I'm sure each had her reasons, but I never asked. I hardly ever spoke to them. I used them for what I needed, and then left them. The money I gave them, the cars, the apartments I rented them, I thought that would compensate them for what I did." His body was shaking and Steele pulled him back into her arms.

"You were a hurt person yourself. How were you to be any better than what you were? Give yourself a break, you lived in hell for quite a few years. No one can judge you, Arsen. Please, don't judge yourself." She rocked back and forth with him as he let out what seemed like years of pent up emotion.

She was mad at herself for breaking him down. Though unintentional, nearly everything she did was making him be a man he wasn't. Arsen pulled back, and she saw his tears were slowing.

It hit her she'd never seen him look more beautiful. He was opening up to her. Letting her see what he never even allowed himself to see. The part of him that was human. Weak and sorry and a completely vulnerable human being, just like everyone else.

"STEELE, you're saving me. I don't know exactly how, but you are saving me, Baby. I feel more weak when I'm with you, but also more powerful in other ways. You've brought something to my life I didn't even know was missing. God, I love you." He took her face between his hands and kissed her.

It was a kiss like he'd never given her before. Not overpowering and not soft, just something which felt as if he was one with her. Like they were equals. And in that moment for one split second she let herself believe she was okay letting him change.

He laid her back on the floor and pulled his mouth from hers.

"I want to make love to you. I never want to fuck you again. Please don't ask me to. I've fucked women for too long. Let me make love to you, Steele, please."

"I understand now. I didn't before, but now I do. Arsen, please make love to me, Baby. You're all I want and need in this world." She opened her arms, and he began unbuckling the leather straps and pulled them all away.

35

ARSEN

rsen ran his hands over Steele's body as she lay on the floor of his Suburban. He'd taken all his clothes off and lay next to her. Thin lines ran over her pristine skin where the leather straps had been.

Things had to change, she had to see he was a man in transition and be able to be there for him, allowing him to make the changes he needed to. Too much bad had happened in his life and it was time for the good.

Steele had brought that good into his life. He wasn't about to let it be him who changed her. She was perfect already. His hand ran over one perfect breast and gave it a gentle squeeze.

He took it in his mouth and ran his tongue around the nipple then suckled it, moving his hand to play with the other pert breast as he did. Steele made a little moan. Arsen didn't even have to fight the instinct to smack her ass to let her know she wasn't allowed to make noise.

Instead, he found her sounds pleasing and arousing. He kissed up her chest and playfully nipped at her neck then found her lips and took them in a soft kiss.

The kiss turned hard as Steele pulled at him, making him come closer and closer until his body was over hers and she was arching up for him. Normally he'd make a woman wait until he said it was time, but Steele made him want to give her anything she wanted.

It was all about her. Arsen knew she was his one weakness, and he was able to accept that fact. He could live with it. He wanted to live with it.

He moved into her and she sighed as he filled her completely. His heart beat hard in his chest as he felt more than he'd felt the night before. He'd come apart in front of her and she didn't try to hurt him while he was weak.

S TEELE HAD HELD HIM, nurtured, and comforted him. Arsen knew he could trust her, like he'd never trusted anyone else in his entire life. In his arms he held the one woman who could help him be the strong man he wanted to be without being a monster to keep him that way.

Slow, long strokes he made as she arched up to meet each one. When he pulled his mouth from hers, her eyes opened and she looked at him. Her hands moved over his biceps as she whispered, "I love you so much, Arsen. I love you more than I even knew was possible. Being with you like this is more than Heaven."

He couldn't speak because tears were threatening him yet again. Arsen kissed her cheek softly and rubbed the tip of his nose to hers. Letting her know he felt the same way she did.

Steele ran her legs around him, running her feet up and down the long length of his legs. He knew she loved the way his muscles rippled with every movement. He moved faster, rippling them more for her.

It was all he could think about, pleasing her, giving her whatever she wanted. She arched up to him, silently asking him to speed up. He moved faster and thrust harder until her breathing was ragged and a thin sheen of sweat shone on her creamy skin.

Arsen knew Steele liked a little of his control over her and he leaned to whisper in her ear, "Come."

. . .

HER BODY EXPLODED AROUND HIM, pulsing and squeezing him as she moaned with her release. He came right along with her. They would have some things to work through to get where each needed to be.

Arsen knew Steele wanted some of how he'd done things and some just weren't good for her so he'd have to let her know those were his new hard limits. She was becoming more and more precious to him with each passing day. And he meant to treat her like one would any precious object.

"I LOVE YOU, Steele. Thank you for being here for me. It's more than I deserve," he said then pulled away from her and began dressing. "We should probably get our clothes on. We should be nearing home."

Steele picked up her strappy leather outfit and smiled at him.

"Um, I don't know how to put this thing back on, Arsen."

He smiled and shook his head as he buttoned up his shirt.

"Just put the coat on. Don't even try to get back into those boots either."

Wrapping the coat around her then tying the belt to keep it closed, she sat on the seat and buckled her seatbelt as the car came to a stop in front of the building Arsen's penthouse was in. And that's when he saw her.

"Oh my God." Arsen's tanned face went pale and Steele followed his wide stare.

"Who is that?" she asked as she looked at the woman who stood at the front of the building at twelve o'clock at night.

"Mistress Sinclair." The words barely had left his lips when he realized Steele had rushed past him and gotten out of the car, running at full speed towards the tall, thin, blonde woman.

It was obvious Steele was in a full rage as she screeched, "You fucking piece of shit, bitch."

Mrs. Sinclair had a smug look on her amazingly unwrinkled skin. The woman was a little over fifty and didn't look it. Arsen winced as

Steele, nearly six inches shorter than the woman, jumped up a little and grabbed a handful of her shoulder-length blonde hair.

In an instant, the two were on the ground and Steele was straddling the woman and beating the crap out of her. Arsen and Paul had gotten out of the car as quickly as they could, but Steele was just too fast for them.

Arsen called out to her over and over, but Steele was in such a screaming, cursing rage, she heard no one, was his thought on why she continued the assault on the woman who'd made him her submissive.

He grabbed her by the waist and hoisted her away and found Mrs. Sinclair had a good amount of blood on her face from a busted lip and a wad of blonde hair was held tight in Steele's small fist.

"Steele, calm down!" He ordered her in a strict tone as she wiggled in his grip to get back at the woman.

"Let me go, Arsen! Let me deal with this bitch!" Steele continued to try to get away from him as Paul helped the older woman up.

Arsen watched as the woman who'd helped make him the hard man he was stood up, her body shaking. She wiped the blood from her mouth with the back of her hand and said, "My God, Arsen! Is this your little Hell cat?"

Steele wiggled and kicked into the air, screaming, "Shut the fuck up! You cannot talk to him!"

Arsen kissed the side of her head and had to hold in a laugh.

"This is my little Hell cat. Didn't know she was one, but she's mine. You should leave. She doesn't seem to like you much."

"We need to talk, you and I." Sinclair looked at him then at Steele. "Preferably alone. I can take one attack but not two in one night. I'm not as tough as I used to be."

Steele stopped wiggling and looked at Arsen.

"Do not be alone with this woman. Arsen, please."

He kissed the tip of her nose and smiled.

"You have nothing to worry about, Baby." He looked back at

Sinclair. "I don't give one shit what you have to say. This woman is my life now. The other three who were a part of the life I had before this little Hell cat came along are gone and you, I want nothing to do with. Thanks for going to the police and telling them I'm threatening you, though. You always have been one magnificent liar." Waving a hand to dismiss the wretched bitch, Arsen turned to take Steele inside.

"I know who killed them, Arsen. I thought it was you and I kept digging until I found out who it was. If it was you, I meant to see you go to prison for the murders. Seems it wasn't though. Seems like once again you are in need of my help, my protection. Are you really going to walk away from that again?"

Arsen turned and looked at her. The woman who'd nearly broke him.

DO I NEED HER?

36

PART EIGHT: FOR KEEPS

STEELE

Red was all she could see as Arsen held her tight around her waist, holding her off the ground, and said the words she never thought she'd hear come out of his mouth, "Maybe I should hear her out."

The tall, thin, blonde woman smiled and looked at Steele.

"My name is Anne, by the way. And did I hear Arsen call you, Steele?" Her voice was calm and told nothing of the blood which still flowed from her busted lip or the swelling of her right eye.

Steele looked up at Arsen.

"I will not let you do this, Arsen. She's a horrible person and you can't believe a word she'll say anyway."

Anne Sinclair's left eyebrow arched in amusement.

"Do not tell me this poor excuse for a submissive is going to tell you what to do, Master Sloan. Even in those clothes, she's so obviously vanilla."

A growl came from deep in Steele's chest as she said, "Let me go,

Arsen. I can make her stop talking if you just let me go." She began to wiggle in his tight grip again.

ARSEN NARROWED his eyes at his old mistress.

"She is not a person I want you to speak about any more, Sinclair. Now tell me what you know so we can be done with this."

"In private, Arsen. It's not a quick thing, and I'd like to see to my wounds your hell cat has inflicted on me. If you don't mind." Anne moved towards the glass doors to the lobby of the building Arsen's penthouse was in.

"Paul, will you see her to your apartment? I don't want her in my home." Arsen walked ahead of Anne. Steele was still held under one of his arms as she kicked and squirmed. "I'll be down to talk to her shortly. I have to deal with a couple of things first."

Anne followed behind him.

"I hope one of those things is teaching that hell cat a thing or two about her position. She is quite the brat. I can give you some pointers on breaking that part of her if you like."

Steele screamed, "Shut the fuck up, you fucking bitch!"

"And the language, Arsen, tsk, tsk..." Anne shook her head and sighed as she walked on the other side of Arsen and Steele glared at her.

ARSEN TOOK Steele to the private elevator up to his penthouse and Paul took Anne to the other set of elevators.

"Help her see to her wounds, will you, Paul?" Arsen called out over his shoulder as he took Steel into the elevator.

Paul gave a nod and the elevator doors closed. Arsen finally let Steele go and placed her feet on the floor.

Her face was as red as a beet and her body was shaking.

"Arsen, please don't go talk to her. She really is not a viable person who you can get information from. You know that. She's already lied on you to the police about you threatening her."

Arsen ran his hand through her disheveled hair. The braid had come loose and her hair hung in tendrils around her red face.

"Steele, you know that I need every clue I can get. I have to at least hear what she has to say then I'll send her on her way."

Steele threw her arms around him.

"No! Please, don't! I'm begging you not to go talk to her."

He pushed her back, gently.

"And I'm asking you to trust me, Baby."

Steele stood perfectly still as she thought about his constant need for trust. It was one of his biggest issues.

"Arsen, it's not that I don't trust you. I mean, I do trust you. That woman is capable of hurting you. I want you to realize you have deep seeded issues with her. It's not a smart thing to put your trust in her."

"And I'm not. I simply want to hear what she's found out." He ran his hands over her back and pulled her to him in a hug.

"Arsen, I'm afraid for you." Steele looked up at him. "Something isn't right. Why would she pop up after all this time? What if she was the one who really killed those women? What if this is some type of set up?"

"Do you think I'm an ignorant person, Steele?" His dark eyes danced as he looked at her.

She brushed back a section of his dark hair, letting her fingers relish the silkiness of it.

"You know I think you're the smartest person I've ever met. But your past with that woman makes her dangerous to you. Call Paul's phone, talk to her that way."

He shook his head.

"I need to be able to read her body language as she talks or I'll have no idea if she's lying or not."

They got off the elevator, and he ran his arm around her shoulders.

"Arsen, let me come with you then."

Arsen's laugh filled the hallway they were walking down as they went towards his bedroom.

"Steele, you cannot be trusted to keep your cool with her. That's been proven, Baby." He kissed the top of her head. "By the way, thank you. I've never had anyone be as protective over me as you are. It's nice and makes me feel like what we have is deeper than either of us even realized."

Steele stopped and turned to hug him again.

"I love you, Arsen. You might be right about me not being able to control myself with her. I really hate her. And I really would not stop until she's dead. What she did to you was unforgivable."

"At least you agree with me." He opened the door to the bedroom.

"I want you to take a nice, hot bath. I'm going to bring you a bottle of wine and I want you to relax and let that temper settle down a bit. I'll go see what she has to say then be right back up here to tuck you into bed."

A SHIVER RAN through Steele as she began to realize just how many of his rules she'd just broken.

"Arsen, please don't keep me away from you as a punishment for all the rules I've broken just now. I have to be able to touch you. To hold you after all that's happened."

A little grin ran over his caramel lips.

"Steele, there will be no punishments for that. Your anger was justifiable. I would like you to gain control over it, but much like I found myself punching Rowan, I know your anger." His lips touched hers then he pulled back. "Go jump in the tub as I've told you to and I'll be right back."

Steele did as he said but everything in her wanted to follow him down to Paul's apartment and make sure his old mistress didn't play any mind games with him.

I hope she doesn't make him change his mind about me!

37

ARSEN

Arsen's hand moved up to his twitching eye, and he cursed his weakness. "Damn nerves."

He got off his private elevator and went to the other which would take him to Paul's apartment. He was glad his stomach hadn't begun to ache. Anne Sinclair was not able to make him feel all the little ticks he'd had when he was under her.

A quick knock on Paul's door had Paul answering with a frown. He looked over his shoulder to make sure Anne wasn't behind him then whispered, "What a complete bitch this woman is, Arsen."

Arsen gave him a nod.

"I'm more than aware of that fact. I'd like you to stay in here with us. I want a witness the whole time we're together."

Paul nodded and followed Arsen to the living area where Anne was seated on a sofa. A bag of frozen peas covered the eye Steele had punched.

"I see Paul took care of you, Sinclair. Now down to business. What do you have?" Arsen took a seat across from her.

Her eyes darted back and forth between Arsen who sat and Paul who stood behind him.

"We should be alone, Arsen."

Arsen shook his head.

"I will not be alone with you. You've already lied and told the police you're afraid of me. I won't be setting myself up for any further trouble. So spill it, tell me what you found out."

"I have a friend in the lab where the autopsies have been done on the three women you're being accused of killing. Tell me, Arsen, do you have any way of getting a drug called succinylcholine?"

With a shake of his head, he answered, "Not only do I have no way of getting any drug, legally, I also have no idea what that drug is even used for. Do you?"

PAUL'S VOICE from behind him had him turning to look back at the man.

"It's used in anesthesia. It paralyzes the body. If too much is used it can cause complete respiratory failure. I dated a girl in pre-med last year and helped her study a lot."

Anne's eyes darted back to Arsen's.

"Were you aware of that, Arsen?"

"Him dating a girl in pre-med?" Arsen shook his head. "No, but he and I don't get into each other's business like that."

"So, could you get access to that drug, Paul?" she asked.

He laughed.

"No. I just know about it is all. And it doesn't leave any traces in the body. Only slightly elevated amounts of choline and succinic acid are evidence the drug could've been used to kill the girls."

Arsen's mind was working fast.

"As of right now, all the women's deaths have been ruled from asphyxiation. But that drug would also cause the same effects as strangulation." He looked at Anne. "Do you know if that's the case?"

She nodded.

"My friend is just a student and an intern. She said the only thing the women had in common, other than the marks around their necks, are slightly elevated choline and succinic acids. She couldn't get anyone to listen to her about looking for a point of puncture where a needle would've been inserted to deliver the drug."

Arsen rose quickly.

"Then I need to make sure that gets done."

"Where are you going?" she asked him.

"To make a call. I'll get that new detective to make sure they look for that." He strode away.

"Arsen, wait!" Anne was behind him instantly. "That alone won't get you off the charges. I know who did it. I just need your help in finding the man. He works at the California Pacific Medical Center, here in San Francisco." She tugged at his arm to get him to sit back down. This time she sat next to him.

"How do you know this?" he asked in confusion.

"Once I found out the women may have been poisoned, I was able to get into all three women's medical records." She smiled at Arsen.

"Just how did you manage that?" he asked with a frown.

"I'm a billing specialist now. So I did a little illegal searching and found out all three women knew a certain anesthesiologist as they all had little procedures done this last year. Two had boob jobs and one had implants removed. This guy's name was on all three as the one who billed for the anesthesia. He also frequented one of the local BDSM clubs in town. It's called 'Hard' do you know about it?" Her hand lingered on his arm and he felt her squeezing his bicep.

He moved back away from her.

"I haven't been to that one. I knew they all went there, and I didn't want to run into them. So this man may have been the one who killed them. What's his name so I can tell the detective?"

With a laugh, she shook her head.

"You don't get it at all. The San Francisco Police want you out of the picture. You get way too many criminals off the charges they work so hard to get on them. This is an easy way to be rid of you, Arsen. We have to catch him. You and I, together. Just like old times."

"There is not going to be a you and I, Sinclair. Thanks for the information. If you don't want to give me the man's name, I can work to find it on my own. I do have my sources as well. It would be much easier and appreciated if you did though." He stood up and prepared to leave.

ANNE PICKED up her purse and pulled out a piece of paper. She handed it to him.

"I can see you've changed a lot since you were young. Your eyes tell me your set on doing this without me. So I may as well let you have this. To be honest I thought this might get us back to where we were."

He laughed.

"I'LL NEVER BE GOING BACK to that. I'm pretty much on my way out of this lifestyle all together."

"The hell cat got anything to do with that?" she asked.

"Everything." Arsen took the paper from her and looked at the picture of a man in blue scrubs. The name on the tag was Peter Christy, but the man in the picture was Allen White. "How the hell did he manage to get a position at a hospital as an anesthesiologist?"

"You know this man?" she asked.

"Yeah. And he's easy for me to get to now. He's Steele's roommate's fiancé. Looks like we have to give him another visit in the morning. I'll have the little fucker confessing in no time." He turned to leave and felt Anne's hand on his arm.

"Arsen, can I have one last kiss, please?"

Arsen turned and looked into the light blue eyes which once had been a dark blue. Thin lines ran around them and when she smiled she almost seemed likeable.

Only Arsen knew how quickly that sweet exterior could go dark. He ran his knuckles across her cheek.

"Please. Interesting choice of words. Don't you think?"

Her smile changed quickly into a frown.

"Arsen, you know I was only trying to toughen you up. And what I did worked."

"It made me a man who shut himself off. I can take the worst kinds of pain. You made sure of that. You also made sure I knew how to inflict the most pain and I now have to live with the guilt of how I've hurt people. Mentally and physically." He moved his hand off her face and smiled. "So, no, I won't give you one last kiss. Goodbye, Sinclair."

ARSEN WALKED AWAY without looking back and he felt better than he had in a long time.

38

STEELE

Steele had waited for what seemed like forever in the deep bathtub filled with lilac scented bubbles. She sipped some red wine and jumped as Arsen opened the door.

"Finally!" she said as she breathed a sigh of relief. "Well?"

Arsen picked up a towel and held it out. She got out and let him wrap the towel around her. He picked her up and carried her to the bed.

She giggled as he tossed her on it then started taking his clothes off.

"Arsen! Tell me what she said!"

He just shook his head, making her sigh. Once the last stitch of clothing was removed, he crawled on his hands and knees up the bed to her. His grin was constant, and she squealed as he ran his whiskered cheek along her inner thigh.

Unwrapping the towel from her body, his eyes went from playful to lusty and he ran his hand from her breast to her clit and looked into her eyes.

"I want you, Steele."

A half grin she made as her hand ran through his hair.

"I'm yours."

ONE LEG HE TOOK, holding it up. His tongue ran down the inside of it, igniting a shock of chills over her entire body. Arsen took her other leg and lifted it up, doing the same to it.

He pushed them up until her heels were by her ears then he leaned over her and teased her with his erection. Allowing the tip to move over her, but not pressing it to her while he nipped and sucked at her neck.

Her arms moved to press him to her, but he didn't let her move him. He held himself back until she was begging.

"Arsen, please. I need to feel you inside me. Please, Baby."

He let one leg go, and she moved it to wrap around him as she arched up. Arsen pulled his head from her neck and ran a thumb over the nice purple hickey he'd made just behind her ear.

Arsen watched her face as he pushed his cock into her wet depths. Relief filled her as he entered her.

"I love you," she said as she let her breath out.

He stilled and continued to look at her.

"I have no idea why you do, but that makes me more happy than I knew was possible."

Arsen pulled nearly all the way out and slowly moved back in. Steele ran her hands over his biceps and moaned as he slowly stroked in and out. His chest moved over her breasts as he did, making the nipples go tight and erect.

HE TOOK one in his mouth and licked it. Constant strokes of his tongue had it hard, and she wanted him to suck it so bad her body was shaking for him to do it.

She took one hand off his muscled bicep to push his head harder to her breast.

"Please suck it, Arsen. Baby, please."

He took a long suck, and she moaned as it pulled something deep inside her. "Yes," she hissed.

Arsen let her other leg down and took her ass cheeks in his hands, lifting her so his strokes went deeper into her. He groaned as he moved slowly in and out.

Steele ran her hands over his back and quivered at the way his muscles moved as he made the slow strokes. It was beyond sexy. He was like a perfect machine. Every little muscle was defined and moved like a river under his skin.

Just as she thought she was about to fall over the edge with his sucking and the deep strokes, he pulled his mouth from her breast. His dark eyes searched hers. He put his mouth just over hers without letting it touch.

"Breathe me in, Baby."

His breath left his mouth with a heat she'd never felt before. She parted her lips and took his air in and felt something amazing. He was more a part of her than ever and she loved the way he was being so free with her. Giving so much of himself to her.

She heard and felt him inhale the air she let out and it thrilled her. His mouth came down on hers and his tongue roamed hers. Her body fell apart beneath him and she moaned as she arched up.

He was still for a moment then made hard, deep thrusts. Arsen pulled his head back.

"Keep coming for me, Baby. Don't stop, take me with you, make me come."

She looked into his eyes as she kept arching up to meet his hard thrusts, her body squeezing his thick cock with little spasms. And just as his body was beginning to tense, she said, "Come for me."

His eyes went wide as his body did what she asked of him. He clenched his teeth and made a deep groan as his body released. Steele felt her body going into a deeper climax and joined him. They groaned together, long, deep, guttural.

Then he laid his head on her chest as they tried to catch their breath. Steele ran her hand over his head as she thought about how he might be getting softer, but he was still strong and beginning to make a fantastic combination of both attributes.

ARSEN MIGHT JUST BECOME *the perfect man! And he's all mine!*

39

GWEN

Two male voices woke Gwen up from the deepest sleep she'd ever had. Her head was fuzzy, but she could make out what they were saying. One was Allen's of that she was sure, the other wasn't familiar at all.

Her entire body ached. She had no idea how long he'd had her chained up to the little bed in the empty warehouse.

The empty metal building with cement floors echoed as the two men talked. Even though they spoke as quietly as they could.

Allen said, "I need two syringes, Peter."

"Look, I gave you my medical ID. I don't want to get caught actually taking the stuff myself, Allen. And if I can be frank with you, this is getting a little too risky. Why do you have to take his current girlfriend? There's more than enough evidence to put him away for a long time with the three other women's deaths."

"I want this man to hurt as much as he hurt me. I came to the man needing his help, and he lost the case. Peter, it was the only case the man has ever lost. I think it's because he wanted to see me punished for my crime. He is into punishments after all." Allen's voice was riddled with disgust.

"You don't understand a thing about what that lifestyle is about, little man. Look, I'll go along with you using my ID but I won't go further than that. I hated those bitches is the only reason I've even done as much as I have," the other man said.

"It was Arsen who got in your way when you were trying to get into their panties. You have to want to see him hurt," Allen said.

"Yes, I do. Not to mention the fact he turned Anne into a shell of her former self. That woman had been fantastic until she took him under her wing and he shit all over her for her efforts to turn him into something more than a weakling with oversensitivity," Peter said.

"Well then, why not help a little bit more than you have? I nearly got caught last time I was in the hospital. It's not safe for me to go in there anymore. I need you to get me the two syringes of the same stuff we used on the others. And tell, Anne, she can take out Arsen's girl-friend. I'll allow her that pleasure," Allen said.

The other man laughed. "She'll love that. That feisty little bitch did a number on Anne's face last night and she is not happy with her at all. My mistress will be pleased with that. Tell you what, I will get the drug for you, but you have to swear not to tell Anne about my doing it. She forbade me to actually take the drug myself. And when she punishes for something she's forbidden, it's not pleasant at all."

ALLEN MADE A DEEP CHUCKLE.

"Well, that's pretty obvious by what she's doing to Arsen for leaving her. The woman is a force to be reckoned with. I just hope she stays true to her word."

Peter said, "She will. I've seen the fake contracts she's had drawn up. They put her as a silent partner in every investment she could find Arsen has. Once he's convicted and put away, she'll gain access to all that investment return and I know she'll give you the ten percent she promised you. Don't worry."

"She better or she'll find herself having a little accident. That's all I have to say about that."

"Allen, don't even think about talking like that about her."

"Just make sure she does what she said she'd do," Allen said.

"And you don't forget who came to you in prison and told you how to get your guilty ass out of there. You show her the respect she deserves, Allen. Or you'll deal with me."

"Fine! So, tell me how we're going to get Arsen to strangle his girl-friend and mine?" Allen said.

"I'll handle that when we all meet up here once we have the other chick."

GWEN WINCED as she realized she'd been so wrong about Arsen and Allen. Now she and Steele would meet their end with some type of drug and somehow Arsen would be made to strangle them.

I HAVE to get free and get to Steele before it's too late!

40

ARSEN

With Steele wrapped tight in his arms, Arsen inhaled the scent of lilacs on her soft skin. Without thinking, he pressed his lips to her bare shoulder. His heart was full.

With the information Sinclair had given him, he was nearly home free. Allen might be a crazy killer, but he was nowhere near as hard as Arsen could be. It shouldn't take him much to get the little freak to confess.

The police may have wanted his ass out of the courtroom and on the side of the accused, but with a confession they would have no real choice.

Arsen nuzzled Steele's neck and pushed her hair away and saw the purple mark he'd left on her neck. He grinned and kissed the spot.

Soon he'd no longer have to hide their relationship. Once he was out of the mess he was in she and he could move forward. He had big plans for her and he hoped she'd agree with him about them.

Steele groaned and rolled over to look at him as she rubbed her eyes.

"What time is it?"

"I'm not sure," he said then kissed her cheek.

"I'm sorry, I must've overslept. I see the light coming in through the curtain. I know your breakfast is supposed to be ready by six each morning." She tried to get up, but he held her in place.

"Where do you think you're going?" he asked with a naughty grin.

"Your breakfast. I have to get it ready. It's in the book." She looked puzzled.

"Steele, do you really want that?" he asked as he gazed down at her.

"Arsen, we've discussed this in depth. You know I do. So much is changing in you so quickly. I don't want to sabotage anything and make you break. I can be what you need." She ran her hand over his cheek.

He kissed her softly.

"You already are."

One of his hands ran over her soft stomach and he ran it until it touched her hip bone. He pulled it gently as he moved her body over his. Arsen settled her on his hard erection.

She sat up and smiled. "Look who's up!"

He placed his hands on her breasts and gave them a squeeze.

"Ride me, Baby."

Steele moved her body up and down his as he watched her. Her dark hair was just the right amount of messy. The blue in her eyes was bright from rest and happiness filled them.

She was happy just to be there with him, he could tell. Steele moved to lie on his wide chest as she moved her body up and down his. Her mouth moved over his neck and she bit him playfully.

"FEELING LIKE PLAYING a little rough this morning, Steele?" He chuckled.

Steele sat back up and wiggled her eyebrows at him.

"Want to show me who I belong to?"

Arsen smiled and rolled her over quickly, pulling her arms up over her head. He slammed into her hard.

"Who do you belong to?"

With a moan she said, "You. I belong to you, Arsen."

Pulling out and pushing back into her hard enough a little air was pushed out of her lungs, he said, "Damn right you do. You don't make a move or I'll smack that sweet little ass of yours, understand me?"

She giggled.

"I won't move."

He knew she liked a little of the rough stuff. Arsen took both her wrists in one hand and took a handful of her thick dark hair in the other, pulling it back a bit, making her lips part.

Arsen kissed her hard. His tongue moved through her mouth, claiming every last bit of it as his. Arsen could be whatever it was Steele wanted. He was going to prove to her she was what his world revolved around.

Deep strokes had her breathing hard as her body struggled not to move. Her legs wound around his waist and for a second he forgot he'd told her not to move.

He smacked the side of her ass and she quickly moved them.

"Sorry." She giggled, and he knew she'd done it on purpose.

Arsen drove into her deeper and harder. The animal in him took over, and he pulled out and spun her around, drawing her back to him by her hips until their bodies collided.

Almost instantly she began to climax.

"Arsen! God!" Her body shook as it pulsed around his hard dick.

He slammed into her harder and faster as her orgasm continued to make his cock feel as if he was about to explode. Arsen held it back until he no longer could and he erupted into her.

Arsen gave her hair one last tug then let her body fall to the mattress as she caught her breath. She lay on the bed spent and looking prettier than she had minutes before.

He moved off the bed and stood at the side of it. Her ass was begging for a quick swat, so he gave her one and she erupted into a fit of giggles.

She rolled over and her gorgeous face nearly brought him to his knees. He loved that girl with every single thing in him. He knew it without a doubt. "Get your fine ass up and let's shower then I want you to teach me how to ride your horse."

Steele sat up quickly.

"Really! You want to go ride, Tripper? Arsen, that would be fantastic!"

"I don't have any cowboy boots," he said with an exaggerated drawl. "Will sneakers do?"

"They sure will!" she hopped out of the bed and he picked her up into his strong arms. "I can't wait to introduce you to him. He's such a sweet horse."

"I can't wait to meet him," he said then kissed her cheek.

How much longer can I hold out before I ask her?

41

STEELE

The afternoon was going by much too quickly for Steele. She leaned back against Arsen's broad chest as he sat behind her, holding her horse's reins. He'd caught on quickly, and she was enjoying the day with her two favorite males.

His thickly muscled legs were on either side of her and she rested her hands on them. They moved with each step the horse took and she loved how they felt as they did.

"You know, Arsen. You haven't told me what she said."

He moved her braid and kissed the back of her ear where she found out he had left a good sized hickey.

"You know what? You just reminded me that I need to find that little fucker and deal with him. Thanks for reminding me. I've been kind of drunk on your love since last night."

Her heart fluttered.

"Drunk on my love? That sounds so sweet."

"Yeah, you're making me all sweet, you little hot temptress." He squeezed her in his strong arms.

"So," Steele said as she waited to hear what Anne Sinclair had said to him that had him in the best spirits she'd ever seen him in.

"Allen White has been impersonating an anesthesiologist, and he was able to procure a drug that leaves little trace it was given. It also causes the body's muscles to stop working. The victim dies of asphyxiation. Sinclair found out from a friend who's an intern at the place they're doing the autopsies at. She said they weren't looking for any needle marks and that we needed to get Allen White to admit what he's done."

"Well, how the hell is that, Arsen?" Steele felt agitated the woman was poking her nose into Arsen's affairs. "I mean, she had to have been asking and investigating on her own. Why would she do that?"

Her body had stiffened in his arms and he handed her the reins and massaged her tense shoulders.

"Relax, Baby. She's just that type of person. A real nosy woman. But in this case, I'm damn glad she's that way."

"I don't like it. I smell a rat, Arsen. A scrawny, old, blonde rat with crow's feet."

"You sound like a jealous woman, Steele. You aren't insecure enough to be jealous, are you?" He snickered a little as he deepened the massage.

"I'd like to call it concerned. And here's another thing I'd like to know. Did the old bat ask you to get back together with her?"

His silence told her the answer and her body went hard as a rock.

"Now, Steele, don't go getting your panties in a wad. You have a man who will be propositioned from time to time. You have to...."

She interrupted him.

"Trust you! I know! Dang it, Arsen, I knew she was going to do that." She looked back at him with horror on her face. "You didn't kiss her or anything, did you?"

He smiled and kissed the tip of her nose.

"Baby, you should know me better than that. My lips will never touch another's now I know what a real kiss feels like."

She smiled and turned back around, finding his words and actions comforting.

"I can't believe you like me so much. I'm so plain and dull."

"I don't like you, Baby. I love the shit out of you." He turned her back to look at him. "Nothing about you is plain or dull. Please stop saying that. I want you to feel every bit as special and perfect as you truly are."

She shook her head as she looked into his dark eyes. "I have no idea how I got so lucky. You're perfect, Arsen. You are the man of my dreams. I held out for you, I knew you'd come along one day. I saved my heart just for you."

The horse slowed to a stop as he kissed her. When he eased his kiss she giggled as she said, "Arsen, have you ever done it in a barn?"

"Looks like I'm about to," he said as he took the reins from her and tapped them, making the horse start back up, headed to the barn as the sun began to set behind them.

42

GWEN

"Please, Allen. Please," Gwen begged him.

Allen looked at her long and hard then took the key out of his pocket and unlocked the lock which held the chains. He quickly grabbed her by the wrist and hoisted her off the small bed.

Gwen's legs were weak, and she stumbled as he pulled her along behind him.

"Thank you, Allen. I really didn't want to spoil the bed."

"Just try to make it quick," he said as he took her to the bathroom. Just before he let her go in he looked up at a small window at the top of the wall. "Take all your clothes off."

"What? Why?" she asked.

"Just do it!" he snapped at her.

She began taking off her clothes. Gwen knew he thought she wouldn't try to escape if she was naked. But he was dead wrong.

After she was undressed she asked, "Can I go in now. I'll be as fast as I can."

Allen's eyes traveled over her body. He smiled as he looked up at her.

"Tell you what, Gwen. Take a shower while you're in there. I think

I'd like a taste of what you have before, well, never mind about that. Just take a shower and I'll be here waiting when you get out."

She nodded and went inside the small bathroom. She turned the water on in the shower right away and after relieving herself she started figuring out how she could climb up and get out the window.

A few old towels were laid out on the counter top and she wrapped one around her. Climbing on top of the toilet, she jumped and was able to grab the window ledge.

She was weak from lack of food, water, and the time stuck in that bed, but she managed to pull her body up and pushed the screen out. The drop was probably ten feet, and she knew she could really hurt herself.

Gwen let her body fall out the small window, moving her body so she'd hit shoulder first. As her shoulder hit the cement, she rolled with the fall.

Once she'd stopped rolling, she took a breath which she didn't realize she'd been holding and found her shoulder hurt some, but her adrenaline had kicked in and the pain was bearable.

Her towel had come loose, and she had to wrap it back around her and she began to run. It was dark, and she had no real idea where she was, but a woman running down the street wearing only a towel would be easily noticed.

"Gwen!" Allen shouted as he ran out of the metal building. "Stop!"

Gwen didn't even look back. She just ran faster towards the lights she figured must be a street. A couple of cars' headlights moved along the road and she nearly cried with relief.

A hill separated her from the road and as she came over the hill she nearly fell down with disappointment. A tall fence with razor wire at the top of it kept her from getting to the road.

With no shoes on, the rocks along the fence hurt her feet. But she kept running along the fence. There had to be an opening some-where along it.

"Gwen!" Allen shouted, and she looked back to see he was still pretty far behind her.

She turned and gathered speed to stay away from him. If she couldn't get out, she would hide from him.

Abandoning the fence, she cut back up the hill and ran to the closest empty building. The whole place had been abandoned. It was a series of old metal buildings.

She found this one had open rafters and there was a ladder. She propped it up against the wall and climbed until she got to the long steel beam which ran the length of the large building.

It was wide enough if she laid down on the top of it, he wouldn't be able to see her. The ladder would give her away though and she heaved it up and laid it on the beam as well.

Her position was secure, and all she had to do was wait. She'd left the prison of the bed for the prison of a beam high up in the air, but this prison was one she could eventually make an escape from and the other one led to certain death.

Just like she knew it would, the door squeaked open. Allen's face peered into the darkness.

"I know you're in here. Just come on out and I won't hurt you. I'll even set you free, Gwen. I promise. Just come on out and let me help you."

He moved around the room making clicking sounds with his shoes as he did. Gwen lay perfectly still on top of the beam, not even daring to glance down at him.

His loud shout rang out and made her body clench, "Gwen! God damn it! Get out here or so help me!"

After a few more steps she heard him mumbling to himself as he left the building and she could hear him going into the next one.

She had no idea what she should do. Gwen just laid there and cried silently. Helplessness flowed through her and she was left with doubt she'd ever really be able to get herself free from this man.

How am I supposed to get out of here and make sure he doesn't get Steele?

43

ARSEN

The day had been perfect in Arsen's mind. He and Steele were riding back to his apartment in his Jag. He looked over at her and found a piece of hay had lingered in her hair after their tumble in it back at the barn.

He chuckled as he pulled it out and handed it to her.

"Here you go. A little memento of our time in the barn, Baby."

She giggled as she took it from him.

"Thanks, I'll put it in our book."

Arsen groaned with the mention of the book. He had thought she would take one look at all those rules and toss it away. Instead she acted as if he'd written her a love story in it.

But the day had been too perfect to start an argument over the damn rules she seemed so determined to learn how to live by. Arsen reached over and gave her cheek a stroke with the back of his hand.

"I THOUGHT we might spend the night cuddled up on the sofa watching a movie and eating popcorn. What do you think about that, Steele?"

Her eyebrows shot up.

"I think that's really normal, Arsen. It sounds great, but I thought we were going to go see Allen. You seem to keep forgetting about him."

"He isn't going anywhere and I can't seem to get my mind off you. Tomorrow I can deal with him." Arsen ran his hand down her arm and took her hand in his.

Steele laid her head back on the leather headrest and closed her eyes.

"This seems a little too surreal, Arsen. Like the calm before the storm or something. You're too laid back and nothing like yourself." She opened her eyes and looked at him. "I mean, I'm absolutely loving it, don't get me wrong. It's just not like you to deal with this business of knowing about Allen and doing nothing about it."

"You're really all I can think about. I can't explain it. I know I have a huge undertaking with getting Allen to confess and maybe I'm not in a hurry to get into that." He pulled her hand to his lips and kissed it softly. "I can't seem to get enough of you, Baby. Sue me."

Steele shook her head and sighed.

"Tonight then it can just be us, but first thing in the morning you have to deal with it."

"I will. Now what movie do you want to watch? And what's the best popcorn. I haven't eaten the stuff in so many years I have no idea what kind to buy." He pulled into the parking lot of a grocery store and smiled. "It's been forever since I've actually went into one of these things. I have Paul pick things up for me."

He parked and got out to open Steele's door. She placed her hand in his as they walked into the store.

"Paul's pretty much your right-hand man, isn't he?" she asked.

Arsen pulled out a shopping cart and grinned.

"He is. Wow, this is so odd. I'm grocery shopping."

Steele's eyes rolled. "Yep, just like any normal person, Arsen. I really need to get you out more. It's like you're from another planet or something."

He chuckled and pulled her to him, his arm wrapped around her shoulders and the other pushed the basket.

"We should make some s'mores in the fireplace and roast hotdogs too. What do you think about that?"

Steele grabbed a pack of hotdogs out of the refrigerated bin and tossed them into the basket.

"I think you and I should do a camp out soon."

"I can get a tent!" His eyes went wide. "That's what we can do when we get back home. We can get online and buy a tent and a bunch of camping supplies and go to Big Bear maybe next weekend."

"Or just rent a cabin up there," she said with a smile. "Arsen, camping can be rough. A lot of work."

"I don't care. I want to have you all alone in a tent in the woods. Now that sounds romantic." He kissed the side of her head and an old woman who was passing them in the aisle looked at them.

"How sweet you are, young man," she commented as she passed them.

Steele smiled back at the woman. "He is very sweet, mam."

The woman's eyes ran over Arsen. "You're one lucky girl."

"I am," Steele agreed.

ARSEN CHUCKLED and gave her another kiss on the cheek this time.

"I'm the lucky one."

The older woman sighed and walked on by. Steele shook her head.

"Who knew this sweet man was under all that arrogance?"

"I wouldn't say I was arrogant, Steele. Maybe closed off, but not arrogant," he said as he threw a bag of hotdog buns in the basket.

"You were definitely arrogant. And I'm sure you still will be when it's called for. You'll need to be when you talk to Allen." Steele pulled a bag of marshmallows off the shelf and placed it in the basket, picking up the buns and putting them in a safer position so they wouldn't be squished.

"Let's leave Allen and all that crap out of this evening's conversation, please." He held up a can of chili. "Chili with the hotdogs?"

"Yes! Oh, let's get some corn chips and cheese and make chili pies too. We can just totally pig out on this junk. Tonight only though, then back to eating right I promise," she said as she grabbed a bag of the chips.

"Of course, Steele. Back to the rules tomorrow. If that's what you want." He pulled her to his side again, holding her by the waist.

They went past a couple of young women who were looking at the wine. Steele asked, "Should we pick up some wine, Arsen?"

One of the women's head spun to look at him.

"Oh! It's you!" she said in surprise. "Do you remember me?"

He blinked and shook his head. "Should I?"

The young brunette put her hand over her mouth then said, "Oh, sorry. This must be your new sub. Sorry." She turned away.

"Who are you?" Steele said with a tense tone.

The woman didn't turn back and Steele pulled her by the shoulder.

"I'm no one. I thought he was someone else. Sorry." Her cheeks were red and she wouldn't look up.

Arsen pulled at Steele. "Come on, Baby. She was mistaken. You're embarrassing her."

Steele allowed him to move them along, but she looked back at the woman and she knew they knew each other from the club. She looked at Arsen.

"You don't want to admit you know her?"

"Can't say I do know her, Steele. I have no idea what her name is. So, I don't know her." He went around the corner and pulled out a gallon of milk. "Since we're going all out, I think I want to make milkshakes. You pick, vanilla or chocolate."

"Which do you prefer, Arsen? And tell the truth," she said as she glared at him.

"I like strawberry. If you must know. But most don't, so you can choose." He placed the milk in the basket and moved on.

"I happen to like strawberry too. But you didn't get what I was saying," she said as she took a half gallon of strawberry ice cream from the freezer.

"I got it, Steele. I'm just not doing that with you today. It's been too good of a day to argue. I have a checkered past. You are well aware of that. Now please stow the attitude and forget about that little encounter. I just remembered why I don't do grocery stores."

WILL my past forever haunt me?

44

PART NINE: FOR LOVE

ARSEN

As Arsen emerged from the bedroom, wearing a dark blue Armani suit and ready to go to work, seeking out Allen and making him confess, he smelled the wonderful scent of fresh coffee and bacon. A smile crossed his handsome face.

Then it turned quickly into a frown as he heard a man's voice coming from the kitchen. It was Tanner Goldstein's, and he had not been invited.

As he stepped into the kitchen, he found Steele wearing an apron over one of the new dresses he'd ordered her. She was pulling biscuits from the oven as Tanner sat at the table, drinking coffee and reading some paper he must've brought with him.

Neither noticed Arsen as Steele said, "He should be right out, Tanner."

"Ummm. About that, Steele. What exactly is going on here?" Tanner put the cup of coffee down and looked at her. Waiting for her answer.

Steele fidgeted with the pan of biscuits and Arsen knew she was trying to think of what to say. He made his presence known.

"Good morning, Tanner. Did I miss a phone call or something?"

Tanner stood and shook Arsen's hand.

"Not at all. I just got an early start this morning and thought I'd stop by. We really need to get working on our defense, Arsen."

Steele turned and seemed nervous as she placed the food on the table. "When the doorman called up to say Tanner was here I was already getting your breakfast ready, so I invited Tanner for breakfast, Mr. Sloan. I hope you don't mind."

Arsen cocked his eyebrow. So she was going to act as if they weren't together. He went along.

"Of course, it's fine, Miss Gannon." Arsen looked at Tanner. "I'm keeping her, Tanner. Hope you don't mind. I'll be using her as my intern."

Steele's eyes lit up. He tried hard not to smile with her obvious delight. He'd not even offered her the position, but as it flited through his mind, he blurted it out and there it was. She'd be his new intern, among other things.

He saw her smiling as she moved around the kitchen and poured them all glasses of orange juice. Arsen took a seat at the table as did Tanner.

"I've been visited by Anne Sinclair, Tanner. She seems to think the police are against me. What do you think I can do about that?"

The buzzer sounded off and Arsen gave Steele a nod.

"Can you answer that?"

She rushed off to answer the doorman's call and when she came back she told him, "A Detective Fontaine is on her way up to see you, Mr. Sloan."

He frowned and knew Steele was going to have a hard time handling the flirting the woman was most likely going to do. His voice was laced with sarcasm, "Great."

"A new detective, I see," Tanner said as he tapped his finger on the table top. "When were you going to let me in on that, Arsen?"

He shrugged and took a sip of his coffee and wished it was a nice glass of Scotch instead. The day was starting out pretty crappy.

"Miss Gannon, can you please meet the officer at the elevator and see her in here? Please ask her to join us for breakfast as well."

Steele ran off to do as he'd requested and Tanner leaned in close to Arsen. "Not ready to let me in on what the hell really is going on between you two?"

"She's my assistant. I think she'll learn the most this way." Arsen picked up a biscuit and began buttering it.

"What else are you teaching her, Master Sloan?" Tanner's eyes stared into his with a penetrating gaze which told Arsen he was pulling nothing over on the man.

"None of your business. I'm breaking no laws and that's all that matters." Arsen stood up when Steele came back into the dining area of the large kitchen. She wore a frown as she looked at him.

THE REASON WHY, he already knew. Detective Fontaine followed behind her. A foot taller, and wearing a very nice dress herself, her long legs ran out from under a red dress and her heels were a shiny black.

Fontaine's long blonde hair flowed over her shoulders and Arsen knew Steele was not happy about him leaving out how attractive the detective was.

Tanner stood too and offered his hand to the woman.

"I'm Mr. Sloan's attorney, Tanner Goldstein. You are the new detective on his case, I see."

She shook his hand and Arsen moved to pull a chair out for her.

"Good morning, Detective Fontaine. Did my assistant offer for you to join us this morning? She made a nice breakfast."

The woman nodded and Steele put another place setting down in front of the chair Arsen had pulled out for the woman. Her arm brushed his as she moved back after setting it down and he looked at her, catching the glare she gave him.

There will most definitely be an argument later!

· · ·

AFTER THE DETECTIVE SAT DOWN, Arsen pulled out another chair.

"Miss Gannon, if you will please take your seat, we can get on with this."

She sat down in the chair and his hand moved over her shoulder lightly, trying to diffuse some of her obvious anger. He sat down next to her and pressed the side of his leg to hers underneath the table where no one could see.

Fontaine's light blue eyes went back and forth between them.

"Your assistant comes to make you breakfast, Arsen?"

Steele's head snapped up.

"Mr. Sloan to you!"

Arsen's eyes went wide, and he tapped the top of her hand with his.

"That's quite alright, Miss Gannon. She can call me by my first name."

Steele clenched her jaw and said, "I apologize, ma'am. I had no idea he allowed you to call him that." Her eyes stayed on the table in front of her and Arsen sighed as he knew what was going to come later.

Tanner cleared his throat and said, "Have you found anything new on the case, Detective?"

She looked at Tanner and pulled a paper from her purse. Then laid it on the table.

"We're about to go search Arsen's playroom at Club Fierce. I'd love for you gentlemen to join us."

"Of course, we will," Tanner said then took a sip of coffee.

Steele's hand ran over the top of Arsen's leg under the table and she looked at him. With a whisper, she asked, "Are you okay?"

HE TOOK her hand in his under the table and gave it a squeeze. He wasn't okay. Not even remotely, but he was trying to hang on to his fear.

Allen White was on his mind and he wanted to get to the man first thing, but those plans were going to have to be postponed. And Arsen found his appetite was gone.

Going back into the place wasn't a thing he wanted to do. It was a place he was trying desperately to leave behind him, but it just kept coming back to haunt him, over and over again.

"I'd like to see the autopsy reports on all three victims," Arsen said, making Tanner and the detective stop eating and look at him.

Then Tanner said, "I have the reports, Arsen."

Arsen cocked his head at his attorney.

"And how long have you had them, Tanner?" His tone was stern and riddled with aggravation.

"A week." Tanner took a bite of his jelly filled biscuit and Arsen had to stifle a growl.

"I'd like to have seen them. Can you tell me if there was anything unusual about them?" he asked.

"No, they all died of asphyxiation." Tanner looked at the detective. "Isn't that right?"

She gave a nod.

"There's just the one common thread. Your hand prints around their necks." Her eyes moved to Steele. "Those women seemed to like that sort of thing, Miss Gannon. Do you?"

Steele jerked her head up to look at the woman. "What I like is none of your concern."

Fontaine's eyes flew to Arsen's.

"Feisty one, isn't she? Tell me, Arsen. Are you finding her difficult to train?"

Arsen's tone stayed flat.

"Steele needs no training. She is her own person and I respect that about her." He gave Steele's knee a little squeeze.

Tanner cleared his throat to ease the tension.

"So, when should we go?"

"Right now," the detective said as she got up. "I'm finished with breakfast. Thank you for the hospitality."

. . .

STEELE GOT up and began to pick up the dishes. Arsen took his plate to the sink, following her.

"You're coming with us. I'll have the maid come clean things up."

She turned and looked at him with surprise.

"You have a maid?"

He nodded.

"An older woman who lives in the building. I let her off this last week, because of you, but I'm getting her to start back up."

Steele looked around him to be sure the others had left the kitchen.

"The book, though. It had all kinds of housework in there."

He smiled and tweaked her nose.

"I know it did. It seems I could've put all kinds of crazy things in it and you still would've agreed to it."

She sighed.

"You aren't taking me seriously about this, are you?"

"LET'S DON'T ARGUE. Come on, we need to go. Remember, you've never been to this place." He looked back to make sure no one was watching then looked back at Steele and placed a little kiss on her lips. Leaning in, he whispered, "I love you. Thank you for making breakfast. It was delicious."

She smiled.

"I love you too, And you're welcome, Arsen. You're also in a lot of trouble for not telling me how gorgeous that woman was."

"I know." He placed his hand at the small of her back and ushered her towards the living room where the others waited. "Maybe I'll let you cuff me next time."

She giggled a little, and he playfully swatted her ass before they got into the living room.

All four of them walked into the elevator. It was a bit cramped and Steele was pressed next to Arsen's side. The detective to his other side was close as well.

·   ·   ·

Detective Fontaine leaned closer, whispering, "If there's anything you'd like to admit before we go through all this trouble, now would be an excellent time to do that, Arsen. I could slip you into my car and we could make a little stop at my apartment before we got to the station. If you know what I mean."

Steele's hand threaded into his and she gave it a squeeze.

"Nothing to admit and not interested, Fontaine."

Steele released his hand before they walked off the elevator. His hand touched the small of her back, urging her to walk in front of him. He could feel her heart pounding and knew she was going to cut into him as soon as she found herself alone with him.

"Miss Gannon and I will go in my car and lead the way." Arsen made his way with Steele to where Paul was waiting for them.

"Good morning," Paul said with a grim look on his face. "Looks like you've already had quite a morning, boss."

"Yes, I have. To add to the fun, you'll be leading the other two cars to Club Fierce. This should be so much fucking fun!" Arsen held Steele's hand as she slid into the car.

He slid in next to her as Paul closed the door.

Her beautiful face was pale as she turned to look at him. Before she could open her mouth to start what he knew was an argument that would affect his already sour mood, he pulled her to him and kissed her hard.

Her arguing could be done later. Right now he might be taken in if they found any reason to when they looked around his private room at the club.

Arsen released her from his kiss.

"I need you, right now, Baby. Get rid of the panties."

She quickly did as he said. Arsen felt his body begin to shake, his eye twitch and the fear of going to prison and never having what he knew he could have with Steele filled him.

45

GWEN

The sound of birds chirping woke Gwen up as she had fallen asleep high up on the beam in the abandoned warehouse. Then the sound of a car starting made her sit up.

She listened like her life depended on it because it did. The car sounded like it was pulling away from the area and she quickly put the ladder down. Then climbed down off the beam near the ceiling she'd hid on many hours earlier.

Running to the door, she pulled it open only a little and found the back of Allen's car moving down the steep road, away from the buildings. He'd see her if she followed.

She wrapped the towel around her tightly and made her way back to the building she'd been held in. To get her clothes back on and find a way out of there was all she could think about doing.

As she made her way into the building, she was pretty sure she'd been kept in, she saw a small table. On top of it were three syringes filled with some type of drug. She grabbed them and took them with her.

Allen would not be using those to aid him in killing anyone. She quickly found the room she had been in and her clothes were lying in a pile right where she'd been made to take them off.

She pulled them on, but she still had no shoes on as she didn't have any on when Allen took her from her apartment. Making sure to take the syringes with her, she headed out to find a way out of the place.

To be able to see all around, she went and got the ladder from the other building and took it outside. Leaning it up on the side of the building, she climbed up and got on the roof.

A small ledge ran around it and after she emptied the three syringes, she left them up on the roof. After doing that, she looked around and found her only chance of escape was through the water. She'd have to swim around to get out and then it looked like she'd have to walk through some very tall grass to make it to the road which looked pretty desolate.

She climbed down and knew she had to try no matter how hard it looked to be. After a little prayer, she set off towards the water.

46

STEELE

His need for her was obvious as she moved to sit on his lap, facing him as he sat on the leather seat of the Suburban. Arsen's body was quivering and his eye was twitching.

She had no comforting words. There was no way of knowing what was about to happen. They were on their way with the police to his private room at the BDSM club and anything could happen.

She had been upset with him for leaving things out about the beautiful detective, but that didn't matter anymore. Not when Arsen so obviously needed her.

Steele looked into his dark eyes as she slid her body over his hard erection. His eye was twitching, and she placed her finger to it. His hands took her waist, and he lifted her up and down as they looked into each other's eyes.

Arsen was afraid. For the first time, she saw the real fear of his situation coming out in him. She wanted to take it all away for him. Make it all better.

She knew she couldn't actually make anything better, except for that moment in time. For the brief moments before they made it to the club, she could let him know she was with him.

Body, mind, and soul, she belonged to him and always would no matter what the outcome was.

He filled her as she moved up and down his long length. She placed her lips on his and kissed him. It started out gentle then it grew into a hungry, hard kiss.

She felt his urgent need, and she gave him all he wanted of her. She'd give her life for him if need be, she definitely could give her body to comfort him.

Steele took one of his hands and moved it to her breast. He moaned as he squeezed it through the fabric of her dark blue dress.

Arsen had laid the dress out for her to put on after they took a nice, shower that morning, which had been hot in more ways than one. Then he chose a suit which matched the dress perfectly.

She thought how adorable they would look, dressed comparable to one another. Arsen was a true romantic and didn't even realize it.

The night before had been so normal, so down to Earth.

The two had eaten junk food and watched a sappy love story while making out now and again on the sofa. It was a blissful, normal night, and she'd loved it and could tell he did too.

After the day of riding her horse and the night of doing sweet things, she'd found the hard as nails man to be anything but that.

He'd told her he could be himself with her. The man he never knew he wanted to be until he found her.

Steele's body moved over Arsen's hard cock and both were breathing hard. Her dress had buttons closing the top of it and he undid them, pulling one breast from her bra and placing his mouth on it.

He bit the nipple, igniting a groan from her. Then he sucked it hard. His hands bit into her waist as he tightened his grip on her and moved her faster.

She supposed it wasn't enough for him when he lifted her all the way off and placed her on the floor on her hands and knees. He tossed her dress up over her back and began ramming into her from behind.

With hard pants and low moans, she found him pounding into

her. Animalistic in nature and she knew he needed the intensity to help him stop thinking about what might happen. She was his drug to ease the fear, and she was glad to be what he needed.

His body went tense and she could tell he was clenching his teeth as he said, "Come!"

HER BODY DID as he had commanded and his cock pulsed inside her. A loud groan came from him as he let go of all the fear he'd had.

They stayed still until it was all over then he pulled away from her and offered her a handful of tissue to clean up the mess his attention to her had left.

In silence, they cleaned themselves and sat back down on the leather seat. He reached over and buckled her seatbelt.

"Please try to remember I want you to wear this."

Her hand grazed his perfectly manicured bearded cheek, and she said, "I love you, Arsen."

His hand moved over hers and he looked at her.

"I love you."

She saw the tears glistening in his eyes, but they never fell. She knew he wasn't about to let them fall. Holding it all together was what he was trying to do. So she would help him to do that.

"Arsen, I don't want you to think for one second that I'll stop seeking justice for you if they take you in after this. I'll get that little bastard myself and make him confess. I swear it to you."

His smile was sweet when he said, "I let that one slide, Steele."

"My cursing is necessary when talking about Allen White, Arsen." She ran her hand through his hair.

He took her hand and kissed her palm.

"I can see you're very passionate about that. But, I don't want you in harm's way. If they take me in, you have to promise me not to go find Allen. I mean it. The man is more dangerous than you can fathom."

"Arsen, I can't promise you that. I have to do something. I can't just sit back and watch you go down for something you didn't do. I can't..." Her words were stopped by the finger he placed to her lips.

"Paul can take care of it. He has the means to do it and I have faith in him. If they take me, I want you to stay at my apartment. Only go back and forth to school with Paul. Stay safe until I can get free. And come to every meeting they have as part of my legal team. And stay the fuck away from Allen and even Gwen if she's going to be with him." He pushed a lock of her dark hair back and kissed her cheek then whispered, "Promise me."

It was the last thing she wanted to promise. In the end, though she said, "I promise, Arsen." She would do anything for him.

If it meant sitting back and letting Paul do the dirty work, then she'd do it, if that's what Arsen wanted.

She looked out the window as they entered the alley where the entrance to the BDSM club was. Three police cars were there, waiting for them.

Then it was her turn to feel the fear of losing Arsen run through her veins. It left her cold and on the verge of tears.

47

ARSEN

.

The smell of the club fresh in the morning after a night of debauchery had his stomach lurching. Sex and alcohol filled his nostrils and made him fight the urge to turn around and leave the dimly lit place.

Steele was at his side as they led the way into the club and towards his private room. Shadows seemed to be everywhere just outside the lit areas. He had the distinct impression others were hiding away in the dark to witness the fall of the great defense attorney who was Arsen Sloan.

A familiar aroma wafted past him and he turned to see if he could see the person hiding in the dark. If he was able to walk away to look, he was sure he'd find Anne Sinclair.

She made her own perfume, vanilla, lemon, and a touch of whiskey. He was positive she'd come to watch him go down. Or maybe she was going to try to help him.

With that woman, he could never be sure.

As they came down the hallway he thought about what was about to happen to him. It seemed like a march down the corridor to his death sentence.

The back of Steele's hand rested against his and he glanced at her, finding her looking at him. Her eyes told him to have faith. He was trying, but the fear was pressing him and it was taking a toll on him.

His stomach began to ache, and he prayed his old weakness of throwing up when he was upset didn't come back.

He stopped in front of the door to his private room and unlocked it then took Steele's hand in his and stepped back for the detective and the other officers to enter what had been his secret life.

"Can you turn the lights on in here?" Detective Fontaine asked him as she passed in front of him to enter the dark room.

He let Steele's hand go and walked in first, turning the lights up as far as they'd go. It wasn't completely bright as the light was yellow. Arsen stepped back out of the room and into the hallway with Steel and Tanner.

They watched as piece by piece, Arsen's things were taken from the room. Each and every single thing was picked up, placed in plastic bags and spirited away to become evidence in the case against him.

The sound of electric screwdrivers had him peeking in. He found several officers taking the bondage bed apart and others took it out in pieces. In the end, the room was completely empty.

The detective came out last and winked at Arsen.

"What a collection, Arsen. We'll be in touch. Don't leave town." She sashayed away, her skirt moving with each step.

"I hate that woman," Steele whispered.

He ran his arm around her waist and pulled her to his side as Tanner followed the detective and they were the last in line so no one saw them. He kissed the side of her head.

"At least, it looks like I get to go home and that's more than I expected." He made his way out of the club but stopped as an older woman stepped out from behind the door of the coat check room.

"Mr. Sloan. Are you going to wish to continue to pay the rent on that room?"

He shook his head and handed her the key.

"No matter what happens now, I'll never be back here."

She nodded and Arsen and Steele went up the stairs and left the building.

As they climbed into the back of his car Steele looked at him.

"So that's really over for you, Arsen?"

He nodded. "It is."

Arsen found Steele studying him. He placed her seatbelt on and kissed her cheek.

"That had to have been brutally hard, Arsen."

"It was and now it's over. Saved me the work of having it done myself. No big deal, Steele." He sat back and rubbed his temples.

She knew it was a big deal. A really big deal. So much was happening to this man at one time. It wasn't fair, in her opinion.

Her hand ran over his leg.

"We should go to my apartment and see if we can find Allen. This needs to stop. I'm getting worried about your mental state, Arsen."

Arsen pressed the button to roll the window down to the front seat.

"Paul, let's go to Steele's apartment. And do you still have that gun in the glove box?"

"It's there, Boss," Paul answered.

"Good. I'll need your help. Make sure you have it on you and that it's loaded, please." Arsen sat back and ran his arm along the seat behind Steele.

She looked at him with her mouth ajar. "Arsen, you can't kill him!"

He chuckled. "I know that. Just try to relax. It looks as if we're going to have one long-ass day."

Arsen settled back and tried to find the hard man he'd been before Steele came into his life and had him actually giving a shit if he lived or died. If he had freedom or not, and if he could be around to make a new life with her or not.

SEEMS like that man has all but disappeared!

48

GWEN

The water was deeper than she ever expected and she'd been without anything to eat or drink the entire time which she thought might have been a couple of days.

Her body was weak and the constant swimming she was having to do in the frigid water was hard and she was fearing she wouldn't even make it out of the water.

She also found she was going to have to climb up a steep bank once she did get to the water's edge. The odds just kept building up against her.

Something rough brushed the bottom of her leg and she pulled them both up and paddled her arms faster. The idea there were sharks in the water was one she'd pushed back in order to even get into the water.

It spurred her on to move much faster and ignore the weakness in her arms and legs. The edge was much closer, and she found herself at it. She stuck her hands into the mud wall and hoisted her body from the water.

Once all the way out, she paused and looked back to see if she could see anything. The water was deep even at the edge and she moved up even faster as she saw something coming up to the surface at a high rate of speed.

She made it over the edge and fell onto the high, grassy top just as something sprung from the water and fell back, making a splash. She'd not been able to see what it was, but she guessed it must've been a shark.

Gwen lay back on the dry grass and tried to catch her breath. Her heart was beating harder than she thought it ever had in her life.

"If I lived through that, I can live through anything," she said to herself.

But as she laid there, it became harder and harder to make herself get up. Her body was giving out on her. With no food and no water, it was without fuel. Any residual energy it did have was just used up swimming, climbing, and freaking out about being eaten alive by a shark.

Her eyes closed.

"I just have to rest for a little while. Just a little while," she muttered to herself as she fell asleep.

49

STEELE

As they looked all over the apartment, it became obvious Gwen had not been back at home. The blanket was still gone and her phone still right where Steele had left it.

"He's taken her, hasn't he?" Steele asked Arsen.

"We need to report her missing." Arsen took his cell out and handed it to Steele. "Call 911 and tell them your roommate is missing and you believe a parolee named Allen White may have taken her."

Steele's hand was shaking as she took the phone.

"What did I get her into, Arsen?"

"Don't blame yourself. This is entirely my fault. Make the call while I find myself something to drink." He walked away, leaving Steel alone in Gwen's bedroom.

After making the call, she found Arsen in the living room. He'd had to go out to his car to get a bottle of Scotch and had it on the table in front of him. A small glass of the amber liquid was in his shaking hand.

She sat down next to him.

"They're sending out an officer." She bit her bottom lip. "Arsen, where could he have taken her?"

He shook his head.

"There's no way of knowing. I can't believe we were right here in this tiny-ass apartment when he took her and we didn't hear a thing."

The ice rattled in the glass as he lifted it to take a drink. Steele placed her hand on his leg. He was tapping his foot incessantly.

"Arsen, you need to try to calm down, Baby."

"This is all my fault. I brought all this into your normal life and now your innocent roommate may be dead or ever worse than that. This is what I've done to your life, Steele. I should've left you alone that night. I could've gone home, but I waited for you." His dark eyes were drooping at the corners as he looked at her. "I'm so sorry."

She shook her head. "Don't! Don't do that! You're the best thing that's ever happened to me, Arsen!"

With a roll of his eyes, he said, "I am the worst thing that's ever happened to you. One day you'll look back at this time in your young life and think what a nightmare it was and how lucky you are I got sent to prison and out of your life." He took a long drink.

Steele stood up and wagged her finger in his face.

"Stop that! I will never look back and be thankful if you're taken from my life. Not ever! Please don't even think like that. Now I guess I need to point out that we now have another person of interest to get the police on."

He laughed.

"They're not going to think Allen killed those women. Not just because he might have kidnapped your roommate. That doesn't make any sense. Sorry to let you know that. But it's true." Arsen took the last gulp of his drink and sat the glass down.

A knock came at the door and Steele went to open it. A small, male officer was at it. He smiled at her like he was there for something nice instead of horrible. "Good afternoon, Miss Gannon. I heard you're missing a roomie."

"Gwen was kidnapped by a man who should've never been released from prison. Allen White is the man's name. Your department should know where you can find him. I suggest you get on that." Steele led him into the living room.

His eyes went to Arsen. He smiled. "Hey, I saw you earlier. That's some stuff you had in that room." He looked back and forth between the two and his gaze ended on Steele. "You let him do that to you?"

Arsen cleared his throat.

"Please don't do this right now. Her roommate, who is also her best friend, is in more danger than you can imagine. We need your help."

The officer looked a little apologetic.

"Yeah, sorry. Um, where did you see her last?"

Arsen went over and placed a hand on the small man's shoulder. He made the officer look like a dwarf next to his tall and large frame.

"I'm going to need you to take out your pen and notepad and write these things down. This is a serious matter and I need you to treat it as such."

Steele looked at Arsen and saw his body and mind were worn out. She went to his side and ran her arm around his waist.

"Sit down, Baby. I'll make sure he does the right thing. You rest. It's been a terrible day for you." She took him to sit back down and poured him another glass of Scotch. "Drink this and relax. If you see I'm not giving him enough information, then you can chime in."

He took a sip and gave her a nod.

"I'll be right here, Baby. I'm sorry. I really am."

The officer had his pen and pad out and asked.

"Who saw her last?"

"I DID," Steele said. "Arsen and I spent the night here and had met her new boyfriend. He's an old client of Arsen's. Arsen lost his case, and he went to prison but managed to get paroled. And I want you to take this down as well. It's extremely possible Allen White murdered the women Arsen is being charged with."

The officer's brown eyes went wide.

"What?"

Steele nodded and Arsen sighed. Arsen said, "Just worry about finding the young woman for now. Don't let anything else get into your head, except finding her before it's too late. He's not a quick killer. He takes his time. There's still a chance she's alive somewhere. Please tell me someone has some type of tracking device on him or his car."

"I'll find out." The officer walked towards the door. "I'm going out to the car to call in some more officers to help with this. Just sit tight folks. This is probably going to take some time." He left them alone and Steele went to sit by him.

"You know this is out in the open now? This thing you and I have." She leaned her head on his shoulder.

He nodded and kissed the top of her head.

"So be it. I don't think we were really fooling anyone, anyway." His arm wrapped around her, holding her tight to him. "I love you and I never meant to hurt you, Baby. Seems no matter what, I'm doomed to hurt women."

"You are not. Stop beating yourself up." Steele stayed in his arms as the officer came back in.

"We're going to need you to go to the station and give us your fingerprints, Steele. We already have Arsen's and Allen's on file. I assume you both have been in her room and touched some things?" he asked.

They both nodded.

The officer gave them a weak smile. "Okay, then. After we make the calls to her family to be sure she's not with any of them, we're going to get all we can from here. You'll have to stay somewhere else in the meantime, Miss Gannon. But we'll need to know where that is. I need you to understand that along with Allen White, you both are persons of interest in this case. No leaving town."

Steele sighed and took Arsen's hand.

"So, off to the police station we go and I'll leave all my information there. I'll be at his address if you find out anything."

The officer gave them a wave.

"Get down there and we'll get working on this right away."

Arsen took Steele and led her away from the apartment. She looked back as she got into the back of his Suburban. Part of her knew if she'd never gotten into the car she was getting in now, this would not be happening.

As Arsen got in next to her she found herself falling into his chest and sobbing. "I don't know what I'll do if he's killed her, Arsen!"

"Shh." He held her tight to him. "Don't think like that. Just have faith she's going to be alright. We have to keep thinking positive."

PLEASE LET *them find her in time!*

50

ARSEN

I t seemed like time was always against them. It took hours for Steele to be fingerprinted at the police station. And then the two found themselves waiting to talk to Detective Fontaine.

She'd been assigned to this case as well. Something which Arsen knew was pissing Steele off.

"Does no one else work here?" she asked as they sat in little chairs on the other side of her little desk in the little room they'd been placed in.

Arsen patted her leg.

"Maybe this is for the best."

The door opened and in came the detective.

"My, oh my! So nice to see the two of you again. Imagine my surprise when I heard Arsen was staying at the apartment the night that a young woman went missing. Well, I was flabbergasted. Then I see he had an alibi as he was in your bed, Miss Gannon. And here I thought you were just his assistant. You assist him in many ways, don't you, Dear?"

"There's no reason to act that way, Fontaine," Arsen said as he ran his arm around Steele's shoulders. "This poor girl is going through hell. Let's try to be professional, shall we?"

She made a little huffing sound then gestured to them and said, "How long has this been going on?"

Arsen answered, "We met the night before I found out this one was part of my legal team."

"And you swept her off her little, young, innocent, and very vanilla feet, didn't you, Arsen?" The detective sat back in her chair and watched the couple as they held onto each other. "You seem very close now. Not so much this morning. But now, you two look like you actually love one another."

Steele wasn't even looking up. So not like her to take this woman's crap and Arsen felt he was the reason for that.

"Please try to remain professional, Fontaine."

"Do you two have a contract?" Her words had Steele looking up.

Arsen tightened his hold on her. It was he who answered.

"No."

He prayed Steele would not tell what she considered to be the truth. Their contract was no more real than Santa Clause. He never meant it to be real and was just waiting for her to say she didn't want it any longer and he'd tear it up.

Now the damn thing might really be a problem, fake or not.

Steele asked, "What would it matter if we did?"

Fontaine's eyebrows went up.

"The man you're all hugged up on might be a killer of his submissive partners, Miss Gannon. It wouldn't be in your best interest to get into that with him. Nor in his best interest to get involved with anyone in that way. At least not until this is all figured out."

"He's innocent," Steele said as she glared into the detective's eyes. "I need you to stop fucking around with us and find my friend. Can you just do that, please?"

"You forget that you two could've been the ones who have her or have killed her. I need to know what kind of things have been going on. Did you guys ever have like some threesome with Gwen or foursome with her and Allen White?" The detective smiled at Steele.

Arsen ran his hand over his face as he felt Steele's body go tense. He tried to hold her down as she stood up.

"Now you listen to me, you fucking bitch. I do not like you, not one fucking bit. The fact you came onto the man I love is a thing that has me wanting to beat the shit out of you. So, now you know that he and I are together, I better not even see you wink at him or I'll tear you a new one."

"Physical threats?" Detective Fontaine asked with a wink.

STEELE PLACED her hands on the desk and leaned in close. Her tone was low and even as she said, "Physical promises, bitch. We're leaving and you need to go find my friend. My boy here is a very good lawyer and if she's found dead because you were fucking around with us so you could get your rocks off on our sex life, it's you who'll be sorry."

Arsen got up and ran his arm around Steele's waist, picking her feet up off the ground.

"She can be a real Pitbull, Fontaine. Do yourself a favor and find her friend and don't ask us about what it is we do anymore. You know where we'll both be. Let us know the moment that you find Gwen."

HE TOOK Steele out of the room and placed her on her feet once he shut the door between the two women.

"I hate her," Steele said under her breath.

"Really? I could not tell that," Arsen said with a sarcastic tone.

Leading her out of the police station he took her to where Paul was waiting by his car.

"You guys ready to go home?" he asked as Steele got in.

Arsen gave him a nod.

"Please, Paul."

Please don't let anything else go wrong today!

51

STEELE

In a tub full of hot water, Steele leaned her back against Arsen's muscled chest. He took a glass of red wine and placed it to her lips. She sipped it then he took a sip and set it back down.

"It feels good having it all out there. I'm relieved." Arsen ran his hands through her hair. He'd washed it and conditioned it and she was feeling much more relaxed after his pampering.

She rolled over in his arms and placed her lips on his. Then looked at him. "Are you really glad? I mean this is a lot for you now. A real girlfriend and a real relationship on top of all the other crap. You think it's what you really want?"

He pulled her over him, and she found his hard-on pressing to her.

"Want a ride?" He smiled.

She slipped over him and slid down his long shaft. She moaned as he filled her.

"That feels amazing."

He kissed the tip of her nose.

"To answer your question. It is what I really want, Baby. I've never wanted anything more."

He lifted her and set the pace. Her body moved up and down on him easily in the deep water of the large bath tub. Their wet bodies slid against each other's and she twisted her hands into his hair which had grown nearly to his shoulders.

Arsen took her breast into his large hands and squeezed them, stroking both nipples with his thumbs. Steele moaned with the sensation.

Moving up and down him with an urgency she was startled when he stopped her. His hands on her shoulders. Holding her still. His dark eyes she found looking at her when she opened hers.

"You don't come until I tell you to." He pulled her mouth to his and moved his hands off her shoulders and fisted both hands with locks of her long hair.

He kissed her hard, his tongue running all over her mouth. She suddenly felt her body reaching the point she knew she had to wait for. His kiss was taking her over the edge just like his dick was as it filled her over and over.

She was falling over the edge and she couldn't stop it. Steele tried not to let him know she'd climaxed. The moan which threatened, she managed to keep in and she thought she'd gotten away with it when he pulled his mouth back from hers.

He shook his head slowly.

"Naughty girl. What did I tell you to do?"

Her eyes were wide.

"I couldn't help it."

"Get out of the tub," he ordered her.

"Arsen!"

"Do as I've said." He let her go, and she got up and out of the tub.

"What are you going to do?" She grabbed a towel and wrapped it around herself.

With no emotion in his handsome face, he said, "Take that towel off and go lean over the side of the bed and wait there for me. You seem to need reminding of a thing or two."

Steele gave him a look but his eyes were dark and she dropped hers and went to do as he'd told her to. As she leaned over the bed she found her stomach tensing.

Is he really going to spank me?

WITH HER HEAD laid on the bed, Steele saw him walk out of the bathroom with a white towel hung around his waist. His chiseled abs moved with each step he took towards her.

He stopped at the closet and pulled a leather belt out of it and bent it in half. She found her heart beating hard in her chest. Moving past her, she heard the drawer opening and then felt something soft being pulled across the skin on her back.

Her eyes were covered then with the soft material and he moved her hands up over her head. He wrapped something around them, binding them together.

His hands ran over her ass. Her body went hot in an instant. The leather of the belt she felt moving down her back then over one ass cheek.

She bit he lower lip as she waited for the first strike. Instead she felt him lean over her and grab her by the hair, pulling her head up. His body was against her back, his lips near her ear.

"Are you to come whenever you want when I tell you to wait for my command?"

"No," she whispered.

A little bite he gave her neck.

"What?"

"No Sir," she said as she blew out a breath.

The bite had her body tingling. She had no real idea of what he'd do, but somehow, she trusted him not to hurt her.

She felt the leather moving between her legs. It was soft and supple as he raked it over her clit.

"You want to come again, Baby?"

A low moan came from her as her answer. He leaned over her again. His mouth touched her ear.

"I'm going to use something else this time. See if you can figure out what it is."

Her mind went blank.

"Arsen! What is it?" Her words came out in a shriek.

The deep sound of his laugh had her trying to get up, and he grabbed her and flipped her over on her back and hoisted her up. Her bound hands were placed over the bedpost, keeping her in place.

"Don't you trust me, Steele?" The leather belt ran over her stomach.

She shivered.

"Yes."

"Good. You do remember that I love you." The belt ran down her stomach and he laid it over her sex, leaving it on her.

The cool leather rested against her clit. The constant lightweight of it had her throbbing for more. Then a humming sound filled her ears. The smell of cherries filled the air and then a warm, moist vibrating thing touched the opening of her vagina.

Arsen pushed her legs further apart. Then pushed the thing into her. It vibrated parts of her she didn't realize would even like that. She felt him move his body next to hers.

He turned her face to his and kissed her as his other hand moved the vibrator in and out of her. It was an odd feeling. Like she was kissing one person and letting another fuck her.

She never thought about such a thing and found herself extremely aroused. His tongue stroked hers as his other hand moved down and rubbed the leather over her clit.

It was amazing. He pulled his mouth away.

"Do not come until I tell you to."

She moaned a little, and he kissed her again. His mouth was wet and hot and the way he kissed was amazing. She could really focus on how his mouth blended with hers.

His tongue ran over her teeth. Something happened, and the

vibration went faster. He pumped it faster and took the belt away to use his finger to stimulate her clit.

She had to focus on his kiss to stop herself from climaxing. Her legs were shaking from the need to release. When he finally pulled the vibrating thing out of her, he placed the wide tip right on her clit and she knew she couldn't hold back much longer.

He moved his body over hers as he continued to kiss her. Her head moved along with him and when he pushed himself into her she arched up to meet him, desperate to let it out.

Arsen didn't make even one stroke. He stayed perfectly still then pulled his mouth away. "Come."

HER BODY CRASHED around his and he groaned along with her as her body pulsed around his cock. "Fuck, that's amazing, Baby!"

He pressed into her as deep as he could go then pulled out and slammed back into her. Steele's body was shaking as he began his assault on her. Slamming into her hard and fast.

It felt as if a Wild-man was on her. After repeated, hard thrusts he suddenly pulled out of her and took her bound hands from the bedpost.

She was jostled around as he moved her. He took her by the ankles and moved up with them until her heels were by her ears and she felt him press his hard cock into her again.

He took her bound hands and placed them over his head and around his neck. Then he moved them both as he seemed to be sitting back on his feet.

He began lifting her body, making her stroke him. She was amazed as he lifted her over and over. She had to say something as she was just too stunned. "Wow! You're really strong, Arsen!"

His words came out a little strained as he was exerting himself.

"Uh, huh. And no coming until I say."

"Of course, sir," she said with a little giggle. "I wouldn't dream of it."

"And no talking. You're distracting me."

In their position, their mouths couldn't reach the others to kiss so her mind wandered to what they must look like. A human pretzel was what she came up with.

THE WAY his muscles felt around her body had her mesmerized. The sight deprivation let her hear everything. The little sloshing sounds their connected bodies made was kind of sexy and she found that along with the muscles moving around her and the little pumps he was making inside her too much.

Her body was about to let go and she had no idea how she was going to control that in the crazy position. So she resorted to the old Kegel trick and in no time Arsen was telling her to come as he climaxed.

As they caught their breath, Arsen began to untangle their bodies. He laid her back, removed her arms from his neck and let her legs go back down.

"You're very supple. Not everyone can do that position." He kissed her forehead and put her bound hands back over the bed post.

"More?" she asked. "And I didn't have any real choice in getting into that position. You kind of pretzeled me into it."

His lips pressed against her clit and she arched up as it was still pulsing and tender to the touch. The mere touch was about to set her off again.

"Of course more, Baby. You pulled your trick on me and I have to get you back." The sound of the vibrator filled the air, and it was on her.

He moved it over her as it warmed up and vibrated her entire sex. She moaned and wiggled.

"Oh my God, Baby! Can I at least come when I want?"

"Hell, no! What kind of relationship do you think this is?" He leaned over and took one of her tits in his mouth. Licking it constantly.

She was writhing trying to hold it back. Her voice was shaking as the vibrator had her whole body vibrating. "But you love me, Arsen!"

His hot mouth moved off her tit, and he trailed gentle kisses over her chest and along her neck. Then his voice spread warmth over her as he said.

"I do love you, now come for me, Baby."

Steele moaned loudly as she fell apart and the sound of the vibrator stopped, but the buzzing feeling in her didn't.

He pulled her hands down and let them out of the bind then rubbed her wrists then her shoulders. Then he took the blindfold off and kissed her cheek.

With a smile, he said, "You do remember our safe word, don't you, Baby?"

She nodded and ran her hand over his cheek.

"I knew I could've used it, but you didn't hurt me."

"I never want to hurt you. You need to always tell me if I do and I'll stop. To excite you is all I want. To love you is my only priority." His fingers ran over her lips and he leaned up on his elbow with his head propped on his palm so he could look down at her.

HER HEART ACHED with how beautiful she thought he was. The man was changing right in front of her eyes and she wished liked hell it could just be like any other normal relationship without the constant threat of prison or any of the other things she felt hanging over their heads.

The truth was his ways did excite her. Even as he ordered her to get out of the tub and wait for him, she felt little fear he was actually going to hurt her. There was a part of her who loved it.

His changes were making him into a man who would be perfect for her and now that their relationship was out in the open everything would be great. If only they weren't being implicated in the disappearance of Gwen, and the murders Arsen was still being considered for.

Arsen laid back with his strong arm around her.

"Good night, Baby. Try not to think about a thing. Worry never solved anything. If you wake up and feel upset or have any bad feelings, wake me up and we can deal with them together. You're not alone, ever. I want you to know that. I'm here for you."

"The same goes for you, my sweet man. I'm here for you."

He chuckled. "Sweet. I don't know if I'll ever get used to that word being used about me."

"Go to sleep, Arsen." She ran her hand up to hold his bicep.

His strong arms made her feel safe, and she loved how they felt around her. Just before she fell asleep, one thought ran through her head.

Please let them find Gwen alive!

52

GWEN

Distant voices woke Gwen up. It was dark out and she was confused at where she was exactly. She listened to try to hear what the people were saying.

A woman's voice she could hear saying, "You idiot! No one told you to take that girl. Now you have the cops looking for you. You're going to have to ditch that car. They'll find evidence you took her and then you'll be back in prison before you know it."

Gwen stayed perfectly still. She remembered what had happened. She'd gotten away. Somewhat anyway. At least she was on the other side of the fence and they couldn't get to her.

Allen's voice was a bit high as he said, "I can't go back. Anne, you have to help me. This was all your idea. To get back at Arsen. The girl was a mistake. I admit that."

"Look, you dimwit," she heard Anne say. "This is getting much too complicated and Arsen will not get what he deserves if I don't step in and completely take charge. So, first things first. You have to be punished for this. Get back inside while I figure out how to deal with you. Strip and put your hands against the wall and wait for me. However long that takes, your ass better be waiting just like I said or the punishment will be ten times worse. Arsen can tell you about not doing as I say. His body still bears the scars of disobeying me."

Gwen's heart went to her throat as she realized the woman must have been the big and powerful Arsen's master at one time.

I have to get to Steele and Arsen before it's too late for us all!

53

PART TEN: FOR EVER

GWEN

Cold night air had goose bumps covering her skin which felt every little prick of the brittle, dry, tall grass she crawled on her belly through. Gwen kept picturing herself as a military hero in a jungle somewhere.

Anything she could do to take her mind off the way her body was shutting down was what she was doing to get to help.

Haunting sounds of Allen's cries as Anne whipped him with something moved through the night air. They seemed so far away and Gwen almost felt sorry for the psychotic bastard who'd kidnapped her.

She had to keep reminding herself that she had a mission. Her body would refuse to move at times and she'd have to stop and rest for a while. Each time she did that meant she was losing precious time.

Anne and Allen had their own mission. To ruin Arsen and kill Steele. Gwen had to make it to someone to get her to the police before it was too late.

.   .   .

IF I CAN MAKE it to the road without dying myself!

54

ARSEN

Steele slept fitfully in his arms, keeping him from sleep. Not that he could with all which was happening. The light from his phone caught his attention as he lay there in the dark, listening to Steele's mumbles as she talked in her sleep.

He reached over to pick up the phone on the nightstand beside his bed to find a text. The number was odd, all sevens. He hesitated before opening it to read it.

With a swipe of his forefinger it was open, and it said

-We need to meet, you and I. Dawn in front of your apartment. I'll be waiting in a blue Camaro.-

ARSEN PLACED the phone back on the table and then he was really awake. Dawn was a mere three hours away.

His mind was racing with who it could be and if they could help him out of his current situations. Any of them.

Arsen's problems seemed to keep building. Like all things which build up too high, he had hopes of everything crashing, but not down on him.

He held the love of his life in his arms. Never had he known love like he knew for Steele. Not even his first love had been so complete.

Finally, a real future with a wife and kids stood before him. Only a tall fence with sharp, pointed tops stood between him and that future. He had to climb that fence to get to the other side, and it felt as if led weights had been placed around his ankles, keeping him from doing it.

He lay his head back and closed his eyes as he thought about what he wanted for Steele and himself. A nice mansion with a swimming pool for their children. It would have to have some acreage with it and a barn for her horse and the many other animals they'd get.

Arsen wanted it all. The picture perfect life of a normal couple with a normal life. His heart wanted it so bad it ached.

Right after Steele had fallen asleep, Arsen had gotten up and went to his office. He got on his computer and made a purchase he hoped would be the beginning of the real thing for him and Steele.

Even though so much was happening, he wanted one constant, one thing in his control to help him get through that horrible time.

To have a plan and start moving towards his ultimate goal was a thing he needed and wanted. He just hoped Steele did to.

She grumbled about something and rolled away from him. He reached over and pulled her back to him as she was close to the edge of the bed and he was afraid she'd fall off with her constant dreams or nightmares. He wasn't sure which.

Her long, dark hair had wrapped around her and he gently tugged it out from underneath her and brushed it back from her face. Arsen could look at her face forever and he planned to do just that.

His mind wandered to his past. Anne had taken him in when he was in his first year at Stanford University. Not sure what he was going to be at that time. He only knew he wanted to be something which had to do with the law.

Arsen wanted to prove to himself he could make something out of himself. He hadn't seen Anne since she'd left him at the emergency room, just a few months before he turned eighteen.

He lived out of the old Chevy Cobalt he'd earned enough money while living in the foster home to buy. Working at the closest fast food place to the house he'd been sent to, he walked to it each day after school and worked until near dawn.

Arsen knew he had a limited amount of time with that roof over his head and he made good use of that time. The car had cost him two thousand dollars, and it got him around once he was out of high school and out of the foster home.

He went to the small, local college and applied for the financial aid he'd need to go to college. The two years in the small college had him in a dorm room with a party crowd.

Arsen knew he couldn't get sidetracked by the other young men. He slept most times in his small car in the student parking lot of the dorms. The other guys always seemed to have girls in their beds with them and Arsen wanted nothing to do with sex at that time.

Sex equaled pain in his memory. He wanted none of either. His heart was still mending from the rejection his first love gave him.

Thanks to staying out of trouble, Arsen made excellent grades and was accepted to Stanford University after completing his Associate's Degree at the small junior college.

On his first day there, after a horrific day of trying to get to all his classes and get settled in, he went to a small bar to get a drink after the tough day. That's where he saw Beth's mother.

SHE WAS TALL, thin, and had long blonde hair. Mrs. Sinclair was not wearing her normal clothing, though. Her heels were tall and her dress was short. Minuscule.

The top of her shirt plunged all the way down to her pierced bellybutton. And Arsen found his mouth watering for the older woman who resembled the love he'd lost in her daughter.

He was too shy to go to her though. Arsen sat at the back of the small bar at a table alone in a darkened corner. He watched as his ex-girlfriend's mother made some phone calls while she sat at the bar. She seemed to be waiting for someone.

That someone finally joined her. Another tall woman, wearing all leather. Her shiny boots had high heels on them and her short, blond hair was in tight curls under a leather cap.

Arsen watched with great interest as the two had another drink and talked as they sat on stools at the bar. Then Mrs. Sinclair got up and made her way to the ladies' room. Which was behind Arsen.

His ability to breathe ceased, and he sat perfectly still, trying to become invisible as she walked towards him. Her boobs bounced, and he knew there was nothing between them and the barely covering top she wore.

Her light blue eyes moved to him and after a moment they lit up. She stopped dead in her tracks.

"Arsen Sloan! Is that you?"

He nodded slowly, unsure of how she was going to act. She was caught, busted by him. This was not the Mrs. Sinclair he, nor her husband and daughter knew. This woman was into some tough shit and he knew it by the way she was dressed and made up.

"Wait here," she directed him as she went to the restroom.

He fidgeted in his seat. Arsen felt like running out of that bar as fast as his feet could take him. But he was paralyzed for some reason. The woman had him wondering about her.

ARSEN KNEW Beth's mother was twenty years older than him. He was twenty-one, making her forty-one, but she didn't look old at all. Not one wrinkle. Not one ounce of fat. Not a trace of gray in her long, silky, blonde hair.

Her hand grazed his shoulder as she came back to him.

"Arsen, how have you been, darling." Her lips touched his cheek and sent chills through him.

"Fine, Mrs. Sinclair." He tensed and butterflies filled his stomach.

Arsen was a skinny thing back then. He'd not yet begun to do his strenuous work outs. It was she who had him start that.

His dark hair was cut short, and he wore a black T-shirt and blue jeans with Nike running shoes. Not quite the polished man he became.

She took the chair on the other side of the table and looked him over. Her hand rose into the air and her friend came over. She smiled up at the woman close to her age.

"This is Arsen, Sheila. What do you think about him?"

Sheila gave a nod.

"He's got potential, I'd say."

ARSEN GULPED. He felt on display or for sale or something. He looked down at the empty glass of rum and coke in his hand which was nearly trembling.

Mrs. Sinclair leaned forward and put her elbows on the table, resting her chin in her hands. Her fingernails were long and painted shiny black. Her eyeliner was dark black too, making her light blue eyes pop.

The other woman's eyes were dark brown and her eyes were lined with a dark green liner. She was attractive in a scary sort of way. Her lips were deep red and so were Mrs. Sinclair's.

The two woman gave off a vibe of sexy fear and Arsen wasn't immune to it. He was nervous though.

Mrs. Sinclair's breasts were about to pop out of her tight dress as she leaned forward and reached out to touch the top of his hand which was nervously running around the edge of his empty glass.

"Shelia's apartment is only a few blocks away, Arsen. She and I were going to go out, but since we found you, we'd like to take you back to her place. How does that sound?" Mrs. Sinclair winked at him, making him extremely uneasy.

His voice was shaky.

"For what?"

Her dark red lips curled into a smile and the other woman who stood next to him placed her hand on his shoulder. Arsen looked up at her as she said, "We want to fuck you, Arsen."

With the eloquent statement, he sat back and looked at both of the women with confusion riddling his expression.

"Why?" he asked.

Mrs. Sinclair laughed.

"You're attractive and young. I assume you can fuck for days with your youth. It's Friday night. I would guess you're free for the weekend. We can have so much fun together, the three of us."

Knots had formed in his stomach and Shelia gave him a wink.

"I'm going to go and get you a drink to help you decide. It looks like you need to loosen up a bit."

With her exit, Mrs. Sinclair got up and moved around to where he sat. She tugged the chair he was in back a bit and settled on his lap...

"Arsen, tell me, do you not find me attractive at all?"

He nodded.

"You look different than you ever did when Beth and I..."

Her finger stopped him as she placed it to his lips.

"No mention of her, please. Nor her father. They believe I'm on a weekend retreat with my church group."

His eyes widened.

"Church? Yeah, I remember you were all about church."

She laughed and her mouth touched his ear.

"I may have lied a little about that, Arsen. The things which take me away from my little family are not quite as holy as I've made them out to be. As a matter of fact, they are anything but holy. I hope you decide to take us up on our offer. We have many toys that are sure to excite you. And Sheila really likes to be spanked if you know what I mean."

He shook his head.

"I have no clue what the hell you're talking about, Mrs. Sinclair."

She moaned and ran her pointed, black fingernail across his

smooth cheek. Then pulled her bottom lip between her perfectly white teeth.

"Ummm. I like the way you say that, Arsen. Say it again. But instead of Mrs. I want you to call me Mistress Sinclair."

"Mistress Sinclair?" he asked as his brows furrowed.

Her body melted into his as she ran her arms around him and laid her head on his shoulder.

"The sound of you saying that has just left me wet."

Her hand took his and moved it under her short skirt. She pressed his fingertips to the edge of her vagina and then pushed two of them inside her panty-less pussy.

Arsen's eyes went wide and his dick sprung to life in his jeans. A fact Mrs. Sinclair who sat on his lap noticed immediately. With a smile, she pumped his fingers inside her as they sat there in the darkened corner of the little bar.

She pumped them as he watched her in complete shock. He felt her wet heated flesh just inside her vagina gripping his fingers as she moaned and more wetness flowed around his fingers.

"You made me come, you naughty boy," she moaned in his ear.

She pulled his fingers out of her and he watched as she placed them in her mouth and sucked the juices off them. His dick went even harder when she got up and kept his hand in hers, leading him to the ladies' room just behind them. He followed like a puppy.

More like a lamb to the slaughter!

ARSEN SHOOK his head as he stopped thinking about that first time with her. Steele struggled in her dream and her wiggling had taken his attention from the memory.

As he looked at her he felt awful for holding her in his arms and recalling the first night with Anne Sinclair. The first night of many he and she shared from then on with him being her submissive partner. A thing he was just beginning to realize wasn't something he actively agreed to at all.

Back to his memory he went. Recalling what Mistress Sinclair did to him in that ladies' room in the back of that small bar that fateful night.

The lights in the small bathroom were bright as hell, he recalled. The bar had been so dark it made Arsen's eyes squint when she pulled him into the tiny bathroom.

She closed the door behind them and locked it, pressing her body up against his as she did. His dick was hard and when her mouth fell on his, he ran his arms around her.

Something inside him was hungry for her though he couldn't explain to himself why that was.

This was his only love's mother for the love of all which is holy was what he was thinking as her tongue moved over his. Her hands were expertly unbuttoning and unzipping his jeans and his cock was in her hand before he realized it.

She jerked it up and down and he groaned with the sensation. She took a few steps back and sat on the edge of the vanity. Her short as hell skirt pulled up and her crotch ready for him.

From a small pocket at the front of her skirt she pulled out a foil packet and ripped it open with her teeth, spitting out the little bit of foil which got into her mouth.

Arsen watched silently as she placed it over his hard dick. Then looked up at him.

"I want you to fuck me now."

His heart was pounding as he knew what he was about to do was more than wrong. In so many ways it was wrong. If Beth ever found out, it would horrify her. If Mr. Sinclair ever found out, it could well be the end of him. If he beat him nearly to death over his daughter what would he do to him over fucking his wife?

But Arsen's dick was ruling his head, and he pressed himself into her as she sat on the top of that small vanity. She was wet and hot and her nails dug into his back as he pushed deep inside her.

"Fuck! You're huge, Arsen!" Her legs moved to encircle him around his waist. "Lift me up and fuck me."

He lifted her off the vanity but it was too much of a struggle to hold her up and make any type of strokes. His dick wanted more and messing around like that wasn't going to cut it.

The floor was where he placed her then he went to work, stroking in and out of her as his breathing changed into something which sounded like he was having a panic attack.

Arsen's body quivered as he all too soon came and he groaned with the climax. Only Mrs. Sinclair was not groaning. Her face wore a frown.

"That's it?"

He looked down at her once he opened his eyes.

"What?"

"That's it?" she asked then pushed him off her. "That's not nearly enough. I'm taking you back to Shelia's. That's not enough for me. When's the last time you had sex, Arsen? Shit!"

Arsen stood up and took the condom off, tossing it in the trash. He placed himself back into his jeans, zipping and buttoning them back up.

"Beth."

Her eyebrows went way up.

"That was nearly four years ago!"

He nodded and washed his hands.

"Yep."

She grabbed his wet hand before he could dry them.

"You're coming with us. We can fix you up where you can make more than five strokes into a pussy before coming, Arsen."

His head was fuzzy from the ejaculation and the one drink he'd had. Sheila was waiting patiently at the table as they came out. Mrs. Sinclair was shaking her head at the other woman.

"We have us as close to a virgin here as you can get without having an actual virgin."

Sheila smiled.

"Did you get him to agree?"

.   .   .

MRS. SINCLAIR GRABBED the shot glass full of a dark colored liquor and handed it to Arsen.

"Drink this." Her tone was commanding, and he tossed it down his throat without even asking what it was. "We're taking him. He'll want what we have to offer. He may not know it yet, but he will soon."

Arsen looked back and forth between the two of them.

"Both of you?"

They nodded, and he shook his head.

"I don't know. You just said I came too quick. How can I possibly...."

He was jerked by Mrs. Sinclair as they began to leave the bar.

"Don't worry, we'll show you how you can. When's the last time you ate some pussy, Arsen?"

He gulped.

"Never."

The women laughed, and it sounded a little evil to his ears.

Shelia's hand gripped his ass as she walked behind him.

"Hope you're hungry boy."

THE WOMEN WALKED some three blocks until they came to an old apartment building. The small apartment smelled like men's cologne and leather. There was one sofa in the middle of the small living room.

Mrs. Sinclair pulled him right past that and into a small bedroom. A king size bed and one chair were all that was in it. His eyes roamed around and he found a door knob had been screwed into the wall and next to it hung a small whip and a pair of silver handcuffs. The keys to it dangled from one of the locks.

A sign hung over the bed. It was just one word written in thick black marker. 'PEACHES' had him wondering what the hell that was about.

Mrs. Sinclair reached into a closet and pulled out an odd looking leather thing. She handed it to him. Go put this on and nothing else, Arsen.

He held it out and noticed his ass and dick would be ready to go, but the leather would cover the front portion of his legs.

"Are these what the cowboys in the old days wore?"

She nodded. "Nowadays men who are into a unique sex life wear them. I intend to take you into that way with me, Arsen. Tonight will be your first lesson."

Mrs. Sinclair smacked his ass and pointed to the attached bathroom. He went inside and looked at himself in the mirror.

"What are you doing, man?" he asked himself.

He washed his face and felt the effects of the shot taking him over. Changing into the chaps had him feeling ridiculous. He turned to look at his exposed, skinny ass cheeks in the mirror and his face heated with a blush.

Turning back, he found his dick visible, dangling between his legs and shook his head.

"I can't go out there like this."

THE DOOR OPENED and Mrs. Sinclair was holding out another shot of something to him.

"Drink this."

"I don't know about all this, Mrs. Sinclair."

Her hand moved over his cheek, softly.

"Just take the drink and lets us teach you all you'll ever need to know about pleasing a woman."

Arsen took the drink as he thought about gaining some knowledge about sex. He was twenty-one after all with no real idea about it. And from what he'd just done with Mrs. Sinclair in that bar's bathroom, he knew he was sorely lacking in that department.

But something inside him wanted more than just to learn about sex with some older women.

"I think you should only do that with someone you love, Mrs. Sinclair."

She laughed and took his hand, pulling him out of the bathroom.

His eyes quickly went to the woman strung up on the wall, facing him.

"I want you to eat Shelia out and make her orgasm. After that, you can tell me if you didn't enjoy it." She got behind him and pushed him towards the smiling woman.

"What if I don't?" he asked as he looked over the woman who was naked and handcuffed, hanging from the knob on the wall. Her blonde curls pressed to it, making them bunch around her face. "Will you let me leave then?"

"I will allow you to leave only after we have fixed that early ejaculation problem you have. Now do as I say." Mrs. Sinclair pulled the chair up and sat down on it close to the side of Sheila. "Kneel in front of her, Arsen."

He shook his head and took a deep breath. Then he did as she told him to.

"I guess I just kiss it like I would a mouth?" He looked at the woman he'd only known as a housewife and mother and a supposedly Christian woman.

How wrong I had been!

She tasted like salt. His first impression of his mouth on the woman wasn't a thing he found pleasant, but his damn dick did. It sprang to attention within seconds of his mouth pressing to her.

Mrs. Sinclair's voice was low and controlled as she told him what to do. "Use your tongue and run it over her clit."

He pulled back. "Where is that?"

She gave a heavy sigh. Reaching out, she pulled back Sheila's folds and touched her clit, making Sheila let out a moan. Mrs. Sinclair arched her brows. "See how quickly that affected her?"

He nodded.

"Yeah."

"Okay, then" she stuck her tongue out and made it into a point on the end and wiggled it. "Do that with your tongue over that little bud."

He practiced a second, and she frowned.

"Not good?" he asked.

She leaned over a lot more and said, "Watch me, Arsen."

HE LEANED back a little and watched as she placed her pointed tongue on the other woman's body and his dick went even harder. He was mesmerized by the way her tongue moved over the swollen, red, pearl-like thing.

He was also mesmerized by the moans Sheila was making. Mrs. Sinclair took her hands and spread Sheila's folds wide open and ran her tongue up and down them then her tongue went into her vagina and Sheila writhed in her bonds and moaned like it was the best thing ever.

All Arsen knew was he wanted to do that. So he pulled Mrs. Sinclair back by the shoulders. "I think I can do that."

SHE SMILED and moved to get behind him. Her front pressed to his back and her hand ran over his rock hard cock. He spread Sheila open as Mrs. Sinclair had done and began to feast on her as Mrs. Sinclair ran her hand up and down his cock.

She did it much better than he did when he did it himself. Her hand was softer and her strokes were slower and less insistent than when he did that to himself.

He supposed it was because he was always in a hurry. It most often happened in the shower and living in a dorm always meant someone was waiting to get into the shower next.

Arsen couldn't believe the pleasure he was getting from licking this woman's pussy. Her moans made him feel like he was the best lover in the world. His dick ached to be inside either one of them.

He just wanted to feel some type of tight, wet, heat surround his cock. He didn't give two shits who it was in, it just needed to be inside a pussy. That's all he knew.

When Sheila screamed his name, Mrs. Sinclair whispered in his ear.

"Put your tongue inside her."

He did and found her juicy. Mrs. Sinclair let his dick out of her hand and stood up.

"Take her cuffed hands off the knob and lie her down on the bed. Keep her ass at the edge so you can stand while you fuck her."

Arsen's hands were shaking as he reached up and took the other woman's hands off the knob and laid her on the bed. She held her cuffed hands over her head.

Mrs. Sinclair's lips touched his ear as she whispered.

"I have a whip." He felt the cool leather move across his bare ass. "You do not come until I say or I'll give you a lash. I'm going to pop you once you're inside her so you'll know the sting and fear it."

He turned to look back at her with fear in his eyes.

"You're what?"

She grabbed his chin and pulled his mouth to hers and kissed him hard.

"Do as I say, Arsen."

"Okay," he said as he tried to catch his breath after the steamy kiss. "I'll do what you say, Mrs. Sinclair."

Pop! Went the small whip, leaving a burning place on his ass as he ran his hand to cover it. "Mistress Sinclair!" she corrected, sternly.

"Mistress Sinclair. Sorry, I forgot about that." He rubbed his ass and turned back to find Sheila smiling at him.

"Your cock is huge and I'm about to come all over it." The sound of foil made him look back at the other woman and she slipped a condom over his erection.

"Thanks," he said.

His hands were shaking as he placed them on Sheila's stomach.

He pressed the tip of his wide cock to her vagina and watched as it slipped inside her.

Immediately, his body was shaking, and he felt the need to make swift thrusts. The first thrust he made coincided with a sharp pain on his ass as Mrs. Sinclair struck him with the whip even harder than she had the first time.

It burned, and he felt a whelp had formed. It didn't quit burning, and it took his attention from the need his body felt to release.

"Move in and out of her slowly, Arsen," Mrs. Sinclair told him.

She was a presence just behind him but she wasn't touching him. A light over his shoulder had him looking back over it and finding her with a small camera in her hand.

"Christ, are you filming this?" he asked in horror.

"Shut up and fuck her." Her words came out harsh and her nails dug into his ass. It made the whelp burn even more.

Shelia began to groan.

"He's huge. It feels so fucking amazing."

Mrs. Sinclair directed him.

"Tell her how she feels, Arsen."

He had no idea how to explain it.

"She's squishy and hot."

Mrs. Sinclair rolled her eyes.

"How about something like this? Her pussy is hot and making my dick scream with need for her."

"NAH, that's not how it feels," he said. "It really does feel squishy and hot and your vagina was tighter than hers is."

Sheila raised her head and her eyes went wide.

"Stop filming! I don't want anyone to ever hear that. Erase it, Anne!"

Mrs. Sinclair chuckled.

"Do some Kegels, Shelia."

Shelia laid back.

"Ughh! Just don't let him talk. It's better if he doesn't. He has no idea of what to say."

Mrs. Sinclair moved to lie on the bed, her head near Sheila's bottom and she angled the camera up to film him.

"I'll narrate." She looked at him through the camera. "Here we have a young male, twenty-one. Isn't that right, Arsen?"

He nodded and smiled at the camera.

"Yep."

"I'd like you to answer with, yes, Mistress Sinclair."

His smile widened.

"Yes, Mistress Sinclair."

"Good boy. I'm going to reward you with a nice blow job in a little while."

His face went red as he pumped away at Sheila. "Crap! You have some shit in store for me, it seems."

"You will be well educated when you leave our company at the end of this long weekend, Arsen Sloan. I assure you." She moved the camera to film the connection their bodies were making.

"You getting that sloshing sound, Mistress Sinclair?" he asked.

Sheila's head popped up off the bed.

"Arsen, shut the fuck up!"

"Sorry," he apologized and went back to pumping himself into Shelia.

"Pull her knees up, Arsen. You can go in deeper like that and you may find something tight on her a little higher up there."

He did as she told him to and Shelia moaned. "Yep, he's stretching some new territory."

Arsen felt it too and his dick twitched with a need to release. But the pain of the whip still was fresh in his mind. He tried to look at the wall and not think about what he was doing.

Then Sheila let out a shrieking groan and her body convulsed around his cock and he was about to come with her as her body just kept pressing and squeezing his hard cock.

Mrs. Sinclair's words came from between clenched teeth, "Don't you let it go, Arsen."

He looked at the wall, trying to block out how her body was trying desperately to pull his along with her into that sweet ecstasy. Somehow he managed to control it.

JUST AS HE DID. Mrs. Sinclair moved back behind him. The leather of the whip moved over his ass.

"Come," she told him with one quick word.

He tried, but the urge was gone.

"I can't."

The whip cracked across his ass leaving heat where it had touched.

"Come!"

The pain of the strike had his body nowhere near orgasm and she struck him again. Over and over she struck him until he was quivering and his knees gave out.

His dick had gone limp and every nerve ending was screaming at him. Mrs. Sinclair wasn't letting up. The whip hit him all over his body as she kept cracking it and screaming at him to come.

Finally, she got close enough he could grab her wrist to stop her.

"Mistress Sinclair, please stop!"

Her eyes were wild as she looked at him. Then pointed to the sign on the wall.

"You don't know how to read, Arsen?"

His voice was shaky with the pain which radiated all over his body. "What?"

"What does that say?" She pointed at the sign again.

"Peaches?" he asked in complete confusion.

"Yes. That's all you had to say if it was too much for you." She pulled away from him and stood back up. "Didn't you know that? Haven't you heard of a safe word?"

He shook his head.

"No."

She held her hand out to help him up from his crumbled state on the floor. "I could've sworn I told you that if it gets too intense you are to say that word and we'll stop immediately."

Arsen shook his head and found Sheila sitting up.

"Yeah, I know I heard you tell him that, Anne. He must've not been listening. His mind was probably busy taking me all in as I hung on the wall, waiting for him." She looked at Arsen. "You okay there, kid?"

He nodded. Red whelps covered his body. He watched as Anne Sinclair un-cuffed Shelia.

"I'm taking him to the shower to wash him down. Care to join us?" she asked the woman Arsen had just finished fucking.

She nodded.

"I'm starving. I'm going to order pizza." Sheila looked at Arsen. "Pepperoni okay with you, kid?"

He nodded and felt Mrs. Sinclair's hand slip into his. She led him to the bathroom and started up the shower. Her finger tips ran over the red whelps which covered his chest.

SHE SMILED UP AT HIM.

"You have to admire the colors. The angry red makes your tanned skin look kind of white. It's beautiful. Don't you agree?"

Arsen did not agree. It hurt. He hurt all over his body as she'd struck him all over it. One had even landed on his dick and it burned as well.

He had no intention of staying with the women the entire weekend. In his opinion they were a little odd. Mrs. Sinclair reached into a little bag in the back of the medicine chest which hung on the wall next to the mirror.

She pulled out one little white pill.

"Open up," she told him.

He shook his head.

"What is that?"

"Just something to stop the pain I know is running all over your body, Arsen. It's not addicting. You don't have to worry about that. Open up or I'll have to paddle your skinny, little ass."

His mouth opened quickly as he had no want to feel any more pain. She smiled and pulled her clothes off then removed his chaps and tossed them to the floor.

Her hand took his and led him into the shower. The warm water burned initially as it ran over the many welts, some which bled a bit. She picked up a clear bottle filled with a foamy dark liquid.

The bottle had a tip on it and she squirted it all over him and ran her hands to rub it all in. "This will take care of the places where your skin was broken."

"Okay," he said. His body was starting to grow numb with the liquid. "What is it?"

"An antiseptic with a pain reliever in it. It'll make sure those places don't become infected." She ran her hand over his dick which was limp. "You know you should think about me. There's so much I could teach you. I can have this body of yours very different in just the matter of one year. Wouldn't you like to have muscles, Arsen?"

He thought about it for a moment.

"Like a personal trainer or something like that?"

With a smile, she said, "Something like that."

Her hands running over his body was making it feel better. That or the pain killers both inside and outside of him.

"I'll think about it."

She took his dick in her hand and gave it a squeeze.

"You'll think about it what, Arsen?"

"I'll think about it, Mistress Sinclair."

SHE SMILED and released his cock.

"Are you going to college?"

"I am. I'm in pre-law. I'm not sure what I want to be. An aid, a paralegal, or what." The pill must've been taking over as he found himself picking up a white bar of soap and rubbing it with his hands until he had handfuls of bubbles. He began rubbing it over her shoulders and she moaned.

"You should be an attorney, Arsen." She turned to face him and moved his soapy hands to her breasts. "You'd make an excellent one. I could help you. I could even get us a nice apartment near the campus. Where is it you're going to school at?"

"Stanford University," he said and her eyebrows shot up.

"Prestigious! My, how did you manage that?" She moved his soapy hands to her pussy and moved his hands to rub it.

"Turns out, I'm smart." He smiled.

"As am I, young man." She moved to close the space between them and pulled his head down to kiss her.

His arms ran around her and his mouth was pliable as the pill made him lucid and his body was much more relaxed. She turned the water off and pulled him out of the shower and to the bed. She laid him back on it and went to the door.

SHE SHOUTED OUT THE DOOR, "I'm going to fuck him. Do you want to watch? I'm going to put the camera on the dresser to record it."

Arsen lay on the bed and chuckled. His mind was nowhere near as cluttered as it had been. Mrs. Sinclair was going to fuck him and video tape it. Possibly while the woman he'd just fucked watched.

He never saw it coming as he sat in the dark bar, drinking a little drink and thinking about what kind of sandwich he was going to get and take home for dinner that night.

HER DAMP HAIR hung in limp strands around her then make-up-less face. Then he saw a few tiny lines around her light blue eyes. But that was okay, he thought.

"Since I was much too hard on you about it the last time. You go ahead and come when you want to. I'll be a lot easier with you this time." She moved down his body, and he felt her mouth go over his limp dick.

His eyelids grew heavy, and he closed them. The way her mouth was sucking at him had his cock making little twinges here and there, but the pill had him not feeling much of anything.

Light filled the room as Shelia came in and turned the overhead light on.

"I want to be able to see it all," she said as she came into the room. "The camera needs light to capture the footage."

He placed his arm over his eyes to block out the annoying light. Mrs. Sinclair's mouth moved off him for a second as she said,

"Hey, can you grab some nipple clamps and put them on him. The liquor and the pill have him not feeling a damn thing. We need to bring some type of sensation up in him. His dick is limp, and that's no fun."

Arsen found himself thinking he felt like their boy-toy. He wasn't sure he liked that at all. He felt it when Shelia placed the first clamp on his little nipple. "Oww!"

"Good," Shelia said then pinched his other nipple with the other clamp.

"Fuck!" he shouted as pain went through him.

It subsided pretty quickly, and he found his cock pulsing as Mrs. Sinclair's mouth sucked hard at it.

A humming sound filled his ears, and he opened his eyes to see Shelia wearing nothing but a strap on nine-inch dildo which was thick and black and moving as she'd turned it on.

"Hey, I'm going to take you from behind while you do that, Anne."

Shelia climbed onto the bed behind Mrs. Sinclair and Arsen watched as she pushed the dildo into the woman sucking his dick. When Mrs. Sinclair moaned, he felt it make his dick twitch.

As he watched the woman with blonde tight curls moving back and forth, her tits bouncing as she did and his line of sight included a woman with long, blonde hair bobbing up and down as she sucked him off he became aroused.

. . .

"FUCK ME, YOU CHICKS ARE FREAKY!" he said as his stomach began to tighten and his dick hardened.

Shelia winked at him.

"Want to make an Anne sandwich, kid?"

He didn't know what an Anne sandwich was, but he wanted to.

"Yep."

Shelia pulled out of Anne and Anne released Arsen's dick. She smiled at him.

"You're going to take me in the ass."

"I am?" he asked.

She nodded. "Get up."

He stood up and watched as Shelia laid down, her black dildo standing up. Anne climbed on and slid down it.

"Fill the rest of me, Arsen," Anne said.

"This is wild," he managed to say as he climbed on the bed and found his dick easily moved into her ass. "This doesn't hurt?"

"No," she said. "Stroke along with me, Arsen."

HER ASS RAISED, and he went all the way into her. Then she went down on the dildo and he stayed where he was, letting his dick pull away from her.

She moaned like she loved it. "Now all at once," she said. "I'm going to grind on this dildo while you fuck my asshole, Arsen. Got it?"

"Guess so," he said as he moved back to fill her.

Anne wiggled on the dildo as Arsen moved in and out of her. It was all going fine for a while. Until he really looked at what he was doing.

He was fucking the mother of the only girl he'd ever loved. The girl who had thought him a loser after her father was able to beat him up.

. . .

THAT WOMAN WAS RIDING a dildo the size of a donkey's dick as she fucked another woman and he fucked her up the ass. It was sick, twisted, and nothing he had ever even imagined doing. Then the pill and liquor hit him hard, and he threw up all over the women beneath him.

THE MEMORY MADE Arsen nearly wretch out loud. He then realized it was fifteen minutes until dawn and at the very least he was going to see who it was that was supposed to be waiting outside to tell him something.

Gently he moved away from Steele and went to get dressed. He called Paul and asked him to go outside, with his gun. But he wanted him to act as if they weren't together.

Paul joined him as he got off the private elevator. Arsen gave him a nod.

"Thanks for getting up at the butt crack of dawn for me, Paul. I have no idea who it was that texted me, but I'm grasping at straws here. I have to listen to anyone who has a thing that can possibly help us."

Paul smiled, and the two bumped fists.

"I got ya, man."

Arsen looked out the clear glass doors of the lobby and saw nothing outside. "I wonder if they'll even come."

"Gotta give them time, boss," Paul said and leaned against the wall. One foot he placed against it and fiddled with a pack of cigarettes.

Arsen's eyes went to it.

"When did you start smoking, Paul?"

"Since I started worrying about you, boss. I give quite a large shit about you, man." Paul's eyes looked a little glassy. "I'll watch over her for you if something happens. I don't want you to worry about that. I'll take her everywhere and make sure she comes to see you on visiting days."

"I hope that's not necessary, but you have no idea how much it's appreciated. You always have been an exceptional person, Paul." Arsen found himself feeling sentimental about so much on that night and early morning.

"I know, Arsen. I know."

"I've been recalling my relationship, if you can even call it that, with Anne Sinclair. I've come to the conclusion she kind of molested my naïve young ass back then. She made me something I wasn't before." Arsen looked away as he felt kind of sick to his stomach.

"When Steele and I have kids, and hopefully at least one will be a son, I would kill any bitch if she did the things to him, Anne did to me. I mean it. I would kill her."

Paul nodded.

"And how about what you did to those women, Arsen?"

BILE ROSE QUICKLY in his throat as his long-time friend reminded him of what Anne Sinclair had turned him into.

"Yeah, I know. I wish they were here for me to apologize to and get help for. The way Steele helped me. The girl hasn't even realized it yet, just how much she's helped me."

Paul laughed a little.

"If I could turn back time," he sang with his best Cher impression. "Right boss?"

Arsen chuckled.

"Yep." He fidgeted a little then said, "Do you think it would be unfair of me to ask Steele to marry me with all this shit over us?"

Paul's eyes went wide and his eyebrows ran clean up to his dark hairline. "Marriage, boss? You sure you're ready for that? I mean, you haven't known her long at all. Not to say I don't adore her. I do. And I do think she's good for you. If I can be honest though. I think you need to be sure you aren't going to hurt her. Make her something she isn't. You know like you said Anne Sinclair made you something you weren't."

A sharp pain stabbed Arsen's heart. His friend wasn't lying. Paul was no yes man. That was a thing Arsen had always respected about the man who drove him everywhere he went.

Arsen nodded.

"You're right, Paul. I should wait. I need to make sure she understands what it is I really want from her. At this point she still thinks I need to be in control of all things, her included, if I'm to be truly happy. That isn't the case though. It's far from what I want."

Paul looked at him with a frown.

"You sure about that, boss? I mean, you and having control over things is your deal, man."

"It has been. Fuck! It had to be. If you had a clue about what I had to do to get out of evil Sinclair's clutches you'd have a much better understanding. That woman ruled my ass with a hot mother-fucking poker for nearly four years. All through law school. Then the bitch took credit for all I had accomplished." Arsen began to pace with the anxiety and anger which began to fill him.

"I suppose that was the final straw when she did that, huh?" Paul asked.

"You would think so, but that wasn't it. I mean it was part of it, but not all of it. See, when I told her I wanted out of our contract which stated we would be in that contract. Get this shit, forever. And that I needed to move on with my life, she threatened me. Her husband and daughter didn't know a thing about us. But Mistress Sinclair made sure to keep a video diary of our activities. She assured me her husband would hunt me down and kill me in cold blood without any hesitation."

Paul frowned. "Um, she was a part of it. Why would he only kill you? He'd probably kill you both."

"SHE HAD A SPECIAL SKILL, the old bitch. She'd managed to record a ton of our conversations. She had me say certain things, I had no idea what she'd do with all that later." Arsen stopped pacing as he saw the blue Camaro pull to a stop in front of the building.

The windows were tinted so dark he couldn't see who was inside.

Paul's hand on his shoulder made his look back as Paul said.

"I guess this little conversation is to be continued, boss. Looks like your five o'clock meeting has just arrived."

Arsen walked out first and a few seconds later Paul walked out and leaned against the brick wall of the tall building which housed them both. He lit a cigarette and acted as if he was just another dude catching a quick morning buzz before heading out to work as he watched his friend.

The window rolled down and as hard as he tried, he couldn't see who was driving. Arsen leaned in then stood up and turned back to look at Paul, then got in the car and it pulled away.

To be continued...

55

PART ELEVEN: FOR FEAR

STEELE

The sound of the private elevator opening up in the entry room had Steele calling out from the kitchen where she was cooking breakfast, "Arsen, where have you been, Baby?"

"Not Arsen," Paul said as he came into the kitchen. "I've been trying to call him and he's not answering. Do you know if he left his phone here?"

"Check his office. I know it's not in the bedroom." Steele paused her stirring of the scrambled eggs. "Wait. You didn't drive him? So he took the Jag? Where'd he go without his phone?"

Paul ducked out of the kitchen and went down the hallway to Arsen's office. Steele followed and saw Paul pick the phone up off the desk.

"Here it is," he said as he turned back to her.

His dark hair lay across his shoulders in waves. Not his usual look. Paul always kept his long hair pulled into a low cue and kept it neat at all times. He was clean shaven that night Steele first slipped into the backseat of the Suburban. Now he had a light beard, unkempt.

"PAUL, YOU OKAY?" she asked as she watched him tap away at Arsen's cell phone.

"Yeah, why?" he said as he stared at the phone.

"You look a little off. Your hair, your face. And do I smell cigarette smoke?" she asked as she looked him over and sniffed the air.

His blue eyes moved to look at hers.

"It's just that I'm getting more and more worried about Arsen." He turned the phone around and showed her the message Arsen had received earlier that morning. "He left with whoever it was who sent this message asking him to meet them this morning. Arsen just got into the car with a wave of his hand and they drove away. I didn't get to see who it was."

Steele's face went pale.

"Was it a man or a woman?"

Paul shook his head. "I didn't get to see a thing. The windows were tinted a dark black."

"What kind of car was it?" she asked.

"A blue Camaro." Paul pushed the button to call the number that was all sevens. A recording came on telling him that was not a valid number and he pushed the button to end the call. "Just as I thought. That number isn't anything we can track him by. I should've chased his ass down and made them stop."

Steele let out a sigh.

"Paul, don't blame yourself. The man thinks he's ten feet tall and bulletproof sometimes."

Paul let out a laugh and walked out of the office.

"You don't have to tell me that. I know that man better than anyone. He's hard headed and completely self-destructive at times. What he did with women was..." He shut up and glanced at Steele.

Her cheeks had turned pink with embarrassment.

"I know. It's okay."

Paul reached out and touched her arm as they walked back to the kitchen.

"He's different with you, Steele. He's better with you."

She nodded.

"I wonder why he would take off with someone."

STEELE GESTURED for Paul to sit at the table. He took a chair, and she brought him a cup of coffee.

"Thanks," he said as he picked up the sugar bowl and put a couple of spoonfuls into the cup.

Steele made up two plates with eggs, bacon, and toast and took them to the table and sat across from Paul. After taking a bite of the eggs and a sip of her coffee, she asked, "Do you think Arsen can truly be happy with a vanilla woman like I am?"

Paul looked at her and smiled.

"You aren't vanilla, Steele. I like to think of you as a brilliant variation of flavors. A little chocolate, a touch of vanilla and some spicy cinnamon."

She smiled with the compliment. Then her cheeks turned scarlet as she thought about how many things she'd done with Arsen while the man across from her drove the car, a mere rolled up window between them.

Steele shook her head with the memories of all she'd done with the man in the back of that car. Her panties went damp with the thoughts which had flashed through her mind.

"IT HAS OCCURRED to me you know a lot about our sex life, Paul," she said as she looked at her plate, not daring to meet his gaze as she felt him staring at her.

He laughed.

"I wear headphones, Steele. I have no wish to hear what goes on in the back of the SUV."

She breathed a sigh of relief, but the fact was he knew what they were doing in the back of that car and that was embarrassing to her.

"Paul, do you think I'm a trampy slut?"

"Look at me," he said with an air of authority she knew he'd learned from Arsen. She raised her head and did as he said. "You are no tramp, Steele. I could tell you weren't one of those girls when I first saw you in your boots and jeans. You and he clicked. You had something. I know you would never have done what you did without that spark that instant connection you two had from the very start."

"That night. Was he really waiting for me?" she asked then sipped her coffee. "It seems impossible to me. He's so damn good looking. I just can't imagine Arsen Sloan sitting in a car waiting for any woman to come outside."

Paul laughed.

"I was surprised by him saying he wanted to wait for you. You're right, he's not the kind of man to wait on a half chance with a woman. He's the guy who goes in takes who he wants and the women are grateful for the time he gives them."

Steele looked away.

"He's had more than his fair share of women, hasn't he?"

Paul cleared his throat.

"I shouldn't have said that. Please have that stricken from the record." He laughed.

Steele did too.

"Paul, I can't help worrying about where he is right now. And who he's with. And what the fuck they're doing."

Paul shook his head.

"I'm sure it's just a person who can help him find out more about the murders, Steele. He'll be back before we know it and hopefully he'll have some great answers that will get him out of all this shit he's in."

"It wasn't Anne, was it?" Steele's eyes were beginning to shine with unshed tears.

"It wasn't her car." He said, making her feel a little better.

. . .

SHE DIDN'T TRUST that woman at all. She knew she had a certain hold over Arsen because of all the abuse and she was afraid of Arsen reverting back to his old self. It had been a fear she'd had since she found everything out about the complex man.

"I'm supposed to be in my first class in half an hour, but I won't be able to concentrate anyway. I'm staying home today. At least until Arsen makes it back." She got up and put her empty plate in the sink.

Paul followed and asked, "You want me to hang out here with you?"

She turned with a smile.

"Would you? That would be so nice of you, Paul. It would help me not to get all crazy and jump to conclusions. I have to admit the pictures going through my mind of Arsen in a hotel room with Anne, or anyone really, keep coming in and haunting me. I love that man and jealousy is a thing which is nearly constant in me for him."

"I assure you he's not doing anything like that. I'm more worried he's put his trust in someone who's out to hurt him." Paul took her by the arm and led her to the living room where they sat on a plush sofa.

"That is worse than what I'm thinking," she said and sighed. "There is just no good scenario is there?"

He shrugged his wide shoulders.

"Well, there is one. He could be with someone who is helping him get to the bottom of all this shit."

She nodded in agreement.

"That would be so fucking fantastic."

The bell chimed with a call from the doorman and Steele made her way to the small box beside the elevator.

"YES?"

"There is a Detective Fontaine to see Mr. Sloan."

"Send her up," she said then sighed. "Fantastic."

Paul was behind her as she turned.

"What do you think this is about?" he asked.

She shook her head.

"No idea. It just keeps getting better and better around here."

They waited for the detective and in a few minutes she was stepping off the elevator with a paper in her hand.

"I need to see Arsen," she said.

"He's not here at the moment. What's that?" Steele asked as she gestured to the paper. "And what about my roommate, Gwen?"

"A warrant for his arrest for the other two women's murders is what this is," she answered. "We have officers looking for her, that's the best we can do with no leads yet. Where is Arsen?"

Paul answered, "He left about five this morning with someone in a blue Camaro."

"Five?" Fontaine asked. "That was quite a while ago. Doesn't he have his phone? Let him know I need him back here ASAP."

Steele sighed and walked towards the living room.

"You may as well come in and have a seat. He left his phone here. He's been gone five hours now. Hopefully, he'll be back soon."

The detective sat down and crossed her long legs, the red pencil skirt raising up a bit and showing more of her leg than Steele thought was professional.

"How long does he usually take, Miss Gannon?" she asked.

Steele looked at her with a confused expression.

"Pardon?"

"To fuck?" Her cold eyes stared into Steele's.

Paul laughed and sat down near the detective as Steele sat on the sofa across from them.

"Whoa. I better stay close to you Detective. This one here can be a real hell cat and I don't want you to get hurt. You should really watch what you say."

Fontaine's eyes ran up and down Steele who was nearly a foot shorter and thinner than the tall woman.

"This little thing? She couldn't hurt a fly."

Steele knew she was being baited so her temper was even.

"Fontaine, you cannot goad me into a fight. Sorry. I'm worried

Arsen has put his trust into someone he shouldn't have. Perhaps you could find out who the hell that car belongs to? You do have the hook up to get that accomplished, don't you?"

Paul smiled.

"Good thinking, Steele." He turned to the detective. "The building has cameras out front. The car should show up on them at five this morning and you could get the plates and call them in. Then we'll at least have a name for who he's with."

She nodded.

"Do you know why he would leave with this person?"

Steele nodded.

"Someone sent him a text from a fake number. It said they needed to talk. I suppose he found it was someone he knew. And someone he trusted enough to get into the car without saying a word to Paul."

The detective laughed.

"Arsen should trust no one at this time and no one should trust him, either. The man is now being accused of all three murders and you, my dear girl, are quite the idiot for being alone with him so much. I get it, the man is a God. He has it all. Wealth, the body, the great looks. That hair is something I dream about."

Steele smiled.

"It's soft and silky and smells like Heaven. I love tangling my hands up in it when his mouth is making me climax."

Fontaine's brows went up high.

"Touché, Miss Gannon!"

"I told you, a hell cat," Paul said as pink flushed his tanned cheeks.

"Speaking of your sex life with the accused murderer," Fontaine said with a smile covering her red stained lips. "How rough does it get?"

Steele leaned up and gave the detective a smile. "Oh, it's hot. But he's never hurt me."

"Perhaps you have a higher pain threshold than others," she said as she uncrossed her legs and leaned back on the sofa.

Steele shook her head.

"Quite the opposite. I have a very low threshold for pain. He's very gentle with me. He's the kind of man who finds out what a woman wants and gives it to her. He's kind of magical that way. Knows what I want before I do."

"So, you aren't worried he's out there right now spanking some helpless female into submission because he can't do that to you?" she asked. "People like that have needs, Miss Gannon. Maybe you don't realize that."

Paul cleared his throat.

"Okay, this is my boss and good friend you're talking about Detective. I need to remind you Miss Gannon here is a law student and an intern for both Tanner Goldstein and Arsen. She is not to be treated the way you're treating her."

Steele smiled at Paul.

"Thank you, Paul."

The detective's eyes moved back and forth between the two rapidly.

"Hmm. What about you two? What's going on here? Why are you two all alone in Arsen's apartment?"

Paul laughed and shook his head.

"I would never go behind Arsen's back and go after any women that's his. It's a matter of respect. And just so you know. If he is ever put in jail or prison, I will be escorting Miss Gannon to see him and anywhere else she goes. So you will see us together often if that happens. It doesn't mean we're fucking each other."

Steele's cheeks went pink, and she coughed. Then Paul stood.

"How about some coffee while you wait?"

The detective nodded.

"That would be nice. Thank you."

The two women eyed one another while Paul left the room. Then

Steele said, "Look, you can help here. I need you to understand some things about the man I love and would gladly give my life for. He's a tortured soul. He doesn't deserve what's happening to him."

"Said every woman involved with a killer ever," Fontaine said with a sigh. "Poor girl. He did it. He killed those women. Now, I think there is a slight possibility the first one was an accident, but I think the sadistic man inside him liked it. It thrilled him. So he found another woman who liked that kind of stuff and went too far with it again, but this time on purpose. Getting his rocks off to it a second time. Then he knew one more who'd let him do that to her and he did it again."

Steele shook her head.

"You don't know him at all. He's not that way. He has a soft streak. He can be tough and arrogant and even mean sometimes. But he has this soft spot."

The detective laughed.

"So you think he has a soft spot for you?"

Steele frowned.

"He does. It's not a thing I particularly like. He was weak when he was younger. Before Anne Sinclair got a hold of him and fucked him up royally. Somehow, with me, he's going back to that weakness again. I hate I'm doing that to him."

"Maybe he's feeling secure for once," the detective said as she looked around the room.

A fresh bouquet of colorful flowers filled a vase on a small table. It was the only thing soft in the room filled with fine, dark brown, leather furnishings. No other soft touches were in the room. It was entirely masculine.

"MAYBE," Steele agreed. "You know that Sinclair woman told Arsen she had a friend who was interning at the place the women are being autopsied at. She said that friend told her all three women had elevated chemicals in their bodies. She said they had been killed with some drug which is easily hidden in the body. I can't remember the name of it. But I was wondering if you saw that on the reports."

"Did she say who the friend is? Because I've been down there and there's only two people who work there and there is no intern." Fontaine leaned forward and tapped her long fingers on her chin.

"There's not?" Steele sat up too and Paul came in with a tray of coffees.

"Here we go, ladies." He sat the tray on the coffee table between them and handed them their cups.

Steele asked, "Paul, you were there when Anne Sinclair and Arsen talked, right?"

He nodded and took his place near the detective again.

"Yeah, why?"

"Tell her what all the old bat said to him." Steele took her coffee and sat back.

After a lengthy discussion about all Anne had said, the detective was showing signs of having an internal battle with what the truth was.

"There's a pretty good chance Arsen is being set up."

Steele made a long sigh and sat up.

"So what are you going to do about this?"

"I THINK I should go downstairs and talk to the building manager and get the plates off that car if possible. If that's Anne who he's with she could be doing something awful to him." The detective stood and took off to go downstairs. She looked over her shoulder. "I'll be back. Stay here."

"Finally," Steele said. "Maybe the damn police will do something to help Arsen instead of trying so hard to make sure he rots away in jail." Steele got up. "I'm going to change out of these clothes and into something more comfortable since I'll be staying here instead of going to classes."

She left the living room and went to the bedroom. The room she now shared with Arsen. Her body began shaking as she thought about where he might be.

Her mind kept taking her to awful thoughts. Him and Anne in a room somewhere. Anne beating him and fucking him.

Steele fell on the bed and tried hard not to cry. She got up and pulled her skirt off and kicked off the high heels. She unbuttoned her blouse and lay back down in her lacey bra and panty set Arsen had ordered for her.

Arsen had given her a whole new wardrobe. A car was being put together made specifically for her. He was taking care of her much better than she had ever taken care of herself.

Thanks to the way he had taught her to eat and exercise, she was firm and getting more fit each day. If he was going back to that life with Anne, it would devastate her.

Steele ran her hands over her body and imagined it was Arsen who was doing it. The last night he'd made her feel so good. He'd taken a long bath with her, they drank a little wine and then he took her to bed.

Heat had flushed her body with his first touch. His lips pressed against hers and took her away from all thoughts of Gwen. Even though she knew she should only be thinking about her friend and what might be happening to her, Steele wanted to be taken away for a little while.

Arsen could manage to do that with a simple touch. That night his touch was anything but simple as he ran his fingertips over her breasts and stomach. His lips touched her stomach, sending chills all over her.

His dark eyes gazed at her as he said, "One day this flat stomach will be round with our baby, Steele."

SHE SMILED and recalled the amazing feeling those words gave her. She hadn't even thought about having kids.

"You want kids, Arsen?"

"With you I do," he'd said. Soft kisses he made all over her stomach.

Her heart swelled with love for him and she knew he was it for her. No one would ever come close to being what he was to her. He would one day be her husband and the father of her children.

It seemed to be far away in a future which was not entirely certain. The dark cloud of prison constantly hung over the man's shoulders. Steele shuddered as his lips pressed against her clit.

His teeth took it gently, and she moaned with the sweet feeling it gave her. He made a low growl and bit it a little harder. It sent waves of pleasure through her.

Her hands fisted the sheet beneath her.

"Arsen!"

His tongue flicked at the swelling pearl between his teeth and with every deft flick of his tongue she felt a jolt go through her, straight to a place deep inside her.

She was wetter than she'd ever been and finally she could take it no longer and groaned loudly as her body shook with the climax.

His fingers gripped into her ass and he moved his mouth to taste the juices he'd set free. His name came from her lips over and over as his tongue went in and out of her, making the orgasm go on and on.

Steele ran her hands down to run through his hair. He finally had had enough of her and moved up her body, kissing every inch along the way. Heat filled her as she waited semi-patiently for him to be inside her.

It was amazing when they were joined together like that. Two parts of the same person it seemed. Her body formed around his thick cock as he buried himself into her wet depths.

His breath was warm on her neck as he pushed himself into her.

"I will never get tired of how you feel when I first go into you. Hot, wet, and wonderful. I love you, Baby."

Somehow every time he told her he loved her it still sent shock waves through her heart. "I love you, Arsen."

So slowly it almost hurt, he moved inside her. Her stomach

clenched with every long, slow stroke. He was making it last this moment with her and she knew it.

It was obvious Arsen was beginning to lose hope he'd get out of the legal mess he was in. He was getting more and more clingy. His hands always on her. As if touching her as much as he could before he was taken away and couldn't do it anymore.

Even then his fingertips were flowing over her body as he made the slow strokes. His mouth was moving over her throat, teeth grazing her flesh. He was being more gentle than normal, more into the moment than he'd ever been.

Her hands ran over the tight muscles of his back and she found herself needing to feel him like he was feeling her. Making it last, taking him all in.

He could be taken from her at any moment and she was beginning to feel she needed to touch him all she could too. They may only have a small time left before the walls came crumbling down, breaking them in the process.

His hand moved back up her side and he leaned back and looked at her as he took her breast in his hand. His dark eyes were soft and filled with emotion. "You are a rare find, Miss Gannon."

She smiled and traced his top lip with her finger. "As are you, Mr. Sloan."

He kissed her fingertip. "I could look at this face forever."

A tear escaped as she wanted to look at his forever, but she knew it might not happen for them. "With luck, you will."

He kissed her cheek where the tear had fallen. His lips moved over her cheek as he said, "No tears, Baby. There is only you and me and right now. Let the future go for now. We don't have any guarantees anyway."

Her hands ran up to take his cheeks between them. She pulled his mouth to hers and tasted him with a deep kiss. She wanted that kiss to last forever.

Their tongues moved in unison with the others. Making sweet love to each other's mouths while the bottom part of their bodies did the same. Every part of them seemed to be touching, moving against the others.

Every deep, slow stroke had his body moving slowly over her clit and she was beginning to feel the intensity from it. She arched up to get him to grind into her more.

Little eruptions were beginning to occur inside her. She tried to hold them back, but they just kept going and building until her body was shivering with the need to let it all go.

He pulled his mouth from hers and looked into her eyes.

"Do it, Baby. Come all over me."

She grabbed his biceps and held them as she did as he told her. He kept moving slowly inside her, making it go on and on. He stopped and let her catch her breath. Then started up again.

With a smile he said, "How many times you want to come for me tonight?"

Her hand moved over his meticulously kept beard. "As many times as you want me to."

He kissed her again, soft and slow like a fine wine, he was taking his sweet time with her. She felt adored by him.

A knock came at the bedroom door, taking her out of her memory and she sat up. "I'll be out in a minute. Nearly done changing."

She shook her head and climbed off the big bed she shared with Arsen. She looked back at it and found a tear rolling down her cheek.

If he was with someone else, she would never trust a man again. If a man could be that sweet, intimate, and loving, and still mess around, then she wanted no part of them.

A PART of her was worried about that so much because he didn't seem to even want with her what he'd done with all the other women he'd had sex with. The detective had struck at one of her major insecurities where Arsen was concerned.

His need to dominate, control, and physically test his partners. He didn't do that with her and she knew it. He was gentle with her and listened to her. Catered to her instead of having her cater to his every little need like he made the others do.

Arsen didn't treat her like the rest and that scared her. Did he go off with someone who he could be himself with? Was he unable to be who he was with her for some strange reason and need that control more than he or she even realized?

She pulled on a soft pair of jeans and a white lace shirt and her favorite boots then went out to face the detective and her shitty ways once again. Steele just hoped the man she loved would come home soon with a great explanation of where he'd been.

Steele found Paul and the detective looking over some papers as they sat next to each other on one of the sofas. Fontaine looked up as Steele entered the room.

"I CALLED in the plates and should know something soon about that. I also got the autopsy reports out of my car while I was down there. Paul and I were discussing the fact that, though small, all three women have higher levels of succinic acids and choline in their systems."

Paul added, "I told her about the fact a drug used in anesthesia is called succinylcholine and could've been the real killer of these women."

Steele sat and listened as the detective said, "I think Anne Sinclair is the one who did the crimes or had them done. She has information she shouldn't have about their deaths. You see, I made a call just to be positive. There are only two people who work there and are privy to this information. Both have worked with the department for many years and are very trustworthy individuals."

"If Anne lied about having an insider," Steele said. "Anne could've done it. She didn't take Arsen's leaving well at all. She left scars on his back from the beatings she gave him as she tried to reign him back in when he was through with her. Her way of domination was more than he could take."

The detective frowned.

"It's hard to think of that man as anyone's submissive partner. He's all man."

Steele looked at her.

"He is. That's how fucking bad Anne Sinclair is. Now, what are you going to do with that warrant now?"

The detective picked it up from the coffee table and tore it in half.

"THIS INVESTIGATION IS GOING in another direction as of right now. Anne Sinclair has moved to our main person of interest. I'm not saying Arsen is off the hook, but I think we've been sent in his direction so she can get some revenge on the man she loved to control so much."

Steele let out a breath she didn't realize she'd been holding.

Finally!

She wanted Arsen to be there so damn bad so she could hug him and let him know it was all going to be alright. It was almost over. But he wasn't there.

The fact was Arsen and Gwen were missing and Steele was helpless to do anything about any of it.

"So, what are we going to do about finding Arsen and Gwen?"

The detective frowned.

"Look, Arsen can't officially be called missing yet. I know I've been messing with you, but the fact is he could really be fucking around right now. While hurtful, it's no crime, Steele."

"So you aren't going to send out an APB for that car?" Steele asked. "Because I think you should do that."

Fontaine shook her head, making her long, blonde hair fall around her shoulders. Steele noticed Paul looking at her with a little gaze in his eyes as she said, "I can't yet."

Steele stood up and paced.

"This is a lot of crap! Why do your hands have to be so tied?"

"It's the law," she answered. "You should know that, Miss Law Student! Sit down! You're annoying me."

Steele looked at the tall woman with her too promiscuous

clothing for a cop and asked as she gestured to the woman, "You don't dress like any cop I've ever seen. What's up with this?"

PAUL LOOKED at Fontaine too as if he was interested in knowing as well. The detective ran her hands over her low cut white blouse which was tucked into a tight, red skirt paired with red heels.

"If you must know, I was a model. I don't like to look like a cop. I like to look like a model. Okay?"

Paul nodded.

"No wonder you're so beautiful."

Steele rolled her eyes.

"Good God!"

The detective smiled at Paul and ran a hand over his cheek.

"Thank you, Paul."

"You're welcome." He looked at Steele. "What? I like tough as nails women."

STEELE PLOPPED BACK DOWN on the sofa and shook her head.

"Anyway, back to what's important. What can Paul and I do since we don't have to obey all your little timelines and shit like that? I mean can we go look for that car?"

With a shrug of her shoulders, she said, "Once we get the name of who it's registered to, I suppose you could see if you could find the person through the internet and who am I to say you can't go looking for your boyfriend?"

"Then that's what we'll do! Finally, a break," Steele said as she sat back. "Now if that damn information would get to you, we could get busy finding my man. I can't wait to give him the good news."

Her eyes darted up to Paul as he said.

"So, Fontaine, how about dinner tonight?"

Steele rolled her eyes and looked away. She didn't want to witness the devastation the bitch detective was about to pull down on the poor guy.

. . .

"How sweet," she heard the woman say in a high pitched voice. She looked back to find the detective's hand running yet again over Paul's face. "How about you shave though, before we go? I love the way you look all clean shaven and your hair pulled back."

"I'll go do that now." He jumped up then hesitated as if thinking about doing something. Then he reached out and took Fontaine by the hand and pulled her up.

He took her into his arms and kissed her as Steele's jaw dropped. Fontaine's left foot lifted up behind her and her arms ran around Paul as she moaned.

Steele couldn't look away. It was like a train wreck. You know there will be total devastation, but you have to keep looking anyway.

Paul pulled back with a smile.

"Just wanted to let you know what kissing me felt like with a beard." He let her go and walked away.

Fontaine pressed her fingertips to her lips and turned back to look at Steele.

"Wow! Just, wow!"

Steele finally smiled. "He's an amazing kisser, isn't her?"

The flush on the detective's face let her know he was. The women found themselves giggling, and the detective sat back down. Steele began to feel a bit better about Paul getting together with the woman who had made no secret about her wanting a little roll in the hay with Arsen.

Maybe with Paul to occupy her, she'd forget about flirting with Arsen.

Fontaine leaned forward and whispered, "Do you know if he's into the BDSM stuff too?"

Steele shrugged.

"Not sure. But I don't think so. If he tries to spank you, give it a try before you stop him. The first couple of whacks are pretty damn exciting."

They broke into giggles again and both blushed. Fontaine's cell phone rang, and she picked it up and answered, "Detective Fontaine."

Quickly she took a pen and pad of paper from her purse and wrote something down then got off the phone.

"I have a name and address for you. But you aren't going to like it. You sure you want it?" she asked Steele. "I mean I wouldn't go there if I was you. It might lead to an altercation and that might end you up in jail. Going to a woman's house and kicking her ass is a crime after all. No, I'm not giving this to you. You will definitely end up in jail."

Steele stood up and moved quickly and swiped the pad out of Fontaine's hand. The name Beth Campbell was at the top and the address was right underneath.

"FUCK!" Steele threw her hands up in the air and stomped her foot. "Fuck! Fuck! Fuck!"

"Know her?" Fontaine asked with raised brows.

"The name of the girl who was his first love was Beth. She's Anne Sinclair's daughter. This is most likely her." Steele fell back on the sofa and put the pad of paper on the table.

"Anne Sinclair was fucking her daughter's old boyfriend?" Fontaine asked with shock and a lot of disgust on her face. "That's sick!"

Steele pulled out her cell phone and went to search the woman on social media. In no time at all she'd found her and when she pulled up her friends and family it was all there. Her mother was Anne Sinclair.

Arsen had gone off with the one other female he'd ever loved and been gone a damn long time.

"I'm sorry, Steele. I really am. All shit aside, the man's a fool to let you go." Fontaine went to sit by Steele and ran an arm around her shoulders. "This sucks. Everything might well be over with Arsen's troubles and you two could be getting on to a life together then in one fell swoop, an old flame comes in and takes him away from you. Life sucks."

Paul came back in all smiles and a clean-shaven face with his hair pulled back neatly and a killer Armani suit on. He stopped and looked at the two women on the sofa.

"What the hell? I thought you two hated each other."

Fontaine hugged Steele.

"I don't hate anyone. I'm just kind of bitch is all. We found out whose car that is and the fact Arsen's been gone so long just hit her."

"Like a brick upside the head," Steele added. "He's with Beth. <u>The</u> Beth. The fucking Beth who let her father beat him nearly to death. The fucking Beth who left him the destroyed kid he became because of her. Then her mother swooped in and nearly finished him off. <u>That</u> fucking Beth." Her eyes went to Paul.

His mouth hung open and then he gulped.

"We have to save him. What's the address?"

Steele laughed.

"Save him? Ha! From what? Come on, Paul. Wake up. Smell the fucking shit. Read the writing on the wall! He's with her, fucking her. Lying in a bed somewhere holding her and telling her he forgives her and wants her to marry him and have his babies. That's what's taking so long."

Paul's head shook.

"No, Steele. He wouldn't do that. Something's not right. You have to trust him."

"That's what he always tells me. Trust him. I have to trust him." Steele's body was shaking and Fontaine hugged her tighter. "I did trust him. I trusted him when he tied my hands up. I trusted him when he hung me up and smacked me with his belt until I cried. I trusted him so many times. One too many though it seems."

SHE BEGAN to cry and Fontaine let her bury her face against her neck.

"Shh. It's going to be okay, Steele. There are other fish in the sea."

Paul threw his hands in the air.

"Stop crying, he's not doing what you two think. I know the man. I know him like you two don't. Steele, he loves your ass. Completely loves you. I've never seen him like this. You have nothing to worry about, I promise you."

"I need to be alone," Steele said then pulled herself out of Fontaine's arms and ran to the bedroom.

Paul called out, "Steele, don't do anything stupid. Promise me!"

She slammed the door behind her. The man she loved was with his old girlfriend. The social media site had said she was married with three kids. Steele knew the woman would throw all that away to be with Arsen again.

The billionaire who now was built like a brick house and gorgeous. Fuck yes, Beth would throw away her marriage and kids for the man and Steele knew it without a doubt.

Steele was a shaking mess as she fell on the bed and cried her eyes out. Paul was just sticking up for his friend. Defending the Bro Code. Steele wasn't stupid.

It had all been too good to be true and now it was over. The end of it all. Arsen was off the hook, mostly anyway and he was done with Steele.

That much was obvious.

She pulled her clothes off and went to get in the deep jetted tub to try to blast away the sadness. Her body ached to feel his touch. Her heart ached so bad she felt it in her soul.

Steele wasn't sure she could take it. The pain was too great. Their nights and days had been filled with pleasure and it was over. She would die alone because he'd ruined her for any other man.

No man would be able to ignite in her what he had. No other man would capture her attention the way he had. No other man was Arsen.

Gorgeous, crazily lovable, Arsen.

Steele lay her head back and let the tears flow as she thought about the way he touched her. The way he made her feel.

His lips on her lips, their hips touching as he moved inside her. When he was behind her, the way his hip bones made contact with her ass. Everywhere his body touched hers sent little jolts of electricity throughout her body.

And that is over!

HER HANDS MOVED over her body, pretending they were Arsen's. She cried as she touched her breasts and knew his hands would never squeeze them again. She ran her hands over her stomach. The place he told her only the night before he wanted to see filled with their child.

That wasn't going to happen. No. He'd have children with Beth. His first love. His true love.

Steele might have been a little something to him, but the second Beth showed up, BOOM! He was hoping in the car with her and gone in a flash.

He didn't even tell Paul, his best friend, goodbye. He just got into her car and went away with her.

Steele ran her hands down to where he made her the most happy. In between her legs Arsen had made her feel like no other ever had or ever would. His mouth brought her complete pleasure as did his large cock.

Now he was most likely plunging it into Beth's horrible pussy. Making her come over and over again. Sending her to another place where only the two of them existed.

Steel went under water and stayed until her lungs burned with the need for oxygen. She wanted to drown. Let him find her dead in his bathtub for all she cared. Then he would know what he'd done to her.

Why did he have to wait that night outside that damn club for her? Stalk her? Make her his?

He should've left her alone. She would've better off. Now she was broken. More broken than she ever knew she could be.

With the flip of a switch she went from being the most in love she'd ever been to being at the lowest place in her entire life.

Steele pushed her head up from underneath the water and gasped for air. She shook her head.

What was she doing?

Was she really going to give him up without a fight?

Was she going to kill herself and let Beth have her man?

"No, I am not!" she said out loud.

"That bitch gave him up. She can't have him again. She had her chance and she let him go. Fuck her!" Steele climbed out of the deep tub and grabbed a towel.

"Bitch, better get ready!" She marched to the closet finding a nice set of yoga pants and a matching shirt. She was going to dress for this little encounter.

Putting on clothes she could move in, she was preparing for the battle for her man. Arsen was damaged and Anne and Beth were people he had to be protected from.

Steele had been sent to him. Not only to love him, but to help him be strong in the face of those who had hurt him so badly they nearly broke the man.

If Arsen had fallen victim to Beth's charms again then Steele would help him see why Beth was not good for him. It wasn't as if that was a lie. The girl had watched her father beat him and yelled at him to get up and fight a man twice his age and size.

Beth wasn't good for him, no matter how much she may have changed, and Steele was, at the very least, going to fight for the man she loved more than life itself.

After putting her hair in a braid to be sure her hair couldn't become a target if Beth was going to fight back, she marched out to find Paul and Fontaine exchanging phone numbers as they sat so close to each other their legs were touching.

"IF YOU DON'T MIND my interrupting your little date, I'd like to go to this woman's house. I'm going to fight for my man. I will not go down without a fight," Steele informed them.

"I can't let you go and assault anyone, Steele," Fontaine said with an exaggerated eye roll.

"I'm going one way or another. I memorized the address, Fontaine." Steele headed towards the elevator and Fontaine got up as Paul took her hand and pulled her up with him.

"I have to take her. I told Arsen I wouldn't let her out of my sight." He pulled her along. "You can come with us if you want. I'll let you ride up front with me. It's a bench seat, so you can sit right next to me."

Steele looked back to see Fontaine grinning like a school girl.

"I have to take my own car. I'm still on duty. I'll lead the way and I'll go talk to whoever it is that's home there. Think you can keep her locked in the car until I get things figured out?"

Paul smiled and kissed the tip of her nose.

"Not a problem. I have the master control up front. I got your back, partner."

"Dear, Lord!" Steele said as they all stepped into the elevator. "This is going to be excruciating!"

Paul laughed as the doors shut.

"Now, now, princess. Others like to go to the ball too, you know." He slipped his arm around the detective and pulled her in close to his side.

"Whatever that means," Steele said. "I just want to get to Arsen as quickly as I can. The wait is killing me."

The trip down the elevator from the penthouse to the ground floor seemed to be taking forever. Everything was taking forever in Steele's mind. She couldn't get to Arsen fast enough.

She knew the chances of him being at that address were slim to none, but Beth's husband might be and that was one step closer to her finding Arsen.

If Arsen thought Anne was harsh, he's going to have to come up with a new word for me!

56

GWEN

Inch by painful inch, she'd crawled through the tall grass until she finally came to the edge of the road. The sun was up and had been for a while. Morning dew was still covering the grass, and she was soaked from it.

Her body shivered with the wet cold. She knew she had little time. Exposure, exhaustion, starvation, and dehydration were all combining to take her life away.

She just kept praying and focusing on breathing each breath. The idea of saving Steele and Arsen kept her going. If she never did another thing in her life, she would've accomplished saving a couple of people from terrible fates.

The sound of wheels smashing the gravel along the road made her look up, and she saw the headlights of a car coming towards her through the foggy morning. The person pulled to a stop and got out.

She saw a tall, slender woman with blonde hair. She didn't say a word as she was too weak and the woman didn't speak either. She just picked her up and placed her in the back seat of her large sedan.

Gwen was saved. She would make it. She could complete what had taken her nearly two days to work at. The swim, the shark, the long crawl.

It had all come together and had worked for her. She would be able to save Arsen and Gwen now. She closed her eyes and just took in one breath after another and thanked the Lord above for the woman who had stopped and picked her up off the side of the road.

Soon, she'd be hooked up to an I.V. of fluid which would fill her veins and bring her back to life. Food would be in her empty stomach and fresh clothes, be it a hospital gown which would surely be gaping in the back, letting her ass show, but it would be clean and dry covering her tender flesh.

It was all about to be over. The pain, the agony, the near defeat. Allen White would be behind bars in hours. Anne Sinclair and her boy toy as well. All would be over and Gwen would be in a nice, safe, dry hospital bed, sipping on some refreshing beverage.

The radio came on and played some old rock. A little old time rock-and-roll, Gwen thought to herself. Yeah, some good old rock and some food and water and fresh clothes. That was just what the doctor would order.

And when Steele saw her and found out she had the words to bring her complete happiness, then she'd be a hero. She knew Arsen would insist on rewarding her, so life was about to get real fucking easy.

And she'd let him do it too. She'd let him give her a reward, and she'd take some time off school and work and just lounge around for at least a month. Do nothing but sit by the pool and sip Champagne cocktails and eat fancy things she'd never eaten before.

FRENCH FOODS she'd heard of but had never seen. Escargot, Vichyssoise, and other foods she'd never tasted. It occurred to her in all her twenty-one years of life she'd never had one bite of spinach.

She was going to try every food on the planet. Every drink in the world. She was going to live, damn it!

No more living like every day is a given. Gwen would live every day as if it were her last. Try everything. Find a good-looking guy and kiss the mother fucker on the mouth before he even got a chance to speak.

Dance in the rain, watch an old movie where all the actors have died already and fall in love with the leading man. Crazy shit like that is what Gwen was going to do when she got well and got out of the hospital.

Her eyes felt heavy and her body was beyond tired. Though she knew it was over, she was growing kind of worried. The woman wasn't speaking at all. The car didn't feel as if it were speeding to the nearest hospital.

It seemed to be going slow, as a matter of fact. It took everything she had in her to pull her eyelids open. Her vision was blurry and that concerned her. She didn't need to wear glasses so what was happening to her?

Suddenly she realized she wasn't taking breaths. She pulled in some air and her chest hurt really bad when she did.

After all she'd made it through, was this it? Was she supposed to kick the old bucket now? Throw in the towel?

The numbness was moving over her body in slow increments. Her toes, then up her calves, over her thighs and now her stomach which had been in a constant state of pain was growing numb.

Was her body completely shutting down now she was so close to being saved and saving her friend?

If she died before telling anyone what she knew, she'd have done it all in vain. She took in slow breaths and closed her eyes. She was so tired, and it had seemed like it had gone on so long.

The ride was taking forever. If the fucking broad could speed the fuck up she might fucking live.

She wanted to scream at the woman to hurry the fuck up. She didn't have much longer and people's fucking lives depended on what she had to say.

HER WORDS CAME OUT quiet and scratchy. "Hurry, please."

She doubted the woman could even hear her over the radio she had so fucking loud for some damn reason.

Who the fuck picks up a nearly dead person off the side of the road in a desolate area and places them in their car and turns fucking eighties rock up so loud? Who does that kind of thing?

An idiot? A sadistic person? A narcissist who wants to hear what she wants to hear and fuck all the others, especially the dying chick in the back seat?

This woman was a piece of work. The car stopped and the sound of buttons being pushed Gwen heard as the key pad made little clicking sounds. Then there was the sound of scraping of what she thought was a metal gate opening.

WHERE THE HELL *is this woman taking me?*

The car lurched forward, bumping over the rails which held the gate in place. Then she heard it close with a resounding bang. The car moved ahead slowly. One curve it went around then the car went in another direction around another curve.

It was taking a while to get where they were going and Gwen knew it wasn't any hospital. There were no gates keeping anyone from an emergency room parking lot. Not one.

Something else was happening to her. Something awful. Something which would end not only her life but Steele's and Arsen would go to prison.

Why can't things just work out? Why can't things go right for just one minute? One break? One little break in the chain of crap she'd had to deal with since Allen White took her from her apartment?

Gwen laid perfectly still as the car pulled to a stop. She crossed her fingers that she'd been wrong. The woman turned the radio down then shut the car off.

Gwen felt the cool, wet wind as the woman opened then closed the driver's side door. Her shoes crunched against the gravel of the parking lot or whatever it was she'd stopped in.

It took a long time it seemed to Gwen for anyone to come back to the car to get her. Maybe the woman had forgotten about the too weak to speak woman in her back seat.

Maybe she was picked up by a senile woman who shouldn't be driving in the first place. She placed Gwen on her back and that made it harder for her to move than when she was on her belly.

She tried to pick her head up but she couldn't. She couldn't even get her eyes to open. Then the sound of two sets of feet crunching the gravel she heard faintly. They got closer and closer.

They stopped right by the car.

"YEAH, IT'S HER," a man's voice said. "Where'd you find her?"

A woman's voice filled her ears.

"On the road, you fucking idiot. Get her out of there and then we have to clean the car so there's no evidence of her in my car."

Gwen knew the voices. She knew it was not her fate to save her friend and her friend's new boyfriend. It must be her fate to end up back in Allen White's hands.

Her fate to end her life at a mere twenty-one years old at the hands of Allen White and his partner Anne Sinclair.

Gwen felt the air swoosh past her head as the back door opened. Her limp body was picked up by Allen, no doubt. The sound of gravel crunching under shoes she heard again.

She wanted to cry, but her body had no water to make tears. She wanted to scream, but her body had no strength to do that. She wanted to live, and that was a thing her body seemed to not want either.

All was against her. All was over. All was lost.

He placed her on the bed with broken springs. The one he'd chained her to a few days before. He didn't bother to put the chains on her that time. He and Anne knew she didn't have the strength to go anywhere.

·   ·   ·

"GET the bleach and I'll get the vacuum cleaner and we'll get busy on the car. My daughter called me and she's waiting for me at my house. She was excited and said she had a surprise for me. I hope it's a nice purse of a pair of expensive shoes. Her husband makes a lot of money and every once in a while she surprises me with some expensive gift. She's thoughtful that way. I raised a good girl," Anne said as they left Gwen near death on the bed.

Concentrating on taking in slow breaths, Gwen tried not to fall asleep. She had to hold on. Had to try not to die.

Hope should be long gone, but she found she couldn't give it up.

I HAVE GOT to hold on!

57

PART TWELVE: FOR FORTUNE

ARSEN

The hours had passed at a snail's pace as Arsen and Beth waited for her mother to arrive at her home where they were waiting for Anne Sinclair. They sat on the sofa, leaving space between each other.

"When I found the tapes, I couldn't believe what I was seeing," Beth told him.

Arsen ran a hand over his face.

"It's hard to believe after all this time the woman still has those. I thought I'd destroyed them all."

"Seems three made it without you finding them. It seems my mother was adept at hiding things." Beth stood up and went to look out the front window. "Where is this woman?"

"She made my life hell for a number of years, Beth. She changed me. Well, your father and you did too, but Anne really changed me," he said as he looked at his watch. "It's been hours. Where do you think she is?"

"No telling. I can't say I know the woman anymore. I had no idea who she was and what she was capable of doing until I found those tapes and then when I found the files she kept on the women in your life that really freaked me out." She went back to her place on the sofa.

Arsen barely saw the former Beth under the years of cigarette smoking and obvious alcohol abuse. The glass of vodka in her hand was a constant thing since they got into her mother's house at six that morning.

She sipped at it, but it seemed she needed to hold the glass more so than drink the alcohol it held. Her blonde hair was pulled back into a tight ponytail, the dark roots showing.

Arsen was surprised to find he had absolutely no residual feelings for the girl who was his first love. It seemed the way things ended had really cauterized the wound she left in his heart all those years ago.

"I'm REALLY glad you told me about this, Beth. You have no idea how much this shit was going to cost me. Your mother has a knack for fucking up my life. This time would've been beyond devastating."

She ran a finger around the rim of her short glass.

"How did you leave her if she had so much control over you?"

"It wasn't easy and I have the scars to prove it." He looked away at the memories he tried hard not to think about.

"Tell me, Arsen." Beth pulled her feet under her and looked at him with a sadness to her eyes he didn't remember ever seeing in them before.

"One day just before my graduation day, I came home to the apartment she'd rented us. I had a few of my final grades and brought home the papers with them on it. It struck me when she commented how well she'd taught me. And how great it was going to be when I became a lawyer and could support her, finally." He stood and walked to the window.

"So she was planning to leave my father then and marry you?" Beth asked.

He shook his head.

"No. She told me she would never divorce your father. He was the person she stood behind to show the world she was a normal woman with a normal family. Not the freak show she hid from most people."

"Then why did she think you were going to support her, Arsen?" Beth re-situated herself on the sofa and took a tiny sip of the vodka.

"No idea. She used the shit out of me. In all ways. I mean all of them. I suppose she thought because she rented the apartment, that was taking care of me. The fact was, I didn't need her to do that. I had a job at all times. I could've taken care of myself with no problem."

"Then how did she justify that?" Beth asked with confusion riddling her face.

"I don't know. How does anyone know what goes on in the mind of an insane person?" Arsen went back to sit down.

"Sure you don't want something to drink, Arsen?"

HE SHOOK HIS HEAD, making his dark, silky hair which had grown to his shoulders, bounce off them.

"No, thank you. So getting back to how I left. She was away for the week. You know back home with you guys. I had overheard her talking on the phone to one of her friends how she'd built me into the man I was becoming and what a great investment she'd made in me. Like I was a damn animal she had trained."

"That's when you decided you wanted no more of life with her?" Beth asked.

He nodded.

"Yes. So I left. I rented an efficiency apartment and went to a different BDSM club. I found a young woman there who later became my first sub. I have to admit I was hard with her. I had learned from the hardest and that's how I treated her."

"Oh, Arsen." The disapproval in Beth's voice made him flinch.

"Anne came to my apartment once she was able to track me down and she found the poles I had purchased. She put them to good use on my back as she tried to beat me back into submission. I wouldn't go back to that though. No matter how many times she hit me, I wouldn't go back. She eventually gave up. Or so I thought anyway. I had no idea she would go this far to punish me for leaving her."

Beth got up and left the room. Arsen could hear her getting sick in the nearby bathroom. It made his stomach knot. He paced around the room and wondered why he'd said so much to her.

She didn't have to know all of it. But somewhere deep inside him he was glad she knew her mother now. It was Anne's time to be found out. Just as she had made sure his private life had been made public.

Beth came back in with her face shining from the water she'd splashed on it. "Sorry." She sat down. "I just couldn't stomach it any longer. She is my mother after all."

He nodded.

"I suppose I shouldn't say any more about her."

"Probably best." She laughed a little. "All this time we thought she was so into church. Were we fools?"

Arsen sat back down.

"I finally met the one for me and Anne is threatening that relationship as well."

"The one for you? A new submissive?" she asked as she took another drink of the vodka.

"No. Not a sub. A real woman. An equal to me in all ways. And in some areas, she's far superior to me. My body, mind, and soul love and need her. She will be the mother of my children someday. If I can get this legal crap off me then I plan on making that woman my wife." Arsen's eyes drooped a bit at the corners. "If she'll have me, of course."

Beth fidgeted in her seat.

"She's a lucky girl, Arsen. I was an ass back then. I can't tell you how many times I thought about what happened and wondered why I reacted the way I did. I still can't tell you exactly why. I am sorry though. Not that I expect forgiveness because I don't deserve it. And after finding out what my mother did to you, I really don't deserve it."

"I allowed it. I allowed it all. No one held me captive. I came back to that apartment day after day. And as far as forgiving you. I hadn't. But I do now. I see no reason to hold hate in my heart any longer. You were a kid. I can't hold you responsible for what your father did to me."

Beth looked away, tears filled her eyes.

"I don't deserve your forgiveness."

HE SCOOTED over and gave her leg a pat.

"Sure you do." He took the glass of alcohol from her hand and placed it on the coffee table in front of him. "Let it go, Beth. I see you clutching that glass like it's a lifeline. You don't need it. Whatever you're holding on to, let it go. I forgive you. If you've done other things to hurt people, let that go to."

Beth ran her hand over his meticulously kept beard.

"You turned into such a gorgeous man, Arsen."

He drug his knuckles across her cheek.

"Beth, you're more than you're showing right now. You said you have a husband and kids. I think it's time you step up and take charge of yourself and get it together for them and yourself. This part of your life is over. Done. You can't go back a change a thing. But don't let it take the rest of your life from you."

"WHAT'S HER NAME?" she asked him.

His eyes sparkled. "Steele Gannon. She's sweet, kind, and at times stubborn. And I love her with more than I knew I had in me."

"Does she know she's the luckiest women in the world?" Beth asked with a smile.

"I think she does." He winked and chuckled. The sound of gravel crunching in the drive had him jumping up. "Is that her?"

Beth ran to the window.

"Yes! Quickly, go hide and make sure you have that recorder on."

God, *I hope this works!*

58

GWEN

Lying on the mattress, barely breathing, Gwen managed to pull her eyelids open when she heard a noise near her. Allen had several bags of some clear liquid and an IV stand with another bag strung up on it.

"I'm going to get you better, Gwennie." His voice was cheerful, and he was smiling.

She closed her eyes and wondered what the hell was happening.

Not sure how much time had passed, Gwen woke up and felt so much better she couldn't believe it. Her arm was immobilized, and she looked at it to find it secured to a board and an IV was running into it. She moved her head to find Allen sitting there.

"Hi, sleepyhead." He got up and came back with a bowl and a spoon. "I have some soup here, if you care for some."

She nodded. Allen helped her sit up in the bed and gave her a bite of the soup.

It hurt to swallow, but she managed and before she knew it, she'd eaten the entire bowl of chicken soup.

"Thank you," she managed to say.

Allen smiled and went away only to come back with something to drink. He put the straw to her lips, and she took a sip then he yanked it back.

"Not too much or you might get sick."

She nodded.

"What are you going to do with me?"

"Let you go after I get you better. See, I'm going to be leaving town after I do what I'm going to do for someone. I'll set you free then." He looked at her with a frown. "I'm sorry about all this. You are an innocent person in this. I should've never taken you. I'm sorry."

Her head was spinning. He was going to let her go, but then she remembered his plans for Steele.

"Allen, what about Steele? She's an innocent in this too."

"Yeah but taking her will hurt Arsen and that's what I want to do. Sorry about her. You'll get over it though. If I've learned anything it's that people get over stuff." He gave her another sip of the drink which she found tasted like apples.

"It that apple juice?"

"Yes. I know it's your favorite." He gave her a little pat on the shoulder. "I listened to you when we were talking all those times."

GWEN FOUND a little shine in his eyes and thought she might be able to use any affection he had for her to her advantage.

"So I overheard some things you and that woman said to each other. Want to tell me what all happened between you two?"

"Anne Sinclair is the woman behind everything. She came to see me while I was in prison. She gave me the idea to start talking about God and using that to impress the parole board. Then when I got out she found me again. She told he how Arsen deserved to be punished for what he'd done to us both."

Gwen nodded. "She was his master or whatever they call it, right?"

"Mistress. Yes, she was. He ran away from her or something like that. After she put him through college and made him the man he became, he left her flat." Allen stood up and left the area then came back with a chocolate bar and another pillow.

He propped it up behind Gwen and gave her the candy.

"Thank you," she said and took a bite of it. "Please, go one with your story, Allen."

Taking his seat again, he said, "Since I was the only case he ever lost, I think he was punishing me for my mistake. So I think it's perfectly acceptable for me to punish him."

Gwen took a sip of her drink and tried to think of a way to convince Allen that Anne was using him. She took the straw from her lips and said, "I guess you're too close to see it for what it is, but that woman is using you, Allen."

His eyebrows cocked in surprise.

"I don't think so."

She nodded.

"I can see it. You should really think about it. And I heard what she did to you. Are you into that kind of thing?"

He shook his head.

"No. But she has this way of making you think you are. You know?"

"No." Gwen looked down and tried to look as sad as she could. "I hate she hurt you like that, Allen."

"You do?" he asked. "After all I've done to you?"

"I FORGIVE YOU, ALLEN." She looked up and caught his eyes. "I want to help you get out from under her. I can see the writing on the wall, Allen. She means to toss you under the bus when everything goes down. She doesn't want to have you as a loose end."

He looked worried.

"You might be right."

"I think you and I should pay her a visit," Gwen said. "Has she told you where she lives?"

With a shake of his head, he said, "No, she hasn't."

"Hmm. Wonder why not?" Gwen eyed him carefully. "How about

you let me take a shower and freshen up a little then we go find her? We can Google the bitch and give her a surprise visit. Bet she won't be expecting that. Then you can set her straight how you will not be her patsy."

Allen smiled. "You know what, you might be right. I think I will pay her a visit." He got up to help her up. "Let's get you all cleaned up and pay her a visit. I'm done being her whipping boy!"

*T*HANK *G*OD! *Finally, a break!*

59

STEELE

As Paul pulled up behind Detective Fontaine at the address they'd found for Beth, Steele rolled her window down to listen to what was said.

Fontaine rang the bell of the small, blue, wood-framed home with toys littering the front lawn. A tall, pot-bellied man with a large bald spot on his head and light brown hair around the bottom of his head answered the door.

Steele noticed no car was in the drive. Her hands were wringing in her lap as she listened hard to what was said.

Fontaine said, "Hello, my name is Detective Fontaine from the San Francisco police department. I'm here to talk to you about a man we have a murder investigation about. An Arsen Sloan. Have you heard that name before?"

He shook his head and Steele saw a little blonde headed boy peek out from behind the man who was most likely the kid's father. She thought he was probably about four-years-old or so.

"Who's this lady?" the kid asked.

"Get back, Pete. Daddy's talking grown up talk right now. Go play with Becky, she's in her room." The kid vanished with his father's words. "I don't know anybody by that name. I mean I heard about him on television and the paper, but I don't know him. Why would you ask?"

"Your wife does. He was seen getting into a blue Camaro early this morning."

The man looked like he was goin to be sick.

"Beth picked that man up? In our new car?"

Fontaine nodded and Steele felt just about as sick as the man looked like he did as she told him, "At five this morning, she went to his apartment building after sending him a text telling him they needed to talk. Mr. Sloan got into her car without his cellphone or telling anyone who he was with or where they were going. It's been a little over six hours since that time and no one has seen or heard from him."

The man staggered out the door and sat on the top step of the porch, letting the screen door slam behind him.

"My wife is with a fucking murderer?"

The detective moved to allow him some room.

"Sir, have you spoken to her? Did she tell you where she was going?"

"To visit her mother." He put his head in his hands. "Do you know if she'd been seeing that man?"

"She had not been seeing him." Fontaine walked down the stairs and looked up at him. "They aren't involved like you're thinking. She was Mr. Sloan's first girlfriend. Later, after they'd broken up, Mr. Sloan got into a relationship with Beth's mother."

The man raised his head and looked at Fontaine.

"Are you shitting me?"

With a shake of her head, she said, "No, sir. Now, can you tell me what her mother's address is? And please do not try to let her know I'm going over there. I do believe she has Mr. Sloan with her and they plan on confronting Anne Sinclair. I want to get the surprise on them."

"You really think it's just that? I mean, you don't think she's been messing with that guy?" He looked sadly at her.

· · ·

STEELE'S HEART WAS POUNDING. She felt so sorry for the man.

"We've been trailing this man for a while now. I can assure you he hasn't been talking to her at all and they haven't been seen together at all." Fontaine turned to leave. "Thank you, sir. I appreciate your help. I'll go to Anne's house and see what I find out. I'll keep up updated if you like."

"Please do," he said as he watched her leave.

His head fell back into his hands and Steele knew he was not a happy man.

Fontaine came to her window.

"Did you hear all that?"

Steele nodded. "I did. So can we follow you to Anne's?"

"You can. Promise me you'll stay in the car, Steele."

She nodded and rolled the window up. Then watched Fontaine walk up to talk to Paul.

"Hey gorgeous," he said as he rolled his window down.

Steele watched as Fontaine's cheeks went pink.

"I like the sound of that. Follow me, and don't let the hell cat out, please."

"Got ya." Paul reached out and put his hand around the back of her neck and pulled her to him for a kiss.

Steele looked away, giving them some of the privacy that Paul had given her and Arsen. But looked back in time to catch Fontaine's face as they ended their kiss.

With a dazed expression covering her face, she said, "You're very surprising, Paul."

"Wait till later, after our date," he said with a grin Steele could see through the rear-view mirror.

She watched Fontaine kind of float off to her car and stifled a giggle. Paul looked back at her. "You find that amusing, Steele?"

"Sweet, too sweet," she said as she let the giggle all out. "I have to tell you, her reaction to you is priceless."

He pulled out to follow the detective. "I think so too."

. . .

Now if everything else can fall into place that would be fantastic!

60

ARSEN

Hiding just behind a partially opened door of a small bedroom just off Anne's living room, Arsen held a small recording device and waited for Beth to start the conversation with her mother.

Anne's voice was tense as she entered the house.

"Sorry it took so long, darling. I had issues arise I had no control over. So, my surprise?"

Arsen thought how typical that was of the woman. Me, me, me. That's all she ever thought about was herself and what others could do for her.

He was happy he was about to do something for her. Send her ass to prison where she belonged.

"Oh that," Beth said. Some rummaging he heard then she said, "Here you go. Pete made this picture for you of our family. He wanted me to give it to you."

The crinkling of paper he heard then Anne sighed.

"A drawing by a four-year-old. That's it?"

"Mother, Pete worked hard on that for you," Beth said, sternly.

"I thought it would be something good," Anne said. "Well, if that's what you've waited for hours to give me then I'll see you later, Beth. Damn it, what a disappointment."

Beth cleared her throat then said, "Well, I did have some things I wanted to talk to you about. When's the last time you saw Arsen Sloan?"

"What?" Anne nearly shouted. "Arsen? The boy your father nearly killed? That guy? I don't know why you're asking me that. I mean unless it's because of how it came out on the news he killed those women. Seems you dodged a bullet there with that crazy man. Guess your father was right to have beaten him."

"Was he?" Beth asked. "Then why did you stop Dad? Why did you take Arsen to the hospital?"

"Well, I am a Christian woman, Beth. I don't approve of violence."

Arsen had to hold the laugh that almost got away from him back. His hand clasped over his mouth to keep it in.

What a liar!

Beth did let her laugh out.

"Really? So, I suppose that's why you visited Allen White a number of times while he was in prison. To introduce the man to religion?"

"How do you know about him?" Anne's tone had gone to defensive quickly. "I've never told a soul about that, Beth."

"Oh! Well, I may have found a little secret diary thingy you've been keeping." Beth laughed again. "A person who does the things you have done should not keep it all written down anywhere. Much less in a book which is handwritten and has elaborate writing on the front cover of a leather-bound book. The title is amazing. Sounds like a best seller, Mom."

"How did you find it?" Anne asked with a tension to her voice Arsen knew all too well.

"The Destruction of Arsen Sloan, what a title, Mom. And the details are so intricate. Step one, find someone who wants revenge on

Arsen Sloan as much as I do. That was kind of hard to find it seems. Poor Arsen had to lose a case for that to happen."

"That's just a little fiction story I've been working on. None of it is real." Anne laughed. "Darling, you thought it was a true story. How funny."

"LET THAT CRAP GO, MOM," Beth said. "I know about it all now. I even found the tapes. They were truly awful, Mother. I can't tell you how many times I threw up."

The sound of someone plopping onto a cushioned surface let Arsen know Anne had fallen to the sofa.

"The tapes too? Jesus, Beth, when did you find the time to go all through my house? I mean you have that husband and those kids to raise. When did you find the time?"

"Well, let's see. It was when I saw Arsen on television for the first time. When they were talking about how he might be accused of the murder of three women who were his submissive partners at one time. Guess who else they caught on that camera, Mom?"

Anne sighed. "Shit! Shit, I never saw that."

"Yep, you were there in the background with your black wig on." Beth sat down, making the springs on the sofa cushion squeak. "You had on a blue dress which made you look kind of lumpy. Which you're not. So before I accused you of being there, I decided to come and look through your closet to see if the dress was there."

"It was. I knew it had been moved. I knew it!" Anne said. "You came into my home and searched through my personal things! How could you, Beth? How could you?"

"Save that shit, Mom. Come clean. Tell me it all. Every sordid detail," Beth coaxed her mother.

"What do you want to hear? How I found Arsen one fateful night in a small bar? How I made him mine in a way you never could? How he loved me?"

Arsen rolled his eyes. Love was not a thing they'd had. How she didn't know was a mystery to him.

"So he loved you, did he?" Beth asked. "And you repaid him by framing him for murders you had committed by another man?"

"You have no idea how much Arsen Sloan deserves to be behind bars." Anne said.

"Tell me, Mom."

Arsen leaned forward and found he could see the two as they sat on the sofa. The back of their heads, anyway. Anne looked at Beth and said, "Look, I'll cut you in on what I'm going to be getting once he's in prison. How about that, darling?"

He saw one side of Beth's mouth quirk up into a smile.

"Cut me in? On what?"

"I'VE FORGED Arsen's name on quite a few things. I had his social security number, his driver's license number, his date of birth, mother's maiden name. You name it, I have it. So I was able to get my name in on some of his best investments. See he has so damn many he has no time to check each one out for any changes. And the ones I put my name on as an eighty percent owner, I had the address changed on."

"Clever, Mother," Beth said. "Who's address?"

"A post office box in Los Angeles. All I have to do is wait for a judge to find him guilty and off he'll go to prison and off I'll go to the bank with my papers in hand and tell them I want to cash out." Anne patted her daughter's shoulders. "Millions, darling. And I'll share with you. How about I give you ten percent to stay quiet?"

Beth laughed.

"Okay. But tell me how you did it. How did you get those women killed?"

"Arsen made it much too easy. The man must've been looking to hook back up with any of his old subs. I didn't see that coming. But when I did, I got Allen White on the phone and had him move in. I was able to get this drug which leaves traces of things already found in the human body. It elevates a couple of things that occur naturally."

Beth nodded.

"Wow! You did some research, Mom!"

"I did. Then I got that into Allen's hands. All he had to do was inject the women. He did so easily. I tracked Arsen constantly. Within a few minutes of him leaving the women's homes, I had Allen go in and inject them."

Beth smiled.

"So as they slept, Allen did the dirty work. But how did you know he'd choked them all?"

"I watched him do it," Anne said. "It was a thing I had introduced him to. He hated to have it done to him. But he sure didn't mind doing it to others. Those women seemed to have an addiction to it. So when I found he did that to the first one, I jumped on that. Like I said, he made it easy."

"So smart, Mom. So Anne Sinclair is one woman with a lot of mysteries behind her."

Anne laughed. "I am quite a great actress! So, you'll take the ten percent then?"

"Let me think on that, Mom."

"Do not get greedy on me. I worked hard for that money. I made that man and he should've always given me money for what I did for him. Have you seen him? He's magnificent, and I made him that way."

BETH LOOKED CONFUSED. "Just how is what he became your doing?"

"I made him exercise, eat right, do well in college. It was me behind all of that. I taught him how to be a dom. Taught him about a life he had never known. Then the fool goes and finds this little vanilla bore and loses himself in her blandness."

"Huh?" Beth asked. "You lost me. A vanilla? What's that?"

"Someone who doesn't practice the BDSM lifestyle. And that young woman will never satisfy his needs. He's better off in prison than to have a life with her. He'd end up leaving her, anyway. You don't get that kind of thing out of your system. He'll get the urge to hang her up by her cuffed wrists and beat her ass with something. She's too strong willed to stay with a man who would do that to her."

Beth asked, "You know her, or what?"

"Not really. But I went to see him and she came at me like a tigress protecting her cub. That's how she sees him and he's not the kind of man who even wants a female in that role over him. He likes to be taken charge of or he wants to take charge. He's not into being protected and loved and that kind of crap."

ARSEN SHOOK HIS HEAD. Anne could not be more wrong. He wanted all Steele had to give him. Her love, her protection, herself. He knew without a doubt he had changed since he met Steele. For the better.

He knew what love felt like and he'd be damned if he ever let it go. His need to dominate was over. He had never wanted to be dominated, he had merely lacked the gumption to get the hell away from Anne.

Anne's words had damned her. He knew he had enough to put her ass away forever. But he waited. Wanting to hear all she had to say.

Beth said, "So in essence you're saving him from a life of love and boredom? How nice of you."

Anne smiled broadly. The lines on her face pulled all together with the smile.

"It gets better. Allen is going to kill Steele. That way Arsen finds out just how much he's lost by leaving me. I can take it all away from him. Every last thing he cares about. His money, his freedom, and even the love of his life."

Heat filled Arsen as he tried hard not to run out and kill the old bitch. His hands fisted at his side. Anne was more horrible than he'd ever realized. She was the most sadistic woman he'd ever known.

"Mom, how's he ever going to know it was you who took that all away from him?"

"That's what the book is for. I'm going to write all the details until I can't write anymore. Then I'll have the book sent to him upon my death. Then I'll have the ultimate revenge on him. His money will be going to the very people who broke him. You will end up with it all once I'm gone."

Beth's hand moved to her chest.

"Me?"

ANNE NODDED.

"Of course you. I mean it was you who started the whole thing. The boy was head over heels for you and when your father caught you two in bed and beat him, you're the one who broke him. I thought you wanted him broken."

Beth looked down.

"I was a dumb kid. A foolish girl. You and Dad were people I thought were strong. I wanted a person like that in my life. Arsen was always so emotional. So soft."

"I know," Anne said. "He brought you flowers and candy for no reason at all. He bought you little trinkets of cheap jewelry all the time."

"Told me he loved me only a few weeks after he first asked me out," Beth added. "He was sweet, kind, thoughtful. His mother was a horrible person and he wouldn't allow her to meet me. Told me I was too good to have to deal with his crazy mother. He was protective, but not overly."

"He fawned all over you. You remember that time It was raining, and he brought you home after a night at the movies? He took his shirt off and held it over your head all the way up the sidewalk so you wouldn't get a hair on your head wet." Anne broke into laughter. "What a pussy!"

Beth looked back over her shoulder towards the door she knew he hid behind.

"Well, Mom, I wouldn't call him that. That was nice and very sweet."

"He was so skinny back then," Anne laughed. "A real weakling."

Beth turned back to look at her mother.

"Well, he has muscles on muscles now. From what I saw on television."

"I made those," Anne said as she patted herself on the chest. "I made him work out. Pushed him past his limits. I made that body. That was all me."

BETH'S CELL PHONE RANG.

"It's Bill," she said. "I'll forward it to voicemail."

"Nonsense," Anne said. "I'm going to make us a couple of drinks. I see your glass of vodka is sitting there. I'll add some OJ to it for you and brighten it up."

Anne got up and left the room as Beth answered her phone.

"Hey Bill."

Arsen could hear the man yelling from where he was.

"What the hell are you doing with him?"

"Shh. I'll tell you everything when I get home in a little while. I swear you have nothing to worry about." Beth looked back. "Please, be patient. You'll understand everything soon. Have faith in me, Bill."

"I don't like this Beth!" he shouted.

"I know. I promise you will understand soon." Beth got up and walked towards the kitchen where her mother had gone and then back towards where Arsen was hiding. "Bill, I'll call you as soon as this is all over. I love you. Bye." She hung up and stepped around the corner.

Arsen held his finger to his lips. She nodded.

"Are you getting all this?" she asked.

He nodded and waved her back into the living room. She smiled and left him, finding her mother walking back in.

"More snooping, darling?" Anne asked. "You'll find nothing more. And nothing in that room at all. I was going to do something very racy with it but lost interest as things heated up with operation fuck Arsen's world up."

Beth laughed too. "So this Allen White guy. What are you going to do to make sure he never talks or tries to get more money out of you? Or are you paying him anything for murdering all those women?"

"I told him I am." Anne took a long drink from the tall glass she held filled with some kind of amber liquid. "But you don't need to pay a dead man."

"Oh?" Beth looked at her with intrigue. "And how will you accomplish that without getting blood on your hands?"

"Not sure yet, but thinking about how I can inject him with the same drug used on the other women and framing Arsen for that murder as well. What do you think? A good idea?"

Beth nodded and clapped her hands as if she was excited.

"Sounds positively fantastic! Is there nothing you can't pin on the man?"

Anne laughed.

"I know this may be an odd thing to talk to your daughter about. Especially since we've both had sex with the man, but how do you think I can get a taste of that scrumptious man one more time before he's put away forever?"

Beth frowned.

"You want to have sex with him again?"

"Of course. And I know you're married and not as liberal as I am, but you should want a little taste as well. From what I saw that one time, you did not get what that man has to offer. He has the right moves. I taught him so I ought to know."

"I think he would be kind of broken up if this woman you say he's in love with is killed. Don't you? Not really the time a guy thinks about plowing into another female." Beth shook her head at her mother.

"If you showed up to console him, maybe he would give you a little of the new and improved man he's become. And once you had him naked and in bed, I could sneak in with a little something to slip into his drink and then you could help me string him up while he's knocked out and I can have my way with him." Anne looked back at the door Arsen was hiding behind. "Did you hear something?"

"No," Beth said. She tapped her mother's shoulder. "Now get back to telling me how you'd get him to have sex with you if you have him drugged."

Anne blinked then took a drink.

"I've been so jumpy these last few weeks. Anyway, I would give him some ecstasy and when he was aroused, he'd wake up to find me and wouldn't be able to stop himself from doing it. I use to do that to him all the time when he was mine."

"You drugged him a lot?" Beth asked with arched brows.

"At first it was constant. I mean, he wasn't into yet. He would get sick, the little puss. The littlest kinky things would set him off. So I would sedate him to relax him then give him some 'X' or some Viagra and perk him up. Also adding some type of stimulation. A clamp to his balls always accomplished what I wanted."

Beth looked back over her shoulder and her face looked sad. Arsen caught her eyes through the crack in the door then took a step back as he couldn't bear to see the sorrow in them.

His first love had no idea what he'd gone through at her mother's hands. Arsen had no idea how often Anne had drugged him. He didn't recall a lot from the beginning of that whole thing and now he knew why that was.

Anne had left him in a drugged up stupor for the first few months. And then he realized why he let it all happen and how it all became kind of commonplace.

Anne laughed, bringing his attention back to her.

"I had him on three different drugs the first time I took him to a BDSM club. I walked in with the guy on the end of my leash and even though his body had not filled out yet, heads turned. He was pretty sexy even then."

"You drugged him and took him there on a leash?" Beth asked.

"Wearing nothing but some ass less leather chaps. The women were clamoring for him. I had him fuck a few of them then me. It was marvelous!"

Beth's face squished together.

"You let him have sex with other women? I don't get it."

"You wouldn't. You see, I wanted others to know what I had in him. His large cock was a thing so incredible I wanted others to know how great I had it. You know, be jealous of me and what I had found," Anne said.

Beth took in a deep breath and Arsen knew she was holding herself back from puking.

"Okay, so you made him have sex with women he didn't know. Did he even know he was being taken to a club like that?"

"No! He'd never have agreed to go. I had to drug him up and take him. He had fun. I mean who wouldn't have fun fucking the night away with some gorgeous women?" Anne took a long drink.

Arsen had to lean against the wall as he strained his brain to recall that night and just couldn't. So much of that time was blank, gone, forgotten.

HE'D TOLD himself for years he'd just blocked it as it was too hard to wrap his head around the man he'd become. But her admission to drugging him and essentially brainwashing him into thinking he liked that kind of thing was enough to tell him he really had become a man he never would've been if it wasn't for Anne Sinclair.

Beth asked, "Did you drug him the entire time you were together?"

"After six months, I only had to drug him every now and then. He had a defiant streak in him even the beatings couldn't tame. He had to be brought back down in other ways." Anne looked a little sad. "But all along I thought we were getting closer and closer. Until one day he just wasn't there when I got back from spending the week with you and your father."

"Is that when you lost him?" Beth asked.

"I found him after a couple of months. He had a small apartment, and I dragged his ass back and beat the fuck out of him with these poles he had bought. He told me he had become a Dom and would never be a sub again. I left bloody marks all over his back. I hope the ass still has the scars."

ARSEN LEANED against the wall and tried hard not to go out and confront the woman. His body was aching with the memories she had conjured in his mind. She was a monster.

Arsen had been in the lifestyle long enough to know Anne Sinclair was not your stereotypical Dominatrix. She was anything but typical. No Anne was a not into the real ideas behind that lifestyle. She was crazy.

Anne took a young man, drugged him, manipulated him, brainwashed him and broke him. That wasn't enough though. She wasn't about to stop until he was thoroughly fucked.

Arsen had heard more than enough, but Anne wasn't through talking.

"So you should see what I have in store for his vanilla princess," Anne said.

Arsen's entire body tensed, holding himself back. He couldn't believe she was planning even more than just having Steele murdered. She had more planned, and it was going to test him not to make a move and kill Anne Sinclair.

"MOTHER, you really should leave that poor woman alone. If Arsen has turned into the man it seems you've turned him into, then I'm sure she's suffering already," Beth said as she scowled at her mother.

Anne looked at Beth in surprise.

"The man I turned him into? I didn't turn him into a monster who kills women."

Beth's jaw dropped.

"Mom! He didn't kill those women. You had Allen White do that."

"Well, yes. I mean." Anne fanned herself with her hand. "You have me all mixed up, darling. With your accusation of me turning him into something he wasn't. I mean, his good points yes. The fact he's a lawyer. The fact he's attractive, the fact he has a great body. Yes, I did all that. The fact he likes to choke women, no I did not."

Beth stood up and threw her hands in the air.

"Look, just leave his vanilla princess alone. That's all I'm saying."

"If you saw how he was with her you'd be so jealous. I know you would," Anne said. "Just listen to what I have in mind for her."

Beth cast a nervous glance at the door Arsen was behind.

"Mom, please."

ANNE COULDN'T SEEM to stop her mouth. "I'm going to get Allen to take her to this abandoned warehouse. We have her roommate there now. I think she might still be alive, but that's neither here nor there. Anyway, I'm going to use every one of my devices on her until she's begging for mercy and I'm going to record it and make Arsen listen to it. Well, I won't be giving it to him until I'm dead. He'll get that recording along with the book."

Beth looked at her mother with no emotion. "You have to know he'll be set free after he gets those things in his hands. Then he'll come after me. Do you realize that, Mother? Your plans are going to hurt me. A person who was never involved in any of this."

"Oh!" Anne looked shocked. "I honestly never thought about it like that. Well, perhaps I shouldn't give you the ten percent or leave the money I'm taking from him to you after all. I guess I'll leave it to a charity. Maybe one for abused women or something noble like that."

"Mom, do you think maybe you could use some help? Like some professional help?" Beth went to her mother and put her hand on her shoulder and looked into her eyes.

Anne looked into her daughter's eyes.

"There is nothing wrong with me, Beth. You don't understand this lifestyle is all."

Beth laughed. "Mom, that lifestyle may be a little odd for some, but it's not about murder. It's not about making people do that type of thing who don't want to. It's not about any of the things you're making it out to be."

"I feel as if you're judging me, Beth. I knew this would happen if I told you about this. You should leave. I cannot take that look you're giving me. I can't take it. You and your father always expected me to be perfect! I can't be! I can't damn it!" Anne moved away from Beth and grabbed her drink and drained it. "Leave!"

Beth stood still.

"Don't yell at me, Mother."

"How can you stand in my home and say a word to me, you little slut? I guess you don't recall how your father and I found you fucking that man in your bedroom!"

BETH LAUGHED.

"Mom, we were teenagers. He was no man. We were not fucking. We were making love. It was beautiful and wonderful until Dad busted in on me. Arsen treated me like gold. My only regret is that I lost my mind when I saw Dad and you and something in me went crazy. I thought Arsen was some kind of God. More than a mere teenage boy. I was wrong for thinking that way. I was wrong for thinking he could fight my father. A man twice his size at that time."

"He was a weak man," Anne said.

"He was a fucking kid, Mother! A kid. And Dad beat him like he was a grown-ass man! I hate myself for how I reacted. I drink to forget what I allowed to happen to him. I'd never let anyone hurt my kids like that. It was only because of who his mother was and how he had no father that Dad even got away with what he did to Arsen."

"Beth, you're making me feel really uncomfortable. Are you thinking of telling Arsen what you know? Because, Beth I can't tell you how much I cannot allow that." Anne took a step toward Beth. "Tell me you will always remember who your mother is. Who you owe your loyalty to."

"You, Mother. Always you. Is that what you want to hear? Is that what will make you happy? I will never tell Arsen about what you did to ruin his life. I will never do that. Want to know why?" Beth folded her arms over her chest and glared at her mother.

"Why?" Anne asked.

The doorbell rang, and both women turned and looked at the door. Arsen tensed even more.

WHO THE HELL *could that be?*

61

PART THIRTEEN: FOR REVENGE

Intrigue. Passion. Suspense

Gwen managed to get Allen White to see through Anne Sinclair. They went to find Anne and Allen was going to deal with her once and for all.

Gwen took full advantage of her chance to gain her freedom and with the help of a little, old lady, she was finally safe.

Arsen had managed to stay hidden and get all Anne's confessions recorded, but Allen's sudden appearance and his actions had Arsen in a bad situation, one he might not make it out of alive.

Detective Fontaine arrived on the scene along with Paul and Steele, but when they got inside it looked to all like they may have gotten there a few moments too late.

So many questions needed to be answered.

Steele felt Arsen may have rekindled some spark for his first love, Beth. But she needed to let him have the closure with Beth he'd need to heal from all her family had done to him.

Was Arsen changing? And could Steele accept and love the man he was going to become now the threats were gone, and the wrongs had been pointed out and he could move on from the past which had him so scarred?

Is this the end for Arsen and Steele?

62

GWEN

The sun was right overhead as Allen and Gwen drove to Anne Sinclair's house just after noon. Allen glanced at Gwen as he drove down the road at 80 miles an hour. "I can see now she was totally setting me up. That bitch was totally setting me up all this time and I was too stupid to notice."

Gwen looked sadly over at Allen.

"I'm sorry this happened to you Allen. I really am but no one else has to die." She was doing everything possible to make the man feel as if she was on his side.

Gwen knew a thing or two about getting into a person's head and making them think things which weren't true. And she was using all she'd learned in her psychology classes to get into Allen's head and make him believe she was in this thing with him one hundred percent.

Allen looked at her with a sly smile.

"One more person has to die," he said.

Gwen's stomach knotted as she asked, "Who's that Allen?" She knew the man was insane and anything he did he seemed to make a plausible excuse for. In his mind anyway.

"Sinclair, of course," he said with a little laugh. "I'm not going to let her get away with this. My ass is going to get sent back to prison for sure. Unless..."

Gwen looked at him with worry in her eyes.

"Unless what Allen?" Where Allen White was concerned, she was certain about only one thing. He was capable of anything and she had to stay on guard and alert.

Thanks to the IV he had hooked her up to, she felt much stronger than she had since the whole ordeal had begun. But she was still very weak. And if he decided to do anything to her, she was near powerless to stop him. She knew she had to stay agreeable if she was going to use the circumstances to her advantage.

"Unless I can get out of here. Maybe go to another country," he said as he smiled at her.

Gwen was thinking it might be the best thing for him if he thought he could get away with it all.

"Sure, Allen. I'm sure you could get out of the country."

There was no way in hell that man would be able to get out of the country and leave Arsen to hang for those murders. Gwen was going to make sure of that, herself. But what Allen didn't know wouldn't hurt him.

Allen looked at Gwen with a spark of hope in his eyes.

"What do you say Gwen, want to come with me?" he asked with a lilt to his voice. Trying to flirt with her.

The man is certifiable!

IT WAS A LIE, but she said, "Yes, Allen. I'll go with you but first do you think we can go see Arsen and Steele and let them in on everything?" She thought she'd test the waters to see if Allen was going to be about doing the right thing before she threw him to the police.

Allen looked at her and shook his head.

"No, we can't tell them anything. I mean once I'm gone out of the country maybe then I'll send back my confession about killing those women and Anne Sinclair. But I have to be out of the country. Have to be long gone. Name changed and all that kind of stuff. You understand right? Plus, I still hate Arsen, so I'm not sure about all that. I do want him to suffer for what he did to me after all."

Gwen had to stop herself from going off on him. Allen was obviously never going to take responsibility for any of his actions. He was going to blame Arsen until the end, of that she was sure.

"Sure, I understand," she said. And then Gwen knew without a doubt what she was going to have to do to make things right for Arsen and Steele.

Allen took the next two corners like some kind of race car driver, making Gwen grab at her seat. In most cases she'd be yelling at the driver to slow down. This was not most cases though, and she was in just as much a hurry to get where they were going as he was.

He pulled into a short driveway, blocking in a blue Camaro and a large Crown Victoria from the nineties. The car Anne Sinclair drove.

"Shit!" he muttered.

"What?" Gwen asked as she surveyed the scene.

THERE WAS a house not far from Anne's. A little, white brick house with a little, red Honda Accord in the drive. Her heart began to pound. She was so close to freedom she could practically smell it.

"Someone else is here." He looked at her. "Get in the back and lie down. It could get ugly. Whatever you do, stay in this car." He reached into the glove compartment in front of her and pulled out a handgun.

Gwen did as he told her, shimmying over the front seat into the back. She wasn't about to argue with him over anything.

"I'll be right here when you get back, Allen. I promise you." Her fingers crossed behind her back and she smiled.

"You better be. I shouldn't have to tell you what I'll do to you if you get out. I'm more than capable of hunting you down." He spun the bullet chamber of the revolver.

The chambers were all full. He had six shots he could fire. Six chances to kill Anne and Gwen supposed he planned on killing whoever else was in the house too. She would have to hurry to call the police. The other people in the house might be innocent people who didn't deserve to die the way Anne Sinclair did.

Allen caught her off guard as he leaned over the seats into the back. He caught her behind her neck and pulled her to kiss him. Although disgusted beyond anything she'd ever been, she kissed him back.

"Hurry back to me, Allen," she said with a fake smile.

He gave her a smile too and left the car. She watched as he snuck around the back of the house and she cracked the back passenger door open a hair, so she could hear.

After counting to three hundred and not hearing a thing, she got out of the car. The only thing she had on was a ragged T-shirt and jeans with no shoes. He'd taken her shoes off and thrown them somewhere so she couldn't run away again.

Not that she had enough strength to even make the attempt back at the warehouse. But she had enough strength to make it the forty feet across a lawn of carpet grass to get to safety and help. Shoes or no shoes, she was going for it.

Although Allen had let her take a shower, he had no shampoo or soap of any kind and no hairbrush either. Her hair was a nasty, gnarled, blonde mess, and she knew she smelled awful, but she was on her way to the neighbor's house. With the one car in the drive she prayed someone would be home.

Though not far at all, every step had her looking back over her shoulder to see if Allen had come back around the house for some reason. Her heart was pounding so loud she was afraid he could hear it.

Fear ran through her that he'd just come out of nowhere and grab her up again. Or even worse, shoot her and leave her to die.

The sound of a dog barking made her freeze. Then she realized it was pretty far away, and she started moving forward again. She moved more quickly as she could see the front door. A green wreath hung on the front of it, commemorating the Saint Patrick's holiday which she guessed must be near.

Gwen had lost all track of time. She had no idea what time it was or day or even month. It felt like she'd been kept in the warehouse for years, not days.

Her bare feet touched the smooth concrete surface of the well-kept front porch and she took in a deep breath.

"Please let someone be home. Please!"

KNOCKING AS QUIETLY AS she could, she waited and hoped someone would answer the door. When a tiny, old woman opened the door, Gwen let out the breath she'd not realized she'd been holding. The little woman looked Gwen up and down with an odd look.

"Thank, God! Mam, I need your help. I know I look awful, but I've been kidnapped for I don't even know how long. Can I please come in, I need to use your phone to call the police?"

The woman looked her up and down one more time then took a step back.

"Come in, sweetheart. You look near death, darling."

Gwen stepped inside the house and took in the sweet aroma of Ben-Gay, mothballs, and burnt eggs. It was the best thing she'd ever smelled in her life.

"Thank you, mam. You've saved my life!"

Can the cops get here in time to catch Allen before he hurts someone though?

63

STEELE

"So tell me again how Arsen isn't doing anything wrong," Steele said to Paul as he looked at her through the rear-view mirror.

Her pulse had remained high since they left Arsen's penthouse. It had been over eight hours since he'd gotten into that car with his old girlfriend, Beth, and Steele was uneasy about why whatever they were doing was taking so damn long.

Thoughts of them making plans together kept racing through her mind. She saw them holding hands and talking about her leaving her husband and kids and going with Arsen somewhere far away. Then she saw them lying in a bed somewhere and laughing about how stupid she and Beth's husband were.

There just wasn't any good scene she could come up with in her jealous mind.

"He's not doing anything wrong, Steele," Paul said. "Obviously this Beth girl must have something to tell him that's going to help him."

Steele sat back and threaded her fingers together back-and-forth. Her head was spinning with what she would find Arsen and Beth doing. Her stomach was tight and her insides on fire. The green-eyed monster was in full force inside her and she prayed she found her man in a situation which was not compromising.

The ride to Anne Sinclair's house was taking forever. Traffic was backed up worse than she'd ever seen. Steele asked Paul, "What's going on with this crazy traffic?"

His eyes caught hers through the rear-view mirror.

"I heard on the radio a minute ago there's a car wreck about 2 miles up the road."

SHE LEANED back on the soft leather seat and sighed for the hundredth time.

"It could not happen at a worse time!"

Paul chuckled. "Think the people involved in the accident share your feelings, Steele?" Paul's cell phone rang. He looked at Steele through the rear-view mirror again. "It's Fontaine." He answered the phone. "Hey baby what's up?"

Steele's eyes rolled with how quickly Paul was falling for the detective. The woman was a real bitch most of the time. Paul could do much better. Find someone sweet instead of so abrasive.

Fontaine answered him.

"There's just been a 911 call from the house next door to Anne Sinclair's. It's Gwen. Tell Steele, Gwen's okay."

Steele bolted upright in the back seat and wondered if she'd heard that right.

Gwen's okay?

PAUL SAID, "I have you on speakerphone, she just heard it. And man did relief just wash over her face. Thanks for letting us know that. You sure are a sweetheart. Miss me?"

Fontaine's shy laugh came over the phone.

"Paul! I'm working here!"

Steele sat up to listen to everything Fontaine had to say. Her heart was racing after finding out Gwen was alive.

She's okay! Everything is going to be fine! It has to be!

FONTAINE SAID, "Allen White is in Anne Sinclair's house. As we speak, he's got a loaded revolver with six shots. And it's there, the blue Camaro. Safe to say Arsen and that Beth woman are there along with Anne. How you doing, Gannon?"

Her stomach knotted as she now was positive Arsen was inside that house. And now so was Allen White. Along with Anne Sinclair and Beth. Allen White was the only one with any kind of weapon, most likely. Steele knew he would want to see Arsen dead rather than alive.

"I'm holding on, Fontaine. How much longer until we get to them?"

"Fifteen minutes. Just hold tight and stay on my ass, Paul. I'm about to turn on the lights and do a bit of off-roading to get out of this traffic jam. You follow me. I told all other officers to stand down and let me take care of this situation. They know you're with me." Fontaine's lights went on and her siren blasted.

Cars began to move out of her way, giving her just enough room to get past them and onto the median. Paul followed and in no time they were free from the traffic and on the side roads heading to Anne's home.

Steele moved up and kneeled down behind the window separating her and Paul. "Fontaine, can I go in too?"

Fontaine let out a loud laugh.

"Hell no! You stay in the car, Gannon. Paul don't let her out of the car. Okay?"

"Yes, ma'am. You can count on me," Paul said. He turned his head and looked at Steele. "You're not getting out of the car, Steele. No matter what. You're not getting out of the car."

Steele moved back to the seat at the back of the Suburban. "Brown noser!"

She knew she was going to get out of the car the minute Fontaine got out of her way. Steele was going to get out of the car and she was going to go into that house to find her man and bring him back home. End of discussion!

I hope he's alright!

64

ARSEN

The sound of the doorbell ringing had Arsen taking a step back to make sure he was hidden from everyone's view. Anne made her way to the door and Arsen could see her through the barely opened door.

Beth and Anne had been talking for nearly an hour and Arsen had all he needed on the recording device Beth had given him to catch her mother's words.

Just as he knew he had all he needed and was about to spring his surprise on Anne, it seemed she was about to have some company and Arsen would have to wait to tell her how screwed she was.

Light flooded the small entryway as she opened the door.

"What the hell are you doing here?"

"We need to talk," he heard a man say, but he couldn't see him.

"Who has the girl?" Anne asked.

"Never mind about her. Aren't you going to ask me to come inside, Anne?" the man said.

Anne shook her head. "Can't you see I have company? I'll come see you in a little while at your place. The place you should be so what happened last time doesn't happen again. Or did you do as I suggested and end that little problem?"

"If you must know, I have her hiding in the car. If you let me in I can tell you all about it. I took a little walk around your house. I overheard you talking and I know you only have one other person in here with you. So if you'll let me in we can deal with this really quick then I'll be out of your hair, Anne."

Anne hesitated and Arsen had a gut feeling the man was not there for anything good. "You walked around my house, Allen?" she asked and held the door tight in her hand, ready to slam it if need be.

Arsen knew then it was none other than Allen White who was paying his old Dom a visit. He shook his head and leaned against the wall and hoped the woman would close the door. Arsen smelled danger and Allen's scent was all over it.

"Just let me in, Anne." Allen's voice had turned commanding.

Arsen watched as Anne took a step back. "What the hell are you doing, Allen?"

Arsen's eyes caught Allen White as he walked in and Anne backed up. He was holding a gun out, pointing straight at her. Arsen's breath caught in his chest and he had no idea what he was going to do to get the gun out of the man's hand.

"Who are you?" Beth asked. "And why the gun?"

"I'm the man who is about to kill this woman and then you, obviously," Allen answered as he kept moving forward and Anne kept moving backwards.

"Allen, why are you pointing a gun at me, you idiot? We're on the same side. Or have you forgotten that?" The back of Anne's legs hit the front of the sofa, stopping her retreat.

"Are we on the same side?" he asked her. "Because I don't feel like we are. I can see the writing on the wall, Anne. I'm your patsy. Always have been since the first time you came to see me while I was in prison."

Beth's voice was shaky as she said, "Look mister, I don't even know who you are. I'm married with little kids please don't kill me. Let me leave. I swear I'll never tell a soul what I've seen."

Anne sounded stunned.

"I've got things to live for too, Beth. Jesus! This little man isn't about to really shoot us." She looked back at Allen. "What are you doing, you idiot? Don't make me come over there and take that gun out of your hand."

Allen laughed.

"You think you're taking this gun away from me? You're crazier than I thought you were!"

Beth began to cry and Allen pointed the gun towards Beth who stood several steps away from Anne.

"Maybe I'll take you out first as it seems like you're going to be kind of annoying," he told her.

Beth shook her head.

"No. I'll shut up. I'll shut up, I promise. Please let me go, sir. My kids need me!"

Anne spoke up, drawing Allen's attention back to her, "Allen you need to stop this. Put the gun down. What are you doing? Why are you here with that gun? What's going on with you? We have a deal. I'm not going to do anything but what we've agreed to."

He pointed the gun back Anne.

"I've gotten wise to you. I know you're going to throw me under the bus. I know that you're going to tell everyone I killed all those women. I know what you're going to do."

"And who told you this? Someone put this into your head." Anne tapped her temple with one long finger. "That dumb bitch! Gwen put this into your head, didn't she?"

"If you mean the love of my life, yes it was Gwen who talked to me about this," he said. "Gwen showed me who you really are. She explained how I'm nothing but a patsy in your whole scheme."

ARSON WATCHED as Anne threw her hands up in the air. All he could see was her back and Beth's back and he prayed Allen was so focused on them he wouldn't see his eyes peeking at him through the crack in the door

Beth let out a big sob. She started crying uncontrollably and Allen pointed the gun at her again.

"Shut up! Shut up! I can't take that! Shut up or I swear to God I'm going to put a bullet in you first!"

Beth tried her best to shut up. She did everything she could to stop crying.

Anne looked at him and said, "Can I go over there and put my arm around my daughter? Before you kill us, at least let me give my daughter one last hug, you piece of crap!"

"Go ahead," Allen said as he waved the gun, gesturing for Anne to move the few steps to her daughter. "Give her one last hug. Do whatever you want to do. Give her a kiss for all I care. I don't care what you do, but I'm going to kill you both."

Anne walked over to her daughter and put her arms around her.

"It's okay Beth. It's okay. Don't worry, this man isn't really going to kill us. He's kind of crazy, but he's not so crazy he would kill the person who is going to give him more than one million dollars." Anne turned her head to look at Allen. "Have you forgotten how much money I'm going to give you, Allen? Have you forgotten that it's almost in my hands? It's almost in your hands, Allen!"

"I don't believe you were ever going to give it to me anyway, so you shut your mouth," he told her as he pulled the gun up and aimed it right at her head. "Pray to God or whoever it is you believe in, because I'm fixing to send you to wherever it is you're going to go. You're an evil lady so you'll probably go to hell."

"Evil!" Anne shouted.

Beth was choking on her sobs and holding on tight to her mother.

"Mom, I love you!"

Anne shouted, "We are not about to die! Stop the damn bawling, Beth! Shit!"

Arsen couldn't believe that Anne was staring into the face of death and would tell her daughter to stop crying. She was a complete, heartless bitch.

Allen's hand was shaking as he pointed the gun at the women and Arsen knew the time had come. Allen took a couple of steps and pressed the gun to the side of Beth's head.

She was screaming and crying and begging for him to spare her life. Allen's hand was shaking worse and Arsen knew he had to do something.

He slammed the door back as hard as he could. The noise made Allen turn around. He only got two words out of his mouth, "What the..."

Arsen was on him and had wrestled him to the floor. His hand touched the gun which was between them. He felt Allen's finger on the trigger.

Allen shouted, "Get off me! I'm going to kill you, Arsen! Then I'll kill them!"

Arsen wasn't about to let him go. He wasn't about to let him up. The pieces would just have to fall where they may.

He tried to position the gun, trying to push the gun into Allen's gut. Allen's finger was still on the trigger as Arsen wrapped his hand around the gun.

Arsen closed his eyes and prayed for the strength and the courage to do what he had to do. Then he squeezed Allen's hand until the sound of the gun going off rang out in the room.

All Arsen could hear was the women screaming. Then a gurgling sound. He assumed it was the sound of blood coming out of someone's body, He knew someone had been shot, but he wasn't sure if it was him or Allen.

His stomach burned and his heart was pounding. Arsen knew his adrenaline was so amped up, if he was shot, he wouldn't feel it right away.

He closed his eyes and pictured Steele and prayed he'd live to see her again.

It can't end like this!

65

STEELE

The afternoon sun made Detective Fontaine's blonde locks glow as she walked up to the driver's side window, Paul had rolled down. They had pulled up on the side of Anne Sinclair's home, just her cruiser and the Suburban parked right behind it.

Other officers were in the area, but all were waiting for Fontaine's call for backup before moving in.

"Okay, keep her here, Paul." She drew her gun.

Paul wiggled his finger for her to come closer. She leaned in the window as he said, "You be careful baby. We have a date later."

She smiled.

"I know. I will, don't worry, I've never been shot yet."

Paul shook his head.

"I hope you haven't just jinxed yourself."

Fontaine gave him a smile, and he gave her a little kiss. Then she turned around and headed towards the house, staying close to the side of the outside wall. Steele's eyes stayed glued to her as she ducked, going under the large set of windows she figured were in the living room.

. . .

JUST BEFORE FONTAINE made it to the door the muffled sound of a gun blast was heard and she looked back over her shoulder at them and hurried into the house. Paul jumped out of the car and ran towards the house.

Steele hauled ass out of the car and ran for the house as well. There was no way she could sit there not knowing who had been shot.

"Steele, what the hell are you doing in here?" Fontaine asked with her jaw clenched.

She was holstering her gun as Beth and Anne stood screaming and crying and holding on to each other. Paul stood between Fontaine and Steel as all looked at the two men on the floor.

Paul said what all were thinking, "Fuck!"

Blood had already stained the white carpet the men were lying on.

"Arsen!" Steele shouted and ran fast to him. She fell on her knees next to him. Her hand on his back, her mouth near his ear. "Baby, please talk to me. Please."

Arsen's head moved a little and his eyes opened slowly.

"Hey, Baby. What are you doing here?"

She laughed and tears ran down her cheeks.

"Are you hurt?"

"Not sure about that," he said. "I feel odd, but not in any real pain. My stomach burns a little though."

Detective Fontaine kneeled on the other side of him and she took Allen's hand and checked his pulse.

"I think this one is dead." She looked up at Paul who was right behind her. "Help me roll Arsen off this guy."

He nodded and did as she'd told him. They rolled him to his back and Steele stayed right by him. Her eyes went wide as she saw blood covering most of his shirt. "Oh, God!"

Fontaine unbuttoned Arsen's shirt as he lay perfectly still and kept his eyes focused on Steele.

"I'm sorry I left without telling you where I was going. You must've been worried."

"Don't worry about that now." She ran her hand over his forehead, pushing back some damp strands of his dark hair.

Fontaine let out a sigh of relief.

"It's all the other guy's blood. No wounds on Arsen." She gave Steele a wink. "What muscles this man has! Lucky girl."

Steele laughed and ran her arms around his neck and hugged him tight. With the information he wasn't shot, Arsen sat up and Steele let him go and took a step back so Paul could help him up.

Paul pulled Arsen into a hug.

"You scared us all, you son of a bitch!"

Steele was so busy starring at Arsen she almost missed seeing Anne slipping out of the living room. She moved quickly to get to the woman.

"Stop!"

Anne didn't even look back. She took off running. Not nearly fast enough though as Steel caught up to her and had her down on the kitchen floor.

"Stop! Let me go!" Anne screamed.

Fontaine came into the kitchen and placed her knee in the woman's back.

"Thanks, Steele. I can take her from here."

"I didn't do anything!" Anne shouted as she squirmed to get away.

ARSEN AND PAUL walked in and Arsen handed the recorder to Fontaine once she had Anne secured. "Here you go. This will exonerate me and condemn her. Seems Mistress Sinclair has been into some bad things. Revenge for leaving her had her thinking up new punishments for me. It's an open and shut case with her words on this recording."

"How dare you, Arsen!" Anne yelled from her position on the floor. "That's illegal! You can't record someone who doesn't know they're being recorded!"

Arsen let out a sigh.

"I can't listen to her speak anymore. I've had to listen to her voice for far too long as it is."

Beth's voice came from behind them.

"Arsen, can I talk to you?"

Steele's heart clenched, and she looked at Arsen who silently asked her to let him do what he needed to do. She gave him a nod and ran her hand over his cheek.

"I love you, Baby."

"I love you," he said them pressed his lips to her forehead.

He walked towards Beth and took her by the hand, leading her away from the crowded kitchen. Steele watched as a pain filled her chest. But she knew Arsen needed this closure.

Still, it wasn't easy to witness. All the craziness was over. Arsen was a free man, all the hard times were over for him. Steele couldn't help but wonder how Arsen would feel with all the weight off his shoulders.

She wondered if he might want to slow things down between them now that prison wasn't hanging over his head. He may have found some feelings left over for Beth.

Beth was Arsen's age, early thirties, but she looked as if life had been rough on her. Lines around her lips showed she was a smoker and dark circles under her eyes showed she was most likely a drinker too.

Perhaps all that had happened all those years ago had Beth filled with guilt and it was showing on her face and body. Her posture was poor and she had extra weight on her. Arsen could feel sorry for Beth and that could turn into more.

Arsen could feel he needed to save Beth and that would be a powerful thing which could bring the two together again. The woman certainly looked like she needed some kind of help. But she had her own husband to do that for her.

Steele knew if Beth had a choice between the man she'd seen sitting on the porch of their small home and Arsen, she'd be an idiot not to pick Arsen. It circled round and round in Steele's head and it began to ache with fear of Arsen leaving her for his old flame.

Steele left the kitchen and walked through the living room, finding some other officers had come inside and had Allen's body covered with some black thing. She stepped out the front door and the light from the sun made her shield her eyes.

THEN SHE HEARD Arsen's voice coming from the side of the house. He and Beth must have stepped to the side of the house to talk. She took a couple of steps away. Planning to wait in the Suburban but stopped when she heard Beth say, "I'm more sorry than you'll ever know, Arsen."

Steele knew she shouldn't be listening. But she couldn't make her feet move. She stood still and listened.

Arsen said, "Thank you, Beth. You don't know how it helps to hear you say that. All these years I was left wondering if you were ever sorry about what happened."

"I was a very confused girl back then. And I can't even begin to tell you how sorry I am my mother did all she did to you. If I would've had any idea about that stuff back then, I swear I would've put a stop to it." Steele heard material move and thought Arsen's hands must be running up and down Beth's arms.

She fisted her hands at her sides and had to focus on the fact Arsen needed to hear those things from Beth. No one else could help him heal the wounds she and her family had given Arsen.

The sound of his lips making a little smack against somewhere on Beth made Steele take a step away. She couldn't take knowing his lips were touching her anywhere.

Arsen's voice stopped her.

"I know you would've. I knew I could've gone to you and told you what she was doing. I just didn't do it. I take responsibility for my part in it. I told myself for many years that wasn't anything I could've controlled. That was a lie I kept telling myself. Then I had to have all the control in my dealings with women."

"So, you became the dominant then?" she asked.

"Yes. And I did it for all the wrong reasons." His voice was soft and then she heard the sound of him running his hands over Beth again as the fabric moved once more.

"That girl who came, is that her? The one you told me about?" she asked.

STEELE'S HEART stopped beating as she listened as Arsen answered, "Yeah, that's my Steele. My rock, my savior, my everything."

Steele walked away then. Giving him his privacy. Whatever he had to do was his to do, and she didn't need to let her jealousy ruin anything that helped him get over all which had happened to him.

Half way to the car she heard footsteps come up behind her. She turned to find Arsen in his blood-soaked clothes. His arms opened, and she went into them. Her tears flowed as he held her tight.

"I was so afraid." Her body shook.

His lips pressed against the top of her head as he swayed with her.

"So was I. It's all over, Baby. Let's get the hell out of here. I told Fontaine she could talk to me tomorrow. I'm done for the day."

Steele let him lead her to the back of the Suburban and saw Paul coming out to take them home.

It's hard to believe this is really over!

THE SOUND of people coming out and talking in medical terms had Steele and Arsen looking back to find a stretcher coming out the front door of the house next to Anne's.

"Gwen!" Steele said under her breath. "In all the drama I forgot she was in the house next door." She pulled Arsen along with her to go see Gwen as the paramedics wheeled her to the ambulance.

Arsen called out, "Wait a second. We know her."

They waited and Gwen raised her head a little.

"Oh my God! You're alright!"

Steele was crying again as she got to her friend and hugged her.

"You have no idea how happy I am to see you, Gwen."

Gwen laughed.

"You too! Did they catch Allen? And that crazy old bitch he was doing all this shit with?"

Arsen nodded.

"He didn't make it. We got into a scuffle with his gun between us and it went off." He pulled at his bloody shirt. "I wasn't hurt."

Gwen's eyes went vacant.

"He's dead then?"

Steele ran her hand over Gwen's cheek.

"Yes. You okay?"

"Well, no. But I will be. I suppose it's what was meant to be for him. And the woman?" she asked.

"She'll be going to prison for a long time," Arsen answered her.

Gwen nodded. "Good, she's horrible."

One of the paramedics interrupted their little reunion.

"We really should get her to the hospital."

Arsen ran his arm around Steele, pulling her back as he took a step back. "We'll come and see you first thing in the morning, Gwen," Steele said. "I would go tonight, but I bet your family will want you all to themselves."

"Probably," Gwen agreed as they began moving her down the sidewalk to the waiting ambulance.

Paul and Detective Fontaine were standing beside her car as Arsen looked up.

"We're ready, Paul."

Paul pulled Fontaine into his arms and kissed her, grabbing her ass in the process and Arsen stopped in his tracks.

"When the fuck did that happen?"

Steele laughed.

"A little earlier today. Seems Paul moves about as fast as you do. Way to teach the man, Boss."

Arsen chuckled as they climbed into the back of the Suburban.

"I cannot wait to get these sticky, nasty clothes off."

Steele sat on the soft leather seat and pulled him to sit close to her. "Me too."

Running her hand to cup the back of his neck, she pulled his lips to hers and gave him a kiss she hoped he'd never forget.

Now to see where we're headed from here!

66

STEELE

A rsen soaked in the warm water of the deep, jetted bathtub as Steele lit candles in the bedroom. She pulled her clothes off as she made her way to the bathroom and found him lying back in the water with his eyes closed.

She turned on the stereo, playing something soft and romantic. His eyes opened and his lips curled into a smile. He held his hand out to her, and she took it and climbed in.

Straddling him and sliding her body along his. Her hands ran over his chest then up to his face. She took his face between her palms and pressed her lips to his.

She couldn't seem to get enough of him. Something inside her was telling her things were about to be different and she didn't want a thing to change.

Steele wanted things to keep going like they had been. But something felt different with him. He was acting a little quiet, and it was as if he was keeping a secret from her.

She kept thinking the worst. That when he saw Beth again it stirred something in him for her. Steele was feeling vulnerable and uneasy and she needed to feel him.

Feel him all over her, all inside her. She needed him and she hoped he would feel the same for her as she felt as if he was drifting away from her.

His lips tasted like the Cognac she'd made him a glass of and she ran her tongue over them. He moaned and his fingers pressed into the flesh of her ass. His tongue ran into her mouth and hers began a little dance with his as the music led their movements.

He lifted her, and she felt his cock hard and ready for her. He slipped her down and filled her the way she'd been craving. Her heart sped up and her kiss went hungry. She was ravenous for him.

He moved her up and down his long, hard cock as their mouths heated with the fevered kiss they shared. Steele ran her hands up to move through his shoulder length, silky locks.

The jets of water pulsed around their bodies as they slid against one another. Water splashed out onto the floor as he moved her faster and faster. Neither seemed to care much about the mess they were making.

Arsen's hands dug into her waist as he moved her over him. Her insides were tight as she felt every little movement he made. His muscles rippled against her stomach. His skin was like silk against hers.

They moved together like practiced partners yet they'd only been together a short time. Their connection a quick one, Steele hoped was deep enough to last.

Something inside her was afraid though. Her fingernails raked his back, and he moaned as he ran one of his hands up to wrap her hair around his fist. He pulled it back hard, making her mouth leave his.

Her neck was exposed and his teeth grazed it as she kept up the movements he'd shown her he wanted. Up and down she went as his teeth raked over the tender flesh along her throat.

Tugging at her hair, he bit her hard, making her growl with how it was making her feel. Primal and sexy and so hot for him, she felt as if her body was on fire.

Arsen eased his grip on her hair and moved her face down,

pressing his forehead to hers. "Out of the tub and onto the bed. This slipping shit is pissing me off."

She moved off him and climbed out of the tub. The floor was wet, so she tossed a fluffy, white towel on the floor before they got out. Her feet touched it and he had her up in his arms.

He carried her to the bed and tossed her on it.

"Knees, now!"

SHE GOT on her hands and knees and felt his hand tangle up in his fist again and he pulled it hard as he slammed into her. She shrieked, not in pain but in desire for him.

He was rough, nearly to the point of being violent. His body was pounding hers, but she knew it was something inside him finally releasing. Finally, he was losing control and she could tell that's exactly what he wanted to do.

He seemed to want to let himself go and Steele was both exhilarated and scared nearly to death as she'd never been around Arsen when he wasn't in complete control of himself and whoever was with him.

Arsen stopped his pounding and pulled out of her. She looked back to find him grabbing the television remote off the nightstand and clicking on the TV. Some hard rock music channel came on as he pushed the buttons and he turned the sound up so loud she could feel the bass line beating in her body.

The song had hard sounds and his lips pulled into a quirky grin and he grabbed her by the waist and flipped her onto her back as he moved his body over hers.

His dark hair fell across his cheeks as he looked down at her. Steele was feeling anxious as his dark eyes ran over her body then back up to her face. His lips touched her ear as he told her, "I'm going to fuck you like you nor I have ever fucked before."

A deep growl filled him and his nails raked down her arms. Her breath was coming in hard, ragged gasps. It was Arsen but such a different Arsen. A hot as hell Arsen, an Arsen who wasn't thinking. An Arsen who had no more rules.

Steele's body was more than quivering, it was shaking. His knee went between her legs which she'd moved tightly together. He pushed them apart as he looked at her. His eyes were wild and untamed.

The music was loud, hard, demanding and seemed to be setting the tone. His hand moved to grasp the back of her neck and his mouth took hers in the hardest kiss. Their teeth clashed as he pressed his mouth to hers harder than he ever had before.

He pulled back and looked down at her. His hands moved over her body then his mouth took her breast. He sucked it hard as he raked his nails over her sides. Up and down her sides, he raked them over and over again.

Arsen hadn't even entered her yet, and she was about to climax. Her heart was pounding. Her body was more alert than it had ever been and then he pulled his mouth off her tit and looked her in the eyes.

He just looked at her for the longest time. She looked back and saw something different. Something was gone and something was new.

She ran her hands up to catch them up in his hair. She pulled him to her and kissed him. His body was tense as he let it fall down on hers.

Steele pulled her knees up and Arsen pressed his hard cock into her. Then his mouth left hers and he moved it to her neck and bit down hard as he began moving hard and fast into her.

Steele made a noise she never had before. A shrieking moan kind of thing and her body was lucid. The combination of all things had her somewhere else.

The man on top of her was the same man who had been on top of her last night, but he wasn't the same man. This man was wild. This man was wanting. This man was a beast.

Not the kind who needed someone tied down. Not the kind who needed control. Not the kind who needed rules.

Steele finally had figured out what Arsen was striving for. She raked her nails over his back and grazed her teeth over his left shoulder. His body shuddered as she did.

He wanted wild, she'd never done wild, but he was bringing it out in her.

Time to try something new, I think!

67

ARSEN

With the revelations the day had brought him and the threat of a lengthy trial and prison gone, Arsen was feeling different. Extremely different.

The way he thought of sex and life in general was changing. He wanted to experience it all without the control he'd needed since he first became Anne Sinclair's submissive all those years ago.

Steele's blue eyes were wide as he looked into them. She had been so ready to accept his control. She wasn't good at it and he was glad for that as he was done with it.

The music was pounding and his body was itching to do things he'd never allowed himself to do before. Feel every little thing. Steele's body was tight and firm and her tits were perky and begging for his attention.

But his cock wanted to pound into her and that's what won out. He made hard, fast strokes as he watched her reaction to him. He saw fear in her eyes and knew she was seeing him turning into a different man.

Can she accept who I'm becoming?

. . .

ARSEN WAS on a new path and he hoped like hell Steele would take that path with him. The fact was, he would never allow anyone to make him what he wasn't ever again.

Steele and her tenacious way of trying to get him to make her submissive to him was a thing of the past. He prayed she could accept that fact and move on with him. If she couldn't, what they had would be over.

Arsen was aware of the fact Steele might not want him if she thought he was going back to being a weak man. He wasn't going all the way back, but he was changing and the hard as nails man who had to have everything his way would be drastically different.

Moving so fast and hard had his dick throbbing, ready to explode. He let it out without doing his usual thing of making himself wait. It had always been his job to make sure the woman climaxed first, and he saw Steele's surprise at his release.

She seemed so surprised her body didn't join his in the intense orgasm. Once his cock jerked for the last time, he opened his eyes to find her searching them. He smiled and kissed the tip of her nose.

Then pulled out of her and kissed her lips then her chin, moving down her entire body until he kissed the tip of her big toe. He got off the bed and grabbed her ankles and yanked her down until her ass was at the edge of the bed.

Arsen kneeled down to the floor and ran one finger over her clit. Her body shivered as he took her plump ass in his hands and pulled her body up. His mouth came down on her hard and wanting.

A saltiness filled his mouth as he licked and nipped her clit. Steele was writhing and pulling at his hair. Her moans were so loud he could hear them over the loud music.

Her legs began to shake on either side of him and then he felt her body tense as she sat up.

"My God, Arsen! You look amazing from this angle!"

His face was buried in her sweet essence and all he could think about was how delicious she was and how he could never get enough of her.

Little sounds of desire he heard her making as her hands ran over his shoulders and up into his hair. His tongue ran over her swollen clit over and over until her body was shaking and she was screaming his name.

Her orgasm had his cock hard and wanting to feel her again. He stood up and picked her up. She wrapped her legs round him and her arms around his neck and he took her mouth in a hard kiss as he slid her onto his erection.

Squeezing his hard cock, her body was rocking a hard orgasm and he could feel it all. They groaned, and he moved away from the bed and backed her up against the wall then began moving inside her.

Deep, hard thrusts that had her breath pushing out of her lungs and into his mouth in hot, little puffs made him move his mouth off hers so she could take in more air.

He kissed her neck. The way her soft skin felt under his tongue made him want more and he grazed his teeth over it them bit it and sucked hard. He knew he was making marks all over her and he didn't care.

Her body started shaking again, and he heard her screaming his name again as she came undone again. The way her body was pulsing around his hard cock had it pulling the orgasm from him and he let it all go.

Arsen stopped thrusting into her and let himself feel every little squeeze and pull her body did to him. When they finally stopped, he walked back to the bed and laid her back on it.

He climbed up next to her and grabbed the remote, turning off the music. The only sound in the room was them both trying to catch their breath. Then Steele's hand slipped into his as they laid side by side.

She rolled over on her side and kissed his cheek.

"I love you, Arsen."

He turned his head to the side and ran his hand over her cheek and pressed his lips lightly to hers.

"I love you, Steele."

He ran an arm around her and she snuggled into his side. She felt like home. More so than ever before, Steele felt like the other part of him which had been missing for so long.

But can she take the man I am becoming?

68

GWEN

The sun was shining through the large window of Gwen's hospital room as she watched Steele come into her room.

"There she is," Steele said as she carried in a large crystal vase full of roses. "These are from Arsen who had some pressing business to take care of this morning or he would've been here too."

Steele sat them on the window ledge where Gwen could look at them from her bed. "They're beautiful. Tell him thank you for me."

"I will," Steele said then went to sit on the bed beside Gwen. "I heard Detective Fontaine came to visit you early as shit this morning."

Gwen nodded.

"She did. I gave her all the details, and she told me they arrested that other guy who was the man who got them the drugs that killed those girls. He and Anne Sinclair had a little dom-sub thing going on. He'll get less time than Anne, but he'll get some."

"It's good to see some color back in your pretty face, Gwen," Steele said as she ran her hand over her cheek. "I was sick with worry over you. You have no idea how happy I am to see your face."

Gwen sighed.

"Yours too. It was all I could think about, getting to you before Allen got you and killed you."

"You're quite the hero, Gwen. Just so you know, Arsen has told the hospital all bills for your care are to be sent to him and they are to spare no expense on you." Steele pushed back a lock of her blonde hair which had been washed and looked a lot better but nowhere near as pretty as Gwen usually had it.

"That was nice of him. Tell him I really appreciate it. A poor college student is what I am after all." Gwen smiled.

Steele looked around the small hospital room.

"He has another surprise for you when you get out. I think you'll be pretty happy about it."

"I can't let him do any more than this, Steele," Gwen said with a frown.

STEELE PATTED the top of her hand.

"It's too late. It's already taken care of. Since you've suffered such a terrible ordeal he wanted to make sure you felt secure. He got you an apartment one floor under his penthouse. Some movers are moving your personal things as we speak. He had a designer pick out the furnishings and everything to go in it."

"He did not!" Gwen threw her hand over her mouth as tears filled her eyes. "Steele, I can't..."

Steele shook her head. "You can. I'm not even finished yet, so just be quiet and stop saying you can't. I snooped through your purse and got your check book so I could find out your bank account information. Arsen put some money in there for you. He paid all the bills we had at the apartment too."

"Steele!" Gwen shook her head as tears spilled over her cheeks.

"HE GAVE you enough money to get you through without having to have a job for this year, anyway. You can go to school and focus on that and not worry about anything else. Plus, he set up a little investment under your name and you'll receive the dividends on that for the rest of your life."

Gwen wrapped her arms around Steel and cried like a baby. It had all been so hard and she thought she might die at times but it was all going to be okay. And she had the best friends in the world at the end of it all.

"I love you, Steele."

"I love you too, Gwen."

69

ARSEN

After visiting the graves of all his submissive partners who'd been murdered and leaving flowers on them, Arsen made his way back to the penthouse to set Steele straight.

The time had come for him to let her know how things were going to be different and see how she took the news. And see if she thought it would be something she still wanted with him.

He was nervous to say the least. The doors to the private elevator opened, and he stepped inside. Steele was curled up with a book on the sofa and sat up as he came in. "There you are," she said with a smile.

"Wait here," he told her and walked back to his office.

She looked a little surprised. Her eyes went really wide when she saw him come back into the room with the contract in one hand and the book he'd written her with the rules in the other. He placed them on the coffee table then went to the kitchen, coming back with a small metal trash can and a box of matches.

"Arsen, what are...?"

"Sh. Let me talk please. This is hard for me to say. So please just let me talk then you can talk after that."

Steele nodded and sat back.

Arsen picked up the dom/sub contract.

"I don't want this anymore." He tore it in half then dropped in in the trash can.

Tears sprang up in her eyes as she watched the pieces fall. She gulped and looked up at him.

He took the book and said, "This isn't a thing I want to have around anymore. This is over." He tossed it into the trash can as well.

The tears amped up and ran in rivers down Steele's reddened cheeks. She watched Arsen light several matches and toss them into the trash can as well.

Smoke came up in small spirals as the things which had bound them together went up in flames.

"I want you to understand me clearly, Steele," Arsen said as he looked at her with no smile, no sign of any emotion at all. "This is over."

She nodded but didn't say a word. Steele got up and left the room.

Arsen stood there. Still as a statue. He watched the fire burn away what he had made so Steele would feel like she was part of the life he led.

That life was over and he wanted no part of it any longer. All that needed to be erased. And by what Steele had just done, he had no idea if she could take it.

Should I even ask her now?

70

PART FOURTEEN: FOR FREEDOM

STEELE

Steele's hands shook as she pulled her clothes from the closet. Not taking any of the new clothes Arsen had bought for her. Only her old clothes, the one's she'd come there with.

Tears flooded down her cheeks but she managed to hold back the sobs which were threatening to bust out of her.

His footsteps coming into the bedroom had her trying to hide in the closet from him. She didn't want him to see her face. Sure it was streaked with tears and red as well.

Arsen was done with her. She supposed he wanted to move on to a new life. One with no old memories of the bad times. One without her in it.

His hands ran around her from behind and his lips pressed against her neck. "What are you doing, Steele?"

"Packing." Only one word could come out of her mouth while holding back the cries which longed to escape her.

"You don't want something new and different then?" he asked.

She blinked and wiped her eyes.

"What?"

"I meant by burning the book and the contract that I don't want that life any longer. That is behind me and I want it all to stay in the past. None of that has a place in my future. You do, though. You will always have a place there. If you want it." He turned her in his strong arms.

Her eyes were rimmed red with her tears and he kissed her tear-stained cheeks. She looked up at him.

"I don't understand, Arsen. You will have to be a bit more communicative and let me know what it is you want."

"I want you and me to have a normal relationship. Free of contracts and punishments and control," he said. "Normal, Steele. What do you say? Want to be normal with me?"

"Normal? You, normal?" A laugh came from her and she sniffled. "Is that even possible?"

He frowned. "I was a normal guy once upon a time, Steele."

"You want that man back?" she asked.

"I'LL NEVER BE that kid again. No matter how hard I might try, I'd never get him back. People grow no matter how hard they might try not to. It just happens." He kissed her cheek. "I have something to give you. If you want to move forward with me, that is."

Steele looked into his dark eyes and found a new man there in them. They shone brightly and had lost so much of the sadness she'd thought was a permanent part of him.

"I love you, Arsen. All I want is to be with you every single day of my life." Her arms ran around his neck and she pulled him to her and kissed him.

He moaned with the kiss and ran his tongue through her lips. Then he pulled back and smiled at her. "I have something for you, then."

Arsen pulled her out of the closet and into the bedroom. Guiding her to sit on the edge of the bed, he had her sit down as he went to the nightstand beside the bed.

A leather-bound book he pulled out and placed it on her lap. "You seemed to love the book I made for you so I made you another one. One that our children can see. The other was never what I really wanted, anyway."

Steele ran her hand over the cover. The title was hand written in calligraphy. "This is beautiful, Arsen. You are a true artist."

"What do you think of the title, Baby?" He sat down next to her and looked over her shoulder.

"No Truer Love Has Ever Existed, The Arsen and Steele True Life Series," she read out loud. She looked up at him with a smile. "I love the title."

"Good. Open it up and see what else I have written in our book."

Steele opened the book and on the first page, she saw the words he'd written there and she read them to him, "On April eleventh in the year two-thousand-sixteen Arsen Sloan and Steele Gannon married at the Paris Chapel at Paris, Las Vegas at noon."

She turned to look as Arsen as she felt him moving and found him pulling a black box out of his pocket. He moved to get on one knee in front of her and held out the box then flipped the lid up.

Her eyes went wide with the size of the single diamond cast in platinum. She looked at him and the tears started flowing again.

A smile crossed his lips.

"Steele Gannon, you are a rare find. The night I saw you for the first time changed my life. You've been my rock, a thing I never realized I needed before you came along. You're tenacious, feisty, and hard to handle and I love every part of you. You keep me guessing and on my toes and I can't imagine a life without you right by my side. Would you consider becoming my wife?"

He pulled the ring out of the box and she stopped looking at him as the light glanced off the large stone, making her look at the ring. After taking in a deep breath, she let it out and said, "Arsen Sloan, I would love to become your wife."

He slipped the ring on her finger and she noticed his hand was shaking. She pulled his hand up to her mouth and kissed his knuckles. Arsen stood up and eased her back onto the bed and moved his body over hers.

Taking her lips with his, he kissed her long and hard. Steele ran her arms around him and held him to her as they kissed and held one another.

Their time, though short, had been intense and full. She'd learned so much about the man who held her. And now she'd learn so much more about him as they spend their lives together.

Then the date in the book ran through her mind and she pulled away, stopping the kiss.

"Arsen, April eleventh is tomorrow!"

"It is, Baby. Tomorrow, your name will change." He tried to kiss her again.

She turned her head. "Arsen! There's so much to do! We have to get ready! Let me up!"

"I'll let you up in a little while. Right now I'd like to seal this deal with you. If you don't mind that is." He nudged her cheek with his nose and made a low growling sound.

She looked at him and saw the desire in his dark eyes and ran her hands through his silky, dark waves. "Well, if you're feeling frisky, I guess there's time for that."

"There's always time for this, Baby." His mouth took hers again.

I'm going to be Mrs. Arsen Sloan!

ARSEN

Steele's body felt good under his hands. He ran them over every inch of her after he'd undressed her. She was about to become his wife in the matter of one day and he could hardly believe it.

His lips grazed over her stomach as his hands roamed over her perky breasts. He felt her hands go through his hair and her stomach twitched under his lips.

Arsen nipped her stomach, and she groaned.

"Again."

He nipped her flesh again, and she wiggled a little. As he moved up her body, he bit her place after place, leaving little red marks on her pristine skin. Arsen moved up until his hands ran into her hair and he fisted large chunks of it.

Her face was so close and he let his lips barely touch hers. By the way her body was moving under his and her lips were pursed for his kiss, he knew she was more than ready for him.

Arsen didn't settle on her lips. He moved around and took her neck with his teeth. She arched up.

"Please, Arsen."

"We've discussed little about what you want for the future, Steele."

"For the immediate future, I want you, Arsen. I want you all over me. I want you inside me," she said with a moan and a wiggle.

His laugh was deep.

"Do you want your family flown in for the wedding?" he asked.

"If you want." She raked her nails over his back. "Come on, Baby."

He smiled at her want for him. But didn't give in to her yet.

"How many children should we have, Baby?"

"As many as you want," she moaned and moved her mouth to his neck and bit him. "Baby, please."

"Do you like dogs or cats, Steele?" He bit her neck and sucked it.

"For the love of God! Arsen, please!" She writhed under him. "I'm on fire here."

"Dogs or cats, Baby. What kind of family are we going to be?" His hands moved over her sides.

"A DOG FAMILY, Arsen. A salt water fish tank and a cockatoo named Bentley who will have a cage in the corner of the living room. There, our life in a nutshell. Now take me, Baby, before I implode." She ran her hands to grip his large biceps as he laughed.

"Are you saying that you want me, Steele?" he growled in her ear as he ground his erection against her soft core.

"I want you bad, Baby. So please stop asking me questions about the future and let's get going with right now." She arched up to him and he gave into her.

Sliding his erection into her, her sigh of relief filled his ears.

"There you go, Baby."

"Yes," she said as she breathed out. "Yes, Baby. That's what I wanted."

HE SMILED against her neck then moved to take her lips. Nipping at her bottom lip with his first, slow stroke. She placed her hands on either side of his head and held him tight in them. Her mouth opened, and she kissed him hungrily.

She was on fire. He could tell that and she was making him heat up as well. Her hot body gyrated with each one of his strokes. She arched up just as he pulled out and made him stroke her more quickly.

Arsen moved his hands down her arms and took her hands in his and pulled them up over her head and held them to the bed. He held them with one hand and took the other hand and moved it up and down her side.

One hard thrust he gave her, knocking the breath from her. He felt it shoot into his mouth and he eased their kiss. Pulling his mouth from hers, he looked at her.

Another hard stroke he made and her breath puffed out of her mouth. He felt it on his lips which hovered near hers. He took in a deep breath and made another hard thrust.

She opened her mouth and let the air come out and he breathed it in.

"I cannot wait to call you mine, Steele."

"I am yours, Arsen. I always have been."

He growled and kissed her hard and wanting. Moving hard and fast inside her, he claimed her as his. Every last inch of her was nearly entirely his, and his alone.

The fact she was about to be his wife had him feeling wild and free. She bucked under him and he let her.

Their ragged breathing filled the room along with the sound of flesh smacking against flesh. Arsen's body began to shake with his need to release. Steele's words fell soft near his ear. "Just do it, Baby. Let it all go."

So many years holding himself back, stopping the normal urges had him forgetting he didn't have to or even want to do that any longer. He whispered in her ear, "Come."

Her body blasted with his words and she fell apart around him. He released her hands, and they moved over his back, raking it over and over as she pulsed around his cock, taking him along with her.

His heart pounded as he spilled inside her. He lay still on top of her. Their bodies wet with sweat. Their hearts pounded loud and hard. Their breathing was rough.

One soft kiss he placed on her sweet lips. The next day she would be his in name as well.

I cannot wait!

72

STEELE

A white dress, a white bouquet of roses, and a bottle of white wine sat on the table in their hotel suite. The Paris theme of the place was gorgeous and Arsen told her the honeymoon would be a surprise.

Since he told her to bring her passport, she thought it was safe to say he planned on taking her to Paris for that.

Steele's family was there. In several rooms a few floors down. Though not the most expensive place in this city, the hotel had a charm all its own.

Arsen picked the place out because he'd always wanted to visit France, but never made time to do it before. He told Steele he was going to make time for so many things he never did before.

He was really changing. And while she was nervous about it, she knew she could handle it. If she loved him in the first place, she would love him as he morphed into the man who would soon be her husband and father to her children.

Detective Fontaine had to stay back in San Francisco to deal with what she said was a mountain of paperwork on the three murder cases. But Paul came along anyway.

He was Arsen's best man after all. With Gwen still in the hospital, Steele asked her younger sister to be her bride's maid. She was over the moon about it.

Steele's parents were still unsure about the marriage. It was too sudden for them. She hadn't even told them about her and Arsen as she knew if they found out she was living with a murder suspect, who lived a BDSM lifestyle, her father would've come straight out to San Francisco and snatched her out of Arsen's penthouse.

He's a little controlling himself.

A KNOCK at the door startled Steele.

"It's Mom and Dad, sweetheart." Her mother called out from the other side.

Steele went to open the door and found they had changed into the clothes she and Arsen had bought for them. In true Arsen style, he paid for the whole shebang, clothes included.

"My father in an Armani suit," Steele said, adding in a wolf whistle at the end. "My, my, you make a dashing man when you get all cleaned up, Dad."

Her mother smiled and took his arm and wrapped hers around it.

"He does, doesn't he?"

Steele's eyes raked over her mother in a Vera Wang dress that they had found in a shop in Vegas when they flew into town last night. "And you look like a fashion model, Mom!"

Her father looked at his wife with a smile.

"She always does." He kissed the top of her head, making her giggle and slap at his chest.

"It's time, isn't it?" Steele asked as she grabbed the bouquet and took a long drink of the glass of white wine she'd poured herself to take the edge of her nerves.

Her father took her hand and pulled her along with him and her mother to go down to the chapel. Steele looked back at the room one last time. She thought to herself that the girl who was leaving that room wasn't the same one who would be coming back to it in just a little while.

She closed the door on who she was and went to become who she would be.

73

ARSEN

Her naked back pressed up against his bare chest as they laid on the bed together. The entire night had been spent showing each other how happy they were to finally be married.

A picture of the two as they stood at the altar in front of the preacher had been taken by her older brother and Arsen had their book out and was making a sketch of it on the second page.

Steel watched as he moved the pencil over the cream-colored page. He was almost done with it and she seemed impressed.

"Arsen, you really are very artistic. I hope our children inherit that."

His lips touched the side of her head. "I hope they get your heart."

She ran her hands along his thighs which were on either side of her.

"I hope the boys get your muscles."

He laughed. "I hope the girls get your hair."

"Yours is nice too. They could get either of our hair," she said with a little laugh. "I hope they get your gorgeous, naturally tanned skin tone."

Making the last few strokes with his pencil he held the book up.

"There, finished!"

Steele took the book in her hands and looked at the picture of them he had drawn. "You made me look very pretty, Arsen. I love it."

"It wasn't me who made you look so pretty," he said. "We can thank your parents and the Lord above for that."

She closed the book and sat it on the nightstand then took his pencil from him and placed it next to it. Turning in his arms, she ran hers around his neck. "Want to practice making babies again?"

His lips quirked up to the right. "Anytime."

He moved his hands over her back and held her close to him. Her lips pressed to his for a moment then she pulled them back and trailed kisses down his chest and slid her body down his. "While I have you on your back I may as well have a taste of you."

"BY ALL MEANS, TASTE AWAY," he said as he laced his fingers and placed his hands behind his head, leaning back on the mountain of pillows.

Steele's warm mouth covered his chest with her sweet kisses. His body was washed in warmth from her lips touching him all over. When they ran over the head of his dick, it twitched.

She laughed. "Did you make it do that on purpose?"

He shook his head. "You made it do that."

A smile moved over her lips and she pressed them to it again and it twitched for her again. "Wow!"

"You think that's something. Sometimes you can just walk by me and it does that." He gave her a grin.

"Does that mean you like me?" she asked then kissed the tip of his growing cock again.

He shook his head. And she frowned. "It means I love you, Baby."

"Oh, okay then," she said and took the stiffening organ into her hands, running them up and down it.

Her lips touched the tip again then she opened her mouth and slid it over his hard cock. His eyes closed with the sensation and he let out a groan without realizing it.

The way her mouth was making slow strokes over him had him enjoying every sweet moment she had him inside her steamy hot mouth. When she slipped it all the way in, deep throating him, he moaned and moved his hands to run them into her dark waves of thick hair.

"Baby, yeah. Take me all in," he moaned as he fisted her hair and moved her a little faster over him.

SHE MOANED and the vibration of it made him moan too. It was all he could think about. Her mouth on him. The way her head was bobbing up and down was mesmerizing.

Her tongue glided over the tip of his dick and he knew a bit of pre-cum must be oozing out of it as Steele made a sound like she was saying, ummm.

Arsen didn't want to waste a thing, so he pulled her head up and she wiped her mouth with the back of her hand. He sat up and lifted her up and sat her on his cock.

"Let's put that stuff to good use, Baby."

She placed her hands on his wide chest and began moving up and down with long, deep strokes. Her dark hair fell to her waist in waves and her tits bounced just the right amount.

His hands stayed on her narrow waist as he helped her go up and down his length. "How about you put one of those juicy tits in my mouth, Kitten?"

Steele's dark brows arched up. "Kitten?"

"Yeah, Kitten." He smiled, and she leaned forward.

"That sounds kind of cute." She kissed him then placed her nipple to his lips.

His teeth grazed it at first then he gave it a nip and she let out a yelp. He pulled it into his mouth and gave it a hard pull. Her eyes closed, and she made a wonderful little purring noise.

The vibration he could feel coming through her breast in his mouth and her body covering his cock. His hands trailed up her sides and back down again as he lifted her, moving her a little faster.

Steele's hands tangled up in his hair as she held him to her breast and bounced up and down on his cock. Over and over she went until she was squealing with her release and pulsing all around him.

She slowed her strokes as her body had what it wanted. He pushed her back and got on top of her. Slamming into her. Hard, deep, fast strokes he gave her until he could take no more.

His cock jerked, sending his juices into her in swift pulses of heat. Her head hung back over the edge of the bed. Her body jerking more and more out of him until neither could do anymore.

He lay back and pulled her up with him. She lay gasping on his chest.

"The jet leaves in a couple of hours." He told her.

"Are you going to tell me where it is we're going finally?" she gasped out.

He laughed. "No."

She pulled her head up off his chest and stared at him.

"Really? No?"

He nodded. "No."

"So what should I wear to this mystery destination?" she asked as she laid her head back on his chest and he ran his hand through her hair.

"I packed all you'll need to get there and once we're there I'm buying you more clothes." He pulled a section of her hair up to his nose and smelled it. "And I'm taking you to a salon while we're there and letting them do your hair and we'll be getting whatever kinds of shampoos and conditioners and any other products they say will be good for your hair."

"Are you saying my hair is ugly and it stinks?" she didn't even bother to look at him as she asked.

"No!" he said then laughed. "Your hair smells like the hotel shampoo. It's nice but it can be better. I'm going to spoil the shit out of you, Baby."

"Okay," she said.

He pulled her up. "Okay? Did you just simply say the word, okay?"

"I did. I'm now the wife of a billionaire. I should look the part."
She kissed his forehead and leaned hers to his. "I have a lot to learn."

He pulled her to lie on his chest again. "You and learning shit!
Just live, Baby. Live the way you want to. However you want, as long as
it's with me."

"Can I be honest with you, Arsen," she asked as he held her tight.

"I hope you always are, Steele." He kissed the top of her head.

Her hand ran over his tight abs. "First confession, I absolutely
love your six pack."

"Noted." He stroked her hair. "And the rest?"

"Oh, yeah all the rest of you as well," she said.

He laughed. "No, the rest of your confession, Steele."

"OH. That. Okay. The other part is that other than being a lawyer and
having that interest I have in my horse. I have never had a real
interest in anything else. I am vanilla to the hilt, I suppose." Her
finger trailed through the crevices between his formed abs.

"My turn," he said as he moved his hand over her back. "First, I
never want to hear the word vanilla again unless it's about some delicious dessert. That part of our lives is done and those words have no
place in our future. I'll be damned if our children overhear either of
us speaking about such things."

"I can agree to that," she said. "And when are we starting this
family of ours, Arsen?"

"As soon as you stop taking birth control." He pulled her up again
and looked into her blue eyes. "I want to see that perfectly flat tummy
of yours swollen with my child."

A blush covered her cheeks, and she bit her bottom lip.

"Okay."

"Okay again, huh?" he asked with a smile. "I like this being
married thing."

"So do I," she said and lay back down on his chest, making circles
over it with her finger. "Imagine the first time our child calls you,
Daddy."

A mist covered his eyes in an instant. The thought of being someone's father was never a thing he thought he wanted. Arsen Sloan, someone's father. It had never been a figment in his mind.

Since he met Steele, though, it had crept in and now it was all he could think of. A little boy with his hair and her eyes. Or a daughter with her hair and his eyes. He didn't care, he just wanted a bunch of little combinations of them running around, getting all under their feet and into mischief.

"I'LL MOST likely bust out in tears and you better not make fun of me, Steele Sloan." As soon as her name with his last name left his mouth he had to close his eyes, the tears threatened so badly.

He had her. He had the one for him and she lay in his arms and talked of having their children. Then he said, "You are young. It's a lucky thing you have me because I will allow you to grow in ways most men wouldn't. You can be interested in whatever you want. It doesn't make a difference if I like it or not. You can follow your own heart, Baby."

"What a hippie you're turning out to be, Arsen." Steele laughed and kissed his chest. "But thank you for being you."

"I followed what I was molded to be for far too long. It's time to find my own path, with you and our family." He squeezed her and knew she was the right one for him.

Is it possible to love someone so completely the way I love this girl?

74

STEEL

Arsen gave Steele an expensive sweat suit in blue, he said to match her eyes. He wore a very normal looking gray one and some killer shades that made him look like a work of art in it.

Sitting in the waiting area for his private jet to fuel up and be stocked up for the eighteen-hour flight to the first leg of their honeymoon, the couple waited at the airport to leave.

Steele leaned up against him as they sat in the little seats of the small room. "Really, Arsen? Still you will not tell me?"

His lips grazed hers as he said, "I will tell you this, Kitten. You and I will be joining the mile-high club in the jet's bedroom while we are on our way there."

She laughed and batted at his chest.

"Rogue."

"Temptress," he countered.

A GROUP of people came into the little waiting area. All well dressed and all looking a little tired. Steele's eyes ran over the three couples. A tall, dark-haired man with striking blue eyes had his arm wrapped around a tall, blonde woman. Steele felt as if she had seen the woman before.

There was a couple behind them with their arms wrapped around one another. Both had sandy blonde hair and she knew the man. It was a singer named Kip Dixon.

Steele straightened up in her chair as her eyes roamed over the last couple to come in and she had no clue who they were, but they were expecting a baby as the dark-haired woman's belly was round.

"Hɪ," Steele said and waved a little. "Have to get this out there so this doesn't get weird, but you're Kip Dixon, right?" Her eyes looked into the blonde man's brilliant blue eyes.

His Australian accent confirmed it, as he said, "I am. And who might you two be?"

Arsen stood up and pulled Steele along with him.

"Arson Sloan, and my wife Steele. Nice to meet you, Mr. Dixon. I'm a big fan of your music."

"Thank you. I love to hear that. Call me, Kip." Kip gestured to the woman who was sitting down already, probably used to people recognizing the man she was with. "That's my gorgeous wife, Peyton and that man with his arm wrapped around the pretty blonde is Max and his wife's name is Lexi. And over here." He turned to gesture to the other couple, the pregnant one. "These two are why we're here in the first place. Our good friends, Blake and Rachelle. It's their anniversary. Their first. They've been busy as you can tell."

Arsen and Steele sat back down and the woman Kip had introduced as Lexi, the one Steel felt she had seen before, asked, "Where are you two headed?"

"I don't know," Steele said as she looked at Arsen.

ARSEN LEANED FORWARD AND ANSWERED, "It's a surprise."

"A surprise anniversary present or birthday or anything special?" Lexi asked with a Texas accent.

Arsen answered.

"Honeymoon."

"Congratulations," they all said.

"Thank you," Arsen and Steel said.

"So where are you from?" the dark-haired guy named Max asked.

Arsen looked at him and said, "San Francisco. But as soon as we get back from our trip we're going to be looking for an estate. I have a penthouse right now and that's not going to cut it with a wife and family."

The woman next to Kip, his wife, Peyton, looked at the couple with interest. "Did you say estate?"

"Yes," Arsen answered. "It needs to be in California and there has to be at least one barn and a bit of land for my wife's horse. But anywhere in the state is fine."

Blake looked at Kip then back at Arsen.

"What is it that you do, sir?"

Steele laughed. "Do I hear a lot of Texas accents here?"

Blake, Peyton, Max, and Lexi all raised their hands. Steel nodded and looked at the only girl who she couldn't figure out where she was from by her accent, Rachelle.

"And you are from?"

"Cali, Baby," she answered, making them all laugh.

Kip smiled. "So what did you say you do, Arsen?"

"I didn't," Arsen said. "I'm a criminal lawyer. And my wife is in school to become one as well. I'm thinking she and I will team up once she passes the bar."

Steele leaned into him and smiled. "You did?"

He nodded and kissed her forehead. "I did."

Lexi pointed at Kip and then at Blake.

"These two have estates in a small subdivision in Los Angeles. There are some nice places there with property and many have barns. You might take a look around there."

Steele couldn't take it anymore and just asked, "You look so familiar. Is there any way I know you from something?"

· · ·

LEXI BLUSHED and Max patted her leg and answered the question, "My wife was once on the cover of quite a few books and magazines."

Steele nodded. "I knew it. With two hot men, right?"

Lexi nodded and smiled. "Right."

Steele laughed.

"Those books were hot, hot, hot, girl!" She got up and went across the small room and gave Lexi a high five.

The scene ignited laughter from all of them and Arsen smiled at his wife as she took her place at his side once again. She looked at him and said, "Their neighborhood sounds good to me, Arsen. We should check it out."

KIP PULLED a card from his wallet and gave it to Arsen. "Give me a ring, man, when you guys get back from the secret honeymoon. I'll give you the lowdown on the mansions up for sale around us, Mate. Adding a new bro to the pack would be awesome."

Steele smiled as Arsen placed the card in his pocket. "Being added would also be awesome," Arsen said.

Rachelle asked. "You guys planning on starting a family soon?"

Arsen winked at her.

"Tossed the birth control pills in the trash a few hours ago."

Everyone laughed again. Steele felt lighthearted and at ease for the first time in a long time. As if all these strangers in the same room were their friends already somehow.

"Arsen Sloan, your jet is ready," came over the intercom.

They got up and Steele was surprised as all the people stood up too. The men all shook hands and the woman all exchanged hugs. Steele had never felt more like she belonged to a group before.

Kip patted Arsen on the back.

"For real, man. Give me a call when you get back. We'd love to have you in our neighborhood. I keep trying to get this couple to come to L.A. but they're hard core, Houstonians," he said as he gestured to Max and Lexi.

Max laughed.

"Hilda has her family there, man. I can't uproot her."

Steele looked at Max and asked, "Hilda? Is she your mother or something?"

"No, my chef slash house manager. And as close to a mother as I have," Max answers. "But I visit these guys all the time. If you do decide to buy something there, you'll see us plenty. And our little hellions."

Steele's heart filled in a way it never had before. Normal people wanted to be their friends. And in Los Angeles. The changes were moving forward fast, and she was excited about their future.

She waved goodbye as Arsen led her to their jet.

I WONDER if I'll ever see them again...

75

ARSEN

Steele's mouth left his hard cock, and she looked at him with the darkest blue eyes he'd ever seen on her. Lust, desire, and pure need filled them. She moved her body over him as she moved up the bed in the jet.

Her lips cocked up to one side as she said, "You are my husband now, Arsen." She pushed him to lie back as he looked at her with wide eyes. "Mine!"

She made a low growl. Her teeth scraped his neck, and he said, "Kitten, you okay?"

He placed his hands on her arms and held her back a bit.

"Am I getting too wild for you?" she asked.

Arsen's laugh filled the small bedroom of his private jet.

"Now, come on. We both know you cannot get too wild for me."

His hands slid down to her wrists and in one quick motion, he grabbed them and turned her over. He pressed her body to the mattress and held her hands behind her back.

. . .

OPENING the drawer beside the bed he found what he knew would be inside. A pair of handcuffs with the key in the lock. He leaned over her and whispered, "You have the right to remain silent."

Her breath came out hard as she said, "I won't give in willingly, officer."

"But you will," he said as she licked her neck and closed the handcuffs around her wrists, keeping them behind her back.

"Never!" she shouted.

He pressed her face to the mattress.

"Quiet or your ass will feel the sting of my hand!"

Steele wiggled her ass. "Sure it will."

Arsen landed a nice slap to it and Steele shrieked.

"Bet you won't do that again," she said.

He slapped it again and said, "Bet I will."

Holding her to the bed, he ran his thick cock along her ass crack. Teasing her as he pressed it to a place he knew she didn't want it. "Hey! We're just fucking around here, right?" she shouted. "You know I was playing, don't you?"

ARSEN'S SMILE, she could not see with her face pressed against the mattress. He stayed silent and rubbed it against the place she told him was off limits. Then he made an evil laugh.

"Do you think playing with me is safe, Kitten? I'm a big bad dog and kittens shouldn't play with dogs."

"Arsen! Stop! You're freaking me out!"

He flipped her over and ran his hands all over her breasts as his dick pressed on her sex. "Am I?"

Steele let out a laugh.

"Fucker!"

Arsen laughed and moved to sit on the side of the bed and picked Steel up like she was a doll.

"Spread, 'em," he said.

She spread her legs, and he placed her on his lap, facing him. Her hands still cuffed behind her back. His groan filled the small room as he slid her over his erection.

Hers followed, and he began to pick her up and down to stroke him.

"Arsen, where are we…"

He stopped and smacked the side of her ass.

"You have the right to remain silent, remember? I just told you that."

Steele sighed. "K."

Arsen started moving her again and took her right tit in his mouth and sucked on it. Steele made noises he'd never heard her make before. Her heart started pounding so hard, he could hear it.

It made him move her even faster up and down his cock. It was aching for her to come all over it. But he wasn't going to tell her to do it. He wanted her to cum in her own good time.

He let her breast go and moved his mouth to bite her neck. She made little crying sounds he found arousing as hell. She murmured, "Please tell me."

Arsen smiled against the flesh of her neck and moved his mouth to her ear, biting her earlobe.

"No."

Steele fell backward in an instant. Arsen was surprised and held tight to her waist as the top portion of her body was no longer in front of him but now hanging down by his legs.

He pulled her up and when he did he felt the most amazing feeling as her body gripped his cock. She smiled at him. "Let me fall back again."

Arsen did and felt her body tighten around him again and this time, she pulled herself up. It was even more amazing as she did, gripping his cock like it had never been gripped before.

He looked at her as his breath caught in his chest. "Where the hell did you learn that, Steele?"

"The internet," she told him with a smile. "There's more than one way to skin a cat."

She fell back again and started doing some type of sit up as he just held her waist so she didn't completely fall and her tunnel contracted over his hard dick as she did.

"Oh, Baby! Oh, Kitten! Oh, shit!"

Steele held her body out at a ninety-degree angle to his as he climaxed. Though surprised by the action, he looked at her. "Come!"

She fell back as her body did as he said. She pulsed all around him as the top half of her remained dropped to the side of the bed.

When both were spent, Arsen pulled her up and laid her head on his shoulder and rocked with her still on him. His lips pressed to her neck.

"You and I will find happiness. I never knew I could, but you showed me the way, Baby."

He took the key and unlocked the cuffs that had bound her hands. Arsen laid her on the bed and massaged her arms and all the joints to get the blood flowing back to them. Kissing every part of both arms as he did.

"Are you about ready to get cleaned up and off this jet so you can see the first place I'm taking you?" he asked her.

"Though, thoroughly satisfied," she said, "I am ready to see where it is you're taking me. I have my suspicions, though. Just so you know."

He smiled and picked her up to take her to the shower. "Do you now?"

She has no clue!

76

STEELE

Arsen had placed a blindfold over Steele's eyes as they left the jet. And then he held her tightly to his side with his arm around her waist as he led her to yet another flying machine.

She heard the blades before she felt the wind on her skin. The air was warm, almost hot.

"Arsen, where are..."

His lips pressed against hers as he picked her up and placed her in a leather seat and strapped her in. Then he climbed into the seat next to her and shouted over the loud sounds of what she guessed was a helicopter, "Trust me!"

It seemed like forever as they flew through the warm air. She heard an odd language being spoken by the pilot and Arsen spoke back in the language she thought she may have heard before.

Arsen spoke it much choppier then the male pilot did. Her brain was putting it all together as she felt the blindfold being taken off her. The language was Middle Eastern.

Bright light blinded her for a second then Arsen placed some sunglasses over her eyes for her. And there she saw what she had been dreaming of seeing since she was a teenager.

. . .

"Is this for real, Arsen?" she asked as his hand took hers.

"I asked your family where you talked about the most wanting to see. They told me you loved the Transformer movies and really loved the one with the scenes from Egypt in them. Your father told me you said at that time you felt as if you had seen them before. So I knew I had to bring you here to see it all for real."

"I thought we were going to Paris, Arsen," she said as she cried. "You said you wanted to see France. And we were married at the Paris place in Vegas. That was a lot of hints, pointing me in that direction."

Arsen held her to him as the helicopter flew up out of the canyon to make another pass as it was obvious Steele was not paying attention to the sight in front of her.

"We'll go to Paris on our first anniversary. This honeymoon is about you, Baby. I told you I was going to spoil you." His words were punctuated with a kiss.

Steele tried hard not to look at her husband and turned to look out the side of the helicopter.

"Arsen, we aren't in Egypt, this is Petra. It's in Jordan." The magnificent stone structure of what was once only a picture on the screen at a theater filled her vision.

"We will be staying for two weeks and touring all the structures here and in Egypt. Not quite as glamorous as Paris or London, but it is exactly what you told your little sister you always wanted to do one day," Arsen told her.

"You are one sneaky man, Arsen!" Steele shouted as the helicopter moved through the air in front of the most impressive thing Steel had ever imagined seeing.

That was until the man who is now my husband was right by my side!

THE HELICOPTER LANDED and Arsen got out and helped Steele out. They walked up to the enormous door and into what people thought had once been a church of some kind in ancient times.

Inside people had drawn on the ancient walls.

"What a sin," Steele said as she ran her hand over one of the drawings.

"Check this one out," Arsen said as he led her to a large, very primitive drawing of two, giant, black birds, depicted as flying over a crowd of people wearing red, hooded robes and kneeling.

Steele laughed.

"That looks like those things the American Indians called thunderbirds. I don't know what the robe-wearing people are doing in the picture, though."

Arsen grabbed her around the waist and pulled her to him.

"Probably getting ready to sacrifice a virgin to them." He tickled her ribs, making her laugh.

"Stop," she said with a laugh.

He stopped tickling her and pressed her against the wall.

"We're all alone in here, Kitten." His hand moved under the short hem of her dress.

Her hands ran around him, pulling him to her.

"That would make for a great memory, Arsen. You taking me in the lost city of Petra."

His mouth pressed against hers as he pulled her panties to one side and she unbuttoned and unzipped his pants to release his erection. Arsen pressed his hard, throbbing cock into her wet, welcoming sweetness.

THEIR MOANS ECHOED off the stone walls. Moving into her with sharp, deft thrusts, every breath they took made loud sounds in the enormous, empty, ancient room.

His mouth left hers to run it over her neck. She brushed her hair back as he took her ass in his hands and lifted her. Her legs wrapped around him as he moved inside her.

Arsen nipped her neck as Steele ran her nails over his back. The sound of voices were heard as some more visitors to the ancient lost city came into the canyon, their voices echoing off the rocks outside of the structure they were in.

"Hurry," Steele coxed him. "Oh, God, Arsen, hurry!"

He moved quick and their breathing was fast, hard, and loud.

Steele felt him release, and she climaxed along with him. He let her legs fall to the stone floor, and she adjusted her panties as he put himself all back up in his pants and locked the beast away again.

He smiled at her and took her hand in his and walked to the other side of the large room to look at the drawings on the other walls as a group of people walked in.

Steele put her head on his shoulder and sighed.

"You're a lot of fun, hubby."

His whisper moved her hair. "You are very willing, wifey."

I think this marriage is going to go just fine!

77

ARSEN

He held their book on his lap and sketched a picture of Steele as she sat in a chair at the ritziest beauty salon in Cairo he could find. Her hair was in large curlers and she was draped with a dark cape.

"What are you drawing?" she asked him as the stylist left them to go get something.

He turned the book for her to look at.

"You."

"Me! In curlers!" She shook her head.

"It's not simply you in curlers," he said with a laugh.

"It's you in curlers in a salon in Cairo on our honeymoon. There's a difference."

"Okay, when we get back to the hotel maybe I'll draw the next picture. Maybe one of you on the toilet in our hotel room in Cairo on our honeymoon," she said then stuck her tongue out at him.

He shook his head and grinned.

"So young you are, Steele. Bathroom humor."

The stylist came back and started working on doing Steele's make-up. Arsen gazed at his wife and knew she didn't need all this primping to be gorgeous, but he loved being able to do it for her.

. . .

SHE WAS his prize in life. The one thing he never thought he deserved. Steele was his angel.

No matter where life would take him, he'd never be alone again. Steele would be with him through thick and thin. She already had been.

Later, when they walked out of the salon with Steele looking like a fashion model, he kissed her heavily made-up cheek.

"I love you, Baby."

Steele looked at him with heavy, black lashes, and artistically shaded eyelids. "I love you too, Arsen. I always will."

"Promise?" he asked.

She kissed his cheek. "Promise."

Arsen realized his fingers were crossed in hopes the words she said were true and always would be. There was still a little part of him who couldn't believe things were going to be fine.

But I sure as hell hope this lasts forever!

TO BE CONTINUED, *just one more time...*

THANKS SO MUCH FOR READING, please click here to leave your review:

78

PART FIFTEEN: FOREVER AND A DAY

ARSEN

"And that's the end of our story. Up to that point, anyway," I tell my wife of five years as she lies out on the bed next to me, her head on my shoulder.

It's our fifth wedding anniversary today and each anniversary I read Steele the story that begins with the night we met up until our honeymoon. I wrote it all in my handwriting with sketches here and there I made to make the story a little more graphic.

Steele loves the book I made for her. 'No Truer Love Has Ever Existed, The Arsen and Steele True Life Series.'

She lets out a deep sigh and looks up at me with shiny blue eyes.

"What memories that book invokes in me."

Steele and I wrote the book together and got a little help from her old friend, Gwen to get the story as accurate as we possibly could.

Running my hand through her long, dark hair, I say, "I think we should start on one for the kids. You know, document their conception and the pregnancy of each of them all the way through, say their first day of Kindergarten. Brady will be starting next year, you know."

Steele sits up and shakes her head, "Not from the conception, Arsen! That's too much for our kids to know about!"

I laugh and put the book on the nightstand.

"I meant like what we were thinking about or something like that, Kitten. You should know me better than to think I'd want to leave a written record for our kids about our steamy love life. You know our book is going to the grave with you."

She lays her head on my chest and says, "I suppose all those racy memories the book always conjures up in me had me thinking crazy, Baby."

And just like every anniversary we've shared before this one, I have her in the mood for love. Not that it takes much for this feisty vixen.

"You know the kids are with the neighbors for the entire night, Baby," I say as I run my hand over her pink silk nightgown I gave her as a present this morning.

Steele sits up and pulls it off over her head. "I do know that."

I wiggle under the blanket, taking off the boxers I put on after I got out of the shower before we came to bed for the night. "Even though it's late, we can sleep in tomorrow."

"We can do that," she says as she turns to me and wraps her arms around me.

Her lips barely touch mine and the spark zaps through me like a bolt of lightning. Every damn time, it never fails.

My fingers grip her ass and I roll over with her, getting her on her back. Then I move my hands up to tangle in her silky hair, pulling it back.

Her throat is exposed and I move my mouth from hers and kiss all the way down it. Then back up to her ear and I nip her earlobe. "I'm going to fuck you nine ways to Sunday, Steele."

The sound she makes sends my already hard cock into overdrive. Her fingernails dig into my back and she rakes them over me. I pull my head back to look at her. And she gives me a sexy smile.

Pinning her body with mine, I reach over and take the cuffs out of the drawer in the nightstand.

"Assume the position, Kitten."

SHE PLACES HER PALMS TOGETHER, and I put the cuffs on her wrists and pull her arms up over her head and hook the cuffs over the bedpost. Steele bought this bed a few years ago when she saw the design would work perfectly to hold her in place now and then.

I kiss the tip of her nose and then take on the role I know she's looking for right now. The old me role I do for her on occasion. She did fall in love with that part of me after all.

"No moving, no making any noise, and no coming until I tell you too."

She nods and watches me as I run my hands down her throat. Up and down I run them then over her chest, taking the time to massage, pinch and pull each erect nipple until they can get no more erect than possible.

Her eyes never leave me as I manipulate them both. Then I reach over and get the blindfold out of the drawer.

As I place it over her eyes, I say, "I'm going to get something else out of the drawer, Baby. It's a surprise. You'll just have to trust me. Remember, no noise or you'll feel the sting of my hand."

Running my fingertips over her taut stomach, I see goosebumps spring up over her flesh. Taking out the special little device, I bought to give her an extraordinary orgasm on this special day we share, I push the button at the end of it and the humming sound it makes fills our bedroom.

Steele's body tenses. I run the soft tip of the narrowest dildo I could find over her stomach and breasts. Then grab the bottle of lube that smells like chocolate and pour some on her stomach.

Rolling the vibrating device in the lube to coat it and ensure an easy entry into the area she has had me experimenting with these last few months, I notice her body shaking.

I think she has a slight idea of what I intend to do with this thing. My voice comes out huskily as I say, "If you need to stop the only word you can utter is, possum. Nod if you understand."

She nods and takes her bottom lip between her teeth. Her fingers are lacing back and forth together. Steele is nervous and I'm loving this.

Running my hands down her legs, I move them up to bend her knees. Then I take the vibrator and move it over her clit until it's swollen and nearly about to send her into a climax, but I move it just before that happens.

Down I move it, keeping the tip touching her folds as I make my way down. The largest thing she's had me put into her ass is my finger and this is longer and has a little more girth to it, but not much. She should be able to handle it.

Apparently, she had read a book about some threesome with a couple of guys and one girl and has wanted to see what it feels like to have one in both holes. I suppose the writer made it sound kinky but hot. It's had her wheels turning ever since.

Slowly, I ease the dildo into her ass in small increments to allow it to stretch and accommodate the device. "You can let out a moan if you need to, Baby."

Nothing comes from her yet. I keep going until I have it all the way inside her. The humming sound muffled now and I can feel the vibration when I place my hand on her stomach.

Oh cool, this could be interesting for me as well!

79

STEELE

So far the fifth anniversary is coming along fantastic. It seems Arsen has surprised me with something I've been talking about for a while now. My ass is vibrating, and that's a first.

We've managed to find a perfect combination of ways to please each other. A little soft and tenderness at times, rough and rowdy at other times, and technical ways of stimulation at others. It works for us.

His lips touch my clit and I try hard not to wiggle. His fingers are gripping the sides of my ass and he pulls me up and puts his entire mouth on me.

The way his tongue is sliding over my clit is agonizingly hot. My body is aching to be filled by his huge cock and he's a master at making me wait. I fight the urge to arch up as his tongue goes into me.

Finally, his hands move up, running over my sides as he makes his way up my body. The vibration in my ass is already sending little waves of pleasure through me.

His mouth touches my neck then his teeth graze over it as he slides his large, hard cock into me. And now I let out the moan he told me I could.

Shit! This feels amazing!

I KNEW IT WOULD.

Long, deep, slow thrusts he makes and I feel so full it's unreal.

His lips move over my neck as he moans, "Baby, fuck me, that feels so fucking good."

Arsen goes still for a moment, I guess he's enjoying the way my body is vibrating him. Then he starts stroking again. The way I'm beginning to pulse all over tells me this will not take long with this thing.

I just hope Arsen feels the same way.

He starts moving faster, stroking in and out with hard thrusts. A sweat breaks out all over me and our skin starts sliding over the others. I care barely breathe as he moves so fast and hard and the vibration is awesome and igniting parts of me that have never been on fire before.

I can feel his cock jerk inside me then his words bring my sweet release, "Come."

The euphoria that flows through my body as I climax is insane. So thorough, so complete!

I LET OUT another long moan that has a bit of a squeal to it. Arsen's breathing is heavy and ragged. He stays inside me but reaches down and removes the vibrator, turning it off.

The humming sound has left the room, but my body still hums as if it's still there.

Arsen pulls my cuffed arms down and sets me free then takes off the blindfold. His strong hands rub my shoulders as he kisses them.

"So, did you like it?"

I groan and stretch. "Umm hmm."

His lips pull up into a half smile. "I knew you would."

"Five years, Arsen. It's passed so quickly." I run my hand over his stubbly cheek.

He still keeps his hair at shoulder length because that's how I like it. His facial hair is meticulous as ever. The only thing that has changed on him is his dark eyes.

I swear they've lightened up through the years. The first time he laid them on our first born, a boy we named, Brady, a new light moved into them. When our daughter, Trace, was born a couple of years later they went a shade lighter.

Arsen is the best daddy in the world, according to our kids. He gives piggyback rides and plays with them all he can.

HE AND I are both criminal lawyers and we have our own law firm here in Los Angeles where we moved to the year following our marriage. But he and I only go in when we have to. As consultants mostly.

Arsen has more than enough money to not only take care of this family but our kids' families when they have their own as well. The investments he's made will live on for a very long time.

When we got back from our honeymoon, Arsen called that Kip Dixon guy we met at the airport before we left. He and his family live two mansions over and the other couple we met, Blake and Rachelle, have one next door to us.

They don't always live here, they have a restaurant and a huge log cabin style mansion in Colorado too. We all go up to ski and hang out with them once a year.

Max and Lexi, the other couple we met at the airport, have a huge estate outside of Houston, Texas and we go there a couple of times a year as well.

My husband seems to have joined an exclusive little club I've given the moniker, 'The Billionaire Boys Club.' Max, Kip, Blake, and now Arsen are all billionaires and have somehow found each other in this tiny world and became the closest of friends.

Their wives and I found common grounds as well and love to hang out with each other. Thankfully the kids all get along and there are a lot of them. Get-togethers are huge. Thankfully we all have giant homes and estates so we can all spread out when we're together.

Coming to Los Angeles was the best decision we ever made. The move gave us the freedom to go places without any of Arsen's past acquaintances showing up and ruining my mood. It also gave us this awesome group of friends I don't know how we ever lived without.

THE ONLY THING we lost in the move was Paul who stayed and later married Detective Fontaine. They live in Arsen's old penthouse he gave Paul as part of a severance package for his years of dedicated service. Plus, he made an investment for him and that makes enough so Paul no longer has to work.

He works anyway as a private eye. Paul helps his wife out on cases. They make a pretty great team.

Gwen married one of Kip's wife, Peyton's, brothers from Texas. She has three older brothers and one was still available, Tyler Reed. We had Gwen over to visit and the Dixon's had a bar-b-que as her family was visiting and she met him there.

The two of them live back in his hometown, a tiny town outside of Austin, Texas. No kids for them as of yet. But they've only been married a year or so.

I cuddle into Arsen's arms as he spoons me from behind. His lips touch just behind my ear with a sweet kiss goodnight.

I don't think I'll ever get tired of this!

80

ARSEN

The cockatoo, Bentley, screams as the front door flies open and in run my two rugrats.

"Good afternoon, guys!"

"Daddy!" they both yell at the top of their lungs as they don't seem to have an inside voice at all.

Rachelle brings up the rear and her husband, Blake, follows her. Their latest baby is strapped to his chest and waves at me, excitedly.

I have to get up and go kiss her little, pudgy hands. But first, my kids have to jump into my arms and act as if one night away from home and Mommy and Daddy was an eternity.

Brady wraps his arms around my neck.

"Daddy, was my fishy okay while I was gone?"

"Yes, son. I told you I would feed him for you and I did." I put him down and pat him on the head. "Mommy has lunch ready in the kitchen, Buddy."

"Yeah!" he yells and takes off then spins around, stopping all of a sudden. "Thank you for letting us spend the night, Mr. and Mrs. Chandler."

"You're welcome, Brady," they say together.

Our two-year-old daughter, Trace, clings to me and kisses my cheek. "Daddy, I missed you."

"I MISSED YOU TOO, PRINCESS." I kiss her cheek and place her on the floor. "Tell them thank you and go see Mommy."

She runs and hugs Blake's leg. "Thank you, Mr. Chandler."

Rachelle reaches down and picks her up, giving her a kiss on the cheek. "Thank you for coming to see us, Trace. I had fun fixing your hair."

Trace giggles. "Me too! Thank you, Mrs. Chandler."

After placing her feet on the floor, Trace takes off like a rocket to see her mother.

"Thanks. We'll return the favor anytime you want." I give them a knowing smile. They have four kids of their own. Adding in a couple more makes a difference.

Blake reaches into his pocket and pulls out a set of keys. "We'll be heading back to Colorado tomorrow. Think you could check on the house now and again for us? We'll be back in a month."

I nod and take the keys. "Not a problem. We'll make sure those plants are watered too."

Rachelle gives me a smile. "Thanks, Arsen. You two are the best neighbors ever."

They turn and walk back out the door. I wave and watch them walk back through the gate that separates their estate from ours. Then make my way to the kitchen to find out what my wife has whipped up for lunch.

I FIND our eldest arguing about the food like he always does. "Yeah, Mom, but at McDonald's, there's toys with the food. And tuna fish is not on the menu at all. Thank goodness."

"Well, in Mommy's kitchen all food comes with a side order of love. What about that, Brady?" Steele places his plate in front of him as he wrinkles his nose.

"But that smell, Mommy. Yuk!" He pulls the corner up on his wheat bread and takes a huge sniff.

I laugh and take the chair next to him.

"Did you know that fish is good for your brain?"

Trace nods and takes a bite of her sandwich with no argument what-so-ever. She's our good eater and her chunky little body is a testament to that fact.

"Mmmm. Thank you, Mommy. I wuv you."

Steele runs a hand through our daughter's dark curls. Trace has hair the color of mine and her mother's curls which I found she had when she was a kid. Later they turned into waves.

Her eyes are just like mine, though. And for a two-year-old she's very smart and has a vocabulary far ahead of other kids her age. When Brady was two, he barely spoke at all. Mostly grunted and pointed at what he wanted.

I CALLED him our little caveman for a while.

Steele takes the place across from me and has her hair pulled up in a high ponytail. A little red spot on her neck is left over evidence of our heated night.

"Something bit you, Mommy," Brady says as he notices.

"I know," Steele says with a smile then her eyes catch mine and I smile back at her. "There was a mosquito in our bedroom last night and it bit me in several places." She gives me a wink.

"I hate those pesky things," Brady says as he picks up a potato chip and eats it.

Her foot runs over mine underneath the table.

"I don't hate them. They have their purpose."

Neither of us has shoes on and I move my foot over hers and then up her bare leg as she only has shorts on. Her face flushes and she takes a drink of her iced tea then licks her lips all seductively as she looks at me.

.   .   .

I DON'T KNOW how she does it. One look, one touch from her can send me to another realm in my head. She's got me all hot and bothered and wishing the kids would take a nap already.

Running my hand over Brady's shortly cropped dark hair, I say, "Bet you kids stayed up late playing with the neighbor's kids. Bet you two could use a nap after lunch. Hurry and eat up and Daddy will read you a story so you two can fall asleep for a little while. You know, catch up on your rest."

Steele's lips quirk into a sly smile and her toes run up my calf then back down again. She puts the pickle spear she had on her plate to her lips and pulls it in a bit then takes it back out and lets her tongue move over the tip.

My cock jerks to attention. I look at the untouched sandwich on my son's plate. "I'll give you a hundred dollars if you hurry up and eat that sandwich."

His blue eyes go all wide and he says, "Seriously, Dad?"

"Dead serious, Son." I pull my wallet out of my pocket and take out the bill and place it on the table in front of his plate. "You eat it up and the money is yours, Son."

He picks the sandwich up and takes the first bite. After he swallows, he says, "Hey, this ain't really yukky at all."

Steele's eyebrows cock up. "Told you."

Thankfully the kid starts eating because my wife isn't letting up. Her foot runs up and down my leg and my body is heating up so quickly it's insane.

And I still have to read the kids a story!

81

STEELE

Thank God for naptime!

I've taken every stitch off and wait for Arsen to come to our bedroom. He's reading the kids a book, in hopes of them falling asleep for a little nap after lunch.

It cost him a hundred-dollar bill to get our son to eat his tuna sandwich, but I think I can prove to him it was worth it.

The door opens and in comes Arsen, stripping as he comes towards me in what looks like a heated rush. "That took forever."

I giggle and hold my arms out to him.

"Come to me, Big Daddy!"

His underwear hit the floor and I can see he is so ready for me. His hard body smacks against mine as he grabs me up in his strong arms. My arms wrap around him as his mouth takes mine in a hot kiss.

I was keyed up and now I'm about to boil over. His fingers press hard into my flesh like he wants to feel me so deep. It's beyond amazing.

The bed I bought a few years ago stirred so much in me when I saw it, I had to have it and bought it on the spot.

It's a four post bed with smaller posts covering the top end of the bed and has a metal frame around the top of it. You could throw mosquito netting over it if you wanted to. I didn't, though.

We use the rounded metal bars for other things.

Arsen's hands go to my waist, and he takes his mouth from mine, hoisting me up. I wrap my hands around the bar over my head and he takes my legs and places each one over his broad shoulders.

He looks up at me and licks his lips as his face is right there in my crotch.

"Time for dessert."

I LET OUT a loud moan as his hot mouth crushes against my sex. His tongue moves over my folds and dip into my opening a bit then back out to roam over every part of me again.

The way his teeth feel against my tender flesh has my body trembling already. I throw my head back as his tongue strokes my clit and I groan with the sensation.

My body is on fire for him as his fingers squeeze my ass and he pinches it every so often, sending spikes of heat flashing through my entire body.

The sounds he's making as he consumes me has me reeling with the knowledge this turns him on almost as much as it does me. He gives my clit a nip and I yelp with the action.

He bites it harder, making it pulse and then licks it over and over. I fall apart. "Arsen!" My body shakes with the hard orgasm.

His head pulls back, his hands move to my waist, and he pulls me down.

"On your knees."

I turn around and get on my hands and knees and he takes me by the waist and pulls me back to him then slams into me. He stops and moans as he makes the tiniest strokes inside me.

My body is still climaxing and the little muscles in my vagina clench around his hard cock. He gives my ass a smack and starts pounding into me. The orgasm keeps going and I start making crazy sounds as it does.

Another smack he gives me, sending lightning flashing to every nerve ending in my body. I'm moaning so much I can barely even take in a breath.

My body is on fire, pulsing all over and so deep inside it is unreal. Just as the intense orgasm begins to ease up, his hand comes around and he strokes my clit. It sends me back into the spasms of pleasure.

"Arsen! Arsen!"

His dick jerks hard and he groans then says between clenched teeth, "This is it!"

Heat fills me and sends me deeper into the climax. I find myself screaming with the intensity of it. Before it ends all the way, he pushes my body to the bed and pulls out of me then turns me over and climbs on top of me.

Back inside of me he goes and starts pumping again. I am shocked as it seems he has more to give me. His mouth crashes down on mine as he makes hard and swift thrusts.

He moves his kiss from my mouth to my neck where he says, "I can't get enough of you, Baby."

His teeth clamp down on my neck, making another red mark and taking my mind away from wondering what the hell has gotten into my husband all of a sudden.

Arsen's body is hot and wet all over me and it has me in a frantic state. My hands run all over his muscled back as he pounds into me. A loud groan comes out of him and his cock jerks hard inside me.

My body responds by going into another orgasm and I join him in the groan. He stays inside me as my body squeezes him and takes every last drop he has to give.

And just like that, it pops into my head that I forgot to start taking my birth control pills when I switched to a new package two weeks ago.

"Fuck!"

Arsen pulls his head back to look at me. "What does that mean?"

I close my eyes and pray for a second before I answer him, "It means your wife is an idiot."

"No, she's not," he says with a chuckle. "My wife is rather intelligent."

I roll my eyes as he continues to hold me tight and looks down at me. His hair hanging in damp strands around his handsome face. I run my hand over one stray lock that hangs in front of his eyes.

"Your wife has been off birth control for two weeks and just now remembered it. See, you did marry an idiot."

A smile moves over his face and his lips touch mine.

"Let's have another baby, Steele."

"What?" My eyes search his. "Trace is only two and Brady only two years older than her. It's like stair-step kids. I wanted to wait until Trace was four, Arsen."

"Looks like someone else might have other plans." He kisses me again. "Let's do it, Baby. Let's try for another. I'm game if you are."

"You probably just got me pregnant right now," I say as I look up at him.

"Well, I'm not about to stop trying. Just so you know." His mouth moves to my neck and his tongue runs up it.

"You cannot possibly be ready to go another round." But as the words leave my mouth, his cock jerks inside me and it seems like he is.

82

ARSEN

"Of course, I want a bad ass helicopter, Kip," I tell him over the phone. "Tell Max to bring it out here and I'll buy it from him and use it for the law firm. I'll be a hero at work with a helicopter at our disposal."

"He's going to be happy you bought it," Kip says. "Max has found a new one with bells and whistles galore and is dying to get it, but Lexi told him he had to sell the one he has first."

"Who wears the pants around their house?" I ask with a laugh.

We all know who wears the pants in all our homes.

"Speaking of that. Shouldn't you ask your boss if you can buy the chopper, Arsen?"

"Shit! Steele wasn't real happy with me learning how to fly or getting my pilot's license. You might be right. But tell Max I'll let him know by tonight. I think I can get her to see things my way."

"The jewelry store opens at ten this morning, Mate," he tells me.

"I have them on speed dial," I say with a laugh. "After forgetting to look before I pulled out of the drive-way last week, I ran over Steele's bike and had to get her a diamond bracelet and a new bike to make up for my carelessness."

Kip's hearty laugh comes over my phone and we exchange good-byes and I go to get my car keys.

My love, steps around the corner with a frown on her beautiful face. "I heard that."

I freeze. "Which part?"

"The most important part." Her hands move to her narrow hips.

The stance. This is not good.

"OH, THAT PART." I move towards her and run my arms around her, backing her up against the wall. "I love you."

"I love you too. Hence, why I don't like the idea of you up in the sky with so little to protect your awesome body." Her hands go around my neck.

"Aw, how sweet you are." I kiss her neck. "But you have nothing to worry about."

"Good, so it's settled then. You aren't getting Max's old helicopter." Her lips touch my neck.

"No, it's not quite settled." I nip her ear and lick the flesh just behind it.

Her body melts into mine like it always does. I press her harder against the wall. My cock is hard so I grind into her soft core.

Her words come out quiet and she's already somewhat breathless. "Arsen, I'm serious, Baby." Her lips travel up my neck, sending heat right through me.

"Me, too, Baby. I really, really want it." I graze my teeth down the side of her neck then look at her with my puppy dog eyes. "Really badly, Baby."

She looks at me with a tiny bit of dilemma in her blue eyes. I run one hand through her hair then press my lips to hers. Her lips part and let me in. Our tongues twirl around together in a lazy dance.

My hands tangle up in her hair. I deepen the kiss. It's only been a couple of days since we started actively trying for another baby and I think this is a good opportunity to get a little baby making time in and maybe get myself a chopper while I'm at it.

Two birds, one stone!

I PICK her up and carry her to our bedroom while I kiss her. The kids are at their swimming lesson with Kip's wife, Peyton. The house is empty and we're all alone.

Lying her on the bed. I release her lips and stand up. I unbutton my shirt and slip it off then pull hers off. Her pink, lacey bra beckons me to run my fingers over it and I do.

Her chest rises as she takes in a deep breath. I reach around her and unclasp it, setting them free. I gaze at her plump, perky tits and run my fingers down her stomach to the button on her shorts.

Popping them open and taking the zipper down slow and easy, I pull them off. Leaving her matching pink panties on for the moment.

I take off the rest of my clothes while she watches me. She reaches out as I climb onto the bed and runs her hand over my abs and looks at them.

With a sigh, she says, "I really, really love your muscles."

I smile at her and move my body down hers then take her panties off and run my hands all over her, starting at her perfect pink toes. I kiss the top of her right foot. "Do you remember how crazy it made you how over protective I was with you when we first met?"

She nods.

"And when we first had Brady. You were also uber-overprotective. It took you nearly a year to realize he wasn't quite as fragile as you thought he was."

I smile at her and pull her right leg up and trail my tongue over her calf, then say, "I know, I was so afraid of losing you both in the beginning."

Steele laughs a little. "Yeah, it made you a little crazy."

I nod and run my hand behind her knee, pulling it up and placing her foot on the bed. "It did."

Moving back, I kiss the top of her left foot and take it in my hand, running it up the back of her leg. She smiles at me. "But I'm not being overprotective of you by telling you I think helicopters are dangerous.

And I didn't like you up in them when you were learning to fly so what makes you think I want to live with you being able to hop into one whenever you feel like it?"

"Don't you trust me, Steele?" I ask as I bend her knee and place her left foot on the bed.

"You and trust, Arsen." Her tits rise with the sigh she makes.

"I know, right?" I move my body between her spread legs and run my tongue over her clit. "It's just an issue I have and always will, Steele. I need your trust. I crave it."

Her hands run down and she plows them through my hair. "I crave you to stay alive, Arsen."

With a tap of my tongue to her clit again I watch her eyes slowly close. "Feels good, doesn't it?"

"Umm hmm."

After a little nip, I give her my all. Tongue slathering over her clit until I feel it pulsing. Her body arches and I slip a finger inside her. Her breathing goes ragged as she pants.

I move my finger in and out then in again and hook it up to put pressure on her g-spot. Her hands pound on the bed. "Arsen!" Her body arches up and her vagina clenches around my finger and she's soaking wet in an instant.

Running my tongue up her then over her stomach where I stop and leave a kiss, I make my way up to her. Soft kisses I trail over each breast then I rest my body on hers and my lips on her mouth.

Sliding into her wet depths, I feel the pulsing of her walls around my hard cock. In and out I move as her hands roam over my back, whisper soft. Her shallow breaths fall warm against my left shoulder as I release her mouth and her head moves to it.

Keeping a slow rhythm, I kiss her neck with soft kisses. Her hands move up my back and go through my hair.

I love to feel her like this. Like a warm summer afternoon. Lazily our bodies move in unison. Her skin so soft against mine. And all I can think about is how much I love her.

Moving one hand to tangle in her silky hair, I press my lips to hers again to taste her sweet kiss. Cinnamon and honey are what she tastes like. Her hair smells like cotton candy from using the kid's shampoo she bought for Trace.

Her body fits mine like a glove and I never want to feel another's beneath mine again. She is all I want, all I need.

Warmth fills me as I move in and out of her. Her hands move to place them on my cheeks as she holds me to her. Kissing me back. Holding me in a way that tells me she is mine and I am hers.

Small squeezes begin inside her. Not dramatic hard pulsing, just easy little, gentle squeezes. Inside me blossoms with the adoration I have for this woman.

This perfectly, imperfect creature who I share this life with.

MY LOVE for her spills out of me and into her in a gentle wave as we kiss. I reluctantly release her mouth and we take in deep breaths. I look into her sweet eyes. "I love you, Steele. More than you will ever even understand."

Her soft hands cradle my face. "Arsen, I love you. The love I have for you runs so deep and so true there are no doubts in my mind when it comes to you."

I rest my forehead against hers. "I'll let Max know I won't be buying his chopper."

Her hands flow over my back as she says, "No, don't do that. You've never taken me for a ride yet. I'm basing everything on fear. I'm sure you're as excellent at driving that thing as you are at everything else you do. Tell him you want it."

"Really?" I ask as a smile spreads over my entire face and my heart speeds up.

I kiss her on the tip of her adorable nose. She giggles. "That got your heart pumping!"

Pecking little kisses all over her precious face I say, "Thank you." After each kiss.

83

STEELE

Eight months have passed and Arsen did manage to knock me up again. Another boy is heading our way, and it seems he plans on making his debut earlier than expected.

With our other kids safe with Kip and Peyton, Arsen is speeding towards the hospital. "You okay over there, Momma?"

"The contractions are getting much stronger. I'm pretty sure little Brody is about to enter the world. Just hope we make it to the hospital and you don't have to deliver this baby in the back of the suburban." I look over my shoulder and see some toys on the back seat.

His laugh comes out nervous. "Please hold on, Baby."

"I'm really trying. I promise I am."

The pain is ramping up and I have a bad feeling. The other two deliveries were nothing like this. Then warm liquid gushes out of me.

"Fuck!"

Arsen's head snaps as he looks at me. "That did not sound good!"

"My water broke. What a mess!" Tears just start pouring out of me. "The car's ruined. I'm probably going to mess it up even more by having our baby in it. Arsen, I'm so sorry."

"You don't have to cry. It will clean up or I'll get us a new one, Baby. Don't cry." He rakes his knuckles across my cheek.

· · ·

"But it's not going the way we planned at all."

"Nothing ever does, Baby." He laughs and takes my hand just as another contraction hits and this one hurts like hell.

I squeeze his hand as it makes me scream. Arsen shouts, "Breathe, Baby!"

It ends and I take in a breath. "Arsen, hurry!"

"Hang on, please hang on!"

He puts his emergency flashers on and speeds up. Moving in and out of traffic as fast as possible. But I don't think it'll be fast enough as another contraction hits me hard.

I remember to do the breathing and get through it but feel more fluid pushing out of me. The next one hits only seconds after that last one. I turn to look at him as the sun's last rays leave the sky. "Pull over."

"No! No, no, no!" Arsen's hands grip the wheel. "Shit!"

He hits the 'On' star button. A friendly woman's voice asks, "Hello, Mr. Sloan. How can I help you this evening?"

"My wife is having a baby and I'm on the 101. Is there a hospital anywhere near my location?"

"The nearest hospital is thirteen point seven miles away. With the traffic in your area, your ETA is twenty minutes," she says.

He looks at me and I shake my head as another contraction hits me. Through gritted teeth I say, "I don't have that long."

The nice lady tells us, "Take the next exit. There is a convenient store where you can pull into the parking lot. I will alert 911 of the emergency and your location. I'm connecting you to emergency services to talk you through the delivery, Mr. Sloan. Good luck, Mrs. Sloan. And congratulations to you both."

"Thank you," we both say.

Another pain hits me as he takes the exit and I notice his knuckles are white as they grip the steering wheel.

"It'll be okay," I tell him. "At least, you've seen this done twice before."

"I never really paid attention to what the hell was going on down there. I was always so focused on you and keeping you calm. Shit! Why didn't I ever pay attention to all that? Crap! Fuck me, Baby. I'm so fucking nervous!"

"Arsen. You have to get a grip! I need you to be that in control man you're so good at being. Find that guy, quick."

I watch him swallow hard and he pulls into the parking lot and pulls to the side of the store. I can hear sirens but they're far away. He gets out and opens the back door.

Arsen tosses the toys off the back seat and then opens my door and picks me up and places me in the back seat. He pulls out a blanket from the far back. One we used when we went on a picnic last week.

He drapes it over me as he moves my legs to bend my knees. Then he pulls me forward until my ass is at the edge of the seat. Out of the glove box, he pulls out a pocket knife and cuts my panties off at each side.

"Glad you wore a dress, Baby," he says. "And our son has a head full of dark hair."

"How do you know he'll have hair? Brady was born bald as they come."

"Because I'm looking at the top of his little head." He looks up at me and smiles. All calm, all cool, all in control.

That's my man!

The sirens are getting closer and a voice comes over the car speakers.

"Hello, Mr. Sloan?"

"I'm here," he answers,

"How's it going? I'm Donny, the EMT headed your way. How's our mommy doing?"

"I've been better," I say then groan with another contraction.

"I have the top of the baby's head in view, Donnie," Arsen says.

"Well then, do you have anything to catch this kid with?"

Arsen pulls a baby blanket out of the bag I packed a few days ago when I started getting things together for my trip to the hospital I hadn't planned on taking for another month.

"How about a baby blanket?" he asks.

"It'll help. Babies can be pretty slick and hard to hold onto. So use it to ease the baby out with the next few contractions. Do not pull on it. Are we on time or early or late or what?"

Arsen answers as I get ready to push with the next contraction. "We are a month early and it's a boy we're having."

"A month, huh? Be advised we will be taking the baby and Mommy with us as soon as we get there so the child can be taken care of ASAP. Okay, Daddy?"

"Got it." Arsen looks at me. "I'll be right behind you, Baby. Don't worry."

I nod and say, "Get ready, Arsen. I think this is it!"

He looks at me and says, "I love you, Steele. Get ready to see Brody."

I scream out with the contraction. "I love you, Arsen!"

It seems like an eternity then I hear the little cries of Brody and look to find Arsen with tears flowing down his cheeks as he looks at the red, little, wrinkly thing in his hands.

"Hɪ, Son. How are you doing this fine evening?" He sniffles and holds him up. "Look who's here, Momma."

I smile and lie back and take a deep breath as I hear the sirens pull in and stop next to us.

Thank you, God!

84

ARSEN

"And that's how Daddy was the first person to ever get to hold you, Brody." I rock my son in the nursery we made just off our bedroom.

Brody and Steele were able to come home after just a few days at the hospital and the little guy has grown to a decent ten pounds in the last couple of months since his birth in the parking lot of 'Habeeb's Fine Merchandise, Beer, and Cigarettes.'

Brady has told us he's kind of jealous of his baby brother because he was on the news the night he was born. Seems the kid was born to be in the spotlight.

The sound of footsteps come into our bedroom and I look up to see Steele making her way towards us. "Did you get him to sleep?"

I nod. "He likes to hear his story. He falls right to sleep every time."

"Glad he does for you. Man, that colic he has, drives me crazy. Thanks for taking him. I was at my wits end." She runs her hand over my shoulder as she walks behind me and readies his crib.

"I'm glad he needs me like he does." I get up and take him to lie him down. "He makes me feel special."

After I place him gently in the crib and cover him up I turn to find

Steele with her arms wide open. I grab them and pull her to me and hug her with a little swaying motion.

"I think you're special too, Mr. Sloan."

I kiss the top of her head and inhale the sweet smell of watermelon. "New shampoo, Honey?"

"Yes, Trace and I like it. Don't you?" She looks up at me with a grin.

"All those expensive hair products I buy you and you use the kid's shampoo." I shake my head at her.

"Trace likes our hair to smell the same way. What can I say?"

I put my arm around her and we leave the room and go to our bedroom. "I say, you're a sweet mommy to do that for your daughter."

"Trace and Brady want you to give them good-night kisses, but I already read them a book and told them you were taking the Brody shift this time. I'll be waiting for you in our bed and just a little reminder. The doc approved sexual activities for me today." She winks at me. "If you feel like it. I get it if you don't."

I pull her close to me and kiss her lips softly. "You get it, if I don't?"

She nods. "Yeah. That was pretty gross what you had to see when you delivered the baby. My doctor said sometimes it takes dads a little while to put what they saw out of their minds. I understand. I won't hold it against you, Arsen."

"Baby, there is not a thing in the world that would make me think you unattractive. That was a scary but beautiful experience. If anything, it made me respect you even more. Your body had to morph to bring our children into this world. It makes me love you even more to know the torture you would go through to give me children." I kiss her again.

Steele's hands run over my cheeks. "You are too good, Arsen. Almost too good to be true, I think sometimes."

I shake my head. "No, I'm not. And if I am then it's because you helped me to become that man. I am who I am because of you being a part of my life. I shudder to think what I'd be if I told Paul to take me home that night instead of stalking you."

"I shudder to think about all I would've missed out on if I hadn't gone completely against my nature and got in the back seat of your car, Arsen. Then I let you take me like you owned me. Just not me at all," she says as she shakes her head. "Do you ever wonder what had us acting so different?"

"I try not to wonder about it, because what is the use, anyway?" I pull her in tight to me. "But I have now and again. I was no stalker, and you were anything but my type. But there was such a strong pull when I saw you. Like magic."

She nods in agreement. "Like magic, Arsen."

Her arms tighten around me. "I hope each of our children find a love like we have. I hope it doesn't have to start with such a hard time. Man that would be hard to take."

"That's why I'm glad your parents didn't know a thing about us until the day before our wedding. I bet your dad would've stomped my ass. As he would say." I laugh a little, but I know it's true.

That man is tough as hell and fiercely protective over his family. I'm lucky my shit was straight by the time I met him.

"You're going to be just like him, you know," she says. "Maybe that's why we clicked so quickly. I've always been a bit overprotected my whole life. You came in and it felt kind of normal in an abnormal way."

We laugh and hug and then I kiss her once more before I go kiss my other children good night.

I never thought there would be a woman who would come into my life one day and make it all alright. Not even my mother made it alright. Steele is my angel and I'll always treat her like one.

For forever and a day...

And they all lived happily ever after

THE END

Lightning Source UK Ltd.
Milton Keynes UK
UKHW020119230121
377551UK00003B/371